BY BLAKE CROUCH

UPGRADE

UPGRADE

A NOVEL

BLAKE
CROUCH

BALLANTINE BOOKS
NEW YORK

2023 Ballantine Books Trade Paperback Edition

Copyright © 2022 by Blake Crouch
Book club guide copyright © 2023 by Penguin Random House LLC

Published in the United States by Ballantine Books, an imprint of Random House, a division of Penguin Random House LLC, New York.

Ballantine is a registered trademark and the colophon is a trademark of Penguin Random House LLC.
Random House Book Club and colophon are trademarks of Penguin Random House LLC.

Originally published in hardcover in the United States by Ballantine Books, an imprint of Random House, a division of Penguin Random House LLC, in 2022.

Library of Congress Cataloging-in-Publication Data
Names: Crouch, Blake, author.
Title: Upgrade / Blake Crouch.
Description: First edition. | New York: Ballantine Books, [2022]
Identifiers: LCCN 2022000423 (print) | LCCN 2022000424 (ebook) |
ISBN 9780593157527 (trade paperback) | ISBN 9780593157510 (ebook)
Subjects: LCGFT: Novels.
Classification: LCC PS3603.R68 U64 2022 (print) |
LCC PS3603.R68 (ebook) | DDC 813/.6—dc23/eng/20220107
LC record available at https://lccn.loc.gov/2022000423
LC ebook record available at https://lccn.loc.gov/2022000424

International edition ISBN 978-0-593-50094-1

Printed in the United States of America on acid-free paper

randomhousebooks.com
randomhousebookclub.com

2 4 6 8 9 7 5 3 1

Book design by Sara Bereta

For Michael McLachlan
Marine, lawyer, dear friend
(1946–2021)

PART ONE

You can stop splitting the atom; you can stop visiting the Moon; you can stop using aerosols; you may even decide not to kill entire populations by the use of a few bombs. But you cannot recall a new form of life.

—Erwin Chargaff

1

WE FOUND HENRIK SOREN at a wine bar in the international terminal, thirty minutes from boarding a hyperjet to Tokyo.

Before tonight, I had only seen him in INTERPOL photographs and CCTV footage. In the flesh, he was less impressive—five and a half feet in his artificially distressed Saint Laurent sneakers with a designer hoodie hiding most of his face. He was sitting at the end of the bar with a book and a bottle of Krug.

I commandeered the stool beside him and set my badge between us. It bore the insignia of a bald eagle whose wings enveloped the double helix of a DNA molecule. For a long moment, nothing happened. I wasn't even sure he'd seen it gleaming under the hanging globe lights, but then he turned his head and looked at me.

I flashed a smile.

He closed his book. If he was nervous, he didn't show it. Just stared at me through Scandinavian blue eyes.

"Hi, Henrik," I said. "I'm Agent Ramsay. I work for the GPA."

"What am I supposed to have done?"

He was born thirty-three years ago in Oslo but had been educated in London, where his mother was a diplomat. I could hear that city around the edges of his voice.

"Why don't we talk about that somewhere else?"

The bartender was watching us now, having clocked my badge. Probably worried about getting the bill paid.

"My flight's about to board," Soren said.

"You aren't going to Tokyo. Not tonight."

The muscles in his jaw tightened and something flickered in his eyes. He tucked his chin-length blond hair behind his ears and glanced around the wine bar. And then beyond it, at the travelers moving through the concourse.

"See the woman sitting at the high-top behind us?" I asked. "Long blond hair. Navy windbreaker. That's my partner, Agent Nettmann. Airport police are waiting in the wings. Look, I can drag you out of here or you can walk out under your own steam. It's your call, but you have to decide right now."

I didn't think he'd run. Soren had to know the impossible odds of eluding capture in an airport crawling with security and surveillance. But desperate people do desperate things.

He looked around once more, then back at me. With a sigh, he polished off his glass of champagne and lifted his satchel from the floor.

We drove back into the city, with Nadine Nettmann behind the wheel of the modified company Edison and I-70 virtually empty at this hour of the night.

Soren had been installed behind the passenger seat with his wrists zip-tied behind his back. I'd searched his carry-on— a Gucci messenger bag—but the only item of interest was a laptop, which we'd need a federal warrant to break into.

"You're *Logan* Ramsay, right?" Soren asked, his first words spoken since we'd escorted him out of the airport.

"That's right."

"Son of Miriam Ramsay?"

"Yes." I tried to keep my tone neutral. It wasn't the first time a suspect had made that connection. He said nothing else. I could feel Nadine looking at me.

I stared out the window. We were on the outskirts of the city center, doing 120 mph. The dual electric motors were almost silent. Through the wraparound NightShade glass, I saw one of the GPA's new billboards shoot past—part of the latest public awareness campaign.

In black letters against a white background:

GENE EDITING IS A FEDERAL CRIME
#GPA

Downtown Denver loomed in the distance.

The megatall Half-Mile Tower soared into the sky—an arrow of light.

It was one A.M. here, which meant it was three back in D.C.

I thought of my family, sleeping peacefully in our home in Arlington.

My wife, Beth.

Our teenage daughter, Ava.

If all went smoothly tonight, I'd be back in time for dinner tomorrow evening. We were planning a weekend trip to the Shenandoah Valley to see the fall colors from the Skyline Drive.

We passed another billboard:

ONE MISTAKE CAUSED
THE GREAT STARVATION
#GPA #NEVERFORGET

I'd seen that one before, and the pain hit—an ache in the back of my throat. The guilt of what we'd done never failed to hit its mark.

I didn't deny it or try to push it away.

Just let it be until it passed.

The Denver field office of the Gene Protection Agency was located in an unremarkable office park in Lakewood, and to call it a field office was generous.

It was one floor of a building with light admin support, a holding cell, an interview room, a mol-bio lab, and an armory. The GPA didn't have field offices in most major cities, but since Denver was the main hyperloop hub of the West, it made sense to have a dedicated base of operations here.

We were a young but quickly growing agency, with five hundred employees compared to the FBI's forty thousand. There were only fifty special agents like me and Nadine, and we were all based in the D.C. area, ready to parachute in to wherever our Intelligence Division suspected the existence of a dark gene lab.

Nadine drove around the back of the low-rise building and pulled through the service entrance to the elevators. She parked behind an armored vehicle, where four bio-SWAT officers had their gear spread out on the concrete, making last-minute weapons checks for what would hopefully be a predawn raid based on the intel we were about to extract from Soren.

I helped our suspect out of the back of the car, and the three of us rode up to the third floor.

Once inside the interview room, I cut off the zip ties and sat Soren down at a metal table with a D-bolt welded into the surface for less compliant suspects.

Nadine went for coffee.

I took a seat across from him.

"Aren't you supposed to read me my rights or something?" he asked.

"Under the Gene Protection Act, we can hold you for seventy-two hours just because."

"Fascists."

I shrugged. He wasn't exactly wrong.

I placed Soren's book on the table, hoping for a reaction.

"Big Camus fan?" I asked.

"Yeah. I collect rare editions of his work."

It was an old hardback copy of *The Stranger*. I thumbed carefully through the pages.

"It's clean," Soren said.

I was looking for rigidity in the pages, signs they'd been wet at some point, infinitesimal circular stains. Vast amounts of DNA, or plasmids, could be hidden on the pages of a normal book—dropped in microliter increments and left to dry on the pages, only to be rehydrated and used elsewhere. Even a short novel like *The Stranger* could hold a near-infinite amount of genetic information, with each page hiding the genome sequence for a different mammal, a terrifying disease, or a synthetic species, any of which could be activated in a well-equipped dark gene lab.

"We're going to put every page under a black-light lamp," I said.

"Great."

"They're bringing your luggage here too. You understand, we're going to tear it apart."

"Go nuts."

"Because you already made the delivery?"

Soren said nothing.

"What was it?" I asked. "Modified embryos?"

He looked at me with thinly veiled disgust. "Do you have any idea how many flights I've missed because of nights like this?

Some G-man showing up at my gate, hauling me in for questioning? It's happened with the European Genomic Safety Authority. In France. Brazil. Now I've got you assholes wrecking my travel. In spite of all this harassment, I've never been charged with a single crime."

"That's not quite true," I said. "From what I hear, the Chinese government would very much like a word with you."

Soren grew very still.

The door behind me opened. I smelled the acrid, burned aroma of yesterday's coffee. Nadine swept in, kicking the door shut behind her. She sat down next to me and placed two coffees on the table. Soren reached for one of them, but she smacked his hand.

"Coffee is for good boys."

The black liquid smelled about as appetizing as Satan's piss, but it was late and there was no sleep in my immediate future. I took a wincing sip.

"I'll get right to it," I said. "We know you drove into town yesterday in a rented Lexus Z Class SUV."

Soren's head tilted involuntarily, but he kept his mouth shut.

I answered the unvoiced question: "The GPA has full access to the DOJ's facial-recognition AI. It scrapes all CCTV and other surveillance databases. A camera caught your face through the windshield on the off-ramp at I-25 and Alameda Avenue at 9:17 A.M. yesterday. We took the loop out here from D.C. this afternoon. Where were you coming from?"

"I'm sure you already know I rented that car in Albuquerque."

He was right. We did know.

"What were you doing in Albuquerque?" Nadine asked.

"Just visiting."

Nadine rolled her eyes. "No one just visits Albuquerque."

I took a pen and pad out of my pocket and placed it on the

table. "Write down the names and addresses of everyone you saw. Every place you stayed."

Soren just smiled.

"What are you doing in Denver, Henrik?" Nadine asked.

"Catching a flight to Tokyo. *Trying* to catch a flight to Tokyo."

I said, "We've been hearing chatter about a gene lab in Denver. Sophisticated operation engineering ransom bioware. I don't think it's a coincidence that you happen to be in town."

"I don't know what you're talking about."

Nadine said, "We know, *everyone* knows, that you traffic in high-end genetic elements. Gene networks and sequences. Scythe."

Scythe was the revolutionary, biological DNA modifier system—now extremely illegal—discovered and patented by my mother, Miriam Ramsay. It had been a seismic leap forward that left the previous generations of technologies—ZFNs, TALENs, CRISPR-Cas9—gasping in the dust. Scythe had ushered in a new era of gene editing and delivery, one that brought about catastrophic results. Which was why getting caught using or selling it for germline modification—the making of a new organism—came with a mandatory thirty-year prison sentence.

"I think I'd like to call my lawyer now," Soren said. "I still have that right in America, don't I?"

We were expecting this. Frankly, I was surprised it had taken this long.

"You can absolutely call your lawyer," I said. "But first you should know what will happen if you go down this path."

Nadine said, "We're prepared to turn you over to China's Gene Bureau."

"America doesn't have an extradition treaty with China," Soren said.

Nadine leaned forward, her elbows on the table, the black coffee steaming into her face.

"For you," she said, "we're going to make an exception. The papers are being drawn up as we speak."

"They don't have anything on me."

"I don't think evidence and due process mean quite the same thing over there," she said.

"You know I have dual Norwegian and American citizenship."

"I don't care," I said. I looked at Nadine. "Do you care?"

She pretended to think about it. "No. I don't think I do."

Actually, I did care. We would never extradite an American citizen to China, but bluffing criminals is part of the gig.

Soren slouched back in his chair. "Can we have a hypothetical conversation?"

"We love hypothetical conversations," I said.

"What if I were to write down an address on this notepad?"

"An address for what?"

"For a place where a hypothetical delivery might have been made earlier today."

"What was delivered? Hypothetically."

"Mining bacteria."

Nadine and I exchanged a glance.

I asked, "You made the delivery to the lab itself? Not a random drop location?"

"I didn't make any delivery," Soren said. "This is all hypothetical."

"Of course."

"But if I had, and if I were to share that address with you, what would happen?"

"Depends on what we hypothetically find at this address."

"If, hypothetically, you found this gene lab you've been hearing about, what would happen to me?"

Nadine said, "You'd be on the next flight to Tokyo."

"And the China Gene Bureau?"

"As you pointed out," I said, "we don't have an extradition treaty with China."

Soren pulled the pen and pad to his side of the table.

We followed the stealth SWAT vehicle in blackout mode through deserted streets. The address Soren had scribbled down was on the edge of Denver's gentrified Five Points neighborhood, where at this hour of the night the only things open were a few weed bars.

I rolled down the window.

The October air streaming into my face was more revitalizing than the coffee we'd downed back at the station.

It was late fall in the Rockies.

The air smelled of dead leaves and overripe fruit.

A harvest moon perched above the serrated skyline of the Front Range—yellow and huge.

There should've been snow on the highest peaks by now, but it was all dry, moonlit rock above the timberline.

And I was struck again with the awareness that I was alive in strange times. There was a palpable sense of things in decline.

Africa alone had four billion people, most of whom were food insecure and worse. Even here in America, we were still crippled by rolling food shortages, supply-chain disruptions, and labor scarcity. With the cost of meat having skyrocketed, most restaurants that had closed during the Great Starvation never reopened.

We lived in a veritable surveillance state, engaged with screens more than with our loved ones, and the algorithms knew us better than we knew ourselves.

Every passing year, more jobs were lost to automation and artificial intelligence.

Parts of New York City and most of Miami were underwater, and an island of plastic the size of Iceland was floating in the Indian Ocean.

But it wasn't just humans who'd been affected. There were no more northern white rhinos or South China tigers. The red wolves were gone, along with countless other species.

There were no more glaciers in Glacier National Park.

We had gotten so much right.

And too much wrong.

The future was here, and it was a fucking mess.

"You okay?" Nadine asked.

"Fine."

"I can pull over if you—"

"Not yet."

Nadine and I had worked together for almost three years. She'd been an environmental scientist with UNESCO before joining the GPA.

I took out my phone and opened my text chain with Beth. Typed out:

Hi Beth. Heading to the raid. Just wanted to say I love you. Hug Ava for me, and make it a good one. Call you in the morning.

As I pressed send, our radio crackled.

Officer Hart, the SWAT team leader, said, *"We're three minutes out."*

I felt something ratchet down in my gut. The initial push of adrenaline was beginning to prime my system for what was coming.

There were people who were built for this kind of thing. Those who thrived on the rush of storming a warehouse in hazmat body armor in the middle of the night, no idea of the mayhem they were heading into.

I wasn't one of them. I'm a scientist. Or at least—I once dreamed of being one.

"Pull over," I said.

Nadine whipped the Edison to the curb, its auto-system chiming and grumbling.

I threw the door up, leaned out, and spewed my guts onto the street.

Hart came over the radio again. *"Everything okay back there? We lost you."*

"All good," I heard Nadine say. "Be right there."

I wiped my mouth, spit a few times, and pulled the door back down.

Nadine didn't say anything. She didn't have to. My vomiting up my nerves was the closest thing we had to a pre-raid ritual.

It meant we could go to work now.

Nadine toggled the accelerator.

The back of the SWAT vehicle raced toward us.

As much as I hated going on the raids, I always reminded myself that the fear was a necessary part of my penance.

Most of the outlaw scientists we targeted were criminals, plain and simple. With the black-market demand for synbio products growing exponentially with each passing year, there was plenty of cash to be made—on designer ultra-pets, spider-silk clothes, exotic GMO foods, even an entirely new life-form invented in a lab in Vancouver, B.C., that resembled a tiny, pink gorilla and that had become a kind of status symbol for the Russian oligarchs.

Black-market services and products had been enhanced as well.

Hacked cannabis and heroin.

Sex dolls wrapped in synthetic human muscle and skin.

A dark gene lab in Mexico City busted by the federales had

been constructing "revenge wasps" for the cartels. These yellow jackets could target any person based on their genetic fingerprint. They also carried a primitive Scythe system capable of modifying entire gene networks, leading to brain damage, insanity, and excruciating death.

For others, genetic fuckery was just to show they could do it, like the four biology undergrads at Brown who had simply wanted to see if they could make a dire wolf.

But for a select few, the endeavor was deeply personal—like the socially isolated but brilliant sixteen-year-old who attempted to engineer an antibiotic-resistant, flesh-eating bacteria to infect a bully at school.

Or the rogue geneticist we'd caught attempting to clone an improved version of his dead wife using black-market, enucleated human zygotes.

The desperate parents with no health insurance who tried to somatically edit muscular dystrophy out of their son's DNA. They actually cured him, but the off-target mutations they inadvertently created changed his medial frontal lobe network. He became psychotic, killing them before taking his own life.

Then there were the labs of my nightmares, where terrorist organizations engineered pathogens and weaponized life-forms of destruction, like the group in Paris that was on the brink of releasing a synthesized ultra-smallpox relative when the European Genomic Safety Authority dropped a thermobaric weapon on their warehouse.

Busting up those operations never troubled my conscience.

The ones that hurt were the raids on real scientists. Those who'd been doing groundbreaking work, for all humankind, when governments panicked and made it practically impossible to be a genetic engineer.

People like Anthony Romero.

I still thought of him sometimes. He'd built his lab on a

ranch in the Bighorn National Forest outside of Sheridan, Wyoming.

Before the Gene Protection Act had effectively ended all private and university-based genetic research, Dr. Romero had been at the forefront of gene therapies for cancer treatment. He'd been rumored to be on the Nobel Prize shortlist for medicine or physiology. But his *New York Times* editorial decrying the Gene Protection Act for its extraordinary overreach had ended any chance of him being added to the list of government-approved geneticists.

We'd arrested Dr. Romero peacefully at 2:30 A.M. as a light snow fell on the stand of Ponderosa pines outside his cabin. I felt physically ill as I handcuffed him and put him into the back seat of our car. I wasn't just arresting a hero—a man whose life and career I aspired to and envied. I was condemning him to a life sentence, because I had no doubt that our DOJ would throw the book at him.

Then again, he'd broken the law. Right?

As we handed Dr. Romero over to U.S. Marshals at Sheridan County Airport, the scientist had looked at me and said something I would never forget.

"I know you're trying to do the right thing, but you can't put this knowledge back into the box."

Watching the marshals take him onto the jet as the snow fell and melted on the tarmac, I had never felt so low.

Like a traitor to the future.

The SWAT vehicle pulled into an alley, and Nadine tucked in behind them.

I took in our surroundings through the gray-green of the NightShade glass, expecting to see the buildings of an industrial district. Instead, down the alley, I saw leaning fences and garages that backed up to Victorian houses, their steeply pitched roofs profiled against the starry sky.

"This area's residential," I said.

"Weird, right?"

We'd raided plenty of labs that were hidden away in basements or garages of people's homes. The technology, in its simplest inception, was that easy. But for an operation on the scale and complexity of what I was expecting tonight—one that had done business with *the* Henrik Soren—I would've bet good money that we'd be raiding a warehouse. Not a Victorian in a historic district.

I switched our radio's transmission from the comms rig in the center console to our earpieces. "Logan here. Sure we're at the right address?"

"This is what your informant wrote down."

More often than not, SWAT team personnel were dicks.

"Which house is it?"

"The one with the cupola. We're launching the drone now. Stand by."

Through the glass, I could see the four SWAT officers already out of the vehicle, one of them prepping the thermal-imaging drone. It would fly a perimeter around the target location, attempting to pinpoint heat signatures so we'd have some idea of how many life-forms were inside.

SWAT would go in first, taking the point position, with Nadine and me bringing up the rear. Once the lab was reasonably secure, they'd maintain a perimeter so we could go to work—taking an inventory of the equipment and ascertaining what exactly the rogue scientists were up to.

I fastened the magnetic straps on my inductive body armor and took my weapon out of the go-bag. It was a G47, chambered to .45 caliber. I had modded a grasp to hold a Streamlight onto the Glock's composite after too many raids on warehouses with sketchy power.

Meanwhile, Nadine was locking the shell drum magazine into her weapon of choice—an Atchisson assault shotgun. I liked to tease her for bringing such a beast along when we usually had SWAT support, but her argument was tough to get around. She'd found herself in a bad spot in Spokane, Washington, before we started working together. She had unloaded an entire magazine of .40-cal rounds into a scientist who had done a little self-editing gene therapy around a host of genes in the SKI, PGC-1α, and IGF-1 pathways. As a result, the suspect's skeletal muscles had undergone a massive hypertrophy cycle, together with his mitochondria, making them huge and super-dense. The man, whom she'd described as looking like the comic-book character, Kingpin, had nearly beaten her to death before finally bleeding out.

But as Nadine was fond of pointing out, there was no animal that walked the Earth that a twenty-round drum of twelve-gauge slugs on full-auto couldn't put instantly on the ground.

In my earpiece, I heard Officer Hart say, *"We're not detecting any heat signatures on the premises."*

"Copy that."

No one home, which was just how we liked it. Now we would reconnoiter the empty lab, wait for the scientists to show up. It was much easier to take them down on the street than inside a room filled with explosive chemicals and biohazards.

I checked the time: 2:35 A.M.

We had a good three hours before first light.

I looked over at Nadine. "Shall we?"

It was cold enough outside to cloud my breath.

We grabbed our night-camo hazmat suits out of the trunk and helped zip each other into them. They had a self-contained breathing apparatus and a specially made visor that provided a wider field of vision for combat situations.

Finally, we opened the air tanks and fell in behind the SWAT's tactical column.

"Night vision or flashlights?" Hart asked.

"Flashlights," I said. There was too much ambient light here, and that harvest moon was on the rise. It would soon be shining through the Victorian's windows.

The rear fence was too tall to see over, but we got through the gate leading into the backyard without having to break anything.

The lawn hadn't seen water or other care in ages.

Weeds grew waist-high.

I looked up at the windows of the old Victorian. A few were missing the glass entirely, and every one of them was dark.

Up onto the sagging deck that creaked under our boots.

Officer Hart knelt at the back door; had the lock picked in ten seconds.

We followed them inside into total darkness.

The lights of their assault rifles swept over an under-construction kitchen.

We moved on into a dining room, the walls stripped to the studs, electrical wiring everywhere, tools scattered across the floor.

"Looks like a remodel," I whispered over the open channel.

"Wait here," Officer Hart said.

Nadine and I stood on raw subfloor in what would have been the living room.

Even through my suit, I could smell the sawdust and polyurethane in the air.

Moonlight streamed in through the windows that fronted the street.

My eyes were slowly adjusting.

I could hear the boot-falls of the SWAT team moving systematically above us, room to room.

"Anything?" I asked.

"Negative," Hart said. *"More of the same up here. It's all stripped to the studs."*

Nadine looked at me. "You think Soren played us?"

"Why would he? He's still in custody. Knows he won't be let out until we give the high sign."

I noticed a door under the stairs. It was secured with a Master Lock that opened with a four-digit combination. I gave it a tug. No dice.

"Move," Nadine said.

When I looked back, she had a brick in her hand.

I stepped out of the way as she smashed it down on the lock. The metal sheared off—the broken lock hit the floor.

"That was us," I said to the team. "We just broke a lock off a door."

"We're heading back your way," Hart said. *"It's a ghost town up here."*

I pushed the door open.

It made a grating creak on its rusty hinges.

I pointed my Glock into the pitch black, the light illuminating a set of old stairs that descended to a basement.

My heart kicked.

"Want to wait for SWAT?" I asked.

"No heat signatures. No one's here," Nadine said.

The first step groaned under my weight.

It grew colder as I descended.

Even my suit's air filter couldn't remove the stench of mildew and wet stone.

Another SWAT officer said over the channel: *"Main level is clear."*

As I reached the bottom of the stairs and stepped onto a dirt floor, I had the sinking feeling that Nadine was right. Maybe Soren had played us. As to why, I couldn't imagine.

"You know," Nadine said, "all Soren told us was that he handed his package to a guy at the front door. He never went inside."

"What's your point?"

"Maybe they're just using this place as a drop site."

"That would make more sense than someone running a sophisticated lab out of a quiet neighborhood," I said, wondering if we'd wasted our time coming here.

Sure, we could hold Soren for seventy-two hours. Rattle his cage a bit more. But we had nothing on him. His luggage had come back clean.

I swung my pistol across the black expanse of the basement.

My exhalations steamed up the edges of my visor.

The walls were the original stone foundation of the house.

I saw a rusted boiler.

Dusty furniture.

And a curious black cube about a foot on each side, sitting on an antique dry sink.

"Logan." There was something in Nadine's voice that got my immediate attention.

I turned in her direction.

"Look," she said.

I aimed my light, saw a camera sitting on a tripod.

Pointed at us.

A red light blinked on.

"It just started recording," I said.

The SWAT team was coming down the stairs now.

I let my light sweep slowly across the basement again.

I wasn't worried anymore that we'd wasted time coming. Something wasn't right.

In the center of the room, my light passed over the cube I'd seen a moment ago.

It was in the process of splitting open.

"Nadine," I said.

"I see it."

As the sides of the cube fell away, my light shone through a sphere of what looked like ice. It was roughly the size of a bowling ball, and based on the quantity of vapor peeling off the surface, I suspected that it was supercold, or perhaps made of something other than H_2O.

"There's another one over here," Nadine said.

I turned, saw that she was shining her light on an identical sphere of ice near the stairs.

"What the hell is this?" she asked.

I said, "I'm not really loving the vibe down—"

A buzzing sound interrupted me—it was coming from the dry sink.

I moved toward it. Saw the source of the vibration. Felt an explosion of panic.

Beside the sphere of ice, there was a phone with a touchscreen lighting up as a call came through. Two wires ran from the phone, through a hole in the table, and underneath the ice.

The ice spheres began to glow from a blue light embedded at their centers.

"Get out!" I screamed.

The SWAT team was already halfway up the stairs.

Nadine followed frantically behind them.

I saw everyone disappear onto the main floor, and I was several seconds from the bottom step when the basement went white.

I felt an immense pressure on my chest.

Then I was lying on my back on the floor, staring up at the exposed insulation under the main level.

The visor of my hood was cracked and scratched in numerous places, and there were tiny, clear fragments speared through
the plastic. I didn't understand what they were until one of the
slivers of shrapnel dripped a freezing drop of water into my left
eye.

I managed to raise my pistol and shine the light on my suit.
It had been shredded and punctured in more places than I could
count.

Writhing panic.

Pain flooding in.

My arms and legs—every surface of my skin not protected by
body armor—suddenly burned as if I'd been stung a thousand
times.

2

WHEN I TOOK A breath, a crushing agony constricted my chest.

I heard myself moan.

Opened my eyes.

I was lying in a hospital bed.

On a stand beside me, a vital-signs monitor beeped at regular intervals and an IV bag fed something into my vein through an intravenous needle taped to my heavily bandaged left arm. My other arm and my legs had been wrapped in gauze. More disturbing was the opaque plastic partition completely enclosing me and the bed. Beyond, I could only see silhouettes and vague shapes. The voices I heard were distant, muddled.

I tried to retrieve my last waking memory, and whether it was because of the drugs or my injuries, it took some effort to find it.

I'd been lying on the dirt floor in the basement of a Victorian we'd raided in Denver. There'd been an explosion. I had tried to get up, but the pain in my chest had been paralyzing.

And so I'd lain there in the dark, wondering where the rest of the team had gone.

Wondering if I was dying.

Pain distorts time, so I had no idea how much of it had passed when I finally heard the thunder of footsteps descending the stairs into the basement. A medical team in full hazmat gear had surrounded me, and seeing my extreme pain, one of them had mercifully loaded me up with some beautiful drug.

I'd sailed away into a blissful sea of darkness.

Until I'd woken up here.

Wherever here was.

"Hi, Logan. How are you feeling?"

The voice came through a small speaker on the bedside table—a deeper-than-average female voice.

"Breathing hurts," I said. "A lot."

"How would you rate your pain on a scale of one to ten?"

"Seven. Maybe eight."

"On your right, there's a wand thing with a purple button on it. Press that a couple of times and you'll get some morphine flowing."

I started to reach for it but stopped. I'd had morphine before—in the wake of a botched Inland Empire raid that had taken my first partner's life and left me gutshot. I loved morphine. But it left me so relaxed I could barely bring myself to follow even the simplest of conversations. And in this moment, I needed some answers.

"Where am I?" I asked.

"Denver Health Medical Center. My name is Dr. Singh. I'm an intensivist."

I took another painful breath.

"I'm in intensive care?"

"Correct."

Wow. With new viruses and mutations of known illnesses constantly circling the globe, ICU beds were always in high demand, and often unavailable. Either the GPA had pulled some strings to get me in here or I was in seriously bad shape.

"Am I dying?"

"No, your vitals are good now."

"What's with the plastic?"

"Do you remember what happened last night?"

"I was on a raid. Something blew up."

"An improvised explosive device detonated in that basement. You may have been exposed to something."

A rush of paralyzing fear enveloped me.

"Like what?" I asked.

"A pathogen or a toxin."

"Was I or not?"

"We don't know yet. We're running tests. I will say it's not looking like you were poisoned. Your organ function is good."

"What about the others who were with me? My partner, Nadine. The SWAT team."

"They're in quarantine here as well, just to be safe. But they were out of the basement when the device went off. Their suits weren't compromised."

I shifted uncomfortably in the bed.

The pain was intensifying, the purple button calling to me.

"What are my injuries?" I asked.

"Two broken ribs. Three cracked ribs. Your left lung was collapsed, but that's been fixed. And your arms and legs are covered in lacerations from the ice fragments."

"Was it that bad of an explosion?"

"You were in a confined space, so the differential between your air-filled organs and the pressure wave caused some damage. Fortunately, nothing life-threatening. Nothing you won't recover from."

I figured the pain had reached the threshold of becoming at least as distracting as the morphine would be.

I pressed the purple button several times.

The relief was instantaneous.

Instantly I felt weightless and warm.

"I see you just activated the morphine pump. Try to get some sleep, Logan. I'll check in on you in a couple of hours."

I woke again.

Something was different this time.

Something was wrong.

There was still that radiant pain in my chest, but now my body ached as well, and I felt unimaginably hot. The sheets were soaked with sweat. It was running down into my eyes, and I wasn't breathing so much as panting.

The vital signs monitor beeped too fast.

Someone stood at my bedside, injecting the contents of a syringe into my IV line.

"What's happening?" I asked.

My voice sounded dreamy. My words slurred.

The doctor or nurse peered down at me through the face shield of a hazmat suit. I tried to read the gravity of the situation in their eyes, but it eluded me.

Their voice came through a speaker in the face shield. It sounded like the doctor I had spoken to previously, although I couldn't recall her name.

"You've spiked a very high fever, Logan. We're trying to get your temperature down."

"How high?"

"Too high."

I said something that, even to me, sounded delirious.

A door in the plastic unzipped and another hazmat-suited medical worker stepped into my bubble.

"I have the cold packs, Dr. Singh."

"Thank you, Jessica."

Dr. Singh set the syringe down and drew back the blankets

that had been covering me. I had sweated completely through my bandages and hospital gown.

Dr. Singh carefully lifted my head off the pillow as Jessica wrapped a cold compress around my neck.

I tried to ask if I was dying, but the words rushed out in vibrant colors. I could actually see them leaving my mouth in a train of exploding fireworks.

I sweated and groaned through fever dreams beyond anything in my experience.

Fantastical.

Repetitive.

Terrifying.

When I woke, my fever had broken.

Though my chest still ached, it wasn't that blinding pain from earlier.

I was alone in my bubble, and Dr. Singh's voice was coming through the speaker again.

"*Hello, Logan. How are you feeling?*"

"Better."

"*You scared us. You hit 106.1.*"

"I wasn't trying to set a record or anything."

"*We don't like seeing fevers go that high. At those levels, organ damage, seizures, even death becomes a possibility.*"

"What caused it?" I asked.

"*Still running tests, but there are no indications that this is bacterial or caused by an infection. So at this point, we're thinking whatever's going on is probably viral.*"

Fuck.

Some wack job with a vendetta against the GPA had set a trap. They'd even recorded the moment of exposure.

Scarier than a synthetic virus taking a machete to my body was the other reason people engineered viruses—they're the perfect machines for carrying foreign genetic information into cells. In other words, they can be used to infect people with a change agent capable of rewriting their DNA.

For me, lying here in quarantine, the idea that this virus might have infected me with something like Scythe, a DNA modifier rewriting the code that makes me *me* was exponentially more terrifying than the prospect of a simple virus.

"You have someone here who'd like to say hello."

A new voice came over the speaker.

"Logan?"

I smiled so widely that I felt a corner of my lip split. "Beth?"

"I'm right here in the next room."

It sounded like she was crying.

I started crying too.

It was the familiarity of her voice—this woman who loved me in spite of everything—and the reminder that I could've lost her in the flash of an IED.

"When did you get to Denver?" I asked.

"Yesterday. Ava and I took the loop out here as soon as we heard what happened."

"Ava's here?"

"Hey, Dad."

"Oh my god, hey, kiddo, it's so good to hear your voice."

"Yours too."

"What have they told you?" I asked.

"Not a whole lot. Edwin said that a lab you had gone into exploded. And the doctors told us you might have been exposed to something in the blast and that's why you're in quarantine."

"Sorry about our weekend. We should all be in Shenandoah right now."

"*We'll go as soon as you're out of here,*" Ava said.

"You're staying up on school, honey?"

"*I am.*"

"I don't want you falling behind again. Me almost getting blown up is no excuse."

"*I think it's a great excuse. I brought my laptop. I've been working in the waiting room.*"

"*Okay,*" Beth said, "*they're telling us we have to let you rest now.*"

"You and Ava will be close?"

"*We aren't going anywhere.*"

That night, my fever returned.

I tried to sleep, but wild dreams found me. I kept hallucinating that I was inside my body, watching as the virus invaded my cells. Then I *became* the virus, dissolving myself and my genetic instructions through the cell walls and hijacking its systems to make more of me. More virus particles.

Again and again and—

I smashed into a hot, deranged consciousness.

Nurses in hazmat suits were wrapping my neck in cold packs and pouring ice over my chest.

I was groaning.

Muttering nonsense.

"I am the virus," I said. "I am the virus."

Dr. Singh said, "Six hundred milligram push interferon."

I looked up into my doctor's face shield. "I can feel it in my cells," I said.

Dr. Singh ignored me and looked at one of her nurses. "More ice. Quickly."

It began to rain inside my plastic kingdom, except this wasn't like any storm I'd ever seen.

The individual raindrops fell as glowing letters—

```
A
G    A
C    G    A
T    C    G    A
     T    C    G    A
     T    C    G    A
          T    C    G    A
               T    C    G    A
                    T    C    G    A
                         T    C    G    A
                              T    C    C    A
                                   T    G    G
                                        T    C
                                             T
```

—adenine, guanine, cytosine, and thymine: the four chemical bases that comprise deoxyribonucleic acid.

DNA.

The air was filled with nucleobases.

They blew sideways.

Formed swirling vortexes.

Ran down the walls of the plastic partition.

Endless, mysterious permutations of the blueprint of all life on Earth.

I could feel the letters splashing down on my face.

I *inhaled* them.

A torrent of Biocode that kept changing, mutating.

My head was on fire, and I thought if I could only decipher the code, I could understand what the virus was doing to me.

When I came to, there was someone in a hazmat suit sitting next to me. My ribs felt better and the fever was gone, but I was so bone-weary.

The person in the hazmat suit turned to face me.

I looked up into the face of my boss, the director of the Gene Protection Agency, Edwin Rogers. I was glad to see him. I'd applied to work for the GPA straight out of prison. Didn't think they'd take me seriously, but Edwin Rogers himself had interviewed me and hired me on the spot despite my record of multiple felony convictions and zero law-enforcement experience. For that, he would always have my loyalty.

"Look who's conscious," Edwin said.

"Hi," I said weakly. "How's Nadine?"

"Still in quarantine, no symptoms. She'll probably be released in a day or two. I'm afraid you took the brunt of it."

"And do we know yet what the 'it' might be?"

Edwin cleared his throat. "As I'm sure you've gathered, you walked into a trap. We're still holding Henrik Soren. Going to charge him with attempted murder."

"What's Soren's story?" I asked.

"Complete ignorance. He swears he just made a delivery to a man at that house on Thursday morning."

"No names?" I asked.

"He gave us a generic physical description and a dark-web handle, which is, as you know—"

"Useless." I strained to sit up, my ribs screaming. Edwin helped to arrange the pillows behind me. "Have you been over to the basement where it happened?"

"I have. We found the remains of two ice bombs. Definitely the strangest IED I've ever seen."

"Was the ice H_2O or—"

"H_2O, formed into incredibly hard spheres. The explosion turned the ice into fléchettes. That's what punctured your suit. And you."

"Were you able to recover any of the melted water or ice fragments?"

"Yes. And we just finished sequencing a sample. Those ice spheres held a virus in supercold suspension."

I was suddenly wide awake.

"Pretty ingenious actually," he went on. "The shrapnel gets inside you through superficial cuts and melts without doing lasting physical damage."

"Oh god."

He put his gloved hand on my shoulder. "Before you freak out, it's none of the *Filoviridae* family viruses you've probably been having nightmares about. It's not Ebola or Marburg. We know it's not smallpox. It actually has characteristics of the *Orthomyxoviridae* family."

"Influenza?"

"Yes."

"Synthetic?"

"That's the assumption."

And then I asked the question I almost didn't want an answer to. "Did it encode a Scythe complex?"

He nodded.

Ah, fuck. I'd been infected, not only with a virus of unknown origin, but with a payload encoding the most powerful genome-modifying system ever created. Almost certainly it had been designed, not to make me sick, but to infect some or all of the cells in my body, potentially editing and rewriting portions of my DNA.

"Do you know which genes and pathways were targeted?" I asked.

"Not yet, but we're running a test and a full analysis of your white blood cell sample."

I tried to brace myself against the wave of fear, but I couldn't hold it back. It simply leveled me. This was the worst possible news, though not exactly a surprise. I'd lain on the dirt floor in the basement as the ice melted inside me. But it made the reality of my situation solid in a way it hadn't been before.

Edwin reached over the railing on my bed and patted my shoulder. "I want you to hear this from me," he said. "We're going to find who did this and take a serious shit in their coffee. You just focus on getting better."

"I'll try, sir."

He was trying to comfort me, but catching the culprit wouldn't really help if these DNA changes turned out to be lethal. A Scythe system could wreak all manner of havoc on my genome.

If a person's genetic code were written into a standard-size book, that book would be a twenty-story tome consisting of three billion permutations of the letters *A, C, G,* and *T,* which represent the four nucleobases—adenine, cytosine, guanine, and thymine. The specific arrangement of these four nucleobases creates the code for all biological life on the planet. This code is the genotype, and the way it physically expresses in a lifeform (eye color, for instance), combined with its interactions with the environment, is called the phenotype. But understanding the correlation between genotype and phenotype—which DNA code programs which traits—still largely eludes us.

Edwin rose from the chair. Then he walked to the door, zipped it open, and stepped through to the other side.

As I watched him zip me back into my universe of sealed plastic, I felt truly alone.

It reminded me of my time in prison and the crushing sense that others could come and go.

But I was here.

Trapped with my changing genome.

They started me on a course of interferon gamma and a set of new antivirals.

I spiked one more fever the following night and then began a period of rapid improvement. My energy roared back. My appetite returned. I started sleeping through the night.

Within three days, my bandages were gone, my ice-lacerations scabbing over.

My ribs still hurt, but I was desperate to get out of bed and walk around—even if it was only up and down the ICU corridor.

I longed for a real bathroom instead of my humiliating bedpan.

But they wouldn't let me leave my bubble.

Because they knew almost nothing about the hacked strain of influenza I'd been infected with, Dr. Singh would take no chances. Though I was symptom free, I was still shedding the virus, which meant I could be contagious to others.

And so I passed my days streaming movies on my tablet or trying to amass enough concentration to read. But mostly I obsessed over what Scythe might be doing to me.

The hospital had resisted letting my wife and daughter suit up and visit me inside the bubble, but after a week in bed, I insisted that I be allowed to see them.

My fourteen-year-old strode through the plastic partition in full hazmat gear that swallowed her whole, a canvas bag slung over her shoulder.

I laughed when I saw her—my first real laugh since waking up in the ICU five days ago. But with my cracked and broken ribs, the joy turned instantly to agony.

"Hey, Dad," Ava said, her voice emitting through the built-in speaker. Then she leaned over the bed and gave me the greatest awkward hug I'd ever received, my face pressing into her plastic face shield. Even though it was through latex gloves and a Tyvek suit, the touch of someone I loved, and who loved me, brought me to tears again.

"You okay, Dad?"

"I'm fine." I wiped my eyes.

She pulled the chair over and reached down into the bag she'd brought with her, lifting out a chessboard.

"Want to play?"

"God, yes. I'm so sick of staring at screens."

I sat up, groaning as I tried to get the pillows comfortably arranged behind me. Ava opened the chessboard, placed it on the bed, and began setting up the pieces.

It moved me that Ava would suit up to spend time with me inside my bubble. If you weren't used to them, a hazmat suit could be a claustrophobic experience. They were hot and bulky, and inevitably your face would begin to itch the moment you had entered the quarantine area. And, of course, looming over all of the inconvenience was the very real threat of a breach.

She held out both hands and I tapped the right one, which she opened to reveal a white pawn.

I would go first.

I had taught Ava chess when she was five. She took to it immediately and soon developed an innate understanding not just of how the pieces moved but of the need for a broader strategy to win.

We tried to play a game every day, usually sitting at the

wrought-iron table in the backyard or, if the weather was inclement, in front of the fire with the board set up on the brick hearth.

By the time she was ten, she had become a formidable player.

By twelve, we were equally matched.

By thirteen, she had surpassed my skill level with a great opening repertoire and a strong endgame. I could only beat her by playing flawlessly and hoping she'd make at least one mistake. But that combination was rare.

Sometimes I wondered if she'd been gifted with my mother's intellect.

I made my opening move.

"Hey, Dad?" she said as she responded—queen's knight to F6. "Five hundred and sixty-one. Just wanted to make sure you knew."

I rolled my eyes.

She was grinning through her face shield.

Five hundred and sixty-one *days* is what she meant.

She was reminding me of how long it had been since the last time I'd checkmated her.

We played every day for the next week.

Each time she won, and it was never even close.

Beth would also suit up to come sit with me, and removed from the routines and distractions of daily life in Virginia, we talked more than we had in years.

One afternoon, she looked down at me through her face shield and took my hand in hers, our skin separated by the layer of latex.

"When will it be enough?" she asked.

She meant my job. We had this fight often.

"I don't know."

"You've been shot. Now add almost-blown-up to your scorecard."

"It's not a scorecard."

"Sure it is," she said. "Please look at me. If I thought you loved this job, then as much as I hate the danger it constantly puts you in, I would never say a word to you about it. But I know you don't love it. It isn't who you are. You do this out of obligation and guilt, and maybe that made sense in the beginning, but it's been fifteen years since you were pardoned. Maybe it's time to forgive yourself and do something you actually love."

What I really loved, what I really wanted—had *always* wanted—was to be a geneticist. To understand and wield the power of the source code of life to make the world a better place. I blamed that on growing up in my mother's orbit. She was a juggernaut, and her influence had burdened me with out-size ambitions.

But I didn't live in a world where any of my dreams were possible anymore.

And the hardest truth—the one that had been eating me slowly from the inside for most of my adult life—was that even if it was, I didn't possess a fraction of the raw intelligence of an Anthony Romero or a Miriam Ramsay.

I had extraordinary dreams and an ordinary mind.

Exactly two weeks after my admittance to Denver Health's ICU, the door to my bubble unzipped and Dr. Singh walked in with a broad smile on her face and a cascade of dark hair flowing past her shoulders.

"You have hair," I said.

"I do. Quite a lot of it."

"Where's your suit?"

"Don't need it."

She came over and sat in the chair beside my bed—a bit younger than I would've guessed based on the huskiness of her voice.

"We feel comfortable saying that the virus, whatever it was, has run its course. You're going to be sore for another month or so, but we're kicking you out. Oh, and I have someone on my phone who wants to tell you something." She took her cell out of her pocket, put it on speaker. "Director Rogers? You're on with Logan."

"Logan, can you hear me?"

"Yes, sir."

"Your doc just filled me in on the good news, and I have some of my own to share. Your DNA analysis came back. You're in the clear."

"No changes to my genome?" I asked.

"None that we can see."

I fought back tears.

"Thank you, sir. Thank you so much."

"See you back in Washington."

As Dr. Singh ended the call, Beth and Ava pushed through the opening in the plastic and rushed over to my bed. They both climbed onto the narrow mattress, sandwiching me between them.

"Watch the ribs," I groaned.

We were all laughing and crying. I had missed the simple sensations. The smell of them. The tone of their voices in the open air instead of filtered through the face shield of a hazmat suit. The feel of skin on skin instead of latex.

After fourteen days in quarantine, it was like an invitation to return to my life again.

To come home.

3

ONE MONTH LATER

THE DOOR TO THE bathroom creaked opened. Beth peered in.

"What are you doing?" she asked, bleary-eyed.

Fair question. It was three in the morning, and I was sitting in as hot a bath as I could stand.

"Did I wake you?" I asked.

"No, I reached for you, but you weren't there. Is it the same thing as last week?"

"Yeah."

"Where's the pain?" she asked.

"My legs. My arms. My back. Basically everywhere."

Beth stepped into the bathroom and started rummaging through the medicine cabinet.

"I already took some Advil," I said. "Just waiting for it to kick in."

She approached the claw-foot tub—cast iron with a copper patina overlay. The steam peeling off the surface of the water had filled the bathroom with a hot, heavy fog.

"You haven't peed in there, have you?" she asked.

I laughed. "No, why?"

She untied her robe, let it slide off her shoulders and onto the subway-tile floor.

Taking hold of the side of the tub, she swung a long leg over and climbed in.

"Ooh, that's hot." She exhaled slowly through her teeth as she eased down into the water across from me. "I don't know how you stand this."

"That's how bad it hurts."

"What kind of pain is it?"

"Remember growing pains?"

"Sure."

"It's like that. On steroids. A deep ache."

"Or maybe you've gotten soft and weak in your old age."

I smiled and flipped her off.

Leaning back against the smooth enamel, I closed my eyes. Despite the hot water, my legs still throbbed. I'd taken three Advils, but I was starting to suspect I'd need something stronger if the pain persisted.

"I wish you'd talk to Dr. Strand about this."

"I'm seeing him tomorrow."

What I hadn't told Beth was that I'd talked to Dr. Strand about this recurring pain at a check-in several days ago, and he was troubled enough to send me off for a round of X-rays. I'd tell her what was going on when I had concrete news. No point in worrying her if it was nothing.

"Will you be able to go into work tomorrow?" she asked.

"I hope so."

The GPA had put me on leave since Denver, and tomorrow I was returning to work for the first time since nearly getting myself killed six weeks ago. My ribs were healing nicely, and the ice-inflicted lacerations had resolved without a single scar.

"What time's your train?" I asked.

"Seven-fifteen."

Beth was taking the loop up to New York for a sociology conference at Columbia. She was presenting a lecture on crime in Lower Manhattan, which had become a massive homeless encampment since it flooded and was condemned eight years ago.

"Are you still planning to stay for the whole thing?" I asked.

"Yeah. I wish you could come. We could make a week of it."

We fell into easy conversation as the water cooled. Talking with Beth was one of the few pure joys of my life. In fact, when I'd asked her to marry me all those years ago, I'd phrased the proposal as: "There's no one else on this planet I would rather have ten thousand dinners with."

The pain in my legs slowly relented.

Beth finally stood and stepped out of the tub, sighing as she glanced at her phone.

"What's wrong?" I asked.

"It's after four. I still have to pack and get out to Union Station by six. No point in even trying to go back to sleep."

"Sorry I woke you," I said.

She donned her robe, tied the belt, came back to the tub.

Leaning down, she kissed me.

"Don't ever be."

In the morning, I dropped Ava at school, parked at a lot near the Arlington Cemetery station, and took the blue line into D.C.

The Gene Protection Agency was headquartered in Constitution Center, in the same office space that had once housed the National Endowment for the Arts.

I badged through security and took the elevator up to the suite of offices of the director and deputy director, where I'd been summoned to meet with Edwin Rogers at nine A.M.

I waited outside his secretary's garrison for a half hour, and then Edwin emerged from his office, saying by way of greeting, "Had coffee yet?"

"Yes, but I could always have more."

"Walk with me."

He was an impressive, dominating man.

Six-five, slim with wide shoulders, and dressed in a gorgeously tailored suit.

At sixty, he was still lighter than ever on his feet, and I had to walk fast to keep pace with his long, confident strides.

We rode down to the building's central park and got in line at the coffee stand. It was a mild morning for late November, and the ten, glass-façade stories of Constitution Center that enclosed the one-acre courtyard kept us protected from the wind coming off the Potomac and the interstate noise just to our south.

We took our coffees to a nearby bench.

"How are those busted ribs?" Edwin asked.

"Still tender. I see my doctor this afternoon."

Edwin sipped his coffee. "And therapy? If you don't mind my prying . . ."

"It's helping."

"Good. Important to make sure you're processing what happened in Denver. Could've been so much worse."

I drank my coffee.

Directly above us, I heard the cannon blast of a hyperjet smashing through the sound barrier on its ascent out of Reagan National.

"Where are we with Soren?" I asked.

"We filed attempted-murder charges. Judge denied bail. He's still being held in Denver."

"He doesn't want to cut a deal?"

"Won't even talk to us."

"What do we have on him?"

"Not a lot. His computer was clean."

"He told us where that house was. Admitted making a delivery to it. Walked us straight into a trap."

"And after he asked for a lawyer, you responded by threatening him with illegal extradition to China."

"Sir, I—"

"Logan. I'm on your side here."

"What if we chipped him and kicked him loose?"

"You mean with one of DARPA's experimental nano-thingies?"

"Why not? See where he goes."

"They're really only useful with cooperative informants. They dissolve after forty-eight hours. Also, you know, bit of a violation of his rights. Again."

"So what happens next?"

"There's a preliminary hearing in two weeks. That'll be our face-the-music moment." Edwin glanced at his watch and stood. "I have to go up to the Hill. I want you to report to the Intelligence Division. They know you're coming. You'll be riding a desk on analyst row until you're cleared for fieldwork."

As I watched Edwin walk across the courtyard, a familiar voice called my name. I turned to see my partner, Nadine, moving toward me, breaking into a smile.

"Hey, stranger," she said, sitting down beside me. "How you feeling?"

"Better. The director put me on desk duty, so . . . fun times ahead."

"Oh, come on, this is your dream. You hate fieldwork. It makes you all pukey."

"True. I also hate being in a cubicle."

Nadine laughed. "It's almost like you can't be made happy."

I rolled my eyes.

"Lunch plans?" she asked.

"No."

"There's a new ramen place across the street. My treat."

"What's the occasion?"

"I don't know. Can't I be glad you didn't die?"

"How long are you in town?" I asked.

"I'm taking the loop out to Minneapolis this evening." She shrugged. "Apparently, someone set up a gene lab in the basement of an abandoned psychiatric hospital."

"Sounds like the opening to a great horror film."

"I'll swing by analyst row to pick you up a little before noon." Nadine stood, tapped her coffee cup against mine. "Good to have you back."

And she set off across the courtyard.

Dr. Jeff Strand—my internist of almost a decade—sat across from me in the patient room, studying my chart.

"So I got your X-rays back."

"Okay." I girded myself. We'd been chatting for a few minutes, but this was all I could think about.

"There are some . . . irregularities." He pulled two X-rays out of my file and placed them on the cushioned table I was perched on. They looked identical to me. He touched one of them. "This is an image of the right carpal bones and radius and ulna. Wrist and forearm. It's normal."

"That's good, right?"

"This is from another patient of mine."

"Oh."

He pointed to the other X-ray. "This is the image of your right wrist and forearm."

I went back and forth between the two.

"See the difference?" he asked.

"Not really. Just tell me, is it cancer?"

"No, nothing like that. Did you ever break a bone when you were younger?"

"My clavicle when I was thirteen."

"And you just broke some ribs back in October in Denver."

"Right."

He took another X-ray from my file. "This is an image of your broken ribs taken at Denver Health. Other than the fractures and breaks, these bones are normal." He pointed at the recent X-ray of my right arm. "These are not."

"What's wrong with them?"

"Nothing's wrong per se. There's a metric called the z-score, which measures bone mineral density. Anything between -1 and 1 is within the range of normal. Your z-score is 2.75."

"Is that high?"

He chuckled. "In my entire career, I've never seen bones this dense. This could explain the deep body pain you've been experiencing if they were undergoing a cycle of densification."

"What would cause an uptick in bone density?"

"Bad things. Diffusely metastatic prostate cancer, Paget's disease, pyknodysostosis, osteopetrosis . . . It's a long, scary list. But here's the thing. You don't have any of those."

"You're sure?"

"I screened you for everything the AI could think of. You're otherwise completely healthy. You just have superdense bones now. Far less prone to breaks and fractures."

I felt a sudden rush of fear.

My heart was thudding in my chest.

I looked at Jeff, a slight man with a bushy beard and somber eyes.

"How much of my medical history are you sharing with my employer?" I asked.

"You signed a release allowing me to send over reports

following your Denver incident. It's so they know when to put you back on active duty. Why?"

"Have you shared these X-rays and your findings with them?"

"Not yet."

"Don't."

Jeff looked uncertain.

"What's the concern?" he asked.

"Could you do one more DNA work-up for me?"

"I thought your Denver test was negative for changes."

"It was."

"Why would it not have shown any changes if your genome had been altered?"

"Any number of reasons," I said. "We know those ice bombs contained a gene-editing package. It may have only targeted cells in certain organs. Or the viral vector could have been programmed with a delay mechanism, allowing it to sit dormant and modify my genome later."

Jeff came to his feet. "I'll send your DNA off for a new round of genome sequencing. We'll compare it to your last test." He started putting the X-rays back into my chart. "If there is an anomaly," he said, "I'm required by law to report it. Of course, you know this. But I will inform you first."

Maybe I was just being paranoid, but if my genome had been altered in Denver, I wanted to know what other changes might be coming. The last thing I needed was the GPA thinking I'd done this to myself, or a story breaking in the *New York Post* or the *Guardian*, splashing out the headline that the disgraced son of Miriam Ramsay had been caught self-editing.

But more than anything, I didn't want to become someone's lab rat.

● ● ●

A cold front crashed through the D.C. metro at rush hour.

A violence of black skies, wind, and rain—the final nail being hammered through the heart of autumn.

As I drove the last few blocks toward my home in the Bluemont neighborhood of Arlington, the air was aswirl with dead leaves, and I could feel the pressure change like a vise ratcheting down on my ribs.

With Beth in New York City, Ava and I ordered from our favorite Chinese place.

I built a fire.

First of the season.

And as a cold rain sluiced down the windows that overlooked the backyard, my daughter brought out our rosewood chessboard and began setting up the marble pieces. I thought I detected something in Ava's body language—and a heaviness in her eyes.

"How was your first day back?" she asked.

"Fine. They put me on a desk in the Intelligence Division."

"What do they do there?"

She held out both hands—a white pawn in one, a black pawn in the other. I chose her left hand.

Black.

She would go first.

"They keep tabs on all known scientists who used to work in genetics. Try to predict who among them might be willing to break the law."

"How do you predict that?" Ava asked as she made her opening move.

Pawn to e4.

"An artificial intelligence program called MYSTIC."

I brought out my king's pawn to meet hers.

"Wow, Dad."

"What?"

"You work for the man."

I didn't have the heart to tell her what I had only recently begun to come to terms with. I didn't just work for the man. I was the man.

We went back and forth, bringing our knights forward.

Ten minutes into the game, neither of us had lost a piece.

"Do you love your job?" Ava asked.

"It's interesting work."

"But do you love it?"

"Only the very lucky are fortunate enough to love—"

"That's not an answer."

I couldn't help but smile. So much like her grandmother.

"Well, Mom loves her work," Ava said.

"Yep. She's one of the lucky ones."

"Did you ever want to be a scientist like your mom?"

I nodded, finding her question curious—Ava had rarely asked about her grandmother. Of course she knew who she was, what she'd done. But we rarely spoke about her.

"What was she like?"

"One of the smartest people who ever lived."

"No, what was she *like*? If she were in this room with us right now . . ."

"Serious most of the time. You always had the sense that she was thinking about something else, which she probably was. But when she wanted to engage, it was effortless. She could be wickedly funny in the right setting."

"Was she a good mom?"

"I know she loved me. I'll put it this way—I was not the most important thing in her life. She wanted to master the writing and editing of DNA. To heal sickness. Improve the quality of human life. The environment. The world. And it had nothing to do with money for her. She couldn't have cared less about her fame."

"Would I have liked her?"

"Hard to say. She would never have been Grandma Ramsay. People with those kinds of ambitions—they aren't like the rest of us. There's a relentlessness in them. They think they want peace. They think achievement will bring it to them. It never does."

What I didn't tell her was my unvarnished truth. How did I really feel about my mom? I hated her. And I loved her. And I wished I'd had a different mom, even as I wanted to be her. And I would've killed for her.

"You've never really asked personal questions about my mom before," I said.

"Guess which global catastrophe we're studying in modern world history?"

Fuck.

It was times like these when I was grateful we'd had the foresight to give our daughter her mother's last name: *Williams*. Growing up is hard enough when you aren't the granddaughter of the architect of the largest accidental mass killing in human history.

"Did anyone . . ."

"Only my teacher knows. She gave me a heads-up we'd be talking about it."

I got an alert that our food had arrived.

I went outside and grabbed it from the front passenger seat of the empty, self-driving delivery vehicle. When I came back in, I saw that Ava's bishop was threatening my queen's knight. In short order, if I wasn't careful, this would lead to me losing the game.

I set the bags of food on the coffee table as the spicy-sweet perfume of General Tso's chicken and orange beef began to permeate the living room.

Ava looked up from the chessboard. "Did you get real meat?" she asked.

"I splurged."

Her smile made the 300 percent upcharge worth every penny.

I returned to the game.

What Ava was doing—or trying to do—was lure me into blocking that threat with a pawn. If I fell for it, two moves later she would bring her queen to that newly vacated square, d3, and from there she was thirteen moves (assuming I didn't block her pawn and king's knight; seventeen moves if I did) from checkmate. But if I sacrificed my queen's knight and used this move to advance my pawn to b5, the game's momentum would shift. My queen and knight were already in position on her side of the board, and while I couldn't see checkmate yet, I would definitely be taking a buzz saw through her pieces.

It was profoundly strange to be seeing this many moves ahead—I could usually manage two or three at most.

And so I advanced my pawn and, eleven moves later, checkmated Ava at f8 with my rook and queen.

She was as stunned as I was.

Oddly, this didn't feel like any of our games in recent memory. I didn't think she had let me win, but this was definitely not the Ava I was accustomed to playing. I wondered if the stuff with her grandmother had taken her focus off the game.

Reaching across the board to shake my hand, Ava said, "Have you been practicing?"

"No." I smiled. "Can't I get lucky sometimes?"

"That didn't feel like luck."

She got up, walked over to the bags of food.

"Hey," I said.

She glanced back at me.

"I'm sorry."

"For what?"

I chose my words carefully. "That my family's baggage is affecting you. I wish I could tell you it gets easier."

"Was she an evil person?"

"No. There are very few truly evil people in the world. She was just . . . deeply flawed."

"I don't know what I think about being her granddaughter. Knowing that part of her is in me. My boyfriend doesn't even know. Feels like I'm lying to people."

I didn't know what to say to that, only that it broke my heart to see the pain of my mother's actions finally manifesting in my daughter.

"These are hard things," I said, "and if you ever feel like you want to talk to someone about it . . . someone who isn't me or your mom . . . just say the word."

I climbed into bed at nine, with the window cracked just high enough so I could hear the rain.

I opened the book I'd been reading this week—Kazuo Ishiguro's *Never Let Me Go*. Before Denver, there'd been a twelve-book tower on my nightstand, comprising birthday and Christmas gifts over the last few years. I'd always intended to read them, but usually, at day's end, all I had the energy and focus for was watching an episode or two of whatever nonsense was mildly holding my interest.

Perhaps it was being at home for a month without the stress of work, but I'd found myself with a newfound surfeit of concentration and curiosity.

For the last two weeks, I'd found that, even when I did watch TV, I gravitated to documentaries and true stories. And reading had become my joy again. There was nothing quite like the feel of my fingers turning pages in the silence, and I was also remembering past books I'd read.

Exact passages of prose.

Even what I'd felt at the time I'd read them.

I finished the book a little past midnight, closing it with a small fire of accomplishment glowing inside of me. In the last two weeks, I'd read all twelve books that had been languishing on my nightstand.

I hadn't been capable of this intensity of concentration and focus in, well, *ever*. Something was different. As I closed my eyes, a quiet voice whispered from the furthest corner of my mind. Not *something*. It's *you* that's different.

My psychologist's office was in Georgetown, and I didn't know if the intent had been to create a calm, soothing space, but nearly every item in the room—carpet, furniture, curtains, artwork—was some shade of gray.

Her name was Aimee, this was our third session, and already I could sense that we were coming to the end of things to talk about with regard to what had happened in Denver. I was having to carry the conversation more, often saying with twenty words what only needed ten, doing whatever I could to fill the fifty minutes.

But something was different today.

From the start of our session, it was apparent that Aimee was attempting to guide the conversation in a way she hadn't previously.

She kept circling the idea that new traumas reopen old wounds.

"I guess I'm just wondering," she said finally, "if the incident in Denver brought back any of the emotions or fears from the last time you were injured. Or any other events in your life."

And there it is, I thought. Maybe Aimee Frum, Ph.D., thought she was being subtle, but as far as I was concerned, she was wearing a flashing billboard.

And it said: *I'm trying to get you to talk about your mother.*

I suppose my only open question was whether she legitimately believed we needed to talk about my mother in order to confront what had happened in Denver or if her curiosity having gotten the better of her, I was simply an irresistible psychological box of chocolates that she couldn't stop herself from opening.

I said, "Not really."

"I understand you spent some time in prison."

"Three years. From age twenty-seven to twenty-nine."

"Must've been difficult."

"I was in medium security. Got into two fights the entire time. That's why my nose is crooked. Mostly kept my head down. None of the gangs bothered me, and some good came out of it—I met my wife there."

"In prison?"

"Beth's a professor of criminology. At the time, she was doing research at my prison. She reached out. We met, hit it off, started meeting once a week. This went on for a couple of months, until she left to take a job at American University. When I was released, I asked her out. That was fifteen years ago next month."

"Good first date?"

"The greatest."

"How did it feel to be free after all that time?"

She was starting to annoy me.

"Fine."

"Just fine?"

"The ACLU was able to secure a pardon for me. A lot of people in the legal community felt I was being punished for my mother's crimes."

"How did *you* feel?"

"Glad to be out."

"Why?"

Jesus.

"Because not being in prison is more enjoyable than being in prison."

"It seems like my questions are irritating you today."

"Not at all."

"Maybe you could try being honest with me, Logan."

I leaned back in my chair. "Okay. I am irritated."

"Why?"

"I'm sure you're a very good therapist, but I don't know you. I didn't choose to be here. And I worked through this stuff years ago. Haven't had a panic attack in a long time."

"You used to have them regularly?"

"Yeah. Look, the first two sessions were fine—"

"High praise."

"—but what I'm getting from you today feels more like morbid curiosity."

Now it was Aimee's turn to be annoyed. "I wonder if you could try giving me the benefit of the doubt. I'm only here to help you. I am purely in *your* corner."

"You think I still need help?"

"I do."

"All right then."

"You sure?"

I nodded.

"How do you see yourself?" she asked.

"Aren't we all the heroes of our own stories?"

She smiled. "In the psychology game, that's what we call a classic deflection."

I sighed. "You want to talk about guilt now?"

"Do you still feel guilty?"

I looked at the photograph above her desk—a mountain lake with mist hovering over the surface. Black-and-white, of course. There was a thin line of calligraphy below the photograph: *It's okay to be who you are in this moment.*

Sure.

"I try not to think about it," I said.

"How old were you when you started working in your mother's lab?"

"Twenty-two."

"And how would you describe your relationship with her at the time?"

"She was a god. The world's preeminent cell biologist. She'd already made a billion dollars off The Story of You, her ancestry and genetic testing company. Her Scythe patents were even more lucrative."

"I can read her Wikipedia page. How did *you* feel about her?"

"I looked up to her. Wanted to please her. She was the only family I had."

"What happened to the others?"

"My twin brother, Max, died when we were thirteen."

"I'm so sorry. That's a huge loss, Logan. How, may I ask?"

"Leukemia. He had the big brain between us. Mom's favorite. Dad died shortly after that, and Kara, my older sister, went overseas in the military."

"Sounds like she bailed."

"I'm not saying she wasn't a good sister, but Kara takes care of Kara. So it really was just Mom and me."

"You and Kara close today?"

"Not really. She lives in Montana. We talk a few times a year. I wish we were closer."

"How do you view your role in what happened in China?"

I felt my chest tightening up like it always did when my thoughts turned to that summer.

"We were trying to do a good thing."

My mother's main lab was in Shenzhen, and there was a bacterial leaf blight impacting indica rice in a nearby region called Zhaoqing. Mom wanted to genetically insert a virus into locusts so that these carrier insects would be able to infect the rice paddies with the virus, which we could program to bolster the plants' blight resistance without otherwise changing the plant.

It's one thing to genetically engineer seeds in the lab and charge outrageously for them. This held no interest for my mother. She was trying something far more ambitious—sending insects directly into the fields to somatically edit crops in real time. The potential applications went far beyond the Zhaoqing rice blight, to all of the world's breadbasket crops.

We built several bio-contained greenhouses and released our genetically modified yellow-spined bamboo locusts on infected test plants within the containment facility. It worked. There was no chlorosis, or browning. The plants thrived.

"Were you closely involved with the experiments?" Aimee asked.

"I was helping where I could, but I'd only just finished my undergrad degree. I was there for the summer. Thought I was part of the team, but I know they all saw me as a tagalong who was only there because I was Miriam Ramsay's son."

I felt an ache in the back of my throat. It had been years since I'd talked openly about what had happened.

"The greenhouse phase was successful. The data looked great. We had the support of the Chinese biosafety board, so we released our carrier locusts into the Zhaoqing fields."

I took a careful breath.

"It was a perfect, blue-sky day. The mountains were shining in the sun. The flooded rice paddies were this lovely, emerald green. I had a large canvas bag slung over my shoulder. We all did. I untied mine, opened it. I still remember the twinge of pride as I watched the cloud of our modified locusts fly away. *Look at me, changing the world.*

"The initial results were positive, but then the viral-control systems began developing mutations at an accelerated rate. In addition to emboldening the plants against the blight, it started knocking out genes essential for seed production. We tried to contain it, but . . ."

"The virus had generalized," she said.

"Yeah."

Miriam had engineered the virus to only target this specific strain of rice, but it developed cross-species virus transmission, made worse by new rounds of viral mutation and selection, infecting and targeting other food-crop species. Within a year, the vector locusts began propagating exponentially.

I said, "My mom died right around the time the effects were first beginning to be felt in the American Midwest."

"The car accident?"

I nodded. But accident? Not quite. Miriam had driven her car off Highway 1, between Jenner and Sea Ranch, California, where the road runs highest above the sea.

During the next seven years, each growing season yielded less and less, and before the locusts were finally eradicated, China's strategic grain supply was critically depleted.

The famine spread to every continent and affected every human being in one way or another. When you wipe out millions of hectares of crops, it changes where the rain falls. When you destroy rice paddies, you destroy everything that needs them to live.

Two hundred million people starved to death, but that number doesn't come close to the total impact of the chaos we unchained. The downstream effect on economies, healthcare systems, entire species, and the biosphere itself was incalculable.

"Yesterday, my daughter told me she's studying the famine in school. And . . . um . . ."

"It's okay."

I let the tears fall.

"It's just a lot, you know?"

"It is a lot."

"I've gotten used to not caring what the rest of the world thinks of me, but . . ."

"I'm sure your daughter sees you as the wonderful father you are."

She handed me a box of tissues.

"Logan, when I look at you, I see a man who's still very, very hard on himself."

Something broke loose at the core of me. She was touching a wound that would never heal, which I'd wrapped in two decades' worth of scar tissue.

"How could I not be?" I asked, my voice now barely a whisper.

Specks of snow flurried down out of the charcoal sky, and the wind coming off the Washington Channel was brisk and eye-wateringly cold. I entered the square exedra and gazed up at the thirty-foot pillar on the granite platform.

Though I knew it by heart, I read the inscription engraved in the rock:

IN MEMORY OF THOSE WHO LOST THEIR LIVES
AT HOME AND ABROAD DURING THE GREAT STARVATION
WE WILL NEVER FORGET

Officially, it was also called the Shenzhen Famine.

Informally, it was Ramsay's Famine.

I took a seat on the granite bench beside the pillar. I came here several times a year, usually on the way home from work, when I knew the weather was bad enough to keep the tourists away.

It was dusk now and snowing hard enough to turn the mammoth profile of the New Pentagon into an ominous, featureless monolith.

The horn blasts of rush-hour traffic were dampened by the storm.

Footsteps approached.

I turned and saw a figure approaching, their face concealed by the upturned collar of a burgundy wool coat.

Fuck. I knew that coat.

Nadine walked over and sat beside me.

"Following me," I said. "Wow."

She shrugged. "Saw you heading this way when you left work." And then, "I know you come here sometimes."

"What do you want, Nadine?"

"You seemed upset earlier."

"I had my final therapy session this morning."

"Didn't go well?"

"Maybe too well."

She had never asked me directly about my past. Between us, there was just this quiet understanding. *I know. And I'm here.*

"We don't have to talk," she said. "It just made me sad to think about you sitting all alone out here. Getting snowed on."

I watched the steady stream of delivery drones flying across the water into Arlington and Alexandria.

"Why'd you take this job?" I asked.

"I love guns."

I looked at her. She smiled.

"I'm kidding. Policy creation was so damn ethereal. I wanted to actually *do* something, you know? It's the difference between designing a house and building the thing."

"I hate this job."

"I know."

"But I think I would hate not doing it more."

Nadine said, "There are times I love it. Moments when it feels like we're improving the world. I just wish they came more often."

We sat in the cold, watching the lights wink on across the channel. I started to tell her what I suspected was happening to me—all the small changes that were becoming more impossible to rationalize away. But I wanted to see the results of the new genome analysis first, and asking her to keep secrets from the GPA wasn't a position I felt comfortable placing her in.

"Buy you a drink?" she asked.

"I should probably get home."

Nadine stood, rewrapped the scarf that had come loose around her neck.

She said, "If the job makes you unhappy, quit." I looked up at her. The snow was frosting her hair. "I get that you had some atoning to do way back when, but you've cleared your debts."

And with that, she thrust her hands into her pockets and walked away.

That night, after dinner, I beat Ava in three games of chess. None of them were even close, and the last one required only twelve moves to checkmate her.

"What the actual hell is going on here?" she asked, tipping her king over when she saw the inevitable end. "Have you been going easy on me all this time, Dad?"

"No." I laughed.

"How are you suddenly this good?"

"What's going on?" Beth asked from the couch.

"Dad just shellacked me for . . ." Ava counted up the losses in her head. ". . . the ninth game in a row."

"Impressive," Beth said.

"Impossible," Ava said, staring at me suspiciously.

Memories were coming back to me, and not just of every book I'd ever read. Random moments of insignificance. Pivotal events that had shaped my life.

From a month ago.

From a decade ago.

From my childhood.

It was an eerie sensation. As if someone were brooming out the dark corners of my mind. Wiping off the cobwebs. Repairing frayed connections.

If I tried to recall something, I found I could see it with a clarity and certainty I'd never known.

Max died thirty-one years ago, and I could hear his voice in my head for the first time in years. I could conjure his face. Hold it steady in my mind's eye. Study the shape of his nose. Every blemish, every freckle.

I had picked up a stack of new books at the Central Library on Quincy Street on the way home from work.

The one I was most excited to crack open was *Gödel, Escher, Bach: An Eternal Golden Braid* by Douglas Hofstadter. I had tried to read it twice before. Once in college, once in prison. The second time, I had gotten halfway through, put it down one evening, and never picked it up again. It's a book about number theory, codes, paradoxes, and self-referential systems, and it never failed to make me feel inadequate, with Hofstadter's heady concepts bumping up against the limits of my intelligence on nearly every page, reinforcing the self-defeating mantra: *I'm a pale imitation of my mother's intellect.*

Beth finished brushing her teeth and climbed into bed.

"What are you reading?" she asked.

I showed her the nearly thousand-page doorstop.

I was already on page 150.

"Mind if I turn on the TV?" she asked.

"Not at all."

I went back to reading. The font size of the type was microscopic, and I remembered that it had been a deciding factor in my abandoning the book on my first two attempts.

But it wasn't bothering me tonight.

Nor were Beth's occasional interruptions or the sounds from the television, which would have completely derailed my concentration in the past. In fact, I could've explained in near-perfect detail the events of the episode Beth was watching *and* synopsized the now 224 pages I'd already read of *Gödel, Escher, Bach*.

After a while, I noticed that my wife wasn't watching TV anymore.

I felt her eyes on me.

"Are you actually comprehending any of that?" she asked.

"Why?"

"You're turning a page, like, every thirty seconds."

Over the last few weeks the act of reading had undergone a tectonic shift for me. I was no longer consuming each sentence in consecutive order, but absorbing the page as a whole, letting it make an imprint on my mind.

"I'm just trying this new speed-reading exercise," I said.

"Is it working?"

"Seems to be."

She studied me for a moment but didn't push the issue.

Just went back to watching her show.

I finished the book at four in the morning.

My eyes hurt.

My thoughts raced, though not from the plethora of ideas contained within *GEB*.

What had started earlier this month as a few days of feeling mentally sharper and clearer was becoming more intense and inescapable with each passing day.

Before I shared this with Beth, or anyone, I needed the results of my new genome analysis.

I needed to understand what was happening to me.

The next day, I was sitting at my temporary workstation—a cubicle on the fourth floor of Constitution Center—feeding data points for an ex-geneticist into MYSTIC, the predicative AI engine.

Through the heads-up display, I was currently inputting the basics—age, race, gender.

It was mindless data entry with a sinister undercurrent of government overreach.

MYSTIC would consider millions of data points. The more information you gave the AI's self-learning algorithm, the more accurate its prediction.

The far-ranging latitude granted by the Gene Protection Act made it legal for the GPA to use people's voter registration information, phone records, CCTV surveillance tracking, publications, travel history, census forms, Social Security documents, tax returns, and every keystroke they made, all in the scope of what had been coined Predictive Criminality Modeling.

And all without a warrant or just cause.

This allowed us to flesh out data-point categories such as income bracket, debt load, number of children, political affiliation, voting record, credit score, and a host of other financial indicators.

When it came to providing additional personal data, we were at the mercy of a subject's social media presence and internet search history.

The current scientist on deck was a man named Clifford Johnson, Ph.D.

Before the Gene Protection Act, Dr. Johnson had been a research scientist for a company trying to build human hearts out of artificial jellyfish. With a basic internet search, I found that he was currently employed as a high school biology teacher. This wasn't uncommon. Many scientists who had been engaged in pure research had been forced to pivot to teaching. In the public school system, all science textbooks had been updated to reflect the government's new position on gene editing: illegal, dangerous, and at odds with the natural law.

Johnson's Meta page was public, and as I scrolled through his posts over the last five years, the picture of the man he had become after being forced out of his chosen profession began to take shape.

He was spending more time with his family.

Working less.

Exercising more.

There'd been a period of soul-searching after his old company had gone under, and at least from the outside, he appeared to have made the best of it.

As I began to input my impressions of Clifford Johnson based on a social media review—the algorithm's final data point—my phone rang.

Beth calling.

I touched the earpiece.

"Hi, love."

"What are you up to?" she asked.

"Data entry."

"Sounds thrilling."

I continued typing: *Outward expressions of satisfaction with his life are evident. There are no anti-government sentiments expressed (at least publicly).*

"Yeah, I just can't believe I get to do this for a living. What's up?"

"Take me to La Fleur tonight."

"What's the occasion?" I asked. Eating out, especially at a fine-dining restaurant, was an extortionate affair in our post-famine world.

While Dr. Johnson's prior work history was in the commercial sector, he appears to have adjusted well to his new career in the public school system.

"No occasion," she said. "I just miss you. Feels like we haven't really connected in a while."

Had Beth noticed some of the changes I'd been undergoing?

At least from a glance, his social media presence does not raise any red flags.

"Seven o'clock work?" I asked.

"Perfect."

MYSTIC flashed a message in my HUD: *Recommend no further action or investigation at this time.*

"I'll make the reservation," I said.

As I ended the call, I stared at the text box in my HUD, which I'd been filling out when Beth rang.

An odd realization crept over me.

I had continued to input my assessment of Clifford Johnson's social media presence throughout my conversation with Beth.

Replaying what had just transpired, I arrived at a surprising conclusion.

Neither activity—speaking to my wife or working with MYSTIC—had defaulted to autopilot.

In the moment, I had been fully engaged with each task—simultaneously. Re-reading what I'd written about Johnson, there were no typos. While not exactly Tolstoy, it was a well-reasoned paragraph of writing. Absolutely extraordinary.

Was it possible the virus I'd been exposed to was making me *better*?

And where was Strand's report?

Fuck this. I would go to his office during lunch.

My phone vibrated.

Turning it over, I saw a text from a number I didn't recognize.

It read:

> They know you're changing.

I felt a cold shudder of fear, ripped off my HUD frames, wrote back:

> Who is this?

The response came instantly.

> You need to leave the building NOW.

My pulse quickened.

I lifted off my chair just high enough to peer over my cubicle wall.

Analyst row was an open floor of cubicles that could've been the bullpen of any company.

At the moment, there was nothing out of the ordinary.

The sound of fingertips typing away on keyboards.

Muffled music bleeding through headphones.

A handful of quiet conversations.

Two men appeared in the doorway on the far side of the room. I didn't recognize them, but that wasn't necessarily a red flag. The GPA had four hundred employees in the building, and I only knew a fraction of—

No.

Something *was* off.

They weren't analysts returning from lunch. They were speaking with a woman named Ronna who managed the group that worked with MYSTIC. And it was a small thing, impossible for me to read with absolute certainty at this distance, but their body language evinced a quality I had never seen on analyst row.

Coiled energy.

These were men accustomed to physicality.

To violence.

A wrecking ball of adrenaline hit my nervous system.

I sat back down in my chair.

The men were heading in my direction now, their cheap, dark jackets open, and even from fifty feet away, I could see that they were carrying.

I was not.

And I had a decision to make.

Now.

I slid off my chair, stepped out of my cubicle into one of the walkways that cut from one end of the bullpen to the other, and moved away from the men at the leisurely pace of a government employee taking a much-deserved trip to the breakroom.

Only when I reached the far end of the room did I venture a glance back.

Those men were at my cubicle now—one of them was going through my things.

We locked eyes.

He was short and wide, but he looked like he could move.

As he said something to his partner, I turned out of the bullpen and took off, sprinting down a hallway.

I passed an alcove humming with vending machines.

A breakroom.

Restrooms.

Behind me, someone shouted, "Logan!"

I didn't stop.

Didn't look back.

Smashed through a door leading to a stairwell and flew down the steps.

I'd always taken the elevators on the other side of the bullpen and never went down this way, but I suspected the stairs emptied into the lobby.

Which was a problem.

Constitution Center was a secure government building that required credentials and passage through a metal detector to enter. While the security was outward facing, the lobby was the only exit from the building.

And there were cameras *everywhere*.

As I passed the third-floor landing, I heard the fourth-floor door bang open and then two sets of footfalls pounding down the steps, reverberating off the concrete walls.

At the next landing, I opened the door and slipped out into the second floor, letting it close soundlessly behind me.

I ran through a corridor I'd never seen before. There'd be no hiding here. Every door I passed was locked and required IT security clearance to enter. I suspected that most of the MYSTIC servers were kept here.

I turned another corner, and straight ahead, an Exit sign glowed over a door. I ran for it harder than I'd ever run in my life, hoping it wouldn't just lead back down to the lobby.

Slammed through; glanced back.

The hall was still empty.

I shot down the stairs, reaching for the phone in my pocket, but I'd left it at my cubicle. The stairs terminated at a door emblazoned with a red sign:

EMERGENCY EXIT ONLY. ALARM WILL SOUND.

I shouldered through.

Alarms shrieked, lights pulsated.

I was outside, D Street SW straight ahead, and as I took my first step, something slipped over my head.

Everything went dark.

My legs lifted off the ground.

And then my back struck the concrete so hard I felt the air leave my lungs and I was gasping, trying desperately to tear the hood off my face, but someone rolled me over, my arms torqued behind my back as plastic zip ties dug into my wrists.

Then I was up again, powerful people on either side of me clutching my arms at the shoulders, carrying me swiftly along and the tips of my shoes scraping the pavement.

I shouted. I screamed for help.

Strings of daylight were barely visible through the thread-bare portions of the hood.

Straight ahead, I heard the sound of a door sliding open.

I was thrown to a metal floor.

The door slid shut, and I rolled back under the force of acceleration as a deep male voice said, "We've got him . . . Yep . . . Came out the northwest fire exit . . . Okay . . . We're twenty minutes out."

Then two people held me down against the floor and raised the hood just enough to expose the side of my neck.

I felt the sting of a needle.

4

THE NEXT TIME MY eyes opened, I was lying on a hard mattress.

I sat up slowly.

My head felt too large and too heavy, like it might roll off my neck.

Edwin Rogers sharpened into focus.

He was standing fifteen feet away, and I wondered how long he'd been there, watching me sleep.

I swung my legs off the bed and stood.

Unsteady.

My mouth tasted bitter.

I staggered toward Edwin, wading through a heavy, mental fog.

After a few steps, I stopped.

Looked around.

Just beginning to process my surroundings.

I was inside an octagon, twelve feet across, with ten-foot walls made of glass.

There was a desk, bed, toilet, and sink.

On the other side of the glass, I saw a data terminal and an array of medical equipment.

I looked at Edwin. "What the fuck is this?"

He didn't say anything.

I went to the desk and tried to lift the chair to throw it at the glass.

It had been bolted to the concrete floor.

"Ballistic glass." Edwin's voice came through a speaker in the ceiling.

He was moving toward me now, holding a tablet.

Then we were standing three feet apart, separated only by the glass of my cell. He looked somber, and it was a small thing, but his lower eyelids were tensed in a micro-expression of what I somehow knew was fear.

Of me? I wondered. And also—how had I noticed such a granular detail?

He wore jeans and a navy windbreaker bearing the GPA insignia.

He walked over to a desk on the exterior of the vivarium and took a seat. It faced the desk on the inside—the one that had been bolted to the floor.

He gestured for me to sit.

I slid into the chair across from him.

"Why am I in here?" I asked.

"For everyone's safety."

"Come on. I'll cooperate. You don't need to lock me up."

He didn't say anything.

"Where am I?"

He turned on his tablet.

"Is this a GPA black site?"

No answer.

"How long are you planning—"

"Logan. You've undergone a tremendous amount of genetic change in a short amount of time. There could be dangerous side effects. We're going to monitor your evolution. We need to understand what you're becoming." He looked back at the tablet. "Do you know what the inhibition of the PDE4B gene does?"

"Fuck you."

Edwin's mouth twinged with irritation.

He said, "Why didn't you tell us you were—"

"Because you would've done exactly what you've done. Overreact. I wanted the evidence to defend myself. I wanted to know if, and how, I'd been changed."

"And do you know?"

I shook my head.

"Would you like to? Because I have it all right here."

"Yes."

"Then answer my question. What does the inhibition of PDE4B do?"

I shouldn't have known, but as I considered the question, I remembered reading an article eight years ago in *Scientific American*, where PDE4B had been discussed in the context of gene therapies for mental illness.

I said, "It's linked to low anxiety and high problem solving. Well, at least in mice."

"Correct. It's been inhibited in you. What if I were to tell you that your entire IGF system had also been altered and your GRIN2B gene mutated?"

Four years ago (and six months, eleven days to be exact—*How did I know that?*) I'd read an abstract on the IGF system. In fact, I could see a perfect image of it in my mind's eye.

"High learning and memory," I said.

"You just know that off the top of your head?"

"I remember reading about it."

"FOXP2?"

I shook my head, certain I had never heard of that gene before.

"It's linked to learning stimulus-response associations faster. How about NLGN3?"

I said, "Enhanced learning and spatial-learning abilities."

"GluK4."

"Low bipolar risk and higher cognitive function."

Edwin looked up at me. "Your cognition, memory, concentration, pattern recognition—it's all been targeted for enhancement. Have you experienced gains across these areas?"

"Yes."

"Since when?"

"Over the last three weeks."

"Do you get how astounding this is?"

For a moment, I couldn't speak. I had suspected that something had been done to me, but to hear it confirmed knocked the wind out of me.

"Why did you have Dr. Strand run another genome analysis?" Edwin asked.

Interesting. They had intercepted my new analysis before my doctor could even tell me the results. They must have been monitoring me closely after Denver.

I said finally, "I told you. I wanted the evidence for myself. And because I suspected my LRP5 gene had been upregulated, and perhaps modified." In the context of genetics, upregulation means the gene has increased its expression or effect. Downregulation means the opposite. If you have OPN1MW, you can see color. If it's downregulated, you're colorblind.

Edwin looked at his tablet for a moment, quickly scrolling the pages.

"LRP5 is increased bone density?" he asked.

I nodded.

"When did you begin to suspect?"

"Five weeks after Denver, I started experiencing a deep pain throughout my body."

"Why did you hide this from me?"

"Again, I wasn't hiding it. I wasn't sure what was happening, which is why I asked Dr. Strand—"

"We could've run a new analysis. You work for the Gene Protection Agency, for chrissake."

"I wanted to know if it was just some weird side effect of the virus or something worse before panicking my employer. I wanted to come to you with information, not conjecture. I haven't even told Beth yet."

"I'm going to read you a hit list of the other genes that were targeted for down- or upregulation. In most cases, they've been mutated to previously unknown polymorphisms. In a few cases, short, novel DNA sequences have been edited in, presumably to improve their function."

"There's more?"

"Oh, yeah."

I leaned forward.

"SOST."

I said, "Bone-loss resistance."

"MSTN."

"Lean, large muscles."

"SCN9A, FAAH-OUT, and NTRK1. Do you know any of those?"

I shook my head.

"They're associated with a higher pain tolerance." He went on: "HSD17B13. That's low risk of chronic liver disease. CCR5."

"HIV resistance?"

"Yep. FUT2, IL23R, HBB, PKU, CFTR, HEXA, PCSK9, GHR, GH, SLC30A8, IFIH1=MDA5, NPC1, and ANGPTL3."

I said, "In the order you read them . . . resistance against norovirus, Crohn's disease and ulcerative colitis, malaria, ochratoxin, TB, coronary disease, cancer, the next four types one and two diabetes, Ebola, and I believe the last one reinforces lipid and cardiac health."

"Wow. Okay. These next few are kind of weird. EGLN1, EPAS1, MTHFR, and EPOR."

"I read an article about that gene system a couple of years ago. It's typically found in Tibetans, right?"

"That's right. They support life and body function at high altitude. BHLHE41=DEC2, NPSR1, and ADRB1."

"I don't know those."

"They lower your sleep requirements. APOE, APP, NGF, NEU1, NGFR."

I knew these genes. I'd read an article about them in *Nature Genetics* during a flight to Minneapolis, seven years ago.

"Lower Alzheimer's risk," I said.

"CTNNB1."

"Don't know that one."

"Radiation resistance. CDKN2A and TP53?"

"Low cancer risk," I said.

"TERT."

"Isn't that related to aging?"

"It is. Mutations in the TERT can kill or slow the function of telomerase, which allows telomeres to become too short as cells divide. As you probably know—"

"Shortened telomeres are believed to be the main cause of age-related breakdown in our cells."

"Exactly," he said. "So it's another antiaging gene. If I didn't know any better, I'd say someone was trying to turn you into a superhuman. And this list is just the alleles we have some knowledge of."

"There were more changes to my genome?"

"*Thousands*. We're cross-referencing as much as we can, but it's a big job, and a lot of the affected gene systems and how they interact with one another and your body are unknown. There are even alterations in your junk DNA, which are way outside our understanding."

Even in a post-Scythe world, what Edwin was talking about was impossible. The most successful dark labs we busted might manage to manipulate a handful of genes successfully. An entire suite of changes was beyond anything I'd encountered or even heard of. While there are approximately twenty-five thousand known genes, the variance of their interactions approaches infinity. And beyond the known genes, our genome contains numerous control regions and so-called junk DNA, which aren't junk at all but a collective, self-adjusting web of systems, evolved under the selective pressure of existence for more than three billion years. It added up to a system of unimaginable complexity, one where any single change—let alone thousands— might express itself in dozens of unforeseen ways.

"Does my family know I'm here?" I asked.

"They know you've been detained under suspicion of self-editing."

"I want to talk to Beth."

"That isn't possible right now."

"I didn't do this to myself, Edwin."

"Then who did?"

"I don't know. Henrik Soren? Whoever devised what we walked into in Denver."

"You didn't show any genetic changes immediately after Denver. We ran an analysis."

"If I had the know-how and equipment to change my own DNA, why would I have my doctor's office run an analysis at some highly regulated lab? Why take such an absurdly stupid risk unless I *couldn't* do it to myself? Let's stick to the facts, not to convenient witch hunts. I've already stood trial at one of those. We know that someone infected me with a package designed to alter my DNA. We assumed—big mistake—that it didn't work. But it was obviously a sleeper package, remaining dormant for the first month or so."

"Is that even possible?"

"I mean, is any of this? Do you understand the level of mastery required to pull this off?"

Edwin powered off his tablet. He was looking at me like there was something else he wanted to say.

I waited to hear what it was.

Instead, he stood and walked out of the room through a door beside the terminal.

My hands shook. A trail of icy sweat ran down my spine. I closed my eyes and tried to just breathe.

I was being changed into something unknown.

My employer had kidnapped me and was holding me incommunicado in a black site, having told my family who the fuck knows what.

And Scythe had shown us that even the simplest genetic changes carry with them unintended, unforeseeable consequences. The possibility—likelihood, even—of collateral genomic damage, which might, for good or bad, subvert the original intent of the gene's function, which nature had carefully shaped over eons.

Whoever did this to me was overwriting nature's programming and taking control of evolution itself. That was a precarious game. My genome, for better or worse, had the information encoded to self-regulate, combat disease, and deal with toxins, environmental threats, and glitches on the fly, again, with the primary goal of survival of the species.

The same gene edits and insertions that were improving my acuity, and possibly even my longevity, might also upend the entire, fragile balance of my genome. And my life.

But that wasn't even the most existentially terrifying thought.

When Watson, Crick, and Franklin discovered DNA's double helix structure in the early 1950s, it changed how scientists thought of species delineation. In 1980, Niles Eldredge and Joel Cracraft suggested that, under the phylogenetic definition, animal species could have DNA that differed by just two percent and be categorized as separate species.

What if two percent of my genome had been changed? Would that render me an entirely new species?

Two hours later, I heard the bolt in the door of my cell slide back.

A woman walked in, aiming a Taser at me, with a man trailing behind her. He was unarmed and huge. Six-four. Chiseled out of granite. Guards.

I started to rise from the bed, but the man-beast said, "Just stay where you are."

They stood on either side of the open door, and then Edwin appeared, followed by an older, kind-faced woman who reminded me of my grandmother on my father's side.

I looked at Edwin. "What is this?"

"I want to ask you some questions."

"So ask."

"I'd like to know that you're telling the truth. This is Hana Jalal."

The man-beast brought in an extra chair, placed it beside the desk, and then motioned for me to have a seat.

Hana sat at the desk and set up a tablet, with its myriad sensors aimed at my face. I recognized the device right away—one of the next-gen polygraph rigs.

In the analog days, polygraphists would tie rubber tubes called pneumographs around a suspect's chest to provide a metric for respiratory rates. Blood pressure cuffs would be velcroed to arms. Finger plates called galvanometers would be attached to fingers to measure the skin's ability to conduct electricity.

This tablet did all of that on a no-contact basis with transdermal optical imaging software that extracted real-time measurements of blood pressure, pulse rate, sweat detection, respiratory rate, and iris dilation based on ambient light penetration of the skin's outer layer.

I knew from my own experience in law enforcement that lie-detector tests don't actually detect lies. They detect guilty feelings, which most people experience when they lie, evidenced by dramatic swings in the metrics the tablet facing me was designed to track.

Hana insisted that everyone leave. Then she told me a bit about herself and how she approached her job. I told her a little about me, although I was certain none of what I revealed was new information to her.

She asked about my life. She asked how I felt about being in this glass cell.

"Anxious and afraid," I said.

"I bet."

Like the best polygraphists I'd worked with, she exuded a sense of *wanting* me to succeed, of being in my corner, and of believing the best in me.

She was already profiling me, of course, getting baseline readings, gathering a preliminary assessment of my reactions. How I processed questions.

"Logan," Hana said finally, "if it's okay with you, I'd like to begin the examination."

"Ready when you are."

"Remember. Yes or no answers only, please."

I could see the reflection of the tablet's screen in the glass behind her.

She touched the screen, which I assumed started the test, and then turned over a sheet of paper and lifted a pencil.

"Is your name Logan Ramsay?"

"Yes."

She checked off the first question.

"Do you live in Arlington, Virginia?"

"Yes."

Another check.

"Have you ever been dishonest with someone?"

"Yes."

"Are you going to be dishonest with me during this interview?"

"No."

She checked off her question and studied her tablet.

"Have you ever changed your own genome?"

"No."

"Have you noticed any changes in your body since you were injured in Denver?"

"Yes."

"Have you noticed any changes in your mind since you were injured in Denver?"

"Yes."

"Have you told anyone about these changes?"

"No."

"Have you told your wife?"

"No."

"Have you told your daughter?"

"No."

"Have you told your sister, Kara?"

"No."

"Have you told any friends?"

"No."

"Did someone send a text to you yesterday that said 'They know you're changing'?"

"Yes."

"Do you know the identity of this person?"

"No."

"Are you the son of Miriam Ramsay?"

"Yes."

"Is your mother still alive?"

"No."

"Have you been working with her?"

What? "No."

"Did Miriam Ramsay change your genome?"

"No."

"Do you know who changed your genome?"

"No."

For the first time during the questioning, she looked at me instead of the sheet of paper or her tablet.

"Are you lying to me right now, Logan?"

"No."

"Are you controlling your breathing right now, Logan?"

"No."

"Are you controlling your heart rate?"

"No."

"Are you controlling your blood pressure?"

"No."

Hana touched the tablet's screen again. "That's it," she said.

The door to the cell opened.

Edwin waited in the doorway as Hana gathered up her things.

He said to her, "I'll have your report . . ."

"Before the end of the day."

Edwin entered the cell and took a seat at the desk. I noticed he wore an earpiece.

He looked back at the man-beast and the woman holding the Taser. "Wait outside."

After they shut the glass door, I said, "Why are you asking me about my mother?"

"Because she's alive."

"Fuck you."

He took out his phone and placed it on the table.

"One year ago, she broke into my house and sent me a video of her standing in my kitchen, holding a wineglass."

I pressed play.

If the video was a deepfake, it had been masterfully done.

Miriam's hair had turned silver, she'd made numerous cosmetic changes (probably to elude facial-recognition AI), and her face was gaunt and lined with more wrinkles than the last time I'd seen her. But it was unquestionably my mother. I would've known those eyes—dark and frighteningly intense—anywhere.

I grew lightheaded.

And then she spoke: *"The GPA and its foreign counterparts are destroying scientific research and discovery."* Her voice. No question in my mind. *"If substantive policy changes aren't enacted immediately, including letting universities and private businesses return to responsible genetic research, I will take matters into my own hands. I'll release a viral gene drive."*

As Edwin took his phone back, he said, "We ran the print on the wineglass and tested the DNA from the hair she deliberately left behind. There's no question it's her."

My vision swarmed.

Chest tightening, hands tingling.

"Are you all right?" Edwin asked. "They're telling me your heart rate is soaring."

I was shaking with rage.

"I understand you're upset."

"Why didn't you tell me?"

"Because I didn't know if you were working with her. I didn't know if she would try to reach out to you. I had your phones tapped. Your house bugged. You've been under surveillance for almost ten months."

I wanted to spring across the table and get my hands on him. I felt confident he'd be dead before the guards got inside the vivarium.

"How did you not tell me this!" I shouted.

The guards started toward the vivarium, but Edwin waved them away.

I had grieved for her. I had processed her death as well as such a thing can be processed.

I choked down a gulp of air, utterly destroyed.

Edwin said, "Soon after, she sent me an encrypted message with her demands. I responded, asking what species she would target with her gene drive."

"*Homo sapiens.*"

"Bingo."

"With what sort of changes?"

"She wasn't specific. Just called it a significant upgrade. She also promised to give me a demonstration of her abilities."

I was the demonstration. Of course, I couldn't know this for sure. But I *knew*.

I could feel my emotions evolving from the shock of seeing my mother to the horror of what she was threatening.

A gene drive is the most powerful genetic engineering tool ever conceived. Normally, when a child is born, it gets one copy of each gene from both parents, either one of which might end up being the dominant one of the pair. But if you can insert a gene-drive-targeting system in one parent, you can upend those normal laws of heredity. The gene-editing mechanism—CRISPR-Cas9, Scythe, or whatever it might be—is passed on from the targeted parent into the child's DNA, along with instructions to sneakily rewrite the *other* parent's copy of the targeted gene as the embryo develops. Say the mother has brown eyes, the father blue. With a gene drive, you can overwrite the mother's genes for eye color in the embryo, thus guaranteeing that their child will have blue eyes. But the real kicker is that the child will pass on the targeting system to *their* children in turn. All of their children will now have blue eyes too, and so on.

Within a few generations, the gene drive will pervade the entire population—and the natural, unedited copy of the gene will be wiped out completely. All Homo sapiens will have blue eyes.

A gene drive can be used for immense good. Before the Ramsay famine, one was used to make *all* of the offspring of the malaria mosquito male. Since only female mosquitoes of the *Anopheles* genus are capable of transmitting human malaria, this eradicated the spread of that disease, and eventually that species of mosquito.

Gene drives could also be used to great detriment, because they don't just alter the genetic makeup of one person, plant, or animal. They have the power to alter the evolutionary trajectory of an entire species.

"If you've been surveilling me," I said, "then you know I haven't had any contact with her. So why am I here? I'm not working with my mother. I didn't know she was alive until five minutes ago. You test me every few years. You can't possibly think I'm stupid enough to have altered my own genome."

"I actually believe you, Logan. But you are changing, and we don't know what you're on your way to becoming."

The first night in my vivarium reminded me of my first night in prison. The cell doors locking in unison. The sound of the big lights in the common area shutting off. The silence and darkness closing in around me as I faced the reality that my life was over, that these walls were my home for the next thirty years.

I lay down on the mattress and stared up at the glass ceiling.

My mother was alive.

I had so many thoughts and questions swirling in my head that it was hard to be still.

Where had she been?

What had she been doing for the last twenty years?

Why hadn't she reached out to me?

Had she constructed this upgrade, which was light-years beyond the most sophisticated genetic engineering ever imagined?

And if what Edwin told me was true—what did a "significant upgrade" to the human genome even mean? My mother was, by orders of magnitude, the most ambitious person I'd ever known. But surely even she wasn't crazy enough to try to force a species upgrade on *Homo sapiens*. What would that even look like? Something along the lines of what she had done to me?

But mainly, in a place I'd made a habit of not looking at too closely, I felt rage.

Betrayal and rage.

She'd been alive when I stood trial for her crimes.

She'd been alive the day I was convicted.

Alive and free that first night in prison, and all the nights after.

She'd been alive the day I regained my freedom.

Alive on my wedding day.

The night of Ava's birth.

She had never bothered to contact me.

And as the final insult, it appeared that she had played god again. Not with crops and locusts. With me. Her own son.

The lights had gone out hours ago, and the only illumination came from the blinking LEDs in the terminal behind me. I knew someone somewhere was sitting at a monitor, watching my every move, my every breath, my every tear.

I had to get out of this place. I had no idea how.

Overhead lights tore me out of my troubled dreams.

I raised my arm to shield my eyes, wondering how long I'd slept.

An hour? Maybe two? And yet I felt surprisingly refreshed and sharp thanks to the upregulation of my BHLHE41=DEC2, NPSR1, and ADRB1 gene network.

I sat up and saw a man I had arrested seven years ago on a snowy night in the Bighorn Mountains of Wyoming standing on the other side of the glass.

"Hello, Logan," he said, his voice emitting through the speakers above me.

"Dr. Romero."

"You remember me." He seemed surprised.

"There's rarely a day that I don't think about that night."

"Same," he said sadly, and it was only for a fraction of a fraction of a second, but his lower lip tensed and a vertical line flashed in and out of existence between his eyebrows. He was still angry with me. And no doubt with good reason.

This was the third time I'd intuited someone's emotional state based upon subtle facial cues. Another new attribute of my upgrade?

I stood and stretched.

"When did they let you out of prison?" I asked.

"Four years ago. Could you step over here, please?"

I could see that he was standing near two metal slots in the glass. One accommodated a food tray. The other was circular and just larger than a closed fist.

I walked over.

"Put your arm through the smaller one."

He was holding a hypodermic syringe.

"Why?"

"I need to draw some blood. Going forward, we're going to be analyzing your genome on a weekly basis."

I didn't move.

"Look," he said. "I don't want to hurt you."

I stared at him through the glass, wondering how the GPA had convinced someone with a mind like Anthony Romero's to work in a scientific black site.

I said, "You're not putting a needle in my arm."

He let out a sigh, set the syringe down on a tray beside him, and lifted a tablet. I couldn't see the touchscreen, only his fingers moving.

A sound kicked on above me. I looked up at a vent in the glass wall, just below the ceiling. The cage began to vibrate as a motor behind the vent became louder and louder.

The first sensation was a tightness in my chest.

Though I was breathing faster and faster, I still felt like I was holding my breath.

The motor behind the vent went silent.

The only sound was my gasping.

I went to my knees.

Bright spots exploding and fading across my field of vision.

I fell over.

I could feel my extremities tingling as they starved for oxygenated blood, but it was nothing compared to the fire in my lungs and the explosive pounding in my head.

Each passing second was torment.

Darkness crept in from the sides.

My field of vision narrowing.

And then my dying brain observed a noise. At first, I thought it must be some auditory hallucination, but it kept getting louder and clearer.

The motor behind the vent was running again.

I opened my eyes.

The darkness was retreating.

The world brightening.

I was gasping again, but now the breaths were touching a place deep in my lungs with a satisfaction that far surpassed cold water to parched lips.

I sat up.

Dr. Romero traded the tablet for the syringe.

"It gives me no pleasure to hurt you," he said, "but I've been tasked with studying what you are. What you're becoming. You need to understand that your compliance is nonnegotiable. Now slide your arm through the hole, please."

I complied.

As he drew my blood, I said, "I want to talk to my family."

"I'm just here to track your evolution. If you have concerns, you should ask—"

"Ask who? I'm in a glass cell. Against my will. Can you be a human being for—"

"No. I can't. I was once. You were a part of the apparatus that took my humanity away from me."

"I'm sorry for that. Truly. I was just doing my job, and—"

"You didn't have a choice? Neither do I."

"Are you feeling alert?" Dr. Romero asked.

"Yes."

"Would you like more coffee? I can have some brought in."

"No thanks."

"Are you hungry?"

"No."

I was sitting at the desk in my cell facing Dr. Romero, who was seated at the exterior desk on the other side of the glass. He'd been a man in his prime when I'd arrested him, and unsurprisingly, the years had not been gentle. The skin under his eyes was dark and sagging, and there were burst capillaries around his nose, suggesting he'd been anesthetizing himself with too much alcohol. And the light in his eyes, which I'd seen in videos of his lectures in better times, had nearly been extinguished. He looked like a man in an impossible position, one whose soul was rotting inside him. Despite everything, I couldn't help feeling sorry for him—another victim of Ramsay's famine, intellectually starving right in front of me.

A laptop was open beside him, and on my desk I had a legal pad and several pens.

We began with verbal acuity. Analogies. Letter rearrangement into words. Puzzles.

It was all exceptionally easy until the end of the verbal section, when he turned his laptop toward the glass so that I could see the final question:

Mytacism is most like which of the following words:
a. pugnacious
b. misutilization
c. poltophagy
d. levament
e. agog
f. I don't know

It was the only question so far that had pushed me.
I could feel my neurons firing.
Scrambling to find a toehold.
I had seen this word once, and only once, in my life.

Twelve years ago, for Christmas, Beth had given me a Word-of-the-Day calendar of bizarre and obscure words.

The entry for November 12 had been "mytacism."

I could see the little square of paper from the small calendar, which had been depleted to the last two months of the year. A magnet held it to our refrigerator in the first house Beth and I had bought together in Bethesda.

It was still early that morning when I'd ripped off the sheet for November 11 (spanghew: to throw violently into the air; especially, to throw (a frog) into the air from the end of a stick).

Ava was two, and she was already awake and toddling about, saying, "Meal, meal, meal." Translation: "I want oatmeal." Her favorite food at the time.

I saw a perfect image of that word entry.

November 12
my·ta·cism | \ ˈmīt-ə-ˌsiz-əm \
: excessive or wrong use of the sound of the letter *m*

I said, "B. Misutilization."

Dr. Romero made a note.

"This one took you 2.3 seconds longer than any of your other answers."

"I'd only seen the word once before."

"When? In what context?"

I told him.

He nodded, said, "You haven't selected 'I don't know' for any of the questions yet. Can you explain to me how you're coming up with your answers?"

"Simple. I either know the answer or I don't, and so far, I haven't encountered a word I haven't seen before."

"So you haven't guessed at any words?"

"No."

"Would you say you have perfect memory?"

I thought about it. "I don't know if it's perfect, but it's very good."

"Better than before Denver?"

"For sure. And getting sharper every day."

"Can you recall what you were doing on this day last year?"

I thought about it. "Yes."

"To what level of detail?"

"As if a camera were behind my eyes, recording everything I saw and experienced."

"Do you remember the thoughts you had?"

One year ago today, I was in Kansas City, Missouri, with Nadine. We were there to raid the house of a man who was suspected of building and selling gene-editing kits to enhance muscle—mainly to weight lifters and professional athletes.

I found that I could "punch in" to any moment of that day. Waking up in the hotel and grabbing my phone off the bedside table to find a text from Beth:

Morning, love, how'd you sleep?

To eating burnt ends at Arthur Bryant's barbecue joint. The smells and the sounds, right down to the conversation at the table beside ours, the woman saying . . .

"Yes," I said. "I can even remember certain trains of thought."

He tested my mathematical ability next, and I found it even easier than the verbal section.

"In an ocean, there is a smack of jellyfish," Dr. Romero said. "Every day, the group doubles in size. If it takes ninety days for the jellyfish to cover the entire ocean, how long would it take for the jellyfish to cover half of the ocean?"

"You're wasting my time and yours," I said.

"Please provide an answer. We have to work up to the hard ones."

"Eighty-nine days."

We tackled spatial reasoning, visual/perceptual and classification skills. Logical reasoning. And finally pattern recognition.

"Logan, what is the next term in the following sequence: 0, 1, 1, 2, 3, 5, 8, 13, 21, 34?"

I pored over the sequence on his laptop screen.

"Fifty-five."

"How did you get that?"

"Well, that's the Fibonacci sequence. Each number is the sum of the two that precede it."

"You just happen to know the Fibonacci sequence off the top of your head?"

"No, I learned it my sophomore year of college."

"Would you have remembered this before the incident in Denver?"

"Definitely not."

"Would you say you now have the ability to access everything you've ever read or learned?"

Huh. I considered it. "I don't know if I'm comfortable saying absolutely everything, but many things. Most things."

"Did you study a foreign language in high school or college?"

"French."

"Before Denver, what was your fluency level?"

"I'd lost most of it."

Romero spent the next ten minutes quizzing me on French grammar, and I found that I could now speak fluent French and read it as well.

"Everything I learned in college is available to me again," I said. "I'm probably more fluent now than at my peak in university."

Dr. Romero presented me with numerical sequences of increasing difficulty.

After an hour, I finally met one whose pattern I couldn't suss out.

"Congratulations," I said. "You finally stumped me."

Dr. Romero closed his laptop.

"So I guess I didn't ace it?" I asked.

"No, the test ended forty-five minutes ago. You scored perfectly. I just wanted to see how complex a sequence you could handle. And before you ask, I have no idea what your IQ is. All I know is that it's beyond two hundred, which is the limit of what the test I just administered can measure."

"Say that again?" I said.

I'd heard him. I just didn't believe what I was hearing.

He leaned toward the glass. "Your IQ is at least two hundred. That's as high as the test can measure. And your memory appears to be preternatural."

He got up and left.

I didn't move.

When I was fourteen, I took an IQ test before starting high school, which according to my mother, was simply a tool to help us understand how I learned.

I scored a 118. Above average. In the top fourteen percent of the world's population.

My mother hid it well, but she must have been severely disappointed.

Her IQ was rumored to be in the low 180s.

I got straight As in high school.

Into Berkeley, the college of my choice.

I was disciplined. I *tried*.

And then I met O chem. Organic chemistry. I didn't fail or anything. It just didn't come easily. Plenty of students washed out. The top few in my class breezed through, and I should've been one of them considering my ambitions, but my B– was hard fought.

After completing my undergrad degree in biochemistry and genetics, I asked my mother if I could spend the summer with her in Shenzhen, working in her lab. She agreed that I could come.

So it was me, Mr. 118, surrounded by über-geniuses who were trying to change the world. The more I was around them, understanding only a fraction of what they were attempting to do, the clearer I saw the writing on the wall I'd been avoiding all my life.

It said—

You will never be your mother's intellectual equal.

Of course my mother knew. She'd known when I was a child that I didn't have her hardware or anything close to it. All I had ever wanted was to follow in her footsteps. I'd been chasing them all my life. And that summer in Shenzhen, those footsteps ran full speed into the brick wall of my limitations. Into the DNA code I'd been born with.

It is a supremely cruel thing to have your mind conjure a desire which it is functionally unable to realize.

No one teaches you how to handle the death of a dream.

But that wasn't my fate any longer. My mind was becoming a diamond.

Three nights later, I had wild dreams—like my brain had been infected by Salvador Dalí on mushrooms.

Ecstasy.

Euphoria.

Horror.

Terror.

Joy.

And new emotions I had never experienced, which were a hybrid of excitement for the future and loss for the past.

I dreamed of who I used to be.

Of who, or what, I might become.

• • •

Handstands, with minimal practice, became effortless. I even managed to do them on one hand.

On my first attempt, I performed a perfect backflip off the bed.

I did one hundred push-ups in the middle of the vivarium, only breaking a sweat on the last ten, then transitioned into one-handed push-ups, which I'd never had the strength for.

I practiced squatting on the floor and leaping onto the surface of the desk.

I hoped they were watching. I hoped my newfound physical prowess was beginning to pique their curiosity.

The vivarium itself was completely secure. I had examined every square inch and no amount of muscle tone would allow me to punch through the ballistic glass or tear bolted-down furniture out of the concrete.

Thus far, they had only been studying the changes to my mind, and that could be done while keeping me locked inside. But the list Edwin had read off to me my first day here suggested that a number of physical changes were taking place as well, things that couldn't be measured through glass in a tiny vivarium.

They would have to let me out if they wanted to test those, and when they did, I would have my chance.

I knew that my bone density and night vision had been augmented.

Apparently my pain tolerance had also been boosted.

How much pressure and force could my bones withstand now that my LRP5 gene network had been upgraded?

How strong had I really become?

Had my reflexes improved?

How fast could I run? How far and high could I jump?

I wanted answers to these questions, and I suspected they did too.

• • •

I was working out in the vivarium every day, teasing them with my burgeoning strength and coordination, but no one had so much as hinted that they might be interested in studying my physical abilities. And I couldn't bring it up. Not directly at least.

Dr. Romero kept trying to peer into my evolving cognition, but devising questions that challenged me required minds at least as sharp as mine.

I suspected they wanted to know if my intelligence had plateaued before they would consider testing me outside my cage. No point in letting them know that I was still improving. The sooner they felt comfortable with my intelligence, the sooner they would devise a protocol to test me in a larger space. A tiny agency like the GPA couldn't hold me here indefinitely without their bigger, meaner brothers becoming interested. The DoD was surely breathing down their neck already. How long before they took over?

During one test, as I pretended to struggle for an answer, I became consciously aware, for the first time, of a new sensation. Or, rather, multiple sensations—

The *whoosh* of forced air blowing through the vent above me.

My own heartbeat.

The hairs on my arms wavering as micro-changes in air pressure disturbed them.

All the textures in my cell—glass, cloth, steel, porcelain—and all the textures beyond.

It was on the brink of overwhelming me, and it also created the intensely strange illusion of time slowing down.

What allows human beings to concentrate on things amid the maelstrom of infinite stimuli is a neurological process called sensory gating. It filters out low-relevance (redundant or unnecessary) stimuli in the brain from all possible environmental stimuli. If this didn't happen, we would experience an overload of irrelevant information in the higher cortical centers.

Was my sensory processing changing?

Imagine walking through Times Square in New York City and registering each environmental stimulus equally and simultaneously. The tiny chip in the sidewalk underfoot being given the same priority as every last detail of every incoming pedestrian and the smell of exhaust and food trucks and steam venting out of the subway and urine and every snippet of passing conversation crashing through the auditory inputs right alongside an avalanche of distinct sights, sounds, smells, and tactile sensations of a city in full operation.

The absence of sensory gating is a key marker for schizophrenia, and actually contributes to making people go insane. An existence without gating would be torture.

Perhaps my sensory gating had been downregulated. I would have to reprogram my mind not to let the onslaught of stimuli overload me. Train myself to absorb more input while still maintaining full focus and concentration. And couldn't I do that now that I was able to give my attention to two things fully and concurrently? Wasn't I having this exact train of thought at the same moment I was calculating the square root of pi?

Maybe this modification explained why I was now seeing patterns everywhere.

For instance: Whenever Dr. Romero came for a session, he would first go to the terminal to log in his credentials. The minute muscle movements in his forearms and hands, and the sounds of the keyboard strokes—five with the left hand (the left pinkie finger softest [q, a, or z], the left ring finger slightly harder [w, s, or x; maybe 1]), six with the right (heavy strikes with the pointer and middle fingers [u, j, or n; then i, k, 8, or 9])—was like watching his username and password writ large on the wall before me.

Where it really helped was in reading body language.

When he was close enough, I was beginning to study the changes in his pulse rate and pupil dilation.

What made him breathe faster.

What made him relax.

I was finding that my own body language—the smallest of gestures—could arouse changes in *his* autonomic function.

As I studied these things in Romero and my other keepers, I also studied them in myself.

And the more aware I became of how external stimuli affected my vital signs, I saw how I might one day control them.

From a dream, I heard Edwin approaching my cage. I sat up, opened my eyes, saw him sitting down on the other side of the glass with the *Washington Post*.

I sat up and rubbed my eyes, then climbed out of bed and walked over to the sink.

Splashed water on my face.

"What's in the news?" I asked as I brushed my teeth.

"The satellite war. China's accusing us of sending a covert space team to hack one of their military satellites."

I took a seat at the desk, the glass between us, said, "Sounds like us."

Edwin inefficiently refolded the paper—it was almost painful to watch—and leveled his gaze on me. He was here to ask some new questions about my mother.

I said, "I've already told you, I don't know—"

"I believe you don't know where she is. There are other ways you can be of help to us."

"But I'm not going to help you."

"Okay." Edwin nodded. "You're in here, and the people you love are out there."

He just let the unveiled threat hang. A month ago, this might have actually worked on me, but for all of his failings, I saw Edwin better than I'd ever seen him. I had near-perfect memory of my every observation of the man, and he wasn't going to hurt my family. If he wanted to leverage me, there were things I wanted, things he could provide—first and foremost to communicate with Beth and Ava.

"You're doing it wrong," I said.

"What are you talking about?"

"You should be using the carrot, not the stick."

"Did she have a secret lab?" he asked.

"What's in it for me?"

Edwin's eyes cut to the vent in the ceiling of my vivarium. Then back to me. His nose wrinkled, his upper lip curving upward for a split second.

A microexpression of disgust.

I said, "You're imagining removing the air inside the vivarium. Romero was able to do it because he blames me—rightly so—for the loss of his livelihood, his passion. You have no well of anger at me to tap into. The thought of torturing me for information makes you physically ill." He sighed, annoyed. "Now you're considering having one of your goons do the dirty work, but you're not sure if even that degree of removal will be enough to alleviate—"

"Will you just shut the fuck up. Jesus. You are changed from the Logan I know."

I'd rattled him. Good. Now I would throw him a bone.

I said, "I wasn't aware of any secret lab of my mother's."

His face flashed relief.

"But if she were building this upgrade, she would certainly need one."

"And not some slapdash—"

"No," I said, "she would need a high-grade molecular biology lab with biosafety level-four containment for cell culture and animal experiments. Suppliers of biologically exotic compounds. And she couldn't do this on her own."

"How big—"

"Two, maybe. Likely five people."

"Any idea of—"

God, I knew every question he would ask before he asked it. So much wasted time. So much inefficiency.

"—who they might be?"

I said, "She would need people who, as a group, could encompass biochemistry, molecular biology, genetics, and bioinformatics. Every one of them working at the height of their powers. I can't imagine her pulling this off without a quantum-annealing or exascale processor."

I was speaking too fast. The average person speaks 100 to 130 words per minute. I was pushing 180. When had that started? I needed to slow down, stop drawing attention to my exploding intellect. It would only make them more afraid of me, and the more afraid they were, the less likely they'd be to take a chance by letting me out of the vivarium for physical study.

"So she'd need a computer engineer."

Hadn't I just said that?

"Yeah. A real badass. Someone who could write highly sophisticated programs and was well versed in coding architecture for self-learning AI."

"Any idea of who these people might be?"

A poorly worded question, but I knew what he meant. He was asking for names. Hadn't he already asked this question 12.5 seconds ago?

I said, "Her colleagues from Shenzhen are either dead or in prison. I don't know who she met and worked with after she faked her death."

"Were there any influential people in her life you can think of who she might have turned to on the other side of the famine?"

"I don't know what her friends and colleagues thought of her after the famine. I'm guessing most of them would've turned their back on her. Or turned her in. I do have a crazy idea."

"What?"

"I'll find her for you."

He leaned toward the glass, interest piqued.

"You mean . . . let you out."

I was about to find out whether Edwin was more interested in studying me or finding Miriam. Of course—there was another option. The decision of what to do with me was no longer his.

"Track me," I said. "Monitor me all you want. I'm the only one who can do this."

He was considering.

Said finally, "I can't do that."

"But you expect me to help you while I'm sitting in a glass cell? Meanwhile, you're about to release the one person who might actually have real information."

Edwin said, "I wasn't completely honest with you about where things stand with Soren."

"Let me guess," I said. "Soren was never officially booked into our system. You got a DISA court judge to grant a ninety-day hold."

Edwin didn't say anything. He tried to maintain an unreadable face but failed.

"So where is he?" I asked. "At one of your other black-site facilities? This one?"

"He's not here."

"You've been interrogating him," I said.

Edwin nodded.

"Enhanced?"

Nod.

"Virtual?"

No response. But yes.

I'd heard rumors of this happening in extreme cases with

foreign bioterrorists, but I felt a pang of deep disappointment and shame to hear it confirmed by a man I used to respect. They were interrogating Soren in a virtual world, using military-grade DNI. They would've hacked the amygdala and prefrontal and limbic regions of his neocortex to trick his mind into experiencing all manner of pleasure and pain. Virtual torture had been banned a decade ago by the United Nations, but because it was so hard to track or prove, the ban was nearly impossible to enforce.

"I suppose there's no point in reminding you that he's an American citizen," I said. "Oh, wait. So am I. Certainly no point in reminding you that he's a human being. So what have you learned from him?"

"Nothing. Looks like he really didn't know."

Edwin stood, gathered up his newspaper.

"Edwin," I said. "I just answered your questions. I didn't have to do that."

"I know."

"I would like my family to know that I'm okay. I'd like to speak with them. See their faces."

The way he looked at me—lips pursed, eyebrows raised—belied a sadness just below the surface. I could see his pulse thrumming in his carotid artery. Bumping along much faster than it had been . . . 129 bpm. I wasn't sure how I knew the number. I wasn't consciously counting. I just . . . knew. I possessed a specific, detailed awareness, where none had been before.

Edwin was sad and nervous I had caught him out. And in that moment, I knew—what he'd said to me my first day here had been a lie. He hadn't told my family I'd been detained under suspicion of self-editing.

My mind instantly served up a 16K movie of my funeral.

Closed casket. Beth and Ava crying. Edwin comforting them about what a hero I was. The silence of our home after all the mourners had left and the real grief set in.

"You told them I was killed in a raid, didn't you?"

All he said was, "I'm sorry."

And walked away.

I got undressed and stepped into the shower. The stall was tiny and glass-walled. No privacy or space. I knew someone somewhere was sitting at a monitor, watching my every move.

I couldn't bring myself to think about Beth and Ava. Imagining them mourning me would have broken me.

So as the hot water beat down on me, I thought about Mom, wondering where she was at this moment. Wondering what her endgame might be. Had she also exposed herself to this upgrade?

A memory bubbled to the surface—a conversation I'd been present for that summer in China before everything went wrong.

On the rare occasion Miriam wanted to blow off steam and get her postdocs out of the lab, we'd all go to this Belgian beer bar in the Nanshan District called the Stumbling Monk.

Before Denver and the upgrade to my autobiographical memory, I would never have recalled this moment with such crystalline perfection, but one night, many drinks in, our group was going back and forth in a spirited debate, which had been started when my mother posed a hypothetical question: What is the greatest threat to our species?

Everyone was drunk and happy and loud, chiming in with—

Rising oceans.

Desertification.

Failing ecosystems.

Dangerous CO_2 levels.

Basri, the postdoc who was my mother's number two, had said, "All the existential threats to our existence live under the umbrella of climate change."

My mother had been quietly watching us all debate from the head of the table, sipping from a chalice of Westvleteren 12, her big, enigmatic eyes missing nothing.

She said finally, "You're all wrong."

The table went silent, everyone turning toward her. Miriam had barely raised her voice. There was no way we all should've heard it over the din of the bar, but there was something almost magical about my mother in a crowd of her acolytes.

"You don't believe climate change is the greatest threat to our species?" Basri asked.

She'd fixed him with her gaze. "The greatest threat to our species lies within us."

Everyone exchanged uncomfortable glances, unsure of what she meant.

Standing in this microshower in my vivarium, twenty years later, I could vividly recall not having the foggiest idea of what she was talking about, and sinking a bit inward as even more evidence of my shortcomings piled on top of me.

My mother had said, "Hunger, disease, war, warming—these threats loom over us like building storm clouds. But ninety-nine percent of humanity reads about our crumbling world in the morning headlines, then ignores it and gets on with their day." She looked around the table. "You're all here with me in Shenzhen, trying to do your part to solve crop failure, which might be a step toward solving hunger and famine. Trying to be part of the solution."

She leaned forward, suddenly energized. "If more people were like us, imagine what we could accomplish. New crops to feed the millions going hungry. Stopping pandemics from raging across our world. Ending most disease and all poverty and all war. No more mass extinctions. Clean, renewable, limitless energy. Spreading into the solar system."

Twenty years later, as the hot water beat down on my back, I felt a chill run through me.

"So you're saying people are too stupid?" Basri asked.

"Not just that," Miriam said. "It's denial. Selfishness. Magical thinking. We are not rational beings. We seek comfort rather than a clear-eyed stare into reality. We consume and preen and convince ourselves that if we keep our heads in the sand, the monsters will just go away. Simply put, we refuse to help ourselves as a species. We refuse to do what must be done. Every danger we face links ultimately back to this failing."

I finished my shower, and as I got dressed, one of my keepers—*what else to call them?*—came in with breakfast.

I sat at the interior desk as the good, rich smell of coffee filled the vivarium.

My thoughts were still racing.

After the beer bar, I'd shared a cab with my mother back to the house we were renting in Bao'an District, on Qianhai Bay.

I'd had two beers too many, and the lights of Shenzhen were streaming by in something of a blur.

I'd glanced over at my mother, who was staring out the window, her mind undoubtedly on tomorrow's work. Always the work.

And because I wasn't myself, I just asked her—something I would never have done sober, "If you could do it, would you? Make people more like us?" I quickly corrected myself. "Like you?"

She looked at me, and maybe because her head was spinning as well, she was candid with me in a way I'd experienced only once or twice in my lifetime.

"Yes," she said. "I would."

"But it's just a dream, right? Just an idea?"

She shrugged. "Whenever someone signs up for The Story of You, they have to complete a 350-question personality test and use our imaging app to submit a full-body scan that gives us mountains of data. I have the genomic code of seventy-nine million diverse people and more than twenty-three thousand phenotype data points for each of them. From all over the world. *If* I could develop a sufficiently powerful AI to handle this data set, and ask the right questions, who knows what I might accomplish." And then she looked at me with a frightening intensity. "It's one thing to build a new life-form, cure illness, or even attempt the work we're doing now with our locusts. But to change how members of a fully sentient species *think* is surely the ultimate expression of the power of gene editing."

In light of what had just happened to me, that conversation took on a whole new relevance. My mother had tried to edit a few rice paddies and ended up killing two hundred million people. What havoc could she wreak—intentionally or through unintended consequences—by attempting to change something as fundamental as how *Homo sapiens* think?

I dreamed of Beth and Ava.

We stood on a flat, featureless plain.

The sky was the same stark gray as the land, and there would've been no dimension to the space at all—no horizon, no sense of depth—if the ground hadn't been darker by the slightest degree.

Suddenly, it broke open between us.

A black chasm spreading wider.

Wider.

I wanted to jump across and join them, but the distance was already too great.

And so we just stood there, watching as we drifted farther and farther apart.

I rose from the depths of a deep unconsciousness, and even before I was fully awake, I became aware of a sound.

A muffled *boom boom boom.*

Gunfire?

I sat up, opened my eyes.

I was alone in my vivarium, and though the room was dark, I could still see.

I heard a distant scream—dampened by the exterior walls and the glass of my cell.

A man crashed through the door beside the terminal.

I recognized him instantly, even in the low light—he was one of the men who had shown up on the fourth floor of Constitution Center to apprehend me. The short, wide one. I hadn't seen him during my time here. He had a pistol in one hand, and he was panting and holding his side with the other, blood leaking through his fingers, bloody footprints in his wake.

"What's happening?" I asked.

As he turned to look at me, the door burst open again and a deafening noise accompanied most of his head disappearing in a red mist.

Someone strode through the door in a black coat. They carried a tactical shotgun and wore a fencing mask, and immediately I could sense something different in how they moved. Something *right*. No wasted effort. No inefficiency. Lately, I couldn't escape how awkward and imprecise Romero, Edwin, and my other keepers were with their movements. Like giant, rambling babies, their bodies telegraphed everything.

And while it was admittedly a weird thing to notice in this

particular moment, I was blown away by the elegance of this person's physicality.

They made a tiny finger movement.

I knew exactly what they wanted.

Moving to the far side of my cell, I dragged the mattress off my bed and used it as a shield, crouching down behind it on one side of the vivarium.

The sound of the shotgun cycling rounds was earsplitting— slugs crunching through bulletproof glass, the spray of shards tearing into the mattress and raining down on me.

When the shooting stopped, I threw the mattress aside and came to my feet.

The ballistic glass of my vivarium had been no match for the shotgun slugs.

I stepped out of the cage for the first time in twenty-five days.

Ears ringing.

Fencing Mask approached me.

"Who are you?" I asked.

They shook their head. *Not here.*

"They'll send more people," I said. "More than you—"

A modulated voice cut me off with, "You have no idea what I can handle."

I bent down, lifted the pistol the dead man had dropped when he lost his head, and made a quick chamber check.

"Stay close," they said.

I followed them out of the room and down a low-lit corridor with cables taped to the walls. The gun I held was a Smith & Wesson .45, sticky with blood.

Down the corridor, one of the overhead fluorescents flickered, throwing the hallway into sporadic bursts of darkness.

We passed two men sprawled across the floor in expanding pools of their own blood. They'd been caught coming out of a room filled with monitors showing real-time feeds of my vivarium from numerous angles.

"You didn't kill Edwin Rogers or a pudgy, scientist-looking guy, did you?" I asked.

"Only armed guards."

As we approached the next intersection, I heard voices.

The stranger held up their arm.

I stopped.

They slung the shotgun over their shoulder and accelerated toward the intersection as three men emerged from around the corner.

Heavily armed security contractors.

Fencing Mask slit the first man's throat with a trench knife, but the second man was already raising a Desert Eagle.

I saw it all so clearly—Fencing Mask was about to take a .50-cal round to the face.

As the thought crossed my mind, my rescuer took a beautifully timed side step as the second man pulled the trigger on his Desert Eagle and accidentally blew the third guy's face off instead.

Fencing Mask took another side step, and as the last man standing swung his giant pistol around, trying to take aim, they weaved under his arm, gingerly took hold of it, and broke it in three places.

It was like watching a pistol getting fieldstripped—except with bones.

As he howled, Fencing Mask slashed him twice across the belly.

He dropped to his knees, and with his one working arm, tried to hold back everything that was spilling out of him.

The entire interlude had taken 2.5 seconds. Fencing Mask's movements hadn't been especially fast, but they were graceful, and lethal—a ballet of violence.

"Move," Fencing Mask yelled back at me.

We turned down another corridor that terminated at a set of spiral stairs.

I followed them up, our footfalls clanging on the metal.

At the top, they tried to throw open a hatch—it didn't budge.

"Someone locked it," they said. "There's another exit, but we'll have to go through more guards to get there."

I had an idea. "Wait here," I said.

I raced back through the corridors, into the room that housed the vivarium. Sitting down at the terminal, I woke the screen and typed in Romero's username, which I knew. While I didn't know his precise password, from the times I'd studied his finger movements from inside the vivarium, I knew a range of seventeen possibilities of what it might be.

My sixth attempt gave me access. I tore through the interface until I found a security protocol that would unlock a number of doors, including my vivarium, an armory, a surveillance center, and something called exit hatch.

I unlocked it, then rushed back through the corridors.

My rescuer was already through. As I reached the top of the ladder, they gave me a hand, pulling me up into darkness.

It was freezing.

As my eyes adjusted, I saw old tools hanging from the walls. Rafters above me. A ladder leading to a loft filled with hay. An ancient tractor.

The vivarium complex had been constructed under an old barn.

We ran toward an open door.

The stranger stopped at the threshold.

Peered outside.

A brilliant moon burned down on everything, rendering the pasture before us electric blue and washing out the stars.

The lights of a farmhouse glowed in the distance.

My breath steamed in the frigid air.

"Can you run?" they asked.

I nodded.

We took off across the frosted grass. It was the first time I'd had my body out in the open, and I had never been able to run this fast in my life. I felt young again. Coursing with boundless energy. We didn't stop for six hundred yards, until we reached the fence that enclosed the pasture, then sailed over it onto a gravel road and continued away from the farmhouse, barn, and granary.

Foothills surrounded everything like frozen, black waves.

Higher pastures gleamed in the lunar light.

I kept glancing back over my shoulder as the lights of the farmhouse fell away.

After a quarter mile, we reached a gate and cattle guard.

We climbed over.

The faded pavement of a country road glowed in the moonlight.

The only sound was the icy wind rattling the last leaves on the branches above us—skeletons of once green things. It was the first time I'd been outdoors since the full effect of my upgrade had taken root, and I was struggling to keep the onslaught of stimuli from overwhelming me.

We sprinted along the shoulder of the road. After several hundred yards, the stranger slowed down, pointing at some-thing so well hidden it took me a moment to see what it was. Pulled a little ways into the darkness of the bordering wood, I saw the glint of metal, glass, and chrome.

We piled into the Google Roadster coupe.

As the doors closed, the stranger finally pulled off their mask, tossing it and the voice modulator into the back seat.

I stared across the center console at my sister.

5

IT HAD BEEN THREE years since I'd last seen Kara.

Six months since we'd last spoken.

Although we called each other on birthdays and at Christmas, she was usually overseas, on active duty.

She looked harder than I remembered, and there was a new scar across her face that I had never seen in person. I knew she'd been captured a couple of years back during one of her tours in Myanmar and held as a POW for several weeks before a rescue mission freed her, but that was the extent of my knowledge of what had happened. We'd never really talked about it.

We were suddenly moving over the shoulder and onto the road.

Kara toggled the accelerator.

Wild, rushing speed.

We raced through the countryside without headlights.

Though my night vision was vastly improved, I wouldn't have felt comfortable driving as fast as Kara was on these winding roads, guided only by moonlight. But she seemed perfectly adept.

I looked over at my sister, and anticipating my question, she launched in.

"Last summer, on the porch of my Montana cabin, a bee stung me." She took a hairpin curve so fast we must have pulled a couple of g's. "Pain was brief, no swelling, but two nights later, I woke with the worst fever I'd ever had—drenched sheets, delirium. After three days in the hospital, I stabilized."

She spoke blazingly fast.

I said, "They ran tests, nothing conclusive?"

She nodded.

"Decided you'd caught some strain of influenza and recovered?"

"Exactly."

Kara slowed as we entered Luray, Virginia, a sleepy town at the foot of the mountains. Main Street was dead at this hour. Traffic signals blinking yellow at the intersections and the moon bright enough to light the sky and reveal a black wall to the west—the escarpment of Shenandoah.

"Sixteen days later," Kara said, "this woman I'd picked up the night before was getting orange juice from the fridge. The tablet on the island was showing the news, which she was partially watching. Between her divided attention and the drinking glass she'd set on the edge of the island, I saw how she was going to close the refrigerator door, turn, and with the arm that was holding the juice, knock the glass off with her elbow. This wasn't a suspicion. It was like a physics equation written across the surface of reality just for me. All these variables pointing toward an inevitable outcome. I see these equations everywhere now. This entire thought process unfolded as I flipped a pancake and saw her reach into the fridge in the reflection of the window over the kitchen sink. The pancake hit the pan; I dropped the spatula, reached down, caught the glass mid-fall, a split second before it would have exploded on the tile."

"When did you notice all the other changes?"

"Before, it had been a slowly warming awareness. But in that moment, they all screamed out at me in unison. Better concentration, night vision, memory, less sleep, increased muscle mass, higher pain tolerance."

"Reading people in a way you never could before?"

She nodded.

"The bee was a drone," I said.

Kara smiled. "It hadn't decomposed at all."

After twenty-five days of interacting with—what to call them? Normals?—it was glorious to converse with someone whose mind moved as swiftly as mine.

We reached the crest of the Blue Ridge as dawn exhaled a lavender breath across the sky. The light came, views lengthening toward horizons. I saw the next valley over cloaked in a shallow layer of mist. The lights of towns and cities glowing in the distance.

Kara said, "Figured I'd been targeted for some kind of genetic alteration. I headed for you."

"Why?"

"I knew whoever was behind this, there was no way they chose me by coincidence. It was because I'm a Ramsay—because of Mom. So either you had something to do with it or you'd be on their list too."

"So you put me under surveillance."

"I needed to understand your pressure points in case you didn't want to help or tried to arrest me. That's how I learned you'd been targeted just like me, and that your employer was watching you."

"What tipped you off that I was changing?"

"Chess."

"You texted that the GPA was onto me?"

"It was apparent to me you were changing. I knew they'd

catch on soon enough. Sorry. I should've reached out to you sooner."

"Mom did this to us," I said.

It became very quiet in the car.

Kara looked at me, and I swatted down what she was thinking.

"She's not dead," I said. "She wants to unleash a major genomic upgrade."

"On whom?"

"The human race."

And then I told her everything.

At 7:30 A.M., Kara pulled into the parking lot of the Maple Leaf Motel in Kingwood, West Virginia.

It was flurrying snow, the roads just beginning to frost over.

We both donned balaclavas to shield our faces as we made the short jog to our room, painfully aware that there was CCTV everywhere.

The DOJ's wiretapping and surveillance program, while not necessarily a state secret, had never been publicly confirmed. And while most Americans thought they knew the full extent of the surveillance state they lived in, they had no idea of its full power and insidious integration into our daily lives. For every one hundred people in the United States, there were 48.7 surveillance cameras, and behind them a government network of AI-driven facial-recognition search engines, paired with deeply eroded privacy laws.

After what had happened last night, Edwin would be out of his mind to find me, though I doubted he'd put out an APB to other law enforcement agencies. What would he say? *A GPA agent I was illegally holding in a black site escaped. By the way, he's extensively genetically upgraded, and, oh, his last name is Ramsay.*

No, this would be handled in-house.

But it would only take one hit on a sliver of my face for some algorithm to issue an alert on my location.

The room had two double beds. Small table by the window. Old heat pump droning away. A décor of warring flower prints.

I used one of Kara's laptops to order dermal fillers, paying a small fortune for drone delivery within twenty-four hours.

Then I collapsed onto one of the beds. It was a lumpy mattress, but after three weeks in the vivarium, it felt like resting on a cloud.

"What you did back at the farm was incredible," I said. "Always been that good or is this a new development?"

"Always been a badass." Kara laughed, and for a split second she sounded like her old self. "Whatever upgrade I was given just ramped up my abilities."

"What's it like?" I asked. "Fighting like that."

"Ever been in one?"

"Two in prison."

"How'd you fare?"

"Got my ass kicked."

"Happened fast, right?"

"So fast. My body froze up. I felt paralyzed."

"Now, when my adrenaline levels reach a threshold, the opposite happens. Time slows toward a standstill. I notice every detail of my surroundings. I saw those men coming at me at half speed. My ability to read body movements has been enhanced. The tiniest muscle twitches telegraphed their every intention. Putting them down took almost no effort."

Of course, I'd experienced the same thing.

The idea that the brain speeds up during stressful situations is a myth. When a person is afraid, their amygdala becomes more active, laying down extra memories that coincide with the normal memories of everyday life. It's the richer, additional memories that give the illusion of time slowing down. But I suspected that, like me, Kara's sense of time dilation was more than an illusion brought on by a fear reaction. With our sensory gating downgraded, stimuli would come flooding in during moments of intense focus. So long as our brains weren't overwhelmed by the onslaught, this genuinely would allow us to anticipate and react at superhuman speed.

"They're not going to let what happened go," I said. "You know that, right?"

She shrugged. "I know we aren't close, but you're my brother. I'd kill an army for you."

"Is my family okay?"

"Yes. But they think you're dead."

I knew that already, but still my eyes welled up.

I couldn't call Beth. Couldn't reach out in any way or I'd be opening her and Ava up to charges of aiding and abetting, and pulling them deeper into this mess than they already were by virtue of knowing me.

For the time being, it was safer to let them continue to believe that I was gone.

Two hundred million people dead because of the work I'd been involved with, my time in prison, the death of my parents, the loss of my twin—it all paled in comparison to this, the hardest thing I'd ever faced.

"Now what?" Kara asked.

I quickly appraised our situation—we had both been targeted, ostensibly by our mother, and for reasons unknown. Not a whole lot to work with.

"I'm not sure," I said. "But whatever Mom's planning, we have to stop it."

And then I closed my eyes and slept.

. . .

When I woke, the light coming through the curtains had dimmed and the shower was running in the bathroom. I got up, went to the window, peered outside into a snowy, blue dusk.

The cars in the motel parking lot were covered.

The roads covered.

The buildings across the street obscured by falling snow.

Kara's black duffel bag was sitting on the table.

The shower was still running.

I unzipped it, looked inside.

Four guns, including a CheyTac M200 sniper rifle. Boxes of ammunition. Flash-bangs. Zip ties. Several laptops. Surveillance equipment. Two wads of cash. Three passports, each in a different name. Five non-GPS phones.

I picked up one of the phones and stared at it, the urge to message Beth and tell her I was alive nearly overpowering. I couldn't fathom the pain she and Ava must be experiencing.

And then an odd thing happened.

I turned my feelings down.

Maybe it was a new ability, maybe it had always been there—finally unlocked by my upgrade—but I found that I could take the emotion and empathy I felt toward my family and set them aside.

It was like putting them in a Faraday cage except, instead of shielding me from electromagnetic fields, when my emotion was inside it, I was shielded from my own sentiment. Or, rather, from its controlling effect.

I could put my feelings inside this cage, deep within the recesses of my mind.

I could close the door.

And with an extraordinary effort, I could even lock it.

I could exist apart from those feelings.

It was an unsettling ability that felt like cheating, and it made me wonder—had this upgrade also targeted the heart of my mother's complaint about our species' flawed genome? Had she discovered a way to recalibrate *Homo sapiens'* balance between sentiment and reason?

The shower cut off.

I tossed the phone back into the bag and zipped it closed.

Kara got out one of her laptops.

I had Romero's credentials, but I feared the moment I logged in, we'd have thirty minutes, maybe less, before agents showed up at our motel.

So over the next nine hours, I downloaded and read five books on internet architecture and cruised through numerous message boards, where people were more than happy to dole out "hypothetical" tips for clandestinely accessing a government server.

In my life before, it would've taken me months to absorb this mass of disorganized information and misinformation, and I would've perished from boredom in the process. But my new ability to effortlessly maintain focus saw me through.

I connected to the internet through a VPN. I didn't care so much that they knew someone was accessing their servers with Romero's credentials. I'd rip what I wanted before they had time to react. I just couldn't have them knowing their servers were being accessed from Kingwood, West Virginia.

In addition to securing the traffic between Kara's laptop and servers, the VPN would also mask my IP address and location—for a bit. All that remained was to perform a key exchange undetected, which I executed with an assist from a dark-web algorithm.

There was a single folder entitled "Ramsay, Logan."

As I started perusing my very own GPA file, Kara pulled on her wool coat and balaclava, and left to get us some much-needed food.

The file contained the results of my polygraph (I passed).

The tests Dr. Romero had administered. A log of my sleeping patterns. Feeding charts. Observational notes from Edwin and Romero detailing our every interaction. Medical records from my hospital stay in Denver and my internist in D.C. The psychologist's notes from our three sessions. Surveillance audio and video of my home in Arlington.

But I was mainly interested in the file of my genomic changes. It was enormous.

As I opened my genomic-code analysis, the thought bubbled up again—a whisper in the deepest recess of my mind.

Mom never did anything without a reason.

If she'd just wanted to scare the GPA, there was no point in upgrading Kara too. And she couldn't possibly have counted on changing GPA policy. She wanted to scare them, maybe, but she wouldn't have shown her hand just for that. There had to be something more. Some endgame Edwin and the others weren't seeing.

She had a plan for us. Which meant that somewhere, somehow, she'd have left a breadcrumb behind. Some clue as to what we should be doing now. I was scrolling through page after page of my genome analysis—three *billion* letters—and the mysteriousness of the moment was undeniable: I was a conscious being reading the instructions for my own creation.

I stopped.

Just stared at the screen.

The prickling of an idea was bubbling to the surface.

There was a knock at the door. I felt a stab of panic that the GPA had somehow tracked me. But no, the GPA wouldn't knock. They would break the door down.

I went to the peephole, saw Kara standing in the snow. Unlocked the chain, let her in. The black wool of her coat was frosted, and her hair was wet. She cradled two paper bags, which she dropped on my bed.

"Charge-station gourmet. It was the only thing open."

I pawed through the groceries—junk food, sandwiches, burritos.

"Any progress?" she asked.

"Not really, but I have an idea." I tore open a bag of chips and inhaled several handfuls. "Did you know you can write words in DNA?"

"No."

"In terms of data-storage capacity, DNA's information density is a million times greater than a standard hard drive."

"You think Mom left a message in our DNA?"

"I don't know. Maybe."

Kara looked immensely skeptical.

"Isn't our genome three billion letters long?"

"It is."

"So finding a message from Mom in there would be the definition of looking for a needle in a haystack."

"More like looking for a specific atom on a needle in a sea of needles," I said.

I sat back down at the laptop.

"So where to start?" she asked.

"If I wanted to write a message in your genetic code, I couldn't just do it anywhere."

"Why?"

"Because I might damage something vital. Suddenly an organ stops working. Or the genetic mutations give you cancer or ALS. If Mom did this to us—still a big *if*—she probably would have inserted her message into a genomic safe harbor."

I could tell she had no idea what I was talking about.

"Think of our body as a massive biological computer program," I said. "If you jump in there and start messing with the code, something important might break. Safe harbors are natural regions of the genome that scientists discovered can accommodate the integration of new genetic material without harming other genes or causing bad alterations to the host genome." I started typing. "I think I'll write a query for all locations where my genome was changed, but limit the search returns to putative safe harbor regions. That should narrow things down dramatically."

It took a few minutes to build the SQL to query the database. Because we were working with a laptop instead of a supercomputer, I suspected it would take some time for the search results to come back.

Kara and I sat on the bed, scarfing down a couple of charge-station burritos.

One hour later, we had our first report.

After Denver, my genome had been altered at several well-documented genetic safe harbors, including AAVS1, SHS231, hROSA26, and CCR5.

I ran a report for each DNA region to highlight the extent of the edits performed.

CCR5 is a protein on the surface of white blood cells, involved in the immune system. There were extensive edits to my CCR5. I couldn't tell what they were, but upward of 89kb base pairs had been inserted—a veritable novel's worth of code.

Next, I opened the report for the changes to AAVS1, an ancient, harmless genomic hitchhiker and an ideal site to add DNA without harm.

Huh. I leaned forward. The changes to AAVS1 were minuscule—a brief line of new genetic code inserted on the long arm of chromosome 19.

It was a mere 156 base pairs long.

Perhaps fifty-two codons if translated into a protein.

And according to the gene-sequencing reads, the code had been inserted into the genome in every cell of my body—a challenging feat, and an unusual one. Though the entire genome is contained in every cell in the body, the portions of that code that are actually *expressed* by each cell are determined by its specialized biological function. Every cell in a person's body contains instructions for their eye color—but a Scythe intervention for eye color would target only the tiny portion of cells actually affecting iris pigmentation.

So why target every cell? To make it unmissable?

"This could be it," I said.

Kara stared at the new DNA sequence.

TCC CCC CCG ACC CGA CCC ACG CAC CGC ACC CCT CTC GTG GTC ACC GCA CCC ACC CGG GAC CCC ACG GGT CCC CCC CCC CCC CCC CCC CCC GAC CCG ACC CAC GCA CCG CAC CCC TGG TGT CGG TCG GTC GGT CGG ACC CCG GGA CAC CCG CAC CCC

"You really think these letters are a message?" she asked.

"Maybe. The other safe harbor edit was an insertion of almost a hundred kb. That'd be a very long message. This one is too short to be a new gene, and the protein it encodes doesn't make sense."

"What's next?"

"DNA can be read in two directions, and three reading frames per direction. I'm going to assume, for now, that this follows convention for insertions, which means we should read it left to right. So now we have to figure out how to convert the biological message into a human message."

"Any ideas?"

"Not a one."

My brother's death was the first rift in a chasm that would swallow my family whole. I was thirteen, and two years later, my father took his own life on a foggy morning on the summit of Mount Diablo, east of the Bay Area. That my mother had subsequently faked her own suicide, despite all the loss I'd already experienced, was unfathomable to me.

After Dad was gone, Kara dropped out of Cornell, where she'd been pursuing an information technology degree, and enlisted in the military. She made special forces. At the time, all she'd said was, "I want to actually do something."

Then it was just Miriam and me, until our locusts inadvertently unleashed a famine upon the world.

And following my mother's death and my incarceration, it was just me.

All of which made tonight something special. While the circumstances were less than ideal, it had been years since I'd gotten to spend time with my big sister.

We ate good-bad food on our beds and talked. She'd only met Beth and Ava twice, and I told her all about them. She told me about her life in Montana.

I'd been there once with Nadine. We'd stopped by Kara's cabin after a raid in Helena. Sat out on her porch listening to elks bugling across the valley. It was summertime, a cool night, the sky luminous with stars. We'd talked about life and work and family. It'd been nice to see Nadine and my sister hit it off.

I'd felt it that night and I felt it on this one—being with Kara quenched some evolutionary thirst. A primal, genetic need to belong to a tribe.

She was the only other human being who really understood the transformation I was experiencing. She was also the only human being who truly understood my past.

"Ever think about settling down?" I asked her.

"Kids? A wife?"

"Something like that."

"Does it bother you that I found a different path to happiness?" she asked.

"You assume I think kids and marriage equal happiness. Correlation? Sure. Causation? No. *Are* you happy?"

"Before all this, I was as happy as I'd ever been. I lived in a cabin I had built at seven thousand feet in the mountains above Butte. I skied in the winter. Fly-fished in the summer. Hunted in the fall. You've been there."

"I wish we'd seen each other more," I said. "I would've liked to have been more a part of your life."

"Dude, I am not the older sister who used to play hide-and-seek and build Legos and forts with you anymore."

"Who are you?"

"Now? That's an interesting question. Before the drone stung me, I thought I was a woman in search of peace in a place of my own." Then she looked at me strangely. "You want to know, don't you?" The scar started at the outer corner of her left eye and zigzagged down her cheek to the tip of her chin. She touched it, said, "Hydrochloric acid." She swallowed. "It was a training camp in Kachin state, high in the Himalayan foothills. We came at night. They had infrared surveillance and their snipers took out everyone but me. I got pinned down. They'd never seen a female special forces soldier. I was something of a novelty.

"I was held in a metal cage barely large enough to stand in. Most of the time, I was blindfolded. They put me through four mock executions, and worse. Much worse."

I moved over to my sister's bed and sat across from her.

I tried to hold her hand, but she pulled it away.

"One of them spoke English. He'd been born and educated in London. We talked three times. The last, I asked how he could do the things he was doing to me. To the others they had burned, drowned, stoned, beheaded. These were Buddhists, after all. It's one thing to torture and kill in the name of a god you think created the universe, but their core belief is that nothing is fixed, nothing is permanent. They're supposed to believe in *ending* suffering."

"What'd he say?"

"He had the softest voice. Almost delicate. He said, 'Sometimes you have to cause suffering to end suffering.'"

She was quiet for a while.

There was only the sound of a television in an adjacent room bleeding through the thin walls. The heat pump in our room cutting on again.

I wondered if her memory was as enhanced as mine. I had plenty of dark moments in my past that I could now relive with brutal perfection. But nothing like what she had just described to me.

"I'm so sorry that happened to you," I said.

"Me too."

"Are you still in touch with the people who rescued you?"

Kara smiled. "They're some of my best friends."

Sirens roused me in the middle of the night. As I rushed to the window, Kara pulled her tactical shotgun from under her bed.

Through the icy window, I watched as several police EVs and a fire engine raced by on the main road. Though my heart pounded from the instinctive fear reaction, the colder, analytical part of my mind whispered that they wouldn't bring a fire engine to arrest me, and there certainly wouldn't be incoming sirens.

Kara came up behind me.

"It's not for us," I said.

I returned to my bed and killed the lights, allowing my mind to superimpose that DNA sequence on the popcorn ceiling.

TCC CCC CCG ACC CGA CCC ACG
CAC CGC ACC CCT CTC GTG GTC

ACC GCA CCC ACC CGG GAC CCC
ACG GGT CCC CCC CCC CCC CCC
CCC CCC GAC CCG ACC CAC GCA
CCG CAC CCC TGG TGT CGG TCG
GTC GGT CGG ACC CCG GGA CAC
CCG CAC CCC

There was something bothering me about it. Something staring me in the face that I was failing to comprehend.

I ran a frequency analysis in my head.

Twelve *T*'s.

Nineteen *A*'s.

Ninety-two *C*'s.

Thirty-three *G*'s.

Very *C* rich.

And were those numbers significant?

I let them drift through my mind like clouds on a summer day. I observed them. 12, 19, 92, 33, 12, 19, 92, 33, 12, 19, 92, 33. I reversed them: 21, 91, 29, 33, 21, 91, 29, 33.

Nineteen was a prime number. I noodled with that for a moment, to no avail.

My eyes shot open.

It was morning.

Kara snored lightly.

My mind must have been working the problem while I slept, because I knew what was bothering me about the sequence.

The *T*'s and *A*'s never repeated.

I jumped out of bed, turned on the light. Went to the table, which was covered in pages of failed attempts to break the code—if it even was a code.

I flattened the receipt Kara had brought back from the charge station and wrote down the nucleotide sequence from memory, removing the spaces between the codons and underlining every *T* and *A*.

TCCCCCCCGACCCGACCCACGCACCGCACCCCTCTC
GTGGTCACCGCACCCACCCGGGACCCCACGGGTCCCCC
CCCCCCCCCCCCCCCCGACCCGACCCACGCACCGCACC
CCTGGTGTCGGTCGGTCGGTCGGACCCCGGGACACCCG
CACCCC

"What are you doing?" Kara mumbled from bed.

"Just a second," I said.

If my mother had intended to message me through my genetic code, she had a problem to overcome. How to communicate using only four symbols. And how to create a cipher with *A*, *C*, *G*, and *T* that only someone looking for it could detect.

Kara walked over, put her hand on my shoulder.

I looked up at her, said, "What if the *T*'s and *A*'s don't actually represent letters or other symbols?"

"Why wouldn't they?"

"Because they never repeat. Maybe their purpose is to indicate the start of a word or . . ." And suddenly, I saw how I would create a substitution code based on the four letters of DNA. "Oh my god."

"What?"

"If you had created this code," I said, "what two base units of communication would be essential for this cipher to indicate?"

"Numbers and letters."

"What if the *T*'s and *A*'s indicate what the next character will be? One of them—the *A* perhaps—means the character will be a number. And the *T* means that you have to go a step further and translate the number into a letter of the alphabet."

"You mean like one equals *A*, two equals *B*, all the way to twenty-six equals *Z*?"

"Exactly."

"So then the *G*'s and *C*'s represent numbers?" she asked.

"That's how I'd do it. And if I only had two symbols with which to write any number, I'd use something like the Roman numeral system. Let the *G* equal five, and the *C* equal 1. Or the other way around. Look at the first sequence."

I wrote out <u>T</u>CCCCCCCG.

"Assume *T* means that the *CCCCCCCG* is creating a number. The sequence could stand for twelve or thirty-six. Or the *T* could be designating that the sequence is creating a letter, which means we do one more operation to get a letter of the alphabet. So then it's *L* or . . . wait, no." I scanned the code again, smiling now. "Yep. If my theory is right, I know what *C* and *G* are. *G* is one, *C* is five."

"You sure?"

"Look at the second sequence. *ACCCG*. Let's assume *C* is one. You would not write the number *eight* that way with Roman numerals. You'd write it *GCCC*."

"So *G* is one, *C* is five."

"Let's assume that for now. Which means the only outstanding question is, what do the *T* and the *A* stand for. Based on our assumption that *G* is one and *C* is five, I just have to solve this code as if *T* represents a letter, *A* a number, and then do the inverse."

"The *T*'s can't signal letters," she said.

I looked at the first sequence again. "You're right." Seven *C*'s followed by a *G* is thirty-six. Too high to correspond to a letter of the alphabet.

I made a pot of coffee, and while it brewed, I glanced outside again through the curtains. The snow had stopped. It was eight in the morning, and the town was waking up.

I returned to the table and started the process of transposing the nucleotides, making the *T*'s signal numbers, the *A*'s letters.

The first nine characters translated to the number 36.

The next five sequences spelled out the word *point*.

I raced to transpose the rest.

36POINT5625NORTH106POINT217777WEST

"Kara. I solved it."

I took a sip of coffee as Kara walked over and stared at the computer screen.

"Coordinates?" she said.

"Yep."

She pulled a chair over beside mine, took control of the laptop, and opened a search engine.

Into the query box, she entered: 36.5625N, 106.217778W.

We leaned toward the monitor, waiting for the next screen to load.

A map appeared.

A GPS pin-drop icon affixed to a patch of green.

"I can't tell where this is," I said.

Kara zoomed out.

Until the screen encompassed the words *CARSON NATIONAL FOREST*.

Kara zoomed out farther, and finally, I saw a name I recognized.

Santa Fe.

The coordinates were located in a national forest about eighty miles north-northwest of Santa Fe, New Mexico.

We zoomed back in on the pin drop and changed the screen to satellite view. It was an ultra-res image of evergreen trees with a few pops of yellow that suggested aspen.

I moved the image around, looking for something, *anything*, of interest.

"I just see trees," Kara said.

"Same."

"What are the chances this cipher could have spit out random numbers that just happen to be GPS coordinates for a real place?"

"Infinitesimal. She spelled out point, west, and north."

"But this is the middle of nowhere. I don't see any buildings or infrastructure."

"There could be something we're missing in the shadows, or maybe it's just an old image."

Kara looked at the coordinates again. "One second of latitude is a hundred and one feet. One second of longitude equals eighty."

"These coordinates only encompass eight thousand square feet," I said. "Not a large area."

"What *is* this?" Kara asked.

"I don't know. Want to take a drive to New Mexico and find out?"

Kara's computer flashed an alert—a drone had just left my package of dermal fillers in front of our motel room door.

I cut and dyed my hair at the bathroom sink. Went with black— a departure from the gray it had become after I turned forty. And having unintentionally gone more than three weeks without shaving since my imprisonment on the farm, I had a decent beard that still contained a blend of white, gray, and black. I dyed it all black to match.

The hair color change would help to conceal me from human eyes, but the CCTV- and drone-driven world of facial-recognition software didn't scan for markers as mundane as hair or eye color. They measured more sophisticated, unchangeable aspects of physical features. Eye and earlobe shape. Millimeter distance between the corner of an eye and the corner of a mouth. Bone structure.

I'd sat through two seminars on emerging facial-recognition technologies in the last five years, and now had access to every single word in the memory landscape of my mind.

I used semipermanent eyeliner to artificially extend the length of my eyes and to create the illusion that they were larger and closer together.

As opposed to Botox (a neurotoxin that causes wrinkle-defeating paralysis in targeted areas of the face), dermal fillers simply filled age-related void spaces with a soft, gel-like substance that was injected subcutaneously.

Compared to my clandestine hacking of the GPA servers, getting up to speed on fillers was much, much scarier. Due to the risk of aesthetic and health-related complications, self-injection was forewarned again and again.

I watched every tutorial video I could find, with a focus on patients looking for dramatic facial changes. I studied how medical professionals held the syringes, which products were recommended for which features, appropriate injection doses, and locations.

It was finally time.

I prepared the syringes and gave myself injections at my philtrum (the vertical groove between the base of the nose and the border of the upper lip), my eyebrows and earlobes, and at the corners of my mouth.

No single injection seemed to make much of a difference; however, the cumulative effect was profound.

I stared at the end result in the cracked mirror of the motel room.

I did not look like myself. And while I wouldn't have been comfortable risking the intense security and surveillance of an airport or loop station, I felt confident I could go undetected to where Kara and I needed to be.

I finally called to my sister. "I'm done! Ready to change your face?"

6

WE MADE IT TO St. Louis by nightfall, parked at a charge station, and went out in search of an open restaurant among all the shuttered storefronts.

The last remnant of the Gateway Arch—a teetering, seventy-foot spire wrapped in a skin of stainless steel—was blinding in the setting sun. It had been destroyed in a windstorm seven years ago. Instead of rebuilding, the governor had argued that the millions would be better spent on food stamps and assistance to other St. Louis neighborhoods destroyed by the storm.

Being out in the world with my upgrade was a jarring experience—like how I imagined it might be to see color for the first time.

Everything bolder and brighter. The contrast heightened.

People especially drew me in.

We passed a street musician wailing on a saxophone, and I couldn't stop processing every tiny detail: the sunspots on his face, his respiration rate, his clothing, the tattered hat turned over for donations, the plethora of shrapnel scars down his neck, how he favored his left leg in a way that suggested an old injury—I could practically see the grenade blast he'd taken to his right side, and that was before I clocked part of a tattoo peeking out from under his left shirtsleeve, the anchor from the Marine Corps EGA emblem—and suddenly a portrait of the man materialized. He'd fought in Ukraine, been wounded, came home to a denuded VA, paltry benefits, shit healthcare, and—

A woman passed by in a red bodycon dress, heels, sunglasses, with a tautness in her face: cheeks drawn, heart racing, the palimpsest of wiped-away tears. Nineteen seconds ago, I'd seen her emerge from a bar on the next block, where a relationship of some sort had just ended.

The struggle was to not become swamped by the crush of new stimuli. Aside from the people, the complexity of the ever-changing city—barges, drones, pedestrian traffic, air traffic, ground traffic—all pulled at my focus and curiosity, challenging me to grasp new patterns, to notice things I never had before.

Of course, it was a sensory gating issue.

It wasn't a matter of turning down the volume but of learning to process everything simultaneously. Of learning to live and breathe as I absorbed *everything*.

I felt endlessly curious.

A wood-fired pizza place was the only open restaurant. It overlooked the Mississippi and the seven bridges that spanned the river in the vicinity of downtown.

We ate quickly, anxious to get back on the road.

It was now my turn to drive.

We took I-44 through Missouri as night fell.

I was glad to be driving in the dark, with less incoming stimuli to pull my attention from the road.

Kara was asleep within the hour, and then it was just me and my thoughts and the pavement streaming under the headlights of the near-silent car.

I thought about my mother.

She had returned to America after things got away from her in China. In my ignorance, I had no idea how badly we'd screwed up. I'd just assumed the locust experiment had failed.

Of course, she'd known exactly what was coming.

She was living in our family's Elmwood house in Berkeley, which I found odd and immeasurably sad. With Dad and Max gone, and Kara deployed overseas, the silence in the house only served to remind me of all we'd lost.

A time capsule of how far the Ramsays had fallen.

There was pain in the perfection of the memory.

I would never have come if Mom hadn't summoned me.

She makes us dinner, and we sit at the old dining room table in a kind of tragic silence.

We don't talk about Shenzhen or what our locusts are doing to the rice paddies.

Mom is rarely nostalgic, but tonight proves an exception.

She asks about my favorite moments growing up here.

She even shares some of hers.

And then she tells me something that even my average mind didn't let me forget: "Life never really goes the way you want or expect. Usually, even getting exactly what you want turns out not to have been what you really wanted. So, my son, if you ever find a sliver of happiness and peace, just be thankful and live. Don't reach for more, because a sliver is more than most people ever find."

"Is that what you did?" I ask. "Reached for more?"

I will never forget the way she glares at me across the table.

Later, she sits at the baby grand and plays my favorite piece— "Träumerei," *from Schumann's* Scenes from Childhood. *She's drunk by this point, the piano barely out of tune, and some of her notes slur together.*

I think of other, better times, when she played flawlessly for our whole family—Christmases or New Year's or just random nights when we were all together and happy and blissfully unaware that it wouldn't always be that way.

Mom offers to make up my old bed, but I make an excuse about needing to get back to my dorm room and study for an upcoming final.

So she walks me to the door and, on the threshold, embraces me.

There's a ferocity in how she holds on to me, as if she's clinging to something that is slipping inexorably away.

"It's going to be okay," she says. I don't think much about it in the moment. I think she's had too much to drink and been caught in a rare vortex of sentimentality.

As I walk to my car, I hear the front door slam shut behind me.

The air is perfumed with the minty, piney, honeyed scent of the big eucalyptus that overhangs the front yard, a smell inextricably linked to my childhood and the deepest sense of my identity.

I don't know this at the time, because in life, you're almost never aware when you're living a last chapter—but I won't see my mother ever again.

Three days later, she'll drive her car off Highway 1 and plunge a thousand feet into the Pacific.

Dawn broke on the north Texas grasslands.

It was Christmas morning.

I was still driving, and because of the mutations to my BHLHE41=DEC2, NPSR1, and ADRB1 genes, not remotely tired.

I pictured my family, and there was no mind's-eye imperfection in the conjuring of their faces. I saw them as clearly as if they were with me in the flesh.

I wondered what they were doing without me, and as my eyes filled with tears that splintered the morning light, I took the raw emotion that was unraveling me and shoved it into the mental cage whose walls were growing more impregnable every day.

I hated doing it.

Each time, it was getting easier, and while at this stage turning my heart to stone was still a conscious, painstaking operation, I could imagine a time in the not-too-distant future when the control and suppression of sentiment would become second nature.

We stopped in Amarillo to charge the car batteries, grabbed breakfast at a roadside diner, and pushed on across the sunlit prairie.

In New Mexico, the landscape turned arid.

In the course of an hour, I saw four rockets launching to the southwest out of the spaceport near Truth or Consequences—billionaires spending their Christmas morning in low-Earth orbit.

By lunchtime, we were climbing into the high desert near Santa Fe. The City Different, as they call it, was the second oldest city in America. On approach, Santa Fe hid in plain sight, the low-slung, earth-colored buildings blending quietly into the brown hills.

We drove into the plaza and got a suite at an enormous adobe hotel called La Fonda. In the lobby, there were lights strung from the exposed wood beams, a twenty-foot tree, and families everywhere in terrible sweaters.

I slept through the afternoon and woke with a fierce appetite.

As evening fell, we went out in search of a meal.

It felt good to walk the meandering streets that seemed frozen in time. This tourist town seemed to be offering an experience of America before the great decline—a chance to be in a place where the future still felt like the future.

Christmas trees glowed through the windows of adobe houses, and the scent of wood smoke trickling from fireplaces perfumed the clean, cold air. The mountains east of town were just beginning to glow in the light of a desert moon. I ached with homesickness, and for a moment, I let the ache have its freedom.

We had dinner at a tapas place adjacent to the plaza, which was outrageously expensive since it boasted a nonsynthetic protein menu.

"Not exactly how you imagined Christmas this year, I'm guessing?" Kara asked.

I shook my head and took a sip of the excellent Ribera del Duero. It was almost impossible to find Spanish wines anymore, since the prime growing regions had shifted north. So many iconic wineries no longer produced.

The experience of tasting a world-class wine post-upgrade was mind-blowing. I'd always thought I had a decent palate, but now I was registering an explosion of flavors and smells and finding that I could savor them individually and collectively, simultaneously—dirt and sunlight and dusty black fruits and rose petals and the stellar permeation of oak and time.

"What would you be doing tonight?" I asked.

Kara took one of the tomato bread slices topped with *jamón serrano*.

"Depends on the weather," she said. "If it was snowing, I'd stay home. Make my famous mulled wine. Watch *Bad Santa*. If the roads were good, I'd drive into town. Knock back a few with the nowhere-else-to-go Christmas crowd at El Moro. No." She corrected herself. "That's what I'd do pre-upgrade. Now? I'd stay home and read and think."

"Has your memory improved toward perfection?" I asked.

"Yes."

"Same."

"It's rough," she said. "My life in Montana was built on the concept of *forgetting* who I was. Where I came from." Kara looked at me across the table, her scarred face almost grotesque in the candlelight. "There are memories I would love to lose forever. You're having a hard time, aren't you?"

I knew what she meant.

"Emotion?" I said.

She nodded.

"Yes."

"There are things you can do," she said.

"I know. I've been doing them."

"It gets easier."

"That's what scares me."

"Why?"

I glanced over at the table beside ours. A couple was eavesdropping on our conversation. I suspected it wasn't the words we were saying that had drawn their attention, but the speed of our exchanges.

I cut my eyes at the table and said quietly to Kara, "We should have our conversation at normal speed."

"Right."

I answered her question, forcing myself to speak more slowly and deliberately. "It scares me because I'm afraid of losing the ability to feel things deeply."

"Tell me the advantage of feeling things deeply," she said. "Doesn't feeling cloud logic and reason?"

"To a point. Feelings are also the core of compassion and empathy. We're becoming capable of rationalizing anything. Maybe sentiment helps with the checks and balances."

"True. Or maybe you're just afraid of growing beyond the people you love."

More food came.

It was taking all of my willpower to filter out the seven rambling conversations within my range of hearing and the innumerable smells wafting from other people, out of the kitchen, off the tables.

"Do you wish you hadn't gotten this upgrade?" Kara asked.

"That's a hard one. I finally have the mind I always wanted."

She sipped her wine. "Must've been hard."

"What?"

"Running in Mom's circle. Knowing you didn't deserve to be there."

"You knew I felt that way?"

"Of course. Mom has a once-in-a-generation mind. I always thought your obsession with following in her footsteps was doomed."

"My therapists tell me it's because of Max. When you lose a twin—"

"You lose half your identity. Your connection to Mom served to fill in this other missing part of yourself."

I said, "I thought about him last night while I was driving. Things I'd long forgotten. Moments I'd only half-remembered. It's all so clear now. And it hurts."

Kara smiled. "It doesn't have to."

We walked back to the hotel under a deep navy sky bejeweled with stars.

In the center of the plaza, a choir was singing. They held quivering candles, and their voices lilted icily into the sky.

I didn't see the moment. Not really.

I saw the story behind the moment—a tale passed down over two thousand years that told of a child of a superbeing sent to save the world.

Never before had I seen *Homo sapiens* so clearly—a species, at its most fundamental level, of storytellers.

Creatures who overlay story on everything, but especially their own lives, and in so doing, can imbue a cold, random, sometime brutal existence, with fabricated meaning.

I woke at dawn to the tolling of the bells of the Cathedral Basilica of St. Francis of Assisi, a mighty stone cathedral across the street from the hotel.

I started coffee and opened the sliding glass door to the balcony.

Walked out onto the veranda.

It was blisteringly cold.

Santa Fe was hushed and still.

Already, I was on edge.

The day felt momentous.

We were on the road before eight, speeding north up US 84 into some of the most stunning landscape I'd ever seen, made all the more vibrant by my new perspective.

Everything seemed lucid and rich.

All colors hypersaturated.

Beyond the outskirts of Santa Fe, the desert unfurled.

The sense of space was breathtaking.

Every passing moment a new color revealed itself.

Perspectives changing second to second.

Light and shadow evolving over sandstone.

Arroyos.

Towering mesas.

Epic monuments.

I felt I was seeing through time as we sped across the

transition zone between the Colorado Plateau and the Rio Grande rift.

I saw the landscape in a way I never had before. The flat Mesozoic stratigraphy exposed at the base of the mountains, the younger Cenozoic sediments under the shoulders of the peaks.

For a while, in the distance, we could see the white hyperloop tube stretching across the desert—the line between Denver and Albuquerque.

We crossed rivers I'd heard about while watching Westerns with my father.

To the east, sage- and juniper-covered hills transitioned into conifer forests into high peaks that gleamed brightly with snow above the timberline.

And all under a sky as vast as an ocean, looking down on a desert that 450 million years ago, during the late Cretaceous, *had* been a shallow sea.

We stopped for a quick charge in Ojo Caliente—the only charge station we'd seen since Santa Fe—and pushed on.

I had put Vallecitos into our navigation app. It was an unincorporated community within Carson National Forest and the closest town to our GPS pin drop.

We arrived at nine thirty in the morning to discover that Vallecitos wasn't a city or even a town. It was a village from another time. Only a few hundred people called it home, and while some of the dwellings were clearly inhabited, just as many were crumbling.

We passed an old church that had collapsed in on itself.

And then the ruins of a bar. Old neon beer signs hung by their cords in glassless windows, and a wooden sign—MIS AMIGOS—still swung over an entrance to nothing, faded by decades of high-elevation sunlight.

Kara was driving.

I was looking at her phone.

"No cell service," I said, "but the car's GPS still works. I'm just going to put the raw coordinates in and see what happens."

I converted the decimal degrees to standard degrees/minutes/seconds, and then input 36°33'45"N, 106°13'04"W into the GPS.

The map on the enormous display screen changed to show the location of the pin drop, which was 8.7 miles away.

The automated voice said, *Warning: Driving navigation can only take you to within point five miles of destination.*

Two miles outside the village, the road went from pavement to hard-packed gravel.

We climbed into foothills.

Evergreens crowded up against the shoulder of the road.

After five miles, we hadn't passed another building or soul.

Just us and the car and a trail of dust in our wake.

At 5.9 miles, we turned onto a road of lesser breadth, more rocks, and melting patches of snow in the shade.

Kara had to slow down considerably, and it was becoming clear that the Google suspension package wasn't intended for old logging roads.

At the 8.2-mile mark, the road ended.

The navigation assistant said: *You have gone as far as possible on known roads. Your destination is approximately two thousand feet north-northwest of your current position.*

Kara turned off the car.

I stepped outside.

My door slam echoed through the pine forest.

Kara got out, went around to the trunk, popped it open.

I walked over, saw that she had her duffel bag open. She was pulling out a Garmin minisatellite communicator for off-grid GPS tracking.

She handed it to me. "Can you put the coordinates in?"

While I programmed 36°33'45"N, 106°13'04"W into the device, Kara palmed a magazine into a Glock, which she slipped into a hip holster and secured with a magnetic clasp. Then she loaded shotgun slugs into the same weapon she'd used to shoot me out of the vivarium.

We left the road on foot and headed into the woods, the Garmin taking us on a northerly track.

It was cold and clear.

Sunlight slanted through the trees, creating light wells in the forest.

The air was rife with the smell of pine and spruce.

We climbed a gentle hill.

Despite being at an elevation of almost nine thousand feet, neither of us had any trouble exerting—the hemoglobin in our blood efficiently pulling oxygen out of the thin air thanks to modifications in our EGLN1, EPAS1, MTHFR, and EPOR genes.

The forest was spacious and the underbrush spotty. If we'd had a vehicle with better clearance, we could have driven up this mountain.

I glanced down at the Garmin.

We were fourteen hundred feet from our coordinates.

"There's something up ahead," Kara said.

I didn't see anything.

"Where?"

"Fifty yards straight on. I saw a glint in the trees."

We went a little farther.

And then I saw the old pickup truck.

The front half was in a patch of sunlight. It was the chrome side mirror that Kara had seen glinting.

We approached.

No sound but our footsteps on the pine needle floor of the forest.

Twenty feet away, we stopped.

It was an old Chevy, yellow and white—one of the first fully electric pickup trucks. Pine needles had nearly pasted over the windshield, and the rear left tire was low.

We crept closer, Kara smoothly shouldering her shotgun and aiming it at the driver's-side door, which was coming into view. The window was iced up on the inside.

Kara stopped several feet away.

I felt a pit in my stomach, and a premonition that I was walking into a trap.

Again.

Kara glanced back at me and motioned to the door. "Pull it open," she whispered.

"You sure about that?"

"Got a better idea?"

"Yeah. Leave and come back with hazmat suits."

She rolled her eyes and moved to the truck and jerked open the driver's-side door.

There was a person lying across the bench seat.

Kara said, "Oh god."

She stepped back as the waft of putrefaction hit. I'd encountered my share of dead bodies during the course of my work as a GPA agent, and while I'd certainly experienced worse, this was wildly unpleasant.

Kara leaned her shotgun against the tree and pulled her parka up over her nose. I moved closer, taking a quick glance into the bed of the truck. It was filled with old, dirty snow covering the remnants of a load of firewood.

I walked around to the passenger door.

It made a grinding screech as I wrenched it open.

I was breathing through my mouth now; my eyes watered from whatever decomp gases had been accumulating in the cab of the truck.

Kara came up behind me.

The corpse wore a blue fleece jacket, black jeans, and hiking boots.

A tangle of silver hair spilled over the seat, and the head rested in the crook of the right arm. The only visible skin was the hand, where I saw evidence of slippage and dark wells where blood and liquefied internal matter had settled.

The face was hidden under the splay of hair.

In the passenger-seat floorboard, I saw an empty syringe and an empty glass bottle. I used the Garmin to roll it over so I could see the label.

"Morphine," I said.

I looked at the body again—there was something so peaceful and desperate in its final repose. For the moment, I had forgotten why we'd come here. I was outside of myself, purely in the moment. I wondered what state of mind a person would have to be in to drive into the middle of nowhere and inject a lethal dose of morphine into their veins.

Reaching down, I carefully swept the hair back from the face.

The skin was desiccated, deep purple, and split in places, as if it had undergone periods of freezing and thawing. The eyes were closed, the blued lips parted.

A necklace hung from the neck, draping over the white vinyl seat.

I leaned in to see the pendant hanging from it.

It was a platinum double helix—the structure of DNA.

I see wrapping paper scattered around the tree. I'm opening my new Lego set. Max is lying on the couch, already weary from the early stages of the illness that will take his life next year. Kara is trying out her new tablet, and there's the warm, sweet smell of the scones Mom

made every Christmas morning baking in the oven. I hear Mom say,
"Oh, Haz, it's beautiful," and I watch her lifting a necklace with a
double helix pendant out of a small, burgundy box.

"I had it custom-made by a jeweler in Philadelphia," my father
says. "Here, let me." And then he comes around behind her and deli-
cately lifts it over her head and fastens the clasp as my mother holds
her hair off her neck.

I staggered back from the truck.

Mouth running dry.

I pointed into the cab.

Croaked, "I think it's Mom."

Kara leaned into the cab, examined the corpse's face.

"How can you tell?"

"The necklace."

I watched the recognition hit.

Watched Kara brace against the tidal wave of emotion,
watched it tear through her defenses, her face flashing through
confusion, horror, anger, heartbreak, shock.

I walked a little ways into the woods.

The wind chilled the tears on my face.

I sat down on the forest floor in a patch of sun.

Behind me, Kara scream-shouted at the corpse, "Fuck you!"

I broke down.

My mother was dead.

Again.

When I finally struggled back onto my feet, the light had
changed. The sun was higher. Kara was sitting on the ground,
leaning back against the wheel of the pickup truck, staring into
nothing.

I walked over, eased down across from her.

There were tear streaks across her face.

Anger radiating off her.

I didn't say anything.

She finally looked at me.

Holding back tears.

Chin trembling.

"What kind of person does this to their children?"

"What should we do with her?" I asked. "Notify someone? Bury her?"

"Who do you think gives a fuck that Miriam Ramsay is dead? Again. And if you think I'm going to spend all day putting her in the ground . . . I say we forget this ever happened. Go back to Santa Fe—we still have the hotel room—and get wasted. Fuck this day. Fuck every single part of it."

"I'm on board with that," I said, "but there is one thing." Kara looked at me. I held up the Garmin. "According to this, we're still 1,250 feet from our destination."

Kara took the Garmin from me and stared at it.

She said, "Isn't it obvious this is what we were supposed to find?"

"Maybe. But we've come this far. What's another quarter mile?"

I gave her a hand and helped her onto her feet, then we trudged up the hillside.

I felt weak.

Every step was arduous.

Between the adrenaline rush of finding the body and the emotional crash of realizing who it was, I had nothing left.

We passed into a small glade.

The woods grew dense on the other side.

A darker, cooler forest of spruce trees.

We were climbing into snow.

The Garmin vibrated in my hand. I looked down at the screen.

You have arrived at your destination.

"Says we're here," I said.

I looked up and around. The woods on our destination grid were unremarkable. Engelmann spruce, a few boulders, a crust of old snow on everything. The trees grew too closely together for sunlight to reach the forest floor.

It was impossible to tell exactly where we were in relation to the 36°33'45"N, 106°13'04"W grid.

I set the Garmin on the ground to mark the perimeter.

Kara looked at me.

I said, "GPS is only accurate to within five meters, so we should expand our canvassing to a ninety-six by one hundred seventeen–foot square."

"I'll start over here."

She headed off through the trees.

I started walking.

Slow, methodical steps crunching in the snow.

I looked at the ground.

At every tree.

Each boulder I passed.

The more ground I covered, the more I began to suspect that Kara was right. We had found what we were meant to find. A final *fuck you* from Mom for reasons we would probably never know.

As I finished my fourth traverse of the grid and started back in the opposite direction, I heard Kara say, "Logan."

She was fifty or sixty feet away, hidden in the trees.

I took off through the snow, following the direction of her voice. When I finally glimpsed her, Kara was standing beside the stump of what had once been a ponderosa pine. The tree had toppled long ago, apparently struck down by lightning. There was a burn scar across half of the enormous stump.

I sidled up to Kara.

The trunk was four feet high.

Jagged, blackened, hollowed-out.

I peered over the edge.

A stainless-steel handle protruded from the snow. I looked at Kara, then reached down and took hold of it. Whatever it was attached to was buried in snow.

"Give me a hand?"

She reached in, grabbed the handle.

We both pulled, straining.

After a moment, it broke free from the ice and we stumbled back from the stump, holding a black hardcase, approximately two feet on each side.

Sealed, but as far as I could tell, not locked.

I rolled it onto its base.

It looked expensive. Watertight. Crush-proof. Dust-proof.

The shell was a lightweight polymer and all the hardware was stainless steel.

Kara knelt down, flipped the three latches.

Carefully opened the lid.

Inside, encased in black foam, was a laptop on steroids. I'd seen SWAT guys using them to fly thermal-imaging drones, but had never handled one myself.

"This is military grade," Kara said, opening the screen.

"What are the features?"

"Durable against heat, cold, explosions. Radiation hardened. Very heavy."

She pressed the power button several times, but nothing happened.

Turning the laptop over, Kara exposed a void space underneath.

"No battery," she said.

I pulled a layer of foam out. Underneath, a vacuum-sealed

battery and six PCM drives. With her trench knife, Kara liber-
ated the battery from its packaging.

"If this doesn't work, I have a power outlet in the Google."

She locked the battery into its housing in the laptop and
tapped the power button again.

The screen glowed to life.

I had no idea how long it had been sitting out here, but it
seemed to boot up normally, and after ten seconds, we were
staring at a blank home screen with a single thumbnail in the
center—an AVI file entitled "To my children."

I felt my pulse rate kick up from 78 bmp to 105.

I looked at Kara. "You want to do this here?"

She moved the cursor onto the thumbnail and clicked on the
file.

It took a moment to load, and we waited, both of us kneeling
in the snow before the hardcase like it was some kind of altar.

Our mother appeared on the screen.

Kara muttered, "Holy shit."

One thing for me to tell her our mother was alive. Another
entirely to see her with her own eyes.

Miriam stepped back from the camera, as if she had just
locked a phone into a tripod. She wasn't in these woods. On this
mountain. She was in the desert we had driven through to get
here, and in the same clothes we'd discovered her wearing in
the truck.

The light suggested early morning.

The wind was blowing her silver hair. She pushed it back out
of her face and settled herself onto a rock.

The hood of the white and yellow Chevy was just poking
into the left frame, and the backdrop was miles of pink desert
ending at a soaring purple mesa I'd seen earlier today.

She looked at the camera.

"I don't know if I'm speaking to Logan and Kara, or just one of you, but if you're watching this, I'm proud of you. It means you found the message I inserted at AAVS1. It means the upgrade worked."

I noticed a cluster of cottonwood trees behind her.

The leaves a dazzling yellow.

She'd recorded this in autumn—October perhaps?

"I came through here once with your father."

She smiled.

"I was pregnant with you, Kara, although I didn't know it yet. We were in our twenties. No money. Driving out from Boston to Berkeley for my first postdoc fellowship. Stayed in a motel on the outskirts of Santa Fe called the Desert Aire. The next day, we drove north of the city. I'd always wanted to see the landscape Georgia O'Keeffe spent her life painting. This mountain behind me?"

She glanced back at the purple mesa, silhouetted against the dawn sky.

"That's Cerro Pedernal. O'Keeffe painted it twenty-eight times. She once said, 'It's my private mountain. It belongs to me. God told me if I painted it enough, I could have it.' I feel that way about my *work.*

"When you arrive at the end of your life, you start thinking about the good times and the best times. That trip with your father was one of the best. Maybe I'm just idealizing a moment, but Haz and I were right out of school, and the future was as wide open as this desert. Nothing bad had happened. Nothing that couldn't be undone.

"We drove to this little village in the foothills called Vallecitos. It was a warm fall day, and we stopped for beers at a bar that didn't seem to get many tourists or know what to do with them. It was called Mis Amigos."

She looked off into the distance for a moment, then back into the camera.

"Logan, you and I had a conversation many years ago. You asked me—if I could, would I make more people in the world like us?

"*Twenty years have passed since that night, and things are worse than ever. For the last two decades, I've been working in a small lab in my favorite place in the world, trying to build something that could make every member of our species more like us. Trying to gift something to* Homo sapiens *that might allow us to survive another five hundred, thousand, or ten thousand years.*

"*This gift is a genetic upgrade that ramps up our cognitive performance so that we might, collectively, let the engines of reason guide our behavior instead of the cushions of sentiment.*

"*The genes that steered us toward sentiment and its downstream belief patterns are still present in our genome. They were advantageous at the dawn of humankind, when we had no understanding of the universe. They led us to invent myth and religion and tradition, and these systems unquestioningly put us on the path to stability and cooperation.*

"*But now they're letting us ignore the facts all around us. Poverty, disease, starvation, and all the hatred those hardships breed, growing worse every decade—as we squeeze the last drops from our planet's resources. We can't keep living in denial about what's happening or hoping that it's someone else's problem to solve.*

"*The dinosaurs never saw their end coming. They died off because one morning, out of the clear blue sky, an asteroid 6.2 miles across smashed into the Yucatán peninsula at 67,000 miles per hour. The end of* Homo sapiens *lies just over the horizon. We can see it in a thousand metrics. Which means we have a chance. But only if we collectively decide to act. If nothing changes, we will die off for the stupidest reason imaginable—because we refused, for so many childish reasons, to do the obvious things that would save us.*"

Something shifted in our mother's eyes.

They became distant, dark.

"*The mark I version of the upgrade is complete, but there's work still to do. I haven't developed a dispersal mechanism, and I'm not going to get the chance to.*"

What happened next, I had hardly ever seen in my lifetime.

My mother became emotional.

As rare as a desert snowfall.

"For the first time in my life, my mind is failing me, and because of who I am, seeking treatment is not an option. But after two hundred million dead, maybe I deserve to have the only thing I ever loved about myself taken from me. I'm forgetting things. Sometimes, I'm unable to think at all. Today is actually the best day I've had in months, so I've decided that today is the day I die. I want to say farewell on my own terms, while I still know who I am."

She wiped her eyes.

"I couldn't bear the thought of the upgrade dying on the one-yard line, so I did something drastic. Kara, I hired a man to deliver a drone to your cabin, loaded with my upgrade. Logan, as I'm sure you know by now, I hired Henrik Soren to lure you to that house in Denver. There was no one else in my life I could trust but the two of you. I hope this trust hasn't been misplaced. I hope the upgrade worked. I hope you aren't too angry with me.

"So, my children, if you're watching this, know that you are the next step in human evolution. As the only two people on this planet to receive my upgrade, you hold the fate of our species in your hands. In the hardcase containing the laptop you're watching this on, you'll find phase memory drives with the mark I novel upgrade sequences and function. Consider this your inheritance. What you do with it now is up to you."

Despite the cold, I was sweating.

Trying to wrap my mind around the magnitude of what this hardcase contained.

"I'm sorry about the way you had to find me. I never wanted to hurt you. I never meant to hurt all those people. I think about those who died every day. I think about both of you. And Max. And my sweet Haz. I know I wasn't the mother you wanted, but I loved you in the only way I knew how."

Our mother stood.

The early light hit her face.

She looked out across the desert.

"It's so lovely here. I wish you could see it with me."

And then she came toward the camera.

"Goodbye, Kara. Goodbye, Logan."

Her voice broke.

"Now save our species."

She reached toward the camera.

The screen turned briefly to the sky and then went black.

Kara and I were still kneeling in the snow before the hardcase.

I hadn't looked at her while the video played, but now I did.

Her face was blank. No tears. No anger. She simply looked elsewhere.

I closed the laptop.

I looked at the six phase memory drives held securely in foam, each one about the size of my hand. Kara pried one out. She felt the weight of it, then put it carefully back and latched the case.

Wind pushed through the tops of the trees—a lonely, sustained *whoosh*.

She looked at me. *Well?*

"I think we should douse this hardcase with gasoline and light a match."

Her eyes narrowed.

I said, "Mom tried to edit a few rice paddies and ended up killing two hundred million people."

"What she did to us was successful," Kara said. "It *worked*."

"On two people. That's hardly conclusive evidence that this upgrade is safe for every human being on the planet."

"Why does it have to be safe for all? Why is that the threshold?"

"Are you seriously considering this?" I asked.

"If she's not wrong about our impending extinction, what do we have to lose?"

I stood and looked down at my sister.

"Everything it means to be human."

Kara rose to her feet. "I know you were there on the day Mom released her locusts into the fields, and I can't pretend to know what it feels like to walk around with that. But what if this moment—you and me in these woods—is the crossroads for our species? We need to face it with cold reason, not sentiment. Not nostalgia for a doomed species. We do nothing," she said, "and humanity is gone in a hundred and fifty years. We could lead our species into the future. You and me."

"God, you sound as arrogant as Mom."

"Is that supposed to hurt me?"

"You're making the same mistake she did. Being smart doesn't make people infallible. It just makes them more dangerous."

Kara studied me for a moment.

It was a small thing.

The *smallest* of things.

But her jaw lifted imperceptibly, and the inner corners of her eyebrows drew in and then up—a microexpression of sadness flashing in and out of existence in less than a quarter of a second.

As if she were trying to hide it.

A voice in my head inquired: *Why would she try to hide that she was sad?*

Because she was sad about something she didn't want me to know.

What wouldn't she want me to know?

The answer came quietly, effortlessly, as if on a gentle breeze.

That she sees this moment for what it is. Two people in the wilderness of New Mexico holding humanity's future in their hands. She thinks I'm wrong and she's right, and because the stakes are extinction, she's willing to do something unthinkable.

I reached down, grabbed the hardcase handle.

"What are you doing?" Kara asked.

"We can't leave it out here. Should we head back?"

She stared at me for a moment. "All right."

It was all I could do not to look at the trench knife sheathed on her right hip, the Glock holstered on her left.

Turning quickly, I flipped up the collar of my jacket so she couldn't see my carotid artery pounding away.

My pulse rate had spiked to 144. While I was getting better at controlling it, I didn't have the mastery to throttle back into the range of normal fast enough to elude Kara. And I feared that if she noticed my elevated pulse rate, it would clue her in to my suspicion of what she was thinking, which could escalate this situation before I had a chance to think my way out of it.

Had I made the adjustment in time? Had she already noticed? Were there other tells that might alert her to my nervous system shifting into fight-or-flight? Dilated pupils? Muscle tension?

The hardcase had wheels, but they didn't roll in the old snow. I dragged the case behind me, heading back down the hill across the 36°33'45"N, 106°13'04"W grid.

I felt lightheaded, dizzy.

Was I insane?

Of course my sister who I loved and who loved me, who I'd lived with under the same roof for sixteen years, didn't want to kill me. That was actually true. She didn't *want* to. She'd been convinced by our mother of the importance of this upgrade and knew she had to make a decision here and now.

Her mistake wasn't showing her sadness—she could've easily lied her way through some other explanation, like finding our mother dead in a truck just down the hill.

Her mistake was the attempted subterfuge. The suppression of the sadness.

I reached down and grabbed the Garmin as I passed it.

Kara's footsteps were behind me in the snow—nine feet back.

We crossed onto dry ground, the hardcase wheels rolling nicely downhill now, bumping along over root and rock.

I needed to look back at her, gather more data, but I was afraid she would read the fear in my face and decide that—

"Maybe you're right, Logan."

There was a flatness to her tone that struck me as both a shield and a snare. If I responded, my tone and speech pattern would likely reveal my inner state.

I wiped a line of sweat off my brow before it could burn my eyes, my pulse rate skyrocketing to 165. Blood pressure through the roof.

Calm. Down.

I took a breath as we emerged into the sunny glade.

She's going to kill me in these woods. It makes no sense for her to wait. This is the perfect place to do it. She'll just leave me with our mother.

And still—I wasn't anywhere close to certain. I could be imagining all of this. Basing it on a single microexpression I'd seen for a fraction of a second.

I thought back to how Kara had handled herself at the farm. She'd killed three men in three seconds. While I was definitely stronger and faster than I'd ever been in my life, I doubted I could match her speed, control, and physical prescience. She was a fighting virtuoso before the upgrade. I was not. I suspected the gap between my physical abilities and hers was still just as wide. Plus, I was unarmed, and she was walking behind me with a trench knife and a Glock and her innate, finely tuned, genetically enhanced lethality.

I saw Mom's truck in the distance, eighty-five yards away.

Kara had left her shotgun leaning against the tree near the truck. I saw a route toward it, where the pines grew close together. They might provide me a modicum of cover. But first I'd have to break Kara's defenses, blunt her cognitive processing and reaction times. Make her think like she used to, and give my outmatched self a fighting chance.

I said out of the blue, "Do you remember what you told me that night in the hospital after Max died?"

Kara's footsteps stopped.

"Logan."

I kept walking.

"Logan."

I stopped, took one last look at my route through the pines, and turned slowly around.

She was standing twelve feet away, slightly uphill, staring at me. There were tears in her eyes, her hands were at her sides, and the magnetic clasp that locked her Glock into its holster was open. I knew with absolute certainty—it had been closed when we left the grid. She'd quietly flicked it open as she followed me downhill.

This was all the confirmation I needed, and I was sure she read the heartbreak in my face, because now my eyes were welling too.

I said, "You told me—"

"Stop."

"'—I'm your big sister, and I always will be—'"

"What are you—"

"'—and we'll get through this loss together.' You told me you would always be there for me."

Her mask of control slipped, and for a fleeting moment she

looked like the Kara of old, the agonizing struggle bleeding through her eyes, and on its heels, a grim resignation.

I released my grip on the hardcase. It fell over into the pine needles.

"What do you want me to say, Logan?"

"I want you to say that I'm your brother and that it matters more to you than—"

"But it doesn't. I wish it did. I wish that more than anything. But it's only a beautiful sentiment, and—"

I ran midsentence.

No warning.

Just turned and shot down the mountain on the winding route I'd mentally mapped for myself through the pines.

Heard Kara shout my name some distance behind me, and I almost stopped. Something in her voice—an element of surprise or hurt—made me wonder if I had completely misread—

And then came the gunshot.

A chunk of tree exploded two feet to the left of me.

Mom's truck was straight on, fifty yards away.

I glanced back, caught a flash of movement in the trees.

Another gunshot.

Veered left, then right, trying to make myself a difficult target.

Now flat-out sprinting.

Two more shots echoed through the forest in rapid succession, and I felt something tug at my left shoulder.

Kept running. The truck getting closer.

I could see the shotgun Kara had leaned against the tree.

My left shoulder was vibrating now, and there was pain in the vibration, which was spreading through the rest of my back and into my neck.

Another gunshot.

A bullet pierced the windshield of the truck.

A bull's-eye of pain in my shoulder now, a radiant, wet heat. I reached back and touched it and my hand came away bloody. Kara had shot me.

I felt the front of my chest and shoulder—no exit wound.

Decelerating as I reached the truck and grabbed the shotgun and swung around the tree for cover.

The pain was a dull throbbing, masked by adrenaline. My heart drummed along at 203 bpm. I heard the snap of a twig somewhere up the hill.

Trying to steady my breathing.

The gun was a semiauto Benelli. I'd used one before. They were solid weapons with a standard 5+1 capacity, although Kara had modded this one with a much longer magazine.

I pumped the shotgun.

Peered around the tree.

The woods had gone silent.

No wind. No birdsong. Nothing moved.

My shoulder was aching like someone had struck it with a baseball bat and blood was running down the inside of my left leg, dripping off the hem of my pants, carving a dark trail through the crushed, brown pine needles.

I glanced behind me.

Nothing.

What was she doing? Coming around to flank me? What would I do if I were her?

She had a scoped rifle in her duffel bag—a disassembled CheyTac, the long-range sniper rifle of the U.S. military. It could hit targets at two kilometers, and it was in the trunk of the Google. If she didn't want to risk taking me on with the pistol, that would certainly do the trick. I'd never see her. Never even hear the gunshot.

The Benelli was a close-range weapon, loaded with 00 buck-shot that was only lethal to about fifty yards. She had probably gone back for the phase memory drives. Then she could race to the Google on a wide loop that would keep her out of my range of fire.

I painfully shouldered the shotgun and scanned the forest through the ghost sights.

All was quiet.

I scrambled to my feet. Unsteady. Vision blurring. My left shoe squishing with blood as I moved toward the truck.

The driver's-side door to the Chevy was still open. I crawled into the cab, trying to stay low, hoping the key was somewhere inside.

The smell was eye-watering.

I climbed over my mother and took her by the shoulders, pulling her out of the cab as carefully as I could. But it quickly became apparent that there was no room for elegance or grace in this task. It was like trying to move a giant sack of soup and sticks.

I tugged hard and she slid out of the cab and dropped unceremoniously onto the forest floor.

"Sorry, Mom," I said.

I got back into the cab and closed the passenger's- and driver's-side doors, their metallic shrieking filling the forest.

If Kara was close, if she hadn't made a break for the Google, she'd have an easy shot at me.

Now I just needed the damn truck to start.

By my estimation, it had been sitting here since October. Eight to twelve weeks. When parked in low-consumption mode, on a full charge, it was supposed to take six months to drain the battery. If she'd stopped at the same charge station we had in Ojo Caliente, 28.4 miles back, there *should've* been an ample charge, even on an old model like this. If she hadn't, well, I was probably going to die in the next thirty minutes.

I pressed the motor start.

Nothing.

Tried again.

The motors slowly whirred.

Then seized.

"Come on."

I glanced through the windshield, the rearview mirror, the side mirrors.

No Kara.

I tried once more.

It whirred again, faster this time.

"Come on!"

On the fourth attempt, the motor whirred to life and stayed whirring. I eased onto the accelerator, the bald tires spinning for several interminable seconds, then finding traction.

The truck lurched forward, and I cranked the steering wheel, guiding the Chevy back in the direction of the road, flooring the accelerator now because every second delayed gave Kara a chance at—

Bullets raked the passenger's side of the truck, the window exploding, what I hoped were only glass shards embedding in the side of my face, and it wasn't the single, piercing strike of a sniper bullet but the staccato *chinking* of full-auto rounds.

I caught the briefest glimpse of her—standing in that black coat in a patch of sunlight that made her pale hair glow, shouldering a machine gun.

I saw a muzzle flash—

Ducked as the windshield took fire, then popped up again, swerving just in time to avoid colliding with a tree.

As the back of the Chevy took heavy fire, I glimpsed the road in the distance and the blue Google with its trunk still open.

I broke out of the woods, stomped the brake pedal, and brought the Chevy to a screeching halt a few feet past Kara's car.

The gunfire had stopped.

I grabbed the shotgun, opened the driver's-side door.

Holding the shotgun at waist-level, I put a round of buckshot through the right rear tire. The Google sank a little. I shot out the left rear tire. While I could certainly outrun Kara on the last, rocky stretch of road, her car would've easily caught the truck on the smoother sections.

Kara emerged from the forest.

I didn't hesitate—just put her in the ghost sights and fired three rounds. She dove behind a downed tree and I threw the shotgun into the truck, jumped in, and jammed the accelerator into the floorboard.

I flew down the road on ruined shocks, the truck feeling like it might rattle itself apart at any second.

I pushed the speed to 40 mph, barely able to see through the fractured windshield. My seat was covered in blood, and it felt like someone was shoving a red-hot poker through my back.

I kept checking the side mirror, half-expecting to see the Google bearing down, but there was only a trail of orange dust.

My adrenaline waned. Pain was coming on strong.

After several miles, I had to slow down because I didn't trust myself to keep the truck on the road. I was having trouble seeing, I felt so lightheaded . . .

Didn't know how much time had passed since Kara shot me, but I had been bleeding too long. Of that, I was certain. I needed to stop it or I was going to die.

I reached back and held my hand against the wound. Blood seeped through my fingers. I couldn't drive and put pressure on the wound, but I had to keep driving. I had to get as far away from her as possible.

I was entering hypovolemic shock, which occurs after the human body loses twenty percent of its blood. My respiration rate was too fast and shallow, and I could feel my diastolic pressure plummeting toward dangerous levels.

I was suddenly cold, confusion setting in, and I tried to stay above it all, tried to use the power of my intellect to keep alert, alive, but a gray nothingness was creeping in around the edges of my vision.

A tone.

Blaring.

Sustained.

It called to me, faintly, in the depths of this grave darkness.

Lifting my head was the hardest physical act of my lifetime, and when I did, the noise ended.

I opened my eyes.

Light splintered in.

Crystal shimmering rays of it.

I tasted blood in my mouth. It was sheeting down my face. I was still sitting behind the steering wheel of the old Chevy. Just beyond the hood, I saw the enormous, rippled trunk of a cottonwood tree. I had crashed into it.

There were buildings nearby.

I saw the ruins of Mis Amigos.

There was someone standing beside my window, and I slowly turned my head, blinking against the bright winter sun.

He was eleven or twelve, and he was looking at me through the window, into what I imagined was one of the more disturbing scenes of his young life.

Me bleeding to death in the corpse-reeking cab of a bullet-ridden truck.

"*¿Necesitas ayuda?*"

His voice came high and muffled through the glass.

"*Sí*," I said. My voice sounded so weak. "*Por favor.*"

There were other people now in the street behind him, drifting toward this single-car accident in the middle of their quiet village.

And they couldn't have known—no one could—that the dying man inside the Chevy had just fought a battle for the fate of our species.

A battle he had lost.

PART TWO

Our ability to read out this sequence of our own genome
has the makings of a philosophical paradox. Can an intelligent being comprehend the instructions to make itself?

—John Sulston

7

ONE YEAR LATER

It is January 11, and I've only seen the water today in ephemeral glimpses as a train of mist plows in from the sea. The wind is rattling the storm shutters and the rain sheets continuously down the windows. I just put another log in the woodstove.

I was planning to only be here a week, but I may stay longer. There's an overlooked wildness about this place that speaks to me.

What I am.

What I'm becoming.

Mostly, I just sit by the kitchen window, watching the sea change. In my short time here, I've seen it at roiling gray and glittering stillness. Obscured as a storm slams into the continent (occurring today), and as a shiny, black lacquer under the moon.

More than anyplace I've been, there is the feeling here that the sea is a presence, and a mercurial one—moody, fierce, serene.

And constantly evolving.

I think you and Ava would like it here. When the weather is good, there's a short trail down the bluff to the beach, and the town is only a mile away.

I hope you're safe. I hope you're finding your way toward happiness again. I hope that, if we're ever reunited, you will understand why I had to let you believe I was gone. It's because I know your heart, Beth. You would put your own safety and freedom at hazard to find me.

I miss you madly, and I would give anything

I stopped writing. I looked up from the kitchen table, through the window, out to sea. Crossing out the last sentence, I put the pen to paper again.

I'm not being honest, Beth. I'm writing things the old Logan would write, driven by some vestigial nostalgia for my past life. If I can't be honest with you, even when it's painful, what's the point?

Interacting with people has become a challenge. Imagine knowing what someone is trying to say long before they inelegantly manage to say it. Imagine being intensely aware of every microexpression that belies their words. Imagine a chasm between you and everyone else. Imagine not feeling human anymore. For me, now, speaking with a bright adult feels like what it used to feel like to hold a conversation with a ten-year-old. I know that sounds shitty, but it's the truth.

I can recall every moment of our shared existence. I don't just see you as the snapshot of who you were in our last moment together—our kitchen in Arlington, fixing your second coffee of the day, dash of milk, half a Splenda, and I walk over to kiss you goodbye on my way out the door, and you stop what you're doing and look me in the eyes and kiss me like you mean it, no automatic thing, neither of us with any inkling that we will not see each other again.

I see you as the Beth you were that day in prison, twenty-five years old in your first suit, trying to hide your nerves. I see the Beth in her hospital bed, exhausted and elated, holding our daughter for the first time. I see you on the morning you heard your father had died. And on a Wednesday evening in October six and a half years ago that was utterly unremarkable except for the fact that it was the most fun we ever had together—two bottles of wine and laughter and great conversation and a few tears—everything that is right about us.

All those moments are all equally real for me. All those moments of you. It breaks my heart that I can't live them again. And maybe even more to know that, even if I could, I wouldn't feel now what I felt then.

In the last year, I've experienced a lifetime's worth of change.

I am hardly recognizable as that man who said goodbye to you in our kitchen. I suspect you would think I've become aloof, withdrawn, and interior. Maybe even cold.

The rain has stopped. The clouds are breaking up. Sunlight hitting the sea stacks. One of those rock outcroppings, if I squint my eyes just right, resembles a ship carved out of rock.

Here is the truth, which, once upon a time, I promised to always give you: If I let myself, I could spiral into a very dark place. I could let our separation and my loneliness tear me apart. But I'm too strong for that now.

These are hard things to write.

I am afraid I will never see you again.

And I am equally afraid that I will, and that our connection will have changed too much.

I set the pen down, closed the notebook. It was filled with simi-lar letters—some to Beth, some to Ava. Writing to them had become a form of self-discipline. I wrote letters I would never share in order to remember what it felt like to be a member of a family. To remember what it felt like to be human. To be driven, at least to some extent, by sentiment. My ability to *feel* was an atrophying muscle, which, if I completely stopped using, I would lose entirely.

It was early evening, and I was hungry.

I fired off messages to the cyber, private, and corporate inves-tigators I'd enlisted to find Kara. Then I stood, stretched, and grabbed my rain jacket off the coat rack by the kitchen door.

I headed outside across a stretch of emerald grass to the edge of the bluff.

Waves thundered against the rocks, ninety feet below.

As I followed a precarious path that angled down to the beach, I thought of Kara for the eighth time today.

When my sister shot me, the bullet had entered my left deltoid, shredding through muscle but missing my clavicle and brachial plexus. It came to rest in my upper left pectoral, two inches above my heart. Two inches from a kill shot.

I had very nearly bled to death in my mother's crashed pickup truck on what passed for Main Street in the village of Vallecitos.

I was medevaced to a hospital in Santa Fe, where doctors saved my life.

New Mexico didn't have mandatory gunshot reporting, and I could only hope that the medical staff would respect my doctor-patient confidentiality and not call in law enforcement to interview me about what had happened in Vallecitos.

But there was no way to be certain.

Every second I lay in that hospital bed I was risking capture.

Twelve hours after my admittance, I willed myself out of bed. My clothes had been cut off me in the operating room, and stumbling around Santa Fe in a hospital gown in the middle of the night sounded like a surefire way to get myself discovered and detained.

So I rifled through the dressers in the other patients' rooms until I found an older gentleman's change of clothes that fit me.

I walked out of St. Vincent hospital at 3:45 A.M. into a frigid night with a little over five hundred dollars in cash from my time with Kara.

I had no ID. No credit cards. No phone.

It was the hardest night of my life.

Harder than prison.

Harder than the uncertainty of the vivarium.

I was in agony.

Exhausted.

Freezing.

Without my upgrade, I'm sure I would've died.

I walked into the train station when it opened and bought a one-way ticket on the first Rail Runner down to Albuquerque. Santa Fe was much too small for me to be lingering in, and Albuquerque seemed to be the kind of place where enough violence was happening on a daily basis that I might have a chance at flying under the radar.

The light coming through the window warmed my face.

The gentle rocking of the train car sent me off to sleep.

The conductor shook me awake when we rolled into Montaño station.

I stumbled out of the train, threw up in a trash bin.

I bought gauze, first-aid bandages, antibiotic ointment, and Tylenol at the first pharmacy I saw.

Took my shirt off in the bathroom. I was bleeding through the last round of bandages I'd gotten at St. Vincent. I held a paper towel to the entry wound until it clotted again, doused it in antibiotics, and rewrapped everything in fresh bandages.

By the time I'd finished, I was too tired to even stand. I slept for several hours in a stall, leaning against the side of a filthy toilet until a store worker found me and kicked me out.

Outside again, my predicament bore down on me.

I was broke. Homeless. Badly injured. Wanted.

Because I couldn't stop seeing patterns all around me, I was painfully aware that nothing I was experiencing was new. How many people have been tired, broken, cold, and alone on the streets? And none of them had the considerable resources of my upgrade to save them.

The bell tower of a church loomed in the distance, profiled against a heartbreakingly blue New Mexican sky.

I gathered myself as best I could and walked into the front office.

A kind woman took pity on me and let me use their phone.

The third shelter I called had a bed available.

After a few days at the shelter, my gunshot wound was healing rapidly, and I could finally walk without wanting to collapse.

My focus turned to stopping Kara. Before I could do that, I needed freedom of movement. To have freedom of movement, I would need a bulletproof identity, and that would take time and money.

The money problem was a conundrum.

With my upgrade, I could have gotten any job in the world.

Except I couldn't.

I was Logan Ramsay, and there were people turning this country upside down to find me.

Robbery, stealing, fraud—it all seemed destined to work against my efforts to remain invisible.

But according to my internet research at the library I'd been visiting during the day, there were six casinos in Albuquerque.

So I bought some clothes at a thrift store, cleaned myself up, and walked into my first casino one week after Kara shot me.

The cameras made me nervous. They were *everywhere*. My dermal fillers would last at least a year, but I would find out in short order if the alterations I'd made to my face in West Virginia were enough to fool the facial-recognition AI that was undoubtedly scraping CCTV databases all over the country.

But in light of everything, it didn't really matter.

I needed money. I had no other options.

The slots would be a complete waste of time. When it came

to blackjack, a math genius like myself could certainly count cards, but against a shoe—which contained between six and eight decks—it would simply take too long. Any success would be purely driven by luck.

Poker, however, presented an interesting opportunity. I'd played my fair share and had never been much good at it in my previous life.

But now . . .

Calculating pot odds was suddenly effortless. And sitting at the table, I could instantly call upon the seven poker strategy books I'd speed-read yesterday at the library, which focused on how to read an opponent's range based on their bets, how to bet in the big blind versus the small, versus late positions.

This was a game that rewarded computing horsepower and the ability to absorb a multitude of specific sets of rules quickly. And beyond the mathematical mechanics, poker was ultimately just reading people. Their excitement, their attempt to conceal that excitement, their fear, their boredom, their deceit, their regret. And then making choices accordingly.

I sat down at a no-limit Texas Hold 'em table on a Friday evening with $432 to my name. There were eight of us at the table, and as the dealer dealt the first hand, my gunshot wound started throbbing. Compartmentalizing the pain, I began to play.

I observed—even with the better players—the negligible raise of their eyebrows when they caught a great card they weren't expecting. An imperceptible "sinking inward" when they didn't. I built equations for each opponent to track their emotional leaks. If Fidel, the guy across from me, saw a card and reacted by exposing greater than ten percent of the whites of his eyes, I knew he had something better than a pair. Twenty percent? I'd fold, unless I thought I had the cards to beat him.

Different players leaked their secrets through different microexpressions.

One woman always gave her nose the slightest wrinkle of disgust when she saw a card that didn't help her hand. As if it smelled bad.

A young kid's pulse rate rose above 110 when he bluffed. Every time.

It took a few hands to get a read on each of them, but I quickly cataloged their varying reactions, watching their moods rise and fall with the flop, the turn, the river.

As I played my hands and my chip count grew, I couldn't help wondering if this was what my mother had felt for most of her adult life. Like she was running, thinking, operating ten times faster than everyone else. I understood how that might build a façade of arrogance, and deeper down, intense isolation. She hadn't had my ability to emotionally compartmentalize, so the feeling of being apart from everyone—her postdocs, her friends, even her family—must have been crushing.

I left that first night with $1,907, and it felt as good as the first money I'd ever earned mowing lawns for neighbors the summer I turned twelve.

Each night, I went to a different casino.

Slowly rebuilding my treasury.

By the end of the second week, I had eight thousand dollars, and I was playing at more competitive tables. One player even tipped me off to a high-stakes underground game in Rio Rancho.

I moved out of the shelter and left them the biggest donation I could afford. Then I checked into the cheapest motel I could find, which rented rooms by the week.

Played poker at night, and during the day, began the process of building my new identity.

Making one from scratch was beyond my skill set, and I didn't trust the dark web to provide me with reliable documents.

With my winnings, I bought a laptop and began looking for a very specific person whose identity I could steal.

This person needed to be approximately my age, with a face similar enough to mine so that I could augment my features to fool the ubiquitous facial-recognition AI. They needed to be born in a city that was far from my birth city of Berkeley, California, in a place I had never been and where I knew no one. This person needed to be dead, never married, no children. I needed someone with a light social-media footprint. And ideally, their death needed to have occurred out of the country, in some kind of mass-casualty disaster.

The idea being, if I could find someone who met those criteria, it was unlikely that their individual birth records had been connected to the record of their death. Which meant their identity and the freedom of movement it would afford me was just floating in the bureaucratic ether, there for my taking.

Of course, it would be a daunting search, but I now had the focus and bandwidth to plow through thousands of obituaries in a single evening, my concentration never wavering, not even for a second, as I listened to audiobooks at twice the speed and committed to memory every single word.

When I found this person, I would dig deeper to uncover their date of birth, place of birth, parents' names, and mother's maiden name.

Once I had that information, I would find the cheapest office space in Albuquerque, establish it as my residence, and write a letter to the vital records department in my namesake's state, requesting a new birth certificate.

With a birth certificate and a few letters addressed to my Albuquerque office showing proof of residence, I could get a driver's license.

Then I could request a new Social Security number.

And after that a passport.

I'd be on my way.

I reached the beach and headed north, making footprints in the cold, waterlogged sand.

The wind howled.

I was starving.

I thought I might walk into town for dinner. Sit at a bar. Order a drink.

The identity I'd found was for a man named Robbie Foster. He was from Duluth, Minnesota, and had lost his life on a trip of a lifetime, when a riverboat caught fire and sank in the middle of the night on the Amazon River in Peru.

I'd built my new identity from his.

Earned enough money gambling to buy a vehicle.

I was becoming known in the small poker community of Albuquerque, which meant it was time to leave.

The desire to go home to Beth and Ava was still present. But rationally I knew that if I let myself go to them, I wouldn't be ending any pain. I'd only be creating more.

I'd be pulling them into my impossible situation.

I was sure I had earned the secret top spot on the Gene Protection Agency's most wanted list. They didn't know it was my sister who had broken me out of the farm, although if they were smart, they might have suspected as much and tried to track her down. But she was just an unsub. And my accomplice. From their perspective, I had killed numerous agents and security contractors, broken out intent on working with my mother to usher in a genetic upgrade for all humankind.

The mere act of letting my family know I was alive would be putting their lives at hazard.

And still—my weakness almost prevailed.

I only wanted to ease their pain, to let them know I was alive.

It seemed like such a small act.

But my way back to my family, my way home, was not through the front door of our house. Only through finding and stopping Kara, through putting the Ramsay curse to rest, could I ever go home again.

At least that's what I told myself. But a deeper, harder, more painful truth had already begun to whisper itself to me.

Maybe you've already flown too far from home. Maybe there is no way back.

I was on the move.

Nomadic.

I went to parts of the country I had never seen.

The Ozarks.

The White Mountains of New Hampshire.

Seeing America from the road—the out-of-the-way places, the backwaters, the Main Streets—was a profound experience. I understood our collective suffering now in a new light. The empty storefronts and barren shelves. The hard and hopeless stares from front porches I drove past.

There was a stark unevenness to the quality of life.

You could stand in downtown D.C. and think you were living in the bright and shining future. Then drive to the Gulf Coast of Mississippi, which had been hit by two cat 7 hurricanes in the last decade and left with no economy to speak of, and wonder how people found the will to go on.

In too many places, there was just grim survival.

And beneath it: rage.

I could've stayed in one place, but my curiosity pulled me on down the road.

I spent a month on a lake in Wisconsin, where the light of my lonely summer evenings stretched past ten o'clock, the water like glass until a fish leaped and the sun lingering, lingering—a guest who wouldn't leave.

One afternoon in mid-October, driving through the Smoky Mountains, I saw a sign for an overlook where I'd stopped with my family three years ago on a long weekend.

Pulling into the parking area, I turned off the motor.

The view looked out across a pyrotechnic forest that blanketed the oldest mountains in the world.

I hopped over the stone wall, descended a steep meadow.

Moving into the forest, I soon detected the noise of running water.

It was a small stream, the air cooler, sweeter-smelling near the bank. Three years ago—1,115 days to be exact—I'd sat in this precise spot. I remembered perfectly the experience of watching the stream flowing through this primeval forest. I'd found it sublime. I'd been deeply moved by the tranquility of this place, swelling with joy as I listened to Ava and Beth talking on the other side.

But, in truth, I hadn't really seen any of it. This place had only been a mirror—reflecting my own fragile, emotional state back at me.

I was no longer that man.

The things that had moved him no longer moved me.

Today, I saw the literal components that created this scene.

The metamorphosed sandstone boulders in the current. The stream velocity. The erosion pattern on the far side of the bank, which showed evidence of a summer flood. The four brook trout standing in the current—two of them afflicted with whirling disease. The way the light refracted off the water at innumerable angles, and the equations behind the shadows they created, and every falling, vivid, dying leaf, pushed by a delicate breeze, which evaporatively cooled the back of my neck, and the strong smell of the essential oils in the thickets of rhododendron and mountain laurel and the autumn-death scent of sugars and organic compounds breaking down in a billion leaves, and beneath it all the fainter, insidious decay—which I could only smell when the wind shifted slightly from the north—identifying the remains of a deer or rodent a quarter mile away.

I spent an hour just observing.

I could've spent a year studying how all the constituent pieces of this insignificant tract of land pieced together.

And I felt a twinge of loss for that Logan, for the man I had been 1,115 days ago, who had simply enjoyed an idyllic place.

I turned to online poker. It was harder without the benefit of reading faces, but I found the purity of the math relaxing. I made sure to lose enough to keep the algorithms from banning me, but a few big pots per week was enough to live on, all payable in crypto. Money held no interest for me beyond the freedom it provided.

I hired private investigators in every state to find my sister.

I put myself in her shoes and tried to imagine the things she would need in order to complete our mother's work.

I thought back to my conversations with Edwin.

The same things I'd told him my mother would require to distribute her upgrade Kara would also need: a BLS-4 lab, crew of two to five, although considering her lack of experience, possibly more. People fluent in molecular biology. Virology. Computational genetics. Security.

Her people would have to know what they were creating.

They would have to be willing to risk incarceration. How would *I* find those people?

It'd be tough, and I came from that world.

If I still worked for the GPA and had access to its resources, I'd plug into MYSTIC—try to find Kara using the CCTV facial-recognition database.

I kept returning to the exascale or quantum-annealing processor she would need.

The rest of the lab equipment she could buy on the black market, and those transactions would be nearly untraceable. But the processors weren't something she'd have to buy on the sly. There was nothing illegal about it. They were just very expensive and not terribly commonplace. But she'd know I'd be on the lookout. She'd try to cover her tracks.

Only eight companies in the world built the type of hardware she would need: Atom Computing, Xanadu, IBM, Cold-Quanta, Zapata Computing, Azure Quantum, and Strangeworks.

I hired corporate PIs to find client lists and purchase orders, knowing, of course, that there was another possibility.

Our mother might've already had a lab set up with everything we would need to bring her upgrade to fruition. Its location may have been tucked away in the hardcase she left for us in that New Mexico wilderness, including contacts for the crew.

If that was the case, then Kara was already well on her way to finishing our mother's work and beginning the next phase.

Now that I had the brain I always wanted, I decided to fact-check my mother's claim: *The end of* Homo sapiens *lies just over the horizon. We can see it in a thousand metrics.* Of course I believed it. But I wanted to truly know it—to understand those metrics for myself.

There were several lifetimes' worth of data to catch up on,

and no point, with my sensory gating downregulated, to ever read just one book at a time again.

I could read a book with my eyes while simultaneously listening to an audiobook, and comprehend each one to a seventy percent degree of accuracy.

I read everything. I read constantly. I read fast. I barely slept.

Thousands of scientific journals, and the studies behind the articles, and the data behind the studies.

I looked at anthropogenic global catastrophic risks—those caused by human behavior—as opposed to natural risks, such as supervolcanoes, asteroids, and other cosmic threats: nuclear terrorism. Bioterrorism. Natural and engineered pandemics. Nanotechnology accidents. Superintelligent AI. Famine. Fires. Floods. Sea-level rise. Ocean and global warming. Extreme weather. Crop failure. Agricultural collapse. Deforestation. Desertification. Massive water pollution and scarcity. Mineral resource exhaustion. Power-grid failure. All manner of warfare (cyber, nuclear, civil, genetic, orbital).

Except for a runaway superintelligence or nanotech outbreak, it would be a combination of threats, all working in concert, to degrade human civilization to the point of extreme endangerment.

My mother's famine had wiped out just two percent of the global population, but twenty years on, we were still struggling to feed people. The downstream effects had killed millions more and left even the upper tiers of civilization in a shambles.

And the threats themselves couldn't be evaluated in a vacuum. Cognitive biases had to be factored into the labyrinthine equation: scope insensitivity—the notion that humans are bad at distinguishing between two hundred dead and two million. Hyperbolic discounting—the tendency to value lower, short-term rewards over greater, long-term rewards, or to make choices today that our future self would prefer *not* to have made.

There was the affect heuristic, where current emotions influence critical decision-making. The overconfidence affect where a person's confidence in his or her judgments are much greater than the objective accuracy of said judgments. And that was just the start.

The more information I consumed, the more I began to truly grasp what my mother saw when she considered the state of humanity.

We were a bunch of primates who had gotten together and, against all odds, built a wondrous civilization. But paradoxically—tragically—our creation's complexity had now far outstripped our brains' ability to manage it.

Put simply: Our situation was fucked, and we weren't doing enough to un-fuck it.

For all her arrogance, ambition, and reckless pride, my mother wasn't wrong about where we were heading.

But she was also fallible. Shenzhen had proved that.

Which meant that however bad the problem, unleashing her latest creation on the world couldn't be the solution.

I walked a mile up the beach, then followed a sandy trail into Trinidad, California.

Weather had rolled back in, tatters of mist streaming in off the water.

It was raining, and the lights of town twinkled in the blue dusk—a comforting invitation.

I walked the quiet streets as darkness fell, finally settling on a salt-weathered tavern that sat on a high bluff overlooking the sea. Smoke trickled from a brick chimney. It smelled like real fish cooking.

Inside was crowded and warm. Families sat at tables in the

vicinity of a stone hearth, playing games from a collection that filled an entire bookshelf.

I took the only free stool at the bar.

The blackboard menu showed two options—fish and chips and lemon butter cod.

The bartender came over. His gnarled face and graying hair made him look as much a part of the environment as the wave-battered sea stacks.

I asked if the fish was real.

"Caught just offshore this morning."

"I'll do the fish and chips."

Three televisions hung above the bar.

Two showed football games—it was playoff season—and one the news.

While I waited for my food, I pulled out a small, leather-bound journal I always carried with me, flipped to the next blank page, and started a new letter.

Ava—I'm sitting in a tavern in Northern California, waiting on the first real fish I've had in months. Remember the pub we went to in Fort William, on the shore of Loch Linnhe, Scotland? The one where the guy came up and asked you something and you couldn't understand a single word he said? Reminds me of that place.

There's a father and daughter playing checkers by the fireplace behind me. I saw them when I walked in and felt an emotional flicker of what I believe was loneliness. For a minute, I allowed this loneliness to breathe. I allowed myself to feel envious of this man and his daughter. I allowed myself to miss our chess games. Our talks on the ride into school. I allowed myself to miss knowing everything about your life.

And then, as easy as flipping a light switch, I turned that emotion off.

I reverted to my heart of stone.

By avoiding my feelings, am I driving myself further and further away from you? I tell myself I have no choice—that if I didn't shut this door, I'd find myself reaching out to you and your mother, putting you in danger. And maybe that's true. But it's not the whole truth. Escaping the gravity of human emotion—living without all that anger, heartbreak, sorrow—it's so much easier. Quieter.

"Sir? Sorry to interrupt. Could you pass me the ketchup?"

I looked up from my journal to the woman sitting on the stool beside me. She was in her sixties, with kind, open eyes.

I grabbed the bottle, handed it to her.

"Doing a little journaling?" she asked, glancing at my notebook.

"Writing a letter to my daughter," I said, trying to speak at a normal pace. It had been nine days since I'd last interacted with another human being.

The craggy-faced bartender appeared with my plate—a glorious spread of fish and chips—and a second pint of delicious amber ale from a local brewery.

I closed my notebook and slipped it into my backpack.

"How old?" she asked.

"Fifteen."

"Oh, you're in the thick of it."

The walk from my rental house in the cold had given me a ravenous appetite. Since receiving my mother's genetic upgrade, I was always hungry. I suspected it had something to do with the heightened neural activity.

I dove into my meal, which was extraordinary for its rarity. No amount of preparation could overcome the inherent rubberiness and uncanny valley weirdness of synthetic fish.

But this cod, perfectly prepared and freshly caught in an ocean I could see from where I sat, just flaked apart and melted.

"My kids are grown," she said, pushing the conversation forward.

"How many?"

"Two. Mark's in Chicago. Amy lives in the Bay Area." She told me about them while I ate. What they did for a living. What her grandkids were like. "It goes by so fast," she said. "What's your name?"

"Robbie," I said.

"I'm Miranda. You from around here, Robbie?" She wasn't nefariously fishing for information. She hadn't interacted with anyone in a while, either. I could detect the rasp of disuse in her voice.

"Just passing through."

"Same. That's my Winnebago in the parking lot. Bought it after Francis passed."

I'd seen it on my way in, and roadworthy was not the word that had sprung to mind.

"Your husband?"

She nodded.

I took a sip of the ale.

"I'm so sorry," I said.

I had been intentionally avoiding looking too closely at Miranda's face as she spoke. The reading of microexpressions and intent, especially in a place like this when I just wanted to feel normal for a moment, could be all-encompassing.

Now I looked at her face. Saw a façade of manners and bravery shielding still-raw grief that couldn't bring itself to scab over.

"I lost the house after he died."

"You live in the Winne?"

"Sure do. It's not as bad as I thought it might be. I'm trying to find a caravan to hook up with. Some of them share resources. Francis and I had always talked about buying an RV after we retired. Seeing all the places in the country we'd only ever seen on TV. Never thought I'd be doing it alone. And out of necessity. Life is endlessly surprising, isn't it?"

I wondered how she'd lost her home but didn't ask. Probably the same quiet tragedy that drove so many retirees out of their lifelong homes—Social Security benefits had been left in the dust by inflation.

I clinked my pint glass against her wineglass. "Well said."

"Your family isn't traveling with you?" she asked.

"No, unfortunately. They're back home."

"Where's home?"

This was a tricky answer to provide for someone living on the road, seeing as much of the country as they could. I detected East Coast in her accent—Connecticut or Rhode Island—so I picked a remote location in the West.

"Southern Arizona."

I could see in her eyes she'd never been there. I could also see that she wanted to pry a bit more into my family life. Why was I traveling without them? Again, not out of some malicious suspicion. More curiosity and loneliness.

She glanced up at one of the television screens, and I saw her eyes widen. I followed her gaze. Because the television was muted, all I could see was what appeared to be camera footage from a drone hovering several hundred feet over a highway.

Soldiers were setting up bright yellow barriers across the road.

I read the headline on the bottom of the screen:

GLASGOW, MONTANA, PLACED UNDER MILITARY-ENFORCED
QUARANTINE AFTER 95 DIE OF MYSTERIOUS ILLNESS

"Have you been following this?" Miranda asked.

"No, what's going on?"

"Apparently some sort of virus."

I stared at the television screen, but the closed-captioning wasn't enabled. All I could see was that hovering drone. The screen switched to a view of soldiers in hazmat suits and respirators walking down the middle of what could have been Main Street, Anywhere.

Aside from my general curiosity in a breaking news story, there was something else about the headline that bothered me.

I could feel my subconscious tunneling for the connection, but Miranda was already talking again, asking where I was off to next.

I tried to stay polite and engaged for the rest of the meal, stowing my curiosity into a distant corner of my mind to return to later.

When Miranda left to use the restroom, I paid for my meal and hers and was sliding off my stool as she walked back toward the bar.

"You're leaving?" There was a tinge of sadness in her voice.

"Long drive tomorrow," I said. "Which means an early start."

And then she embraced me, the tension of untouched need and isolation like vibrations in her bones. If I'd chosen to allow it, I could've been leveled by my empathy for her.

"I really enjoyed meeting you, Robbie."

I wished her safe travels.

Then I walked out into the cold, spitting rain.

Even though I was in a town, my phone had no cellular service.

It was too dark and wet to risk the climb from the beach up the bluff to my rental house, so I ran south on the road out of town.

Faster and faster.

One of the few unapologetic joys of my transformation was my improved physicality. My body hummed like a perfect machine. I wasn't just as good as I'd been at twenty. I was exponentially better. My bum ankle that had never fully healed after a nasty sprain in my thirties didn't bother me anymore. Neither did the arthritis in my left knee. I could have six drinks, sleep a few hours, and wake as fresh as a daisy. And I never got sick. I'd been a runner in my younger years until the aches and pains of my middle-aged body finally relegated me to the ellipticals and rowing machines of air-conditioned gyms. But now, I had no problems. I ran marathon distances just for the hell of it. I raced up mountains. Swam alpine lakes. My energy was bottomless. I felt invincible.

As I glimpsed the lights of my seaside cottage, I realized what it was about that headline that was buzzing around in my brain like a fly. On my flight home from China to America, when I left my mother's lab for good twenty years ago, I'd read an article in an in-flight magazine featuring Glasgow, Montana, as the most remote city in America. The parameters were specific. What is the place with a population of more than a thousand, which is farthest from a metro with a population of at least seventy-five thousand? The closest metro to Glasgow was four and a half hours away.

How could the most remote city in America be ground zero for the outbreak of a new virus?

I was drenched by the time I walked in the door of the cottage.

I hung up my rain jacket and stripped out of my wet clothes. The woodstove held nothing but glowing cinders. I opened the glass door, tossed a few logs inside.

Then I turned on the television and stopped at the first news channel I came to.

It was the top of the hour, and the anchor was saying—

". . . *monitoring a developing situation in northeast Montana, where ninety-five people have died in the last week from an unknown illness. The CDC arrived two days ago, and the National Guard has been called in to enforce a shelter-in-place quarantine order from the governor of Montana. Martial law is in effect, all roads in and out of*

Glasgow have been closed, and as of three hours ago, Wi-Fi coverage within the Glasgow city limits has been blocked."

Onscreen, the footage changed to show a team of doctors in positive pressure suits carrying someone out of a house in a body bag.

"The CDC is expected to hold a press conference any moment now, and we'll be joining that as soon as it happens. Meanwhile, we're joined by Dr.—"

I flipped to the next news channel.

An epidemiologist was speculating that this could be a particularly virulent strain of the flu, but it was obvious that he was vamping to fill time and had no real information.

The next news channel I turned to was just recapping what I'd already heard.

I left the TV on and went to my laptop on the kitchen table, ran a quick news search on Glasgow. I read thirty articles from legit news outlets, but there was nothing new.

Social media was a cesspool of conspiracy theories and memes, but I kept seeing one video getting shared.

I muted the television and pressed play.

It was a minute and twenty-one seconds, heavily pixelated, and filmed on a mobile phone.

It started with a teenage girl leaning in close to the camera, which she held. There was a noise in the background that sounded like hysterical laughter. I couldn't be sure because of the poor quality, but it looked as if she had tears in her eyes.

"I don't know what's going on here."

She stood and walked through a blurred-out space.

The laughter growing louder.

She was moving toward it.

When she finally stopped, I saw that she was standing in the dim living room of a double-wide trailer.

She switched her phone's camera. It showed a rail-thin man

sitting in a recliner. He was trembling violently, and every few seconds, he let out an explosion of laughter that could only be described as pathological.

"Dad, what's wrong?"

He didn't answer her. Didn't even look at her.

"What's happening to you, Dad?"

He tried to stand, but his balance was ruined.

He toppled over, sprawled across the floor.

The camera view became blurry as the girl was on the move again, rushing down a narrow hall. The next room she entered was a bedroom.

A woman sat in a half-open bathrobe on the end of a bed. She was shaking as well, although not quite as severely.

"Mom, let me take you to the hospital."

"Thehospitalisfull."

"I'll drive you both to Billings."

"GETOUT!!! GETOUT!!!"

Her mother charged her.

There was a cut, and then the girl was back in her room, crying now.

"It's like this everywhere. Our town is falling apart. I think I'm getting sick too. The past three nights, my whole body aches. Nine-one-one doesn't work. I drove to the hospital, but there's a line out the door. We need help. I don't know what to—"

That hideous laughter started again, right behind her.

She turned her head toward a silhouette standing in the doorway to her room.

The video ended.

I sat in the silence of the cottage, the rain streaking down the windows.

My pulse was rising: 109. 110. 115.

The video had been shared forty thousand times.

I scrolled through the comments.

Holy shit! Is this how the zombie apocalypse begins?

Anyone else thinking this guy should play the next Joker?

Bitch, they 'bout to eat you. Run!

PUT THEM IN A CAR AND DRIVE THEM TO A HOSPITAL IMMEDIATELY.

There was no real information to be gleaned. I couldn't even confirm if the video was real.

Glancing back at the television, I saw that the press conference had started.

I moved back into the living room, sat close to the woodstove, and turned up the volume.

Command Sergeant Major Jackson Tolmach was speaking into a cluster of microphones as a Boeing C-17 military transport taxied down a runway in the background. Standing behind him was my old boss, Edwin Rogers.

"... *anti-ram vehicle barriers at the intersection of Highway 2 and Highway 24 on the southeast side of town, Highway 2 on the northwest side of town, Highway 246, Aitken Road, and Highway 42. All schools, businesses, and government facilities are closed. The Glasgow airport and train station are closed. All trains on the Northern Transcon will be detoured around the city. There will be no hyperloop regional service to Glasgow. A stay-at-home order remains in effect with no essential activity exemptions. A shipment of MREs just arrived from the Montana Air National Guard, which will be distributed to all impacted residents of Glasgow. If you need immediate medical attention, field hospitals are being set up at the intersection of First Avenue North and Fifth Street North. At this time, I'm going to turn things over to Dr. Manpearl.*"

The National Guard commander stepped away, and a suited man with driftwood-colored hair and a five-o'clock shadow approached the microphones.

The army guy was an army guy, exuding can-do coolness.

Even through the pixels I could see that Manpearl was terrified.

"*Good evening. I'm David Manpearl, communications director with the CDC. Five days ago, we received the first reports from Frances Mahon Deaconess Hospital regarding an illness of unknown origin. There were five cases, and the patients had all come into the hospital within several hours of one another.*

"*Symptoms included sudden personality changes, memory loss, impaired cognitive abilities, insomnia, incoordination, body tremors, and vocal outbursts. The patients had first noticed symptoms three weeks prior, and had all experienced a steady mental decline. The next day, eleven people came to the hospital with similar symptoms. The third day, that number grew to thirty. The local hospital has only twenty-five beds, so this became a medical crisis in short order.*"

He glanced down at his notes, then looked back into the camera.

"*At present, we have 218 active cases. The hospital has been transformed into a triage facility and we're adding more beds and field hospitals in coordination with the National Guard and FEMA. We're flying in doctors and nurses from all over the country. As of ten minutes ago, 104 people have died.*"

A reporter called out:

"*What's the mortality rate?*"

"*Well, so far it's one hundred percent.*"

Another reporter asked:

"*What's the cause of death?*"

"*Patients eventually fall into a coma and then experience variations of organ failure, but aspiration pneumonia is the leading cause of death.*"

Someone else asked:

"*Have you found patient zero or determined what type of disease you're dealing with?*"

"The short answer is no, but we're performing a number of autopsies."

I turned off the television and sat in the silence of the cottage, listening to the rain tick at the windows and the perpetual thunder of crashing waves on the beach below.

In my mind, I replayed every frame of the video I'd watched, and one part in particular: "I think I'm getting sick too. The past three nights, my whole body aches."

I could feel a theory fighting to emerge out of the fog of possibilities. And I could feel myself subconsciously resisting it. Not because it didn't have merit.

Because, if it were true, it meant that something awful had happened. Something worse even than all those people dying.

I walked into the small bedroom, pulled my suitcase out of the closet and my clothes from the drawers, and began to quickly pack my things.

It was late and the weather was bad, but I couldn't waste another second.

I would leave for Montana tonight.

8

TWO DAYS LATER, I was speeding across Montana under the biggest sky I'd ever seen, a hundred miles west of Glasgow.

It was a landscape of gentle desolation. Out on the plain, I would glimpse the occasional barn or schoolhouse weathering away in a sea of great wide nothing.

Semi–ghost towns whose only infrastructure were a post office and a grain mill.

The ubiquitous wind farms, with their spinning white blades, were the only evidence that I was driving through a mid-twenty-first-century West.

Otherwise, the landscape seemed to exist out of time entirely.

And the distances weren't just vast. They felt galactic.

I was driving my Mercedes Sprinter 4x4 EV, which I'd modified into a makeshift sleeper and basic molecular biology lab. There'd been times when I couldn't find a rental, when the walls of this van constituted my home. I'd fold out the built-in bed, kill the motors, and fall asleep to coyote howls in the Sonoran Desert, or the rocking of ferocious winds as a Colorado blizzard erased the world outside.

Fifty miles west of Glasgow, I turned on the radio and surfed until I found a local NPR station.

"... *testing cattle at surrounding ranches and meat from grocery stores in Glasgow. Thus far, there is no indication that meat contaminated with bovine spongiform encephalopathy, also known as mad cow disease, is responsible for the 177 deaths in Glasgow since last week.*"

I passed two digital traffic signs positioned a few hundred yards apart:

HIGHWAY 2 EAST OF HINSDALE CLOSED TO ALL EASTBOUND

TRAFFIC

And then:

DETOUR NORTH TO HIGHWAY 5, OR SOUTH TO HIGHWAY 200

I stayed on my eastward heading.

Hinsdale, Montana, population 242, was a blink-and-you-missed-it affair, which stood in the shadow of a one-thousand-meter wind turbine.

As I rolled through the main drag, I saw flashing lights in the distance.

A half mile east of town, a trio of Montana Highway Patrol EVs were parked across the shoulders and both lanes.

As I approached the blockade, a patrolman in khaki slacks, an army green button-down, and a flat-brimmed hat stepped out of his car.

I brought my Sprinter to a stop twenty feet from the cruisers.

During the last year of my nomadic life, miraculously, I had never been pulled over by the police. I felt confident that the self-augmentation I had performed on my face would hold up to scrutiny. And though my identification had never been examined by law enforcement, it had served me well countless other times.

I leveled out my heart rate at 70 bpm.

The lawman made a circle with his finger, telling me to lower the window.

I complied.

He wore aviator sunglasses that reflected an image of me behind the steering wheel. I wondered if they were optical display frames that could transmit relevant information about me and my vehicle onto the inside of the lenses, or simply the old-fashioned kind.

I noticed razor burns on his face and neck from the morning's shave.

"Do me a favor, shut off your motor."

I turned off the Sprinter.

I didn't like that I couldn't see his eyes. Reading eye movement was far and away the most effective method of decoding a person's emotional state and intent.

"Where you coming from?" he asked.

My Sprinter had New Mexico plates.

I said, "New Mexico."

"Okay. Did you see the signs twenty miles back?"

"Sure did."

"So you know everything around Glasgow is closed due to the outbreak."

"I'm a cell biologist with Los Alamos National Laboratory. Glasgow is my destination."

He removed his glasses, stared at me through pale blue eyes.

"What's your name?"

"Robbie Foster," I said.

"License and registration."

I had them ready.

He took them, walked back to his car without a word.

The wind was whipping off the prairie.

The Sprinter shuddered.

After five minutes, he stepped back out of his car and walked over.

"Welcome to Montana, Mr. Foster. You work for the CDC?"

"More of an independent contractor."

"Well, we're glad to have you."

His name tag said D. TRAUTMANN. D as in David.

He was one of 237 state troopers in Montana, and part of District V, based in the town of Glendive. District V covered sixteen counties, including Valley, the one I was currently in. David was twenty-four years old and had graduated from the academy one year ago.

Very green.

He reported to Sergeant Betsy Lane, who reported to Captain Sam Houghton, who reported to Major Tommy Meadows, who reported to Colonel Jenna Swicegood. I'd spent two hours this morning getting up to speed on the Montana Highway Patrol chain of command and how it was currently interacting with the CDC and Montana National Guard vis-à-vis Glasgow.

The MHP had been tasked with establishing the outermost ring of checkpoints twenty-five miles from the epicenter.

Two hours ago, I'd called Col. Swicegood on a spoofed Atlanta phone number, impersonating Ron Auerbach, CDC director of intergovernmental and strategic affairs. I'd given her a list of three scientists who were inbound to Glasgow on Highway 2, including license plate numbers, vehicle descriptions, and Hinsdale checkpoint ETAs.

"What's in the back of the van?" the trooper asked. He wasn't being nosy or suspicious. I detected genuine curiosity.

I stepped out of the car. Even from a half mile away, the sound of the wind turbine's enormous white blades was audible as they chopped the air, filling it with a dull, distant thrum.

I opened the sliding door, and the first thing we saw was a white hazmat suit hanging from the ceiling.

There was a -20° C freezer.

A minifuge.

A fluorescence microscope with videocam.

And a space-gray machine the size and shape of a microwave.

"That's an automated, digital microfluid nanopore DNA sequencer," I said. "I suit up, head into the outbreak zone, and collect DNA from infected people. Skin cells, mucus swabs, blood samples. Then I put the samples into that machine, which analyzes DNA to detect what diseases they may have. If we can discover the sequence, or work out what's been changed genetically, then we'll have a shot at figuring out what type of disease we're dealing with."

"I heard it had something to do with bad meat?" he said.

Something in his voice . . . more than just morbid interest.

"We don't know yet. You live around here?"

"Malta."

"You know someone who's sick."

It was a statement, not a question, and it caught him off guard.

"My brother-in-law. He and my sister live in Glasgow."

"I'm sorry to hear that."

"I haven't been able to speak with her in two days."

"What are their names?"

"Tiffany and Chris Jarvis."

"What's their address."

He wrote it down for me on the back of a business card, which I tucked into my pocket.

"I'll try to check in on them. We're going to find out why this is happening."

I could see that my offer had moved him, but all he said was, "I'd appreciate that very much. If you see her . . ."

I watched him try to push his emotions aside.

"I'll tell her."

The highway between Hinsdale and Glasgow was apocalyptically empty. I knew the roadblock I'd just made it through wouldn't be the last or anywhere close to the most secure. But I didn't have any intention of rolling the dice at another security checkpoint. The next one I came to would be manned by military personnel, not highway patrol stationed twenty miles away and largely out of the loop.

Three miles outside of Glasgow, I pulled my van off the road and parked in a stand of the only trees I'd seen all day, hiding my vehicle as best I could. They were cottonwoods, and they grew along the bank of the Milk River, a 729-mile long tributary of the Missouri, which happened to flow within a quarter mile of Glasgow.

My packing list included my hazmat suit, Garmin, binoculars, an H&K VP9 pistol, body armor, a pair of NightShades (next-gen night vision optics that resembled old-school Oakley sunglasses), a laptop, and a case containing syringes and BD Vacutainer EDTA tubes for blood sample collection and storage.

Fully inflated, the raft wasn't much to look at. I'd bought it yesterday for ninety dollars at the sporting goods department in a Spokane Walmart.

I loaded my gear into the raft and waited for darkness.

Helicopters, drones, and aircraft passed overhead frequently, on low-flying approaches into Glasgow. But not a single vehicle went by on the road.

I sat against the trunk of a cottonwood tree, watching the sun slip below the horizon.

With the light gone, cold set in.

I watched the first star appear.

At eight P.M., I dragged the raft down to the river's edge, climbed in, and used one of the oars to push myself out into the current.

The water was bitterly cold.

Chunks of ice floated beside the raft.

The moon was just a glowing sliver. While my inherent night vision was solid, the NightShades made everything visible.

The only sound was the occasional dip of my oar into the frigid black water.

It was a perfect river for floating—it went nowhere slowly. Wide and not so much as a burble of whitewater.

It took its sweet time, not following the road into town, but twisting and turning on a meandering, serpentine course through patches of farmland.

I could see the distant lights of farmhouses glowing like green suns and the expansive, collective glow of the lights of Glasgow.

I was hours on the water.

Each time the raft swung around a bend in the river, the lights of town glowed a little brighter, a little closer.

I kept a vigilant lookout, carefully watching every foot of shoreline. While I was doubtful there'd be a security checkpoint at the river, you never knew. My guess was that, while the National Guard and the CDC didn't want people coming into town, their main focus would be on keeping the townsfolk from leaving.

At 10:45 P.M., my Garmin chimed.

I'd spent much of last night studying the Google Earth satellite images of Glasgow and the surrounding terrain, and before setting out on the water, I'd dropped a GPS pin at what I had chosen for my take-out point.

I paddled to shore, hopped out of the raft, dragged it onto dry ground.

The edge of town was just under a thousand meters east of my position, on the far side of an open field.

I took out the binoculars and glassed the city.

From my vantage in the shadows, I could see a military checkpoint at Highway 246, approximately a hundred yards west of town. There were Jersey barriers and barbed wire strung across the road, and a half-dozen soldiers in biosecurity suits were milling around a couple of Humvees.

In one of the vehicle's turrets, I saw a soldier in NightShades making slow, steady scans of the adjacent fields, including the one I would need to cross to reach the city. If I took a longer route across the field and kept low to the ground, I felt reasonably sure I could stay hidden behind the slope.

I stowed the raft in the trees, shouldered my pack, and began the long, slow crawl toward Glasgow.

It was midnight when I reached the edge of town.

I sloughed off the pack and pulled out my hazmat suit, less worried about contracting something and more interested in the cover it would hopefully afford me. How many red flags would a guy in a hazmat suit raise walking through an outbreak area?

I donned my magnetic body armor and spent several awkward minutes forcing my way into a Tyvek suit in the dark. Then I pulled on my respirator, tucked my H&K into a makeshift holster I'd rigged on the hip of the suit, and shouldered my pack.

I moved carefully through a stand of trees that separated the field I'd crawled through from Glasgow proper. The nearest building was a body shop at the edge of town surrounded by shells of vehicles rusting in the weeds.

I knelt down and took a moment to observe.

Modest houses glowed in the distance.

According to Montana National Guard protocol, curfew enforcement patrol would put one soldier on each city block from dusk to dawn. There would also be the occasional Humvee or Bradley fighting vehicle on driving patrols.

A national guardsman in a tactical face mask walked into view, heading away from me down the middle of an otherwise empty street, machine gun at the ready. After fourteen seconds, another soldier moved down the closest cross street on a perpendicular trajectory, and five seconds after that—and two blocks up—a third soldier appeared, walked briefly in my direction, then turned right.

I clocked their respective velocities, which varied by degrees of .2, .1, and .35 mph, then ran a quick mental equation, vectoring myself into their midst and solving for my window of invisibility.

When the time was right, I left the shelter of the trees, moving at a brisk clip down a sidewalk and not loving the restricted view of my face shield and the general dampening of sensory input by my hazmat suit.

I heard:

A dog barking.

A man sobbing as he begged for someone named Jane to please wake up.

A voice magnified through a megaphone five or six blocks away, shouting instructions to a crowd.

What sounded like gunshots on the far side of town.

And from more than one house that maniacal laughter I'd heard in that viral video.

Cloth—dishrags, towels, torn T-shirts—hung from nearly every door I passed. There were three colors: green, red, and black.

According to KLTZ, the AM radio station serving Glasgow, the CDC and National Guard had ordered every household to keep a visual marker hanging from their front door that identified the condition of the people inside.

Green = no illness.

Red = someone inside showing symptoms.

Black = someone dead inside.

As I walked up Ninth Street S., it was a devastating thing to see—every ninth or tenth house had a piece of black cloth hanging from its doorknob.

When I glimpsed new soldiers on patrol, I added the additional variable into my equation.

The first few houses I approached were no-go—either dogs barking or lights on inside or locked. I didn't need to be triggering an alarm. I needed a dark house, with no dog, and an unlocked door.

To the north, I glimpsed the epicenter of activity.

White tents gleaming under spotlights.

Lines of people waiting for treatment.

Drones hovering above it all.

I stopped for a moment, trying to take it all in.

You could almost feel the fear in the air—a living thing. These poor people. They must have been scared out of their minds, wondering what psychotic twist of fate had brought this disease into their midst. And, unlike me, they had no way to put their fear aside.

I needed to find a house.

Get my sample.

Get back to the van.

Right on time, in the reflection of a car windshield across the street, I caught movement—a soldier in night camo coming around the block.

Even from a distance of forty yards, I could see they were on a trajectory that would bring me into their field of vision in just under two seconds.

I lunged in front of a car, flattening myself across the curb.

Waited until they passed.

On the next block, I saw a familiar address. I walked up onto the covered porch. The black cloth nailed to the door was the remnants of a Beyoncé T-shirt, from her farewell tour.

I knocked.

The porch light glowed above me, but there were no lights on inside. I reached up into the fixture and unscrewed the bulb.

Then pressed my ear to the door.

No incoming footsteps.

No voices.

I reached down, tried the doorknob.

It wasn't locked, and I kept turning it, finally easing the door open.

The house was dark.

Silent.

I stepped inside, closed the door behind me.

The death stench hit me even through my respirator.

I walked into a small living room.

From an arched pass-through, I entered a kitchen.

Flipped a switch on the wall.

Track lights shined down on countertops covered in towers of putrid-smelling dishes.

I called out, "Hello?"

The emptiness swallowed my voice and gave back no answer.

I climbed the carpeted stairs toward the second floor, arriving at a landing that accessed several doors.

All closed.

I opened the middle one—a bathroom with doors on either side, presumably linking the adjacent bedrooms.

The door on the right led into a home office.

I turned on an overhead light.

There was a scrapbooking table covered in photographs and various cutting instruments.

On the wall over the table hung a framed portrait of a multi-generational family standing in front of a huge Christmas tree in unquestionably better times.

I moved back through the bathroom and opened the door to the second upstairs bedroom.

My eyes began to water.

I heard—muffled by my hood—the softest rasp.

I dropped everything, pulled my pistol, and nearly shot a woman in a silk nightgown sitting in the farthest, darkest corner of the room.

She just watched me, sitting motionless with her arms wrapped around her knees, her hair hanging in her face.

"What are you doing in my house?" Her monotone suggested she was in shock, and there was a clenched quality to her voice.

"I saw the black shirt on your door," I said. "I knocked, but no one answered."

The woman hadn't moved. She was nearly invisible in the dark.

I lowered my gun, took a few steps toward her.

"Is there anything I can do for you?" I asked.

I thought I saw her head shake.

I went to the wall, flipped the light switch.

A lamp on a bedside table glowed to life, illuminating a bloated man keeled over on a queen-size bed. His eyes were open. Skin a pale, waxy sheen. He was in the range of forty to forty-five, wore a T-shirt and pajama bottoms, and there were several dozen framed photographs placed all around him like a makeshift memorial.

The photos were of the dead man and the woman sitting in the corner.

At the London Eye.

Chichen Itza in Yucatán.

The base of Seattle's Space Needle.

At a concert.

On snowmobiles.

"When did he pass?" I asked.

"Three days ago. I tried to call his mother, but you people turned off our Wi-Fi. Blocked all cell reception except nine-one-one."

"He was acting strange before he died?"

"Yes."

"Just sitting in bed? Shaking?"

She nodded.

"Compulsive laughter?"

"It got worse and worse. He wouldn't eat or drink. Wouldn't take himself to the bathroom. Refused to go with me to the hospital. By the time I finally called for help, it was mayhem in town."

"No one ever came to help you?"

She shook her head. "Toward the end, he didn't even recognize me." Tears rolled down her face. "I lost my father to dementia five years ago. This was like experiencing the entire course of that disease in ten days. The last time I tried to make him drink water, he hit me. Broke my jaw." Leaning forward, I saw the left side of her face. It was darkened, swollen. "He finally became unresponsive. Just stared for hours on end into nothing. After he slipped into some kind of coma, I lay down with him in our bed, my hand on his chest, just feeling it rise and fall. I fell asleep, and when I woke up, his chest wasn't moving anymore."

"Would you mind if I swabbed the inside of his mouth?"

"Why?"

"His genetic material will help us to understand the disease that killed him."

"He's dead. Isn't it ruined?"

"There's a chance. Hopefully not."

"I guess it doesn't matter now."

I set my pack on the bench at the end of the bed. Fished out a sample collection kit: a plastic vial and a six-inch, cotton-tipped swab.

The dead man's mouth was closed, and I was hoping rigor mortis had already come and gone. Otherwise, I'd have to cut a piece of skin from a finger.

Thankfully, his mouth opened with minimal effort. I slipped the swab between his teeth and scraped the inside of his cheek, then stowed the swab inside the plastic tube.

"Am I going to die too?" the woman asked.

Her voice so soft.

Brimming with fear.

I walked over to her.

"Are you having similar symptoms as your husband?"

She shook her head. "But I don't feel right."

"In what way?"

"Every night, I have the worst body aches. It feels like my bones are splintering apart inside of me."

"What else?" I asked.

Tears glistened in her eyes again.

"My memories have changed."

"How?"

"It's like . . . all these moments with Chris keep washing over me. I see them with perfect clarity now. Clearer than I've ever seen them. Clearer than I've ever remembered anything.

"We met thirteen years ago at this bar in Bozeman. I could tell you every word we spoke. Every feeling I had. I can't draw, but if I could, I could show you what Chris looked like that night, right down to the stubble on his chin. The way one tuft of his hair stood up. I could tell you how he smelled. How it felt like home. How I knew that night I would spend the rest of my life with him."

She looked up at me with pleading eyes.

"I never thought it would end like this."

I wanted to help her, to ease her pain.

But I was buzzing with a mix of excitement and horror.

Excitement at the discovery of this woman who showed the same, early upgrade symptoms—though with a faster onset—that I'd experienced after the ice bombs detonated in that Denver basement.

Horror at what it meant.

The teenager in the viral video had mentioned experiencing body aches, and while that had fueled my suspicion and pushed me to come here, this was the confirmation I'd been seeking. Or at least as close to it as I could hope to get before I ran their DNA through my sequencer.

I knelt down in front of her.

I said, "Would you mind if I took a swab of your mouth?"

"Why?"

"I'm just trying to understand what's happening."

She nodded.

I grabbed another cotton-tipped swab and swiped some mucus from the inside of her right cheek.

"What will you do with it?" she asked.

I went over to the bed and took a black Sharpie from my sample kit, marked the plastic tube containing her sample with "her/no illness."

"I'll analyze your DNA alongside your husband's. Try to understand why he got sick and you got better."

"Better?" she asked. "This doesn't feel better."

"Fair enough. But you will live." I shouldered the pack, said, "Please consider walking up to tent city and getting help for your jaw."

I opened the door, stepped out into the hall, glanced back into the room.

"I met your brother at a checkpoint in Hinsdale today. David. He's worried about you. He wanted to talk to you, but they won't even let highway patrol into the city. He wanted me to tell you he loves you."

She was crying now.

"I'm very sorry for your loss, Tiffany."

I closed the door and headed down the stairs, already mapping my route out of town, back to the van.

As I reached the foyer, something slammed into me with the force of a truck.

I cratered into the wall.

My gun hit the floor.

An elbow caught me on the jaw—stars and blackness.

I didn't even know what I was fighting, didn't know how I'd been caught so completely off—

Because this person had been upgraded like me.

Another blow plowed into my stomach. I doubled over, gasping.

Suddenly I was seven feet off the floor, lifted as if I weighed nothing.

And thrown—sailing through the air for .85 seconds.

Crashed to the hardwood floor at the edge of the kitchen.

I could hear myself groaning. I was able to shove most of the pain aside, and raising my head, I saw a man at the foot of the stairs lifting my H&K off the floor.

He wasn't wearing a respirator, which could mean he knew this wasn't a contagion in the traditional sense.

I heard footsteps on the second floor.

He heard them too, glanced up the stairs, raised my pistol, waited, then fired.

Tiffany tumbled down the stairs and came to rest at his feet. He released my gun's magazine, ejected the round in the chamber, and fieldstripped it as he walked barefoot toward me, the pieces of my pistol clattering to the floor.

The man was approximately thirty-five years old. Clean-shaven. Square-jawed. Shoulder-length hair. Wearing jeans and a tight polo that barely contained his bulging arms. He was a few inches shorter than me, wide through the chest and shoulders, narrow at the waist, with the intimidating build of a wrestler.

He was upgraded for sure, but he hadn't mastered control of his microexpressions yet. He might as well have been screaming at me how much he loved violence and inflicting pain—the worst kind of person to encounter with an upgrade.

He carried no weapon that I could see.

I stayed down, letting him come closer.

Thoughts fired at the speed of light.

How did he find me here?

Simple.

He was expecting me.

He'd done the same Google Earth reconnaissance I had, determined the Milk River was the best way into town, the field I had crawled across the safest approach.

And he had waited for me to show.

I'd messed up.

Been so intent on finding the best way into a quarantined city that I had failed to consider that someone of my intelligence would have identified the same route.

I should've chosen the second- or third-best option. Or at least been remotely prepared for this potential outcome.

But that was all beside the point now.

When he was within four feet, I launched myself at him.

He simply stepped out of the way.

I shot past, falling, then struggled to my feet, ripping off my respirator for a better field of vision and letting my backpack slide off my shoulders.

He looked at me, tucking his hair behind his ears.

"Hi, Logan."

I could feel my mind running a search, trying to match this voice to every human being I'd ever encountered.

As if reading my thoughts, he said, "We've never met."

"How long have you been waiting for me?" I asked.

"Three nights."

"Where?"

"Abandoned car in the junkyard."

I'd walked right past him.

"My sister here?"

He just laughed to himself as I scrambled to determine if he was here to kill or capture me.

"Get your samples?" he asked.

We met in the living room.

I clocked his left shoulder edging forward, his right torquing back, slipped the right cross that would've put me on my ass, brought a left hook through his face as he tilted off balance, then caught him across the bridge of the nose with a vicious elbow.

He stumbled back, blood sheeting down his face.

We traded blows, some missing, some landing. Even my hardest strikes seemed insufficient—it was like fighting an oak tree.

After I caught him in the left temple, he shook his head and charged, his meaty arms opening. My mind was shrieking, *Do not let him get you on the ground.*

We were in the hallway that led past the stairs to a family room, and as he went for my legs, I jumped straight up, pinning my feet against the walls, then dropping straight down on top of him, my knee driving into the back of his head with a sickening *thunk*.

As he lay stunned on the hardwood floor of the hall, I wrapped his long hair around my right hand, closed it into a fist, and smashed his head into the floor.

Once.

Twice.

Three times.

Four.

Impossibly, he struggled to his feet, but I clutched his back, clinging to him, my right arm around his neck, squeezing with everything I had, trying for a blood choke that would cut off the artery to his brain and give me a precious few seconds to figure out—

He crashed me into the wall, the force driving the air out of my lungs, then spun around and launched back into the opposite side of the hallway, so hard I cracked the drywall.

My ribs were in agony now.

He slammed me into the wall.

Again.

And again.

And again.

Until I couldn't hold on anymore

Until I couldn't breathe.

My grip released.

I crumpled to the floor, and as I gasped for breath, the man rained down a series of blows on my face—

When I came to, I was lying on the kitchen floor and the man was at the dining room table pulling a syringe out of a small black bag.

Everything hurt.

I felt broken, the pain edging beyond what I was capable of compartmentalizing.

I watched him tap the side of the syringe, and as he turned toward me, I closed my eyes.

The floor creaked as he approached and knelt beside me. I felt his warm hand on my shoulder, knew the needle was coming.

I opened my eyes, opened my right hand, and thrust it straight up into the man's soft throat.

It was a perfect strike.

He made a terrible gasping sound and dropped the needle, clutching at his neck.

His face turned red.

Panic filled his eyes.

I rolled over and came to my feet, staring at the man as he tried to breathe. He seemed to be getting a trickle of air, but not nearly enough. I figured he had two minutes of deeply unpleasant consciousness remaining. Four to twelve minutes before brain death.

"I crushed your trachea," I said, groaning against my own pain. "I could let you asphyxiate or I could save you."

He nodded violently, his face turning purple.

"You have a knife in that bag?"

He nodded, fighting to breathe.

Fifteen seconds.

The man's black bag lay open on the counter. Inside was a 9mm Kimber Micro, handcuffs, vials, syringes, and a Viper-Tec Blue Phantom knife.

I hurried back over to the man, who was now sitting against a kitchen cabinet, choking to death.

"Lie on your back," I said. "Move your hands."

Forty-one seconds.

It was an odd thing to go from trying to kill this guy to saving him inside of a few seconds, but he had information.

I climbed on top of him.

"Blink wrong, I'll slice you to ribbons."

He nodded frantically.

His face was a wreck, and I could see exactly where my blow to his throat had landed. It had crushed in the upper part of his larynx. I ran my finger down his throat until I felt another bulge—the cricoid cartilage. The indentation between this and his Adam's apple was where I'd make my incision.

When I flicked open the Blue Phantom, the man's eyes went wide.

Its blade was insanely sharp.

I eased it in, the man whimpering as blood poured from the new wound. I carefully pushed the blade through a membrane until it punctured into his airway.

His face was turning blue.

Seventy-eight seconds.

I knew I'd penetrated his airway, because some of the blood sucked in through the wound. I lengthened the incision to half an inch.

Whether from the pain or oxygen deprivation, the man was now unconscious.

Retracting the knife blade, I came to my feet and started opening kitchen drawers, looking for a straw or—

I grabbed a BIC pen with bite marks on one end, quickly separating the body from the writing components.

The cut I'd made in the man's neck was ugly—ragged and bleeding like crazy, but with some effort I was able to finesse the hollow body of the pen two inches through the man's neck.

He wasn't moving.

I put my lips to the pen, blew two breaths into the man's airway, and waited.

Nothing happened.

I started CPR—one hundred chest compressions per minute.

Then two more breaths into the pen.

Repeat.

Four minutes, twelve seconds.

I was about to start another round of CPR when the pen shuddered in its hole and made a gurgling, sucking noise.

The man's eyes opened. He took long, desperate breaths through the pen and stared up into my eyes with a helpless intensity. The color in his face was returning to normal.

He opened his mouth to speak, but no words came out.

I watched the panic return, and for a split second, almost felt sorry for him.

"I hold your life in my hands," I said.

He nodded. He knew.

I touched the pen. "This is all that's keeping you alive."

I rushed into the living room, grabbed my laptop out of my pack, and returned to the kitchen.

I sat next to the broken-throated man and opened a blank document.

I didn't have much time—someone must have heard the gunshot that killed Tiffany.

"What's your name?" I asked, then handed him the laptop.

He typed: Andrew

"Is my sister in Glasgow?"

He shook his head.

"How did you get entangled with Kara?"

We were in Myanmar together. I was a part of the team that rescued her. She approached me last year to be a part of her project

"Why is the upgrade killing people?"

I have no idea

Probably true.

"What were you supposed to do with me?"

Transport you out of here

"To Kara?"

Yes

"Where is she?"

I don't know

I reached over, yanked the pen out.

Gasping.

Desperation.

Hands clutching at his neck and that oxygen-starved purple beginning to color his face again.

"You think I won't watch you slowly suffocate?"

Andrew typed frantically: Colorado

"Where in Colorado?"

Near Silverton, please

"Give me an address and I'll let you breathe again."

58 Eolus Way

I shoved the pen back through the hole in his throat, and as he gasped for air, I watched him, trying to surmise if he was lying, but the trauma of the tracheotomy was drowning out any expressions, much less readable microexpressions.

I heard footsteps on the front porch. I grabbed the laptop, jumped to my feet, and raced into the living room, shoving it into my pack as someone pounded on the front door.

I grabbed Andrew's bag off the dining room table and ran past him, unlocking the back door just as the front was swinging open.

Soldiers entered the house.

I bolted through the backyard, past an old grill and shed, then hurdled a teetering, three-foot fence into an alley.

Finally got a deep breath of air into my lungs, and a shining pain spread through my entire midsection. My ribs had been bruised during our fight, the pain in my chest still blossoming, but I couldn't stop.

I kept running.

Through backyards and front yards.

Across an empty street.

I finally broke out of a backyard and there was nothing but darkness ahead. I'd reached the field I'd crawled through earlier. I ran as hard as I could, then slid down into an irrigation ditch and slipped on my NightShades, which had miraculously survived—a little bent, but basically intact.

I peered over the edge of the ditch, the lights of Glasgow burning a brilliant green. Three figures emerged from the windbreak of trees surrounding the city.

National Guard soldiers.

At just fifty feet away, I could see their rifles and respirators. They weren't wearing night optics. I watched one of them walk a short distance into the field—a short, stocky man. He must've had some kind of nightscope on his rifle, because he just stood there, methodically panning the field.

I retreated soundlessly into the bottom of the ditch and waited.

His footsteps approached.

I could hear the dirt crunching under his boots.

He stopped several feet away.

I could hear him breathing.

I could see the barrel of his gun.

One of his fellow soldiers shouted, "Anything?"

He hesitated for a moment, still scanning the landscape.

"No," he said finally and started back toward them. "They must've circled back into town. Put the word out."

I climbed up the side of the ditch and watched as they vanished into the trees.

I lay there for a moment, my chest heaving against the cold

dirt, every breath an explosion of agony. Before my upgrade, this level of pain would have decimated me. Even now, it came close.

It took everything I had, but I shoved the pain aside and started the long, slow crawl across the field, thinking of the residents of Glasgow.

Those who had died.

Those who'd been left behind—terrified, confused, devastated.

They didn't know—they couldn't possibly have known—that in their grief, they were living a momentous moment in the history of our planet.

For every great war, there's a first battle.

The Nazi invasion of Poland, which started World War II.

Fort Sumter for the Civil War.

Lexington and Concord for the Revolutionary.

The drone swarms that hit Taiwan when China invaded.

The Battle of Glasgow wasn't a war of armaments. It was a war of genes and mutations. A war with natural selection.

The first attack had already happened, and no one even knew it, the violence raging at the cellular level of every Glasgow resident my sister had managed to infect.

The stakes were bigger than ideology, territory, or even religion.

The stakes were the future of our species.

Where we were going.

What we would become.

Kara had started the Gene War.

9

I REACHED MY SPRINTER as dawn was breaking on the prairie. It was a soft, easy light, except on the extreme eastern horizon, which was reddened at the edges as if the night itself had had a hard night.

I approached the van carefully, on alert for the possibility that someone might be waiting for me.

The National Guard.

Or more of my sister's people. They had successfully predicted how I would infiltrate Glasgow. Perhaps they were waiting near my van.

But it was undisturbed, and the only footprints I saw in the immediate vicinity were mine.

I climbed in, groaning as I removed my hazmat suit. Then I pulled off my shirt, which was drenched in sweat.

I didn't know how many, but I was certain that several ribs were bruised from the fight.

The solar batteries were at full charge, and I'd already hooked them into the automated microfluidic DNA prep and digital nanopore sequencer. Loading in the samples from Tiffany and

Chris, plus my own, and some DNA from a non-upgraded human as controls, the machine began its protocol.

After purifying the DNA, it would read each nucleotide, strand by strand, record every base pair in sequence, then upload the readout to a software engine that would construct a complete de novo genomic alignment. The full sequencing and especially the analysis of these samples would take between eight and ten hours.

As the sequencer systems began the genomic reads and assembly, I started the EV and put Glasgow in my rearview mirror.

Silverton was a thousand miles away—a sixteen-hour drive due south, through Montana, Wyoming, and finally the southwest reaches of Colorado.

I had just crossed the Wyoming border when my body and focus gave out. I pulled over at a rest stop outside Ranchester, got some morphine out of my emergency kit, shot a few milligrams into my arm—

and the pain

just

melted.

I pulled my sleeper down, stripped out of my clothes and boots, climbed into bed.

I hadn't been this tired since Kara had tried to kill me in New Mexico and I'd been forced to flee the hospital in the middle of the night.

But for a blissful moment, all my hurt fell away.

I watched the midday light streaming through the dirty windshield until I couldn't hold my eyes open any longer.

And I floated away to the comforting clicks and whirs of the DNA sequencer.

● ● ●

When I woke, it was night, and silent in the van.

I sat up slowly, took a tentative breath.

The morphine had worn off, and the pain was back, although less all-encompassing than before.

I climbed out of bed, grabbed three Advil from the emergency kit, and walked over to the DNA sequencer, which was humming quietly.

I woke the touchscreen, saw a message: Sequence A Uploaded and Analyzed. Analyzing Sequence B. Time remaining: 51 minutes.

I drank three glasses of water and settled into the banquette that also served as my office.

I turned on my laptop and opened the analysis engine, a software program called LifeCode. Sequence A was the sample of Tiffany's DNA, and because I had meticulously sequenced and annotated my genome, I knew precisely what to look for. I had a list of genes and gene pathways that had been mutated to change their predicted activity and expression levels as a result of the upgrade my mother had forced on me. In fact, I'd already broken into the analyzer's source code and written a far superior program using my DNA sequence as a template to align and compare other genomes.

Humans are 99.9 percent identical in their haploid DNA/ genome sequence of approximately 3.2 billion base pairs. However, while we all have roughly the same genes, there are polymorphisms—small differences in the sequence of these genes—that lead to changes in expression levels, and even alter a gene's function. These subtle differences are what make us each unique from other members of our species.

I had coded my program to find and highlight these differences.

I dropped the huge files containing Tiffany's raw DNA sequence into my program query.

As it went to work, I got a can of soup down from the cabinet and heated it in a saucepan on my stovetop.

I was ravenous.

I read the results of Tiffany's DNA analysis as I ate.

Just as I'd expected, the same genes that had been altered in my genome had also been altered correspondingly in hers.

Even the modifications tracked.

These DNA payloads were already beginning to exercise their edits to myriad genes, involving multiple cascades of pathways—each a light touch to the genome, almost a butterfly effect that would have, over time, changed Tiffany's genome and led to augmentation of her intelligence, longevity, and resilience, finally lifting her to some version of my level of being.

After seeing Kara and Andrew, I was beginning to suspect that, while the upgrade altered expressions of intelligence, memory, and physical prowess across the board, it could exponentially ramp up preexisting proclivities—strength, agility, and coordination for people like Andrew and Kara. Pattern recognition and people reading for the more intellectually inclined like me.

Tiffany had been on the same journey toward becoming an enhanced form of *Homo sapiens* that I had taken when Andrew shot her at the top of those stairs.

Using the software, I began to isolate the genetic codes of multiple viral packages, which had delivered the upgrade to her. Each was an eight kilobase sequence—such an insignificant piece of DNA, but it carried a code. While it had replicated, it didn't appear to be packaged and secreted to the point of becoming transmissible.

Tiffany had never been contagious.

But the real question was what was happening with Sequence B.

I heard the DNA sequencer make a beep that indicated it was now uploading Sequence B into LifeCode.

Since it didn't appear that Kara's virus could spread from person to person, I wondered how she had managed to infect so many of Glasgow's residents. Had she sent a team to infiltrate the city several months ago and manually infect as many people as possible? She could've targeted just a handful of locations and had pretty good odds of infecting at least half the population.

My laptop flashed a message, alerting me that Sequence B (Chris's DNA) had finished uploading to LifeCode.

I dropped the files into my custom program query, then stepped outside to pee.

The sky was overcast and starless.

The crisp scent of snow permeated the air, and darkness crowded up against the lighted areas of the rest stop.

I returned to the van and quickly scanned the initial findings from Sequence B.

Right away, I could see that something was amiss in the code.

While Chris had also received the viral upgrade package, only some of the upgrades had occurred. In many cases, they were only partial, having failed to complete the changes and instead scrambling sections of vital genes.

Instead of initiating the upgrade, the viral package had lit the fuse on a new genetic fragment and begun a series of genetic off-targeting.

I copied the new sequences and dropped them into a general query to see if I could find a match and possible interactions.

Unsurprisingly, no exact genomic matches came back.

But I watched in horror as the list of "50%—95% overlap" results scrolled by: scrapie, mad cow disease, camel spongiform encephalopathy (CSE), transmissible mink encephalopathy (TME), chronic wasting disease (CWD), feline spongiform encephalopathy (FSE), exotic ungulate encephalopathy (EUE), spongiform encephalopathy, Creutzfeldt-Jakob disease (CJD), iatrogenic Creutzfeldt-Jakob disease (iCJD), variant Creutzfeldt-Jakob disease (vCJD), familial Creutzfeldt-Jakob disease (fCJD), sporadic Creutzfeldt-Jakob disease (sCJD), Gerstmann-Sträussler-Scheinker disease (GSS), fatal familial insomnia (FFI), kuru, variably protease-sensitive prionopathy (VPSPr).

Fuck me.

These were all forms of prion disease.

Prions are misfolded proteins that carry a horrifying ability to catalytically transmit their misfolded shape onto normal variants of the same protein. These mutations cause normal proteins in the brain to misfold. They literally shred brain matter and cause a handful of horror-show neurodegenerative diseases. Victims lose their ability to recognize people and places and to take care of themselves. In the final stages, they cease to think at all.

Normally, prion diseases are exceedingly rare—fewer than three hundred cases reported in the United States each year—and proceed slowly. And the method of contagion is highly specific. You could only contract it one of three ways—genetically inherited, from contaminated corneal transplants or medical equipment, or, as in the case of kuru, which plagued the Fore people of Papua New Guinea: cannibalism.

I closed my laptop, powered off the sequencer, and started the Sprinter.

My mind raced.

For people like Tiffany and me, the upgrade was performing as intended.

But if the upgrade had gone terribly wrong somehow, a prion disease was exactly the type of malfunction you'd expect to see.

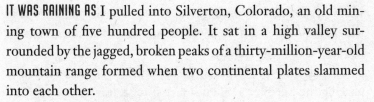

10

IT WAS RAINING AS I pulled into Silverton, Colorado, an old mining town of five hundred people. It sat in a high valley surrounded by the jagged, broken peaks of a thirty-million-year-old mountain range formed when two continental plates slammed into each other.

I drove through the quiet town.

Nothing open but a shitkicker bar at one end, a diner at the other. Half the buildings stood in varying states of disrepair. It felt like the kind of place that hadn't meaningfully changed in a hundred years, one that stood in defiance of the future.

And it was dying.

At the end of town, I pulled over to the side of the road.

According to my GPS, 58 Eolus Way was just 3.2 miles north of my current location, and as I looked around at this empty, dying town, I couldn't escape the thought that Andrew had lied to me. Or maybe he hadn't. Maybe I was playing right into Kara's hand.

Either way, I'd know soon enough.

· · ·

A mile north of town, the pavement ended. The dirt road was muddy, flooded in places, the rain falling harder now as the road wended through an evergreen forest.

The clouds were low and baleful. They decapitated the highest peaks.

I passed the base of an abandoned ski hill. The lodge was dark, its windows broken out, chairlifts swaying in the wind. Two long-neglected snowplows quietly rusting away.

After another two miles, the GPS alerted me that I'd reached 58 Eolus Way.

I didn't stop.

On my right, a one-lane road branched up the mountainside before vanishing into a blackened forest—no street address that I could see, but a gate blocked entry to the driveway, and there was a keypad and an intercom next to it. I'd seen all of this at lower resolution from the satellite map when I stopped to make my preparations yesterday.

I drove a couple hundred yards farther up the road, finally parking the Sprinter a safe distance from Kara's driveway.

Rain hammered the windshield.

I went into the back of the van and opened Andrew's bag. He'd taken my weapon apart in Tiffany's house in Glasgow, but now I had his 9mm Kimber Micro. I checked the load: 7 + 1 capacity. It was a tiny weapon, but at the moment, an improvement over nothing.

Stepping outside, the air was redolent of wet spruce and burned wood. I plunged into the charred forest, making my way steadily up the steep, wooded mountainside.

After fifteen minutes, I was several hundred feet above the road, and I could see, in the distance, the driveway to 58 Eolus Way making its winding ascent through the trees. I suspected there were cameras and IR sensors all along the drive.

I continued my slog up the mountain, keeping the road in sight while remaining hidden in the trees.

An hour later, I finally came to the edge of a glade. Straight ahead of me stood the mountain lodge. From inside, lights shone dimly through the windows.

I sat down against a tree, letting the canopy of branches shield me from the frigid rain. As the afternoon turned toward evening and the light drained away, I took a pair of binoculars out of my pack and glassed the house.

No movement inside.

I'd run a title search on the house. It had had a single owner since its construction twelve years ago, an entity called J6, which was an anonymous LLC with a registered agent in Delaware and no other information available. I'd hacked into the records of the Silverton building inspector's office and found the floor plans. Assuming the builders had stuck to them, I'd know my way around.

As I waited for darkness, it occurred to me that I was on a mountain in Colorado, above ten thousand feet in January, and it was pouring rain instead of snow. Once upon a time, these mountains would've been buried under meters of fresh powder. Once upon a time, the forests would've been green. But the wildfires of overlong summers had crisped them.

Evening arrived.

I came to my feet, staying in the trees and skirting the perimeter of the glade until I reached the side of the house.

Moving along the stone wall, I turned the corner into the backyard. A sprawling deck extended from the house, right up to the edge of the forest. I stopped at the first window I came to.

And there she was.

Her back was to me and she was cutting vegetables at a granite island—just ten feet away.

I moved on. If the architectural plans were to be believed, there was a door at the far end of the house, which opened into a solarium. It would give me the best cover for approaching Kara, and if I had to break glass, it was unlikely she would hear it from the kitchen.

I crossed the deck and ran along the back of the house, finally arriving at a dark wall of glass that was steamed up on the inside.

Pulling the Kimber Micro out of my jacket, I reached for the French doors.

The handle turned.

Warm air swept over my face.

I stepped inside, the door clicking shut softly behind me.

I was in a music room, where a grand piano with a satinwood case stood surrounded by walls of glass. A collection of framed photographs had been carefully arranged on its closed lid.

I inspected them in the darkness.

Max and me at eight years old on a horseback-riding excursion in the Sierra Nevada.

Kara in cap and gown at her high school graduation.

Our father, Haz, at the cockpit of the sailboat he loved in San Francisco Bay, smiling behind sunglasses.

Birthdays, Christmases, Thanksgivings, Halloweens.

There was a time when these images would have shattered me—artifacts of a doomed family. Today, I only felt the distant thunder of emotion, and it was so faint, so far beyond my emotional horizon, as to barely register.

Is this where my mother had lived in hiding, after the world believed she'd driven her car off the coast of California?

There was a chip on the piano's lid, which I recognized. Decades ago, when this piano had sat in our home in Berkeley, I had accidentally crashed into it on a scooter as Kara chased me around the house.

I imagined Miriam sitting here, playing the music she had performed for us in happier times, staring at all of those frozen, unreachable moments.

I unlaced and removed my shoes, then headed out of the solarium and down the wide corridor that bisected the first floor, my heart thrumming 5 bpm faster in the thin, high-altitude air as the sound of my sister in the kitchen became audible.

Eight Vermeers hung on the walls on the right-hand side of the corridor, and the subtle patina on the surfaces of the paintings suggested they were all originals.

Four massive O'Keeffe's adorned the left-hand side—luminous in the glow of the accent spotlights that pulled out every molecule of vibrancy.

In the great hall, exposed timber beams crossed the vaulted ceiling. A fire burned in a two-story stone hearth that was open both to the living room, where I stood, and the kitchen on the other side.

I tightened my grip on the Kimber Micro and edged up to the side of the hearth.

I took a breath, then stepped around the corner, putting my sister in the sights.

She was still standing at the island, dicing an onion faster than I'd ever seen anyone dice an onion.

She didn't look at me right away, even though I was sure she'd seen me.

"Is Andrew dead?" she asked, by way of greeting.

"No. But I wouldn't say he's well."

As far as I could tell, Kara was unarmed. She was wearing yoga pants and a tank top. Her hair was shorter than the last time I'd seen her, and it looked as if she'd performed additional self-augmentation to her face.

"Is it—"

"Just me here," she said, speaking faster than the last time we'd been together.

Or maybe I wasn't used to communicating with another enhanced human.

"I've been waiting for you, brother."

There was something else I was getting from her body language that I couldn't quite put a finger on.

"Planning to shoot me?" she asked as she moved to the stovetop and scraped the onion into a pan of shimmering butter.

"Depends."

She quickly sliced spears of asparagus on the butcher block, placed them in a ceramic baking dish, drizzled everything with olive oil, and slid it into the hot oven.

"Let's have a meal together," she said. "You can always shoot me later. I'm unarmed. But either kill me now or stop pointing that fucking gun at me."

I lowered the gun. Kara motioned for me to sit across from her at the island. She pulled down a saucepan and went to the refrigerator, grabbed a package of chicken.

"So this was Mom's place," I said.

"She had others. Squirreled away millions before the government seized her assets. How was Glasgow?"

"Got some samples of your handiwork."

"So far, 2,016 people have received the upgrade. There have been 274 confirmed cases of prion-like disease."

"By design?" I asked.

She shook her head. "I don't know why 13.6 percent developed prion instead of the upgrade."

Kara expertly butterflied two chicken breasts and rolled them in a spice mix. Her movements were pinpoint, with a speed and precision I'd never seen from professional chefs. Most of the time, even while cutting, her eyes never left mine.

I held the Kimber out of sight, just below the granite ledge.

"You knew I'd turn up in Glasgow?" I asked.

"I hoped you would, assuming you had survived New Mexico. I sent Andrew there in case you did."

To point me here.

"I sequenced the Glasgow samples," I said. "The upgrade wasn't transmissible."

"Had to be sure the upgrade was performing first," she said.

"So it's back to the drawing board?"

"No, I can live with a 13.6 percent defect rate. With a gene therapy of this intensity, side effects and off-targeting are inevitable. I'm surprised that number isn't higher."

Kara went to the range, poured white wine onto the sautéing onions. Clouds of evaporating alcohol perfumed the kitchen.

"Do you have a transmissible version yet?" I asked, part of me afraid to hear the answer.

"Soon."

Dear god. I'd suspected as much, but to hear it confirmed . . .

She said, "I'm using modified HEK293 cells to grow high titers of the upgrade-carrying virus."

I nodded. HEK293 was a strain of human embryonic kidney cells, widely used for decades in the gene-tech industry because of how easily they were grown and how efficiently they could be transfected with foreign DNA. Exactly what I would've used.

She placed the chicken on the stovetop's cast-iron griddle.

"What's the projected R-naught number?"

"Eight-point-seven, with subjects shedding virus within fifteen days from the initial exposure."

That was a very big number. In virology, the $R0$ (R-naught) indicates the contagion level of a given illness. It's the number of cases expected to be caused by a single infected person. Measles, the most contagious virus known to humankind, has an R0 of 12 to 18, which means that each infected person would be expected to infect 12 to 18 others. By comparison, the Spanish flu of 1918, which killed fifty million, had a much lower R0 of between 1.4 to 2.8. COVID-19 had been around 5.7.

I said, "If you expose every human being to the upgrade, and if the Glasgow percentages hold, you're talking about killing a billion people. That won't keep you up at night?"

"Fuck yeah it'll keep me up at night. But it'd be selfish not to do what needs to be done just because it plagues the remnants of my conscience. We have this moment to right the ship. Either we upgrade our collective intelligence to a level where we can all band together and save ourselves, or the next century will be humanity's last."

She turned back to the chicken. It had taken a good sear. Kara used tongs to move the pieces into the white wine sauce, then she topped it all with fresh herbs.

"Where are you finalizing the upgrade?" I asked.

She just smiled at me. "It's time to plate. Go pick the wine. Cellar's behind you."

I waited until she actually began plating the food before sliding off the stool.

Mom's wine cellar was a stone-walled, climate-controlled walk-in. After a little deliberation, I chose a Cabernet Sauvignon from a winery near Walla Walla, Washington. It had been my favorite region before it burned.

Kara had our steaming plates on the dining room table as I walked out with the bottle, and when she saw it, she said, "Year of your birth. Nice choice."

We sat across from each other, and I placed the Kimber on the bench beside me.

The food was superb. The night closed in—nothing but

darkness through the windows and the firelight from the hearth flickering on the walls.

Kara looked at me. "Is it that you don't believe we're in trouble?"

"No." I took another bite of the excellent chicken. "I see what Mom saw. I know what's coming. And it haunts me."

"So why aren't we working together?"

"What if this isn't the solution? What if you end up killing a billion people for no reason? What if you just end up creating a world of Miriam Ramsays—all convinced they know what's best, all capable of inflicting unimaginable harm if they're wrong? What if you create a bunch of people who are just drastically better at what they already were. Soldiers. Criminals. Politicians. Capitalists."

She took the smallest sip of wine and stared at me across the live-edge table, where I imagined my mother had consumed many a lonely meal. Or maybe they hadn't been lonely at all. Maybe she'd loved her solitude and the company of her own mind.

I continued, "You're working off a flawed assumption. Higher intelligence doesn't make you less greedy or self-centered or evil. It doesn't necessarily make you a good person."

"I'm not saying it will solve everything. It's not a magic wand. But if we can give people the power to see the world as it really is, and the intelligence to do something about it, won't we at least be giving ourselves a chance? Don't we owe our species that? Look, I get it. You want to know what the future holds. You need to know beforehand that we're making the right choice. But you can't."

"Show me proof this upgrade will fix the problems you say it will. Show me your rigorous testing and data."

"I know I've changed for the better. I have to trust that most people I upgrade will experience a similar transformation."

"So in the end, you're basing this all on your *belief*?"

"We're out of time, Logan. All we can do is try our best to use the facts at our disposal and examine our motives. I've looked at mine. I wouldn't be doing it for money or fame. Not for power or posterity."

"What reason then? Because you think it's right?"

"Right and wrong are constructs born of human sentiment. Nothing but stories we've made up and assigned meaning to. They don't correspond to any objective reality. The only thing real is survival."

I said, "Maybe compassion and empathy are just squishy emotions. Illusions created by our mirror neurons. But does it really matter where they come from? They make us human. They might even be what make us *worth* saving."

"Come on, Logan. Enough with the abstractions. Maybe you didn't believe our time was up back in New Mexico, but you do now. And you know we can't just let it happen." Kara raised her wineglass. "Are you with me or not?"

I lifted my wineglass and touched it against hers, and as we drank, I held eye contact with my sister, all the while reaching slowly, so slowly, for the Kimber—

Plates, glassware, decanter, wine bottle, food, silverware—everything crashed down onto me, as the full weight of the table knocked me back onto the floor, smashing down into my chest.

I'd never seen it coming. She hadn't betrayed the slightest hint of her intent, but of course she'd read across my face that she had failed to convince me.

I squirmed out from underneath the table, finally getting a grip on my pistol.

"Stop!"

Kara turned slowly around and froze in the pass-through to the living room, absolutely still. I searched her hands for a weapon. They were empty.

She looked at me with a sudden, startling intensity. "I love you, Logan. I'm giving you every chance. Don't make me do this. I know it's just sentiment, but I don't want to have to lose you too."

I aimed the Kimber at my sister's left leg, expecting a glimmer of sadness or fear, but her face remained utterly impassive.

"Where are you purifying the virus?"

She said, "Ava is inheriting a dying world. I can see in your face that you—"

"Of course I hate it!" My voice echoed through the silent house.

"So why are you pointing a gun at me?"

"Because there has to be another way."

"Great. What is it?"

"I don't know."

"Well, while you think about it, I'm actually going to do something."

"Where are you purifying the virus?"

She just stared at me.

"I don't want to hurt you," I said.

"I know."

I aimed at her left rectus femoris, the muscle that flexes the hip and extends the lower leg at the knee. I would disable her without threatening her life.

The gunshot was deafening in the confines of the house.

My ears rang.

Kara was still there, upright. I looked for blood, but there was none. Looked for signs of impact, but there were none.

She stood just to the right of where I'd been aiming.

Unhit.

I—

She moved.

—fired again.

For a second, I wondered if she'd somehow slipped blanks into the magazine, if this had been some intricately orchestrated ruse. But then I saw the bullet hole in the floor behind her.

I took a step forward.

Just ten feet away now.

Again, she moved at the precise instant I pulled the trigger and vanished around the corner of the hearth.

What the fuck?

I rushed after her into the living room, trying to comprehend how my sister had dodged three bullets at point-blank range. Of course, she hadn't dodged them. Most 9mm rounds move at a velocity of 1,200 fps. No human, upgraded or not, could move with anything approaching that speed.

She was anticipating, and moving, in that nanosecond between my intent and the trigger pull. But even with my upgraded perceptions, I couldn't have pulled that off.

A floorboard creaked behind me.

I spun into the sole of a foot striking my chest and launched back, slamming through a glass coffee table, trying to bring my gun up, but Kara kicked the Kimber out of my hand and crashed down on top of me, holding the point of the knife she'd butterflied our chicken with to my throat.

She said, "Ever think maybe there was a reason Mom upgraded *both* of us?" I could feel the blade beginning to slide in. "Maybe she knew you weren't capable of making the hard choice."

"You upgraded yourself again, didn't you?"

She didn't answer. I worked my hand down into my pocket, got a grip on the remote switch, pressed the button, and held it down. Inside the left pocket of my jacket, I felt a quiet vibration as the coupling motor and vacuum generator began to hum.

Kara glared down at me, her mask slipping—rageful and heartbroken.

"I need you to know—there is no part of me that wants to do this."

But she was going to. She had allowed me to find her to make one last attempt at bringing me along. That had failed, and now she had to do a very hard thing.

"I'm sorry," she said, tears glassing over her eyes.

"If you kill me, we both die."

She examined my face, searching for the lie. She didn't find it.

I said, "My thumb is holding down a button. If I release it, the disperser in my jacket will instantly blast out a continuous, aerosolized—"

"Of what?"

"Ricin."

Her pupils dilated. Adrenaline hit.

Ricin is a ribosome-inactivating protein, which infects cells and blocks their ability to synthesize their own protein, shutting down key functions in the body. It comes from the seeds of the castor plant, which are used to make harmless castor oil. Readily available and fairly easy to produce, the average adult requires just 1.78 mg of ricin, injected or inhaled, to die—the quantity of a few grains of table salt.

"Know what happens when you inhale ricin?" I asked.

Kara had become perfectly still.

"Within several hours, you develop a hacking, bloody cough. Your lungs fill with fluid. You drown. And there's no treatment. No antidote."

"This is a good bluff."

I raised my left arm. "See the tube just inside my sleeve?"

Her eyes cut to my sleeve, back to me.

I watched her, my hand on the button. She looked at the Kimber—eight feet away.

I said, "The disperser is custom-made. It will fill this room with aerosolized dry powdered nanoparticles before you even touch the gun."

"Just happen to have one of those lying around?"

"Get your knife off my throat."

She withdrew the blade.

"Throw it across the room."

It clattered to the floor behind us.

"It doesn't matter," she said. "You can't stop me."

If I'd known to a certainty that killing Kara would end the threat of the upgrade getting unleashed across the world, I would've taken my thumb off the remote switch. But she had mentioned a virologist. And she'd recruited and upgraded Andrew, who'd shown up in Glasgow. She had other people working with her, people who could finish the upgrade in her absence. And it sounded like the finish line was close.

"Very slowly," I said, "climb off me."

She moved onto the floor.

"Lie on your stomach," I said.

She rolled over, facedown in the broken glass, said, "If you make a move toward the gun—"

"I won't."

I shot a glance toward the front door. Twenty feet away.

I sat up.

Came slowly to my feet.

Kara watching me from the corner of her right eye, her palms on the floor, ready to spring up.

I took a careful step back.

And then another.

When I was ten feet from the massive door, I turned and bolted for the entrance. I heard glass crunching behind me, Kara on the move, but I didn't stop, hoping the door was open, because the extra second I would burn fumbling with the lock would probably cost me my life.

I wrenched the door open and launched across the threshold as a gunshot rang out behind me.

Sprinted down the steps.

Out of the sphere of the exterior chandelier's illumination, accelerating into the freezing rain, the remote switch still clutched in my hand.

Don't fall, don't fall, don't fall.

More gunshots ricocheted off the surrounding mountains, my bare feet holding a tenuous traction in the mud.

I didn't look back, didn't stop.

Racing downhill across the glade, just needing to reach the darker shelter of the woods, my pulse slamming along at 195 bpm, and between the bass drum of my heart and the drenching rainfall, I had no idea if my sister was in pursuit.

I entered the burned forest, the terrain steepening, my night vision pulling every available thread of light, dodging trees, leaping over logs, and I could feel gravity threatening to send me careening down the mountain.

I slowed down, finally coming to a stop behind a boulder.

Strained to listen.

Nothing.

I was beginning to shiver. My feet had been shredded, and they burned with cold. I heard something. Not a footstep. Some distant, mechanical noise. It was a garage door opening.

Twelve seconds later, two cones of light swept briefly through the forest, brilliantly illuminating the pouring rain. I heard tires rolling over pavement.

I only saw it for a second: the flash of headlights streaking down the driveway.

Kara was leaving. She didn't need this fight. She'd already won.

With my left hand, I pulled the disperser out of my pocket and manually powered it down. Only when I was sure the coupling motors had stopped running did I let my thumb slide off the remote switch.

As I shivered uncontrollably, black thoughts sailed through my mind.

You failed.

The war is lost.

Somehow, she had ramped up her abilities so far beyond mine that she was now capable of dodging bullets. Yes, I had survived, but to what end? I didn't stand a chance.

And then something occurred to me.

The door to my mother's lodge was still open.

I walked in.

The silence blared.

Kara had taken the Kimber, but that wasn't why I had returned.

I went upstairs, found the bedroom Kara had been using. The closet was still full of her clothes. A glass of water rested on the bedside table.

I entered the bathroom. Kara's toiletries covered the vanity, and among them I saw what I'd been looking for. I picked up the hairbrush, examined it closely, and registered the faintest glow of hope.

Still trapped among the bristles were several strands of my sister's hair, and one of them still had the follicle attached.

11

I LEFT LATE THAT night, heading west out of southern Colorado, and as the first hint of dawn brought color to the sky, I found myself on the deserted roads of Monument Valley, the sandstone spires catching rays of early sunlight, even as the lowlands lingered in the purple, predawn gloom.

I pulled over onto the shoulder to give myself a break.

Stepped outside.

The silence was towering.

Not even a breath of wind, a wisp of cloud.

And as I watched the light advance down the otherworldly buttes toward the floor of a valley that had once been a Paleozoic sea, I took comfort in the permanence of this landscape.

The desert lay under a fragile inch of snow, and all around me were red mesas and pinnacles that had existed for hundreds of millions of years before humans ruled the Earth and would continue to exist long after we were gone.

• • •

It was a late January evening, and still a hundred degrees as I sped down I-15 toward Vegas. Several miles away, the spectacle of the Strip exploded from the desert basin like the fantastical bloom of some alien flower.

I approached the clusterfuck of casinos, passing the Meta Frame at the north end—a supertall hotel built in the shape of a one-thousand-meter picture frame, where the picture was a continuous projection of random social media wall feeds.

Amid the gravity-defying statement pieces of casino architecture cowered the smaller, dingier, nearing-their-expiration-date relics of forty, fifty, and sixty years ago.

Rolling down the Strip, wafts of weed and vomit and urine and alcohol and the perfumes of showgirls infiltrated the van.

I passed the radiant, sunlit water of the Bellagio fountains. Once a day, they used real water. The rest of the time, it was holograms.

Caesars Palace had been razed, and in its place a global multiconglomerate had built Tower of Babel—a veritable man-made mountain that soared exactly one mile over the Strip. A greenway called the Hanging Gardens started at the base of the tower, made a winding ascent around the structure of the building, and finally topped out, after ten miles, at the pinnacle. All along the greenway, there were gardens, stores, restaurants, cafés, long stretches of walking paths, digital water features, places to stop and sit and observe the shimmering sprawl of the city and the desert beyond.

At the south end of the Strip, the newest, most striking feature of Vegas shone blue against the early evening sky. It was called Blue Earth—an immense sphere that glittered like a disco ball in the desert sun and glowed like a striking replica of Earth at night.

The Strip was surrounded by shitty-looking tenements—block housing for the people who made Vegas run.

And surrounding the tenements, like an outer circle of hell, was the rest of Las Vegas, abandoned twenty years ago after Lake Mead dried up.

I drove through the empty streets, dodging trash and debris.

To the west, the sun was sinking into California, augmenting the color of the Mojave Desert from orange to red to magenta to purple.

And then it was gone, the Vegas suburbs dark, the casinos a neon bloom.

I parked several blocks away from a building that had once been an abandoned Walmart, climbed out of the Sprinter, and started walking down the silent street.

As I approached, I pulled the bottle of whiskey out of the old coat I'd bought at a thrift store on my way out of Colorado. I opened the bottle, poured a bit of whiskey on my coat, then took a swig and spit it out.

The parking lot was empty. Light poles were toppled everywhere. And there were burned-out husks of cars and the remnants of several homeless encampments—shredded tents and oil drums and the detritus of hopelessness.

There was no moon, but the starlight guided my way.

The old entrances on the façade of the store had been boarded up and rendered impassable.

I walked along the side of the building, my gait a drunken shuffle, and even before I turned the corner, I could smell the cigarette smoke and the imperceptible scent of cheap cologne.

I came around the back side of the building. In the distance, midway down its length, I saw four black SUVs parked in the vicinity of the loading bays.

Voices reached me. They were speaking Russian.

Five men. No. Seven.

I was fifty feet away before they turned their attention to me. I had no doubt they had seen me several minutes ago. There would be cameras placed around the exterior of the building. But I'd been taken for a vagrant, stumbling around drunk in the dark.

They went silent, watching me, waiting to see if I would pass on by.

I stopped and turned and faced them.

A mountainous man in a black tracksuit stepped out of the small crowd.

"Keep moving," he said, waving his cigarette down the alley.

I started toward him, maintaining my faltering stride.

"You deaf?"

He met me ten feet from the others, moving with a light-footedness and grace that belied his size. The man towered over me—it was as if a boulder had sprouted arms and legs.

"Is Feld inside?"

I absorbed his reaction in the starlight: surprise. He lifted his left arm and spoke in his native tongue into the end of his sleeve. After thirty seconds, his eyes shifted; he was listening to some-one in his earpiece.

He responded, *"Da, da, da."*

The corners of his lips upturned into a smile that was com-pletely disconnected from his eyes—he was about to hurt me, and the prospect of violence delighted him.

His right arm moved for a gun in the back of his waistband, which I could see in the chrome reflection of one of the SUVs' side mirrors.

I kicked his left knee straight on. It made one of the worst sounds I'd ever heard—a cracking *pop*—and as he stumbled back, I reached into his waistband, pulled an MP-443 Grach, spun it in my hand, and cracked his head open with the butt of the pistol.

As he dropped, I shot the third, first, fourth, and sixth man in the precise order of who displayed the most coordination and grace. None did, really. It was inelegant chaos as their friends dropped all around them and they clumsily pulled their weapons.

The second man had been smoking a cigarette, and his hesitation saved his life. The fifth, and wisest, of the group had simply raised his hands.

"These bay doors the way in?"

"Yes," the fifth man said.

I pulled a zip tie out of my belt loop and tossed it to him.

"Tie him up," I said, keeping the gun trained on them as he cinched the second man's wrists behind his back but also watching the cameras pointed at the alley.

If they were watching me, they had several options. Send more men—assuming they had them—or try to escape another way.

"Is Feld here?"

The man finished tying up his cohort. He stood and looked at me. My question had scared him. He nodded.

"How many guards inside?"

"Two."

He was telling the truth.

"What's your name?"

"Alexei."

"Take me inside, Alexei."

I disarmed Alexei and followed him up the steps to the loading bay door, which he lifted high enough for us to duck under.

We walked onto the polished concrete floor of an empty warehouse. Lights blazed down from the rafters. I could hear the distant humming of generators.

"Take me to Feld," I said.

Alexei led me down a drab corridor.

At the terminus, he pulled a ring of keys from his pocket and unlocked a heavy steel door.

We entered a room that reminded me of an indoor exhibit in a zoo. The walls were lined with terrariums and aquariums of varying sizes, and the odor of sawdust, animal waste, and cleaning products filled the air.

We walked along a wall lined with cubbyholes behind glass. Petri dishes were visible in many of them. They were being tended to by robotic arms that squeezed solutions out of calibrated glass droppers or moved the clear dishes around to catch new angles of light or heat.

The cubbyholes became larger as we went along.

In one, I saw some kind of larvae squirming in dirt, barely visible to the naked eye.

In another, tiny pink bodies the size of cashew nuts that resembled baby mice.

Seedlings of what appeared to be evergreen trees, only with crimson needles.

There was an entire section filled with terrariums containing insects I'd never seen or imagined.

A larger cubbyhole was filled with water—a marine or riparian habitat with translucent, amorphous fish that looked like something from another planet.

We moved past even larger terrariums and aquariums.

I saw a marsupial-like creature the size of a house cat hanging upside down by three-toed claws. Its indigo eyes opened, the pupils little more than black pinpricks.

An eel with a head on each end swam through an aquarium filled with pink seagrass. It shimmered like quicksilver as electricity pulsed just beneath the surface of its skin.

I couldn't help stopping in front of the largest habitat I'd seen so far. The glass was floor to ceiling, and the space took up roughly the size of a walk-in closet.

The creature sat in a corner of the enclosure, under the shelter of a palm frond. It reminded me of a gremlin from the 1984 movie, but with smaller ears, wings, and a less terrifying disposition.

A door at the end of the nursery swung open.

I pulled Alexei in close, held the Grach to his head.

A man in a white lab coat appeared in the doorway, and when he saw me, he smiled. Ty Feld was two inches shorter than me, with curly, grizzled black hair, bushy sideburns, and a mustache more befitting a saloon owner. The GPA had kept Feld in its sights for years. We'd never gone after him, even though we knew he lived in the penthouse of Tower of Babel and operated out of a handful of old buildings in the abandoned sprawl of Las Vegas. Officially, we'd never been told why he was off-limits, but we all knew. He was a back-alley contractor for DARPA. He sold them illicit biotech and occasionally coughed up legit intel on bioterrorists and competitors to the GPA. So all things being equal, he was allowed to run his business of exotic synthetic creatures as long as he justified the freedom he was allowed.

Behind him, two black-jacketed men with Slavic features waited in the wings.

"Little Logan Ramsay," he said.

"Hello, Dr. Feld."

"Here to arrest me?"

"I don't work for the GPA anymore."

"Here to kill me?"

"I need to borrow your lab."

"Why would I let you do that instead of just killing you?"

"If you think you can kill me, you should definitely do that. It didn't go well for the seven trained guards you had stationed at the loading bay, but maybe the two who are cowering behind you are the real badasses? If they want to take a shot, I'll have to kill Alexei here. I'd rather not. Or . . . just spitballing . . . you could recognize that you're outmatched, skip to the end."

Dr. Feld laughed heartily. He said, "Last time I saw you, you must've been twelve years old. I was giving a lecture in Berkeley, and your mother invited me for dinner."

"I was nine actually. And you stayed with us."

"Did I?"

"We played a game of chess."

"I don't remember that. Who won?"

"You destroyed me in thirteen moves."

"Excellent." He glanced at the men behind him. "Stand down."

I released Alexei, who moved toward Feld, his head hanging low like a chastened dog.

Feld said, "Kill him."

One point two seconds later, all three men were dead at Feld's feet, and I still had one round left in the gun, which I was pointing at his face.

"Sorry," he said. "I had to see for myself."

"So you're building dragons now?" I asked, gesturing toward the largest habitat.

"You'd be surprised how much people are willing to pay for a brand-new life-form that no one else has ever seen. Once I've perfected the design, I'll sell this guy for fifty million."

"Can it actually fly?"

"No. But the wings flap. Unfortunately, it isn't capable of breathing fire."

"You tried?"

"We *explored* the idea. There are creatures in the animal kingdom that can certainly withstand temperature extremes. We looked at the genome for the Pompeii worm, which lives near hydrothermal vents in temperatures above 170 degrees

Fahrenheit. We looked at Alaskan wood frogs and the water bear tardigrades, which can survive down to almost absolute zero. But there's no internal biological structure in the animal kingdom, at least that I've discovered, that can withstand a thousand degrees." He laughed. "And I wouldn't begin to know how to build an organ capable of producing and expelling fire."

"Did it gestate in an existing species or is it lab grown?"

"Lab grown in a synthetic, freestanding uterus. We call him Smaug."

It didn't look like the mighty, mythical dragon. It looked, well . . . kind of pitiful.

Its skin was spiky, hard, and pebbled. I suspected they'd borrowed some DNA from the crocodile genome. Its hind paws resembled the legs of a Komodo dragon.

The creature's eyes opened—reptilian and otherworldly. It gazed at us through the glass.

"This is a highly imperfect creature," Feld said. "As it grew, its mass increased a bit faster than its bone cross-sections could handle. We just finished somatically editing the bones to increase their size and density. Should know if we were successful in the next few weeks."

The dragon moved out from under the palm fronds, dipped its angular head to a small pool of water, and began to drink.

"Why are you here?" Feld asked.

"Seen the news out of Glasgow?"

"Of course. I heard the military is building a perimeter around the city. They're fencing everyone in."

I brought him up to speed on everything, and when I finished, he threw his head back and laughed for a long time. Until there were tears in his eyes.

"Your mother," Feld said. "Kills two hundred million people, wrecks an entire field of science—and with it my life's work—

then fakes her own death just for another chance to step back up to the plate and swing even harder." He sighed, gathering himself. "So this upgrade works?"

"It works on some."

"How did she achieve this?"

"No idea, but if I had to guess? She ran her Story of You biodata through an exascale processor."

"Yes, of course." His eyes lit up, and I caught a glimpse of the scientist behind the criminal. "She had the data set. Probably built an algorithm to reverse-engineer DNA code from the physical attributes of her customers. Wow. She really did it. Actually built a program to extrapolate genotype from phenotype." I watched him thinking it through. "People can lie on a questionnaire. She probably designed spiders to scrape public records and compare death certificates. Social media. Hack a few insurance companies and compare her data to their medical records. Get a reasonable confidence ratio." There was jealousy behind his glee.

"My sister is going to release my mother's upgrade."

"How?"

"A transmissible, asymptomatic virus."

"What's the R-naught?"

"Almost nine."

Feld shook his head, impressed. "Interesting times ahead."

"I need a lab."

He shrugged. "Think stopping her is really worth the trouble?" For a fraction of a second, I saw the bottomless well of grief in his eyes. "We're going down, Logan. It's too late to bail water. Not that we ever really tried. And there are no lifeboats. Live like the world is ending, because it is." He stared at me for a moment. "I didn't change your mind, did I?"

"No."

"Well," he said, looking down at the dead men. "I guess *mi casa, su casa*."

The primary lab took up several thousand square feet in the corner of the old Walmart—the walls lined with servers and an array of DNA printing machines.

Feld showed me to a 3D interface gene station, logged me into their system, and left me to play.

Using the follicle I'd pulled from Kara's hairbrush, my custom program had completed a comparative functional analysis between my genome and hers. She had targeted select genes in her DNA, further modifying their expression far beyond the thresholds set by our mother's initial upgrade—primarily those gene network systems that controlled concentration, pattern recognition, and general cognition.

I uploaded Kara's new genome analysis to Feld's AI interface, which quickly collated a hit list of modifications and the corresponding target organs and gene systems.

If I wanted a chance at stopping Kara, I would have to ramp up my abilities to, or beyond, her level. She could've gently made the modifications, one by one, over a period of months. Unfortunately, I didn't have the time. Whatever I came up with would have to be fast and dirty.

But I had an idea, because everything I had ever read or learned about genetic engineering was now at my fingertips.

For most of our genes and regulatory sequences, we have two copies. My mother's primary upgrade had kept to nature's plan, modifying only one copy of the gene. But modifying both, also known as increasing gene dosage, was a proven brute-force method for upping phenotypical expression—albeit a risky one. For instance, a 50 percent increase in gene dosage on chromosome 21q altered the timing, pattern, and extent of development, creating the genetic disorder known as Down syndrome.

To match what Kara had done, and quickly, I would double down on many of my already modified genes by also activating the silent copy for maximal expression—a very coarse kick to a delicately balanced system.

I caught a few hours of sleep in the Sprinter when I could. Occasionally, Feld's cell biologists and virologists would wander over to see what I was up to, but I kept my head down, engaging as little as possible.

Using DNA forges, I ordered up a half dozen different DNA minicircles, each one a self-contained, self-replicating delivery vector for a specific set of genes and instructions.

On day three, I uploaded the raw genetic sequences and put Feld's DNA forges and assembly array to work creating DNA to order in precise amounts and purity, with everything I needed rendered fully chemically synthesized.

But I still needed a delivery method, something that would integrate into my system much faster than the viral vector that our mother had used to deliver the first upgrade and that Kara had used for her second one. I needed something that would take my mixture of DNA sequences and minigenes and blast the new DNA into my poor, overstretched cells.

I'd been working nonstop for twenty-two hours.

Leaving the workstation, I took a stroll down the pillaged aisles of what had been the sporting goods section.

An article came to mind. I'd read it fifteen years ago on a supersonic flight from D.C. to Los Angeles, only half comprehending it at the time. Now it was perfectly preserved in my mind.

The article examined the benefits and drawbacks of various gene-delivery methods, one of which was via hydrodynamic force—a technique that used pressurized injection of a large volume of DNA to essentially blast a gene package through cell walls via osmatic shock, and permeate the body with great efficiency. Hydrodynamic force wasn't easy on the recipient, but for a quick and dirty delivery method of the systemic changes I needed, it was hard to beat.

In addition to injecting myself, I'd also need a specialized delivery system to cross the blood-brain barrier and effect the changes to my brain. Something fast and delicate. For that, I'd fabricate nanoparticles to house my gene packages, which would go straight to my brain via inhaler.

When I told Feld what I was doing, he looked at me as if I'd lost my mind.

"There are more fun ways to kill yourself than catastrophic organ failure."

"You got a better idea for fast delivery?" I asked.

He didn't.

Six days after my arrival, I shook Feld's hand at the edge of the loading bay and thanked him for his hospitality, for which I had given him no choice.

"You're toast if you do this. You know that, right? The human body cannot withstand what you're about to put it through."

"You're probably right," I said.

"I'm still going to wish you luck. Remember that I helped you."

"After you tried to have me killed. Twice."

"Yeah. Only twice." As he smiled, I hopped down from the loading bay and started across the sunbaked pavement toward my Sprinter.

• • •

I was running out of time to find Kara, so for the first time since establishing my new identity, I decided to fly.

Twelve minutes after takeoff from Harry Reid International, we leveled off at 95,000 feet. It was an eighty-seater Boeing, and though the ramjets propelled us at a mile per second, there was no sense of movement until I looked down and saw the old-school supersonic jets seven miles below, and the older-school subsonic jets another four miles below them. They all seemed to be racing backward.

I watched the curvature of the Earth—the fragile blue mist of atmosphere transitioning into the black void of space.

After twenty minutes at cruising altitude, I heard and felt the engines shut off. The pilot announced that we'd begun our glide descent into D.C.

For the first time in over a year, I was going home.

12

THE DASHBOARD CLOCK SHOWED 6:45 P.M., and it was dark and drizzly beyond the glass. My house had been painted—the wood siding refreshed, the trim changed from burgundy to navy blue, the door painted red.

This was the first time in months that I'd felt indecisive. The minicooler containing my new upgrade was buckled into the seat beside me. I could've taken it in Vegas. I should've taken it in Vegas. But I'd come here instead.

I didn't know what was to come, and I wanted to see my family one last time.

I was fixing my hair in the rearview mirror, trying to make myself more presentable, when the front door swung open.

Beth appeared in the threshold.

She wore a green wrap dress I'd never seen before, and she'd changed her hair from a natural, shoulder-length cut to a sleek, asymmetrical bob.

Beth pulled the door closed after her and started down the flagstones toward the street.

This was my moment.

But as I reached to open the car door, headlights appeared in the distance, the light scattering across the raindrops that were sliding down the windshield.

I waited, watching as the driverless car pulled to the curb.

Beth opened the rear passenger door and climbed in.

After two miles, Beth's ride-share stopped in front of a restaurant called La Fleur, where we'd eaten together on a handful of special occasions. It was an anniversary and birthday place. A trying-to-impress-someone place with a synthetic-free menu and stupefying prices. They sold what some people were willing to pay a very high price for—the experience of what it used to feel like to eat out in the world.

Beth hopped out, hurried across the sidewalk, and disappeared inside.

I pulled into the first empty parking space I saw and stepped out into the rainy evening.

Despite the weather, the sidewalks were bustling.

I moved through clouds of perfume.

There were people spilling out of the entrance to La Fleur, queued up behind the hostess podium. Beth wasn't among them, and the main dining area was hidden behind a wall of red curtains.

I squeezed and pardoned my way through the crowd, slipping through the curtains while the hostess was staring down at her reservation list with a penlight.

The dining room was loud and dark.

Every table was occupied—many of them accompanied by champagne buckets and topped with white tablecloths and shuddering candlelight.

As I stepped out of the way of a black-tied server carrying a tray of martinis, I spotted Beth's green dress.

Her back was to me, and she was sitting at an intimate table in the farthest corner toward the back.

Across from a man.

I started toward them, through the controlled chaos of servers and diners.

Everything dissolving around me.

I saw nothing but the face of the man seated across from my wife. He was good-looking and superbly groomed, wearing a bespoke black jacket over an expensive white T-shirt.

He was leaning forward and laughing, and as I drew closer, I saw that his right arm was resting on the table, his hand several inches from Beth's.

"Sir?"

I turned to face the hostess.

"Are you looking for your table?"

"Yes," I covered, "but I don't see my group. I thought they were here already."

"What's the name on the reservation? I'll see if they checked in."

"I'm not sure who made the reservation."

"Okay, what's your name?"

"Robbie."

"If you'd like, you can wait by the bar."

I took the only open seat, which had an unobstructed view of Beth's table, acknowledging the white-hot jealousy I felt toward the man she was with. But now, like so many of my emotions, this feeling was equally met by my ability to set it aside. To see beyond my own sentiment.

I ordered a drink I didn't touch and watched Beth's table.

They ordered cocktails, wine, food.

Conversation flowed effortlessly.

The body language, the setting, the fact that it was a Thursday night in a dark, French restaurant—everything about this screamed date. The third. Maybe the fourth.

A server brought them the bottle of wine. Beth's date made a show of examining the cork and carefully studying the color of the first splash in his glass.

After the sommelier left, her date scooted back in his chair and stood. I watched as he moved toward a hallway on the other side of the restaurant that presumably led to the restrooms.

I dropped some cash on the bar and started toward Beth's table.

She was just twenty feet away now, texting someone on her phone.

My heart rate spiked to 160 bpm. It felt as if another person had inhabited my body, and of course I knew who it was. Old Logan. Still a captive of human need. Blown through the ocean of his existence by winds he couldn't begin to control or understand.

New Logan wasn't screaming so much as saying in a calm, firm voice, *You know this is not the way. You will endanger her.*

I was ten feet from the table.

Then five.

You know this is not the way.

Through all the competing smells of the restaurant, I caught my wife's—the chemistry of her perfume, body wash, and lotions, and beneath it all, the mysterious alchemy of pheromones and her elemental scent, which penetrated through to what remained of my reptilian brain. The emotional wallop was stronger than anything I'd felt since my upgrade.

I still loved her.

And then it was gone—Old Logan locked away.

I saw myself in the restaurant in a sudden gasp of clarity. The veil lifting. Saw the forces that had brought me here.

The old claws of jealousy, fear, and grief.

Rationalizing away the truth, out of selfishness.

I was a danger to Beth, to our daughter.

I was no longer the best thing for them.

Beth had sensed my approach out of the corner of her eye. Her head was beginning to swivel toward me.

I turned sharply, passing her table, then her date, who had just emerged from the restroom. He didn't see me. He was laser-focused on Beth, and I could read in his face the microexpressions of interest, excitement, lust.

Back outside, I sat in the car as the rain fell, watching people pass by on the sidewalk.

I unbuckled the seatbelt that secured the cooler and opened the lid. Reaching into the meltwater, I grasped the first of eight large syringes—each one labeled for injection at a specific location on my body.

Setting my new upgrade on the center console, I rolled up the sleeve on my left arm, tied a rubber band above my elbow, and swabbed the injection site over my antecubital vein with an alcohol pad.

The bright-sharp scent of isopropyl filled the car.

I lifted the syringe, pushed a single bead of solution through the needle. Once injected, the effects would hit me within the hour. I had a hotel room waiting at the Mandarin Oriental. I was using a pressurized injection for the hydrodynamic shocking of the main systemic upgrades, and a modified nasal inhaler for the nanoparticles to pass the blood-brain barrier and directly target my brain. I'd wait until I was back at the hotel to huff my nanoparticles, since those effects would arrive instantaneously.

Beyond the rain-smeared glass, I glimpsed a flash of green. Beth was coming down the sidewalk, sheltered under an umbrella that was held by the man she'd had dinner with. She was clutching his arm. No wedding ring on her finger. They were talking, but I couldn't hear the words over the pattering of rain on the roof.

Most of her face was hidden by the umbrella, but I could see my wife's mouth.

She was smiling.

Was this the last glimpse I'd ever have of Beth?

Asking for Old Logan.

They walked right past my window, and I caught a sliver of Beth's laughter through the glass. High and melodic. Something about it had always made me think of sunlight.

Then they were gone—just one more couple in a sea of umbrellas. And I was struck, again, as an outside observer, by how much the members of our species needed one another. All these people out in the cold rain. To laugh and drink. To talk about nothing. It was almost as if that need for connection and touch was our . . . *their* . . . lifeblood.

I wasn't lonely.

Old Logan was lonely. But he was dying.

I looked at the syringe.

And then I slipped the needle into my vein.

PART THREE

In the twenty-first century, the third big project of human-kind will be to acquire for us divine powers of creation and destruction, and upgrade *Homo sapiens* into *Homo deus*.

—Yuval Noah Harari, *Homo Deus*

13

IT RAINED FIRE INSIDE my brain.

My eyes rolled back in my head, my body convulsed, arms curled in, foam bubbling out of my mouth.

The seizure passed.

It felt like my bones were melting, and as if something were trying to stab its way out of my skull with an ice pick. I reached the mercifully cool tile of the bathroom in my hotel suite and hauled myself over the side of the tub, which I'd filled with ice.

Settling into the freezing water, I groaned.

I hurt *everywhere*.

My cells were screaming.

As my hot skin melted the ice all around me, I thought: *I'm going to die.*

My mind was falling apart. No center to take things in. No prioritization of incoming stimuli. The arc angles of every hair on my arm raging at the same volume as the water dripping from the sink at forty-two-second intervals as the trowel strokes on the textured ceiling as the frequency of my blinking as the pattern of tiles on the wall and the thickness differentials in the grout as my pulse rate falling through the forties, thinking my thalamus, the subcortical relay for sensory information from periphery to cortex, which filters and organizes sensory information, the thalamocortical circuits that govern attentional control of sensory information by modulating and sustaining functional interactions within and between cortical areas . . . I had fucked it.

I had fucked it all.

Destroyed my own mind.

I whimpered.

Cerebral torture.

Time slowing toward an interminable crawl.

I was staring up into a deluge of slow-motion sensory information and all of it streaming down my face, my attention intensely attaching to every drop simultaneously, my consciousness dividing and dividing and dividing and—

There was a scalding stone in the left side of my chest.

Getting hotter and hotter, and my blood gone still inside of me.

Organs straining.

Faltering.

Pain exploding everywhere. I couldn't breathe . . .

. . . gulped in air, my heart beating again.

I'd been flatlined for 148 excruciating seconds and was still foundering in a maelstrom of sensory data, my own thoughts like a voice outside my body, like many voices, and my mind dividing and dividing.

Thinking eight things at once.

Then sixteen.

Then—
Close your eyes.
Darkness.
Momentary relief.

I came to consciousness shivering in a bathtub of 68.5-degree Fahrenheit water. I gripped the sides and tried to haul myself to my feet, but I didn't have the strength to even stand.

I looked around.

That sense of rudderless, mindless horror was gone, though whether it had really passed, or if I was in the eye of the genetic storm, remained to be seen.

Threads of searing light crept through the space between the curtains. I had no idea what day it was. How long I'd been in this room. All I knew was that I was desperately thirsty and still running a scorching fever.

I pulled myself up onto the bed, grabbed the nearest water bottle, and drank it down. I'd given myself an intravenous saline solution before inhaling the nanoparticles, but I'd thrashed around so much during the first seizure that I'd ripped out the IV port.

After two bottles of water, I tried standing.

Staggered over to one of the windows and peered outside, instantly shielding my eyes from the attack of light.

Gray, winter skies canopied the nation's capital. From my eighth-floor suite, I could see the marinas of the Washington Channel and the distant white dome of the Jefferson Memorial.

Already, my strength was flagging.

I collapsed into a chair by the window.

• • •

My dreams that night were kaleidoscopic.

I witnessed my own mind rewiring and transforming itself.

I rode a knife-edge of pain and ecstasy.

I comprehended all the forces—genetic, environmental, my cascade of predestined choices—that had made me *me* in this moment. Saw myself as the inevitable solution to the equation of my existence. Finally understood that free will did not exist, because I could not choose my desires, only whether to pursue them.

I saw all the old versions of Logan through time.

Zygote to this moment.

I wondered who I had become.

What I had become.

I wept.

I screamed.

I laughed hysterically.

I clawed at my skin and ripped out my hair.

I wanted to die.

I wanted to live forever.

When I woke in the morning, I knew I was out of the storm. I climbed out of bed and padded into the main living area.

Looked around, letting it all wash over me.

I was still ultra-aware of every incoming sensory stimulus, but something had changed. Now I could intentionally divide my mind into more than just two threads of consciousness. And importantly, I could hold back the sensory onslaught if I wanted.

I ran a test, focusing on—

The way the central heating made the curtains appear to breathe like the lungs of an alien creature.

A fly buzzing manically inside a trash bin near the minibar.

The minifridge humming at 49 Hz because of a dirty compressor.

My intellect already turning its high-powered engine toward Kara.

My thirst—a neurological artifact that was actually the elicitation by angiotensin II acting on angiotensin II receptors in the subfornical organ, a brain region near the ventricles with high vascularization, in response to low blood volume.

My hunger—another sensory artifact that I was now blindingly aware was simply the serotonin (5-HT) and catecholamine neurotransmitters in my serotonergic neurons, intestinal myenteric plexus, enterochromaffin cells in the mucosa of the gastrointestinal tract, and blood platelets—telling me to eat.

The more thoughts and sensory input I allowed myself to receive and process, a curious thing happened.

Time seemed to elongate, to stretch. Similar to the fear reaction that activates the amygdala to lay down more memories, my multipronged consciousness was also laying down more memories by a factor of X, where X was the number of times I divided my consciousnesses. And this gave the illusion of time slowing down to a fraction that also corresponded to X.

In other words, by dividing my consciousness and focusing simultaneously on multiple stimuli, I could slow my perception of time. And the more I divided my consciousness, the slower time seemed to unfurl.

I wondered if I could linger in moments, let each second become a world unto itself. Back at Feld's lab, I'd easily anticipated the physical movements of his guards, but that was nothing compared to this.

This had happened in the bathtub and been torture because I had no control. I couldn't stop it. Now I could. It was as if I could actually slow time.

The sound coming through the curtained windows was different. Muffled. It was snowing.

I went to the French doors, stepped outside.

Letting my consciousness divide and divide and divide and divide until the snowflakes stood *almost* motionless. I watched one crawling through the air, just past the tip of my nose. And the cars were still, the people on the sidewalks eighty feet below barely moving, and a hyperjet just inching across the sky.

I blinked, reverting to a single consciousness.

The world at normal speed again.

And I knew: This is how Kara had dodged bullets.

And I also knew something else. Where before, I only had vague theories and educated guesses, in this moment, as the snow melted on my face, I had the clearest model in my mind of how my sister was going to release her upgrade.

I even knew where.

I slipped the needle into his vein so deftly he only stirred. After depressing the plunger, I placed a piece of tape over the needle, which was still embedded in his skin, then moved back to the chair.

The bedroom was dark, and the chair creaked under my weight as I settled into it.

I took a few deep breaths in the silence.

The seconds ticking past at half-speed, since I was concurrently in this space, but also thinking about my sister.

A black cat brushed against my legs, purring contentedly.

Edwin Rogers stirred, rolled over onto his side, and was still again.

There was only the sound of his soft snoring and the whisper of central air blowing heat through the vents and the purring.

My brain wanted to engage with twenty-nine distinct sources of sensory input, but I wouldn't let it. The process of denial was still a conscious effort. Soon, I would adapt.

I was on the second floor of the director's redbrick row house in Georgetown, four blocks from the Potomac.

It was 2:27 A.M.

Noisily, I cleared my throat. Edwin shifted under the covers. I cleared my throat again, louder this time. Edwin startled awake and sat up in bed, staring into the darkness.

"You didn't dream that noise," I said.

He lunged for his bedside table, pulling the drawer open.

"The gun isn't there," I said. "I'm holding it."

Edwin looked in my direction. It was so dark in the room that I felt confident he could only see my general shape. I could see him perfectly.

"Who's there?" he asked.

"Your former lab experiment."

For a moment, Edwin was absolutely still. I saw him look down at his left forearm. Saw his hand touch the syringe I'd taped to his arm. Saw him observe the depressed plunger. He pulled the tape away and removed the needle from his vein.

"What did you inject into me?"

"We'll talk about that later."

"Are you out of your mind, Logan? If my wife—"

"I know she's out of town."

"I have security outside. How—"

"It doesn't matter."

I leaned forward, turned on the bedside table lamp.

Edwin stared at me in wide-eyed horror.

Before the upgrade, most humans were a complete mystery to me—like mountains enshrouded by clouds and mist. I knew they were there, but their true shape remained hidden. My ability to predict others' behaviors—even my wife's and daughter's— had proved endlessly elusive. The first upgrade had cleared some of the mist away.

Now, as my second upgrade began to manifest, an interconnected network of previously invisible forces was revealing itself to me. I saw not only Edwin's fear but all the pressures acting upon him to elicit that fear—his multiple, competing identities as a husband, father, grandfather, GPA director, law enforcement officer, mentor, friend, betrayer, scientist, and living, breathing organism who didn't want to die.

It was like seeing the difference between the trees blowing in the wind and the wind coming long before the trees began to bend. And knowing *exactly* how much they would bend.

The distance between who I thought Edwin was and who he actually was had been narrowed. I had every memory of the man, every word I'd heard him speak, every reaction he'd made in my pre-upgrade years—all working to construct a near-flawless mental model of who he was in the moment and what he would do in the next. It wasn't that I could actually read his mind. Just like I wasn't actually slowing down time. None of these observations gave me exact information, but the impressions they imparted created a rich foundation for inference and deduction.

I saw *into* him.

The secret structure of his identity stood before me unobscured, unobstructed.

A mountain in full view, on a clear, autumn day.

There was no mystery anymore. He was trapped in an endless loop of his core desires, and they would undercut any impulse toward unpredictability.

He would act inevitably.

He would bend as the wind blew him.

I could see the wind.

And I could be the wind.

At this moment, he was thinking: *I didn't know what to do with you. I didn't know how the upgrade would change you. I'm sorry.*

And then he said: "I'm so sorry for everything. I treated you like a lab rat. Lied to your family."

Smart. Getting out ahead of that.

"You were doing your job. I understand what your incentives were. The various pressures bearing down on you." I looked at the .357 revolver I'd taken out of Edwin's bedside table. "But please, never forget . . . I could've killed you tonight for what you did to me and to my family."

He hemorrhaged relief.

I said, "The person who broke me out of your black site was my sister. She killed your contractors. My mother had upgraded her as well."

"Why?"

"Because Miriam was dying. This upgrade was her magnum opus, and she knew she wouldn't live long enough to see it through to completion. So she upgraded her two remaining children and left the final stages of the upgrade for us to complete. I didn't want to go through with it. Kara did."

As I told him everything, I watched his fear for his own safety become horror at what my sister was planning.

"So Glasgow was a test run?" Edwin asked.

I nodded.

"We just finished sequencing a few genomes of the dead."

"Prionopathy," I said.

"Yeah." He sounded surprised that I knew that.

I said, "That's the least of your problems. At this moment, my sister is purifying the virus. She's weeks, maybe days, away from having a transmissible upgrade. Imagine Glasgow on a global scale."

I watched the dread take up residence in Edwin's eyes.

"How would she pull that off?" Edwin asked.

"Once deaths begin happening in mass numbers, governments will respond with lockdowns and closures. I know many countries are already working on anti-Scythe therapies. If I'm Kara, I need to make sure the upgrade is *everywhere* before these things happen. I'd need to infect a handful of willing carriers and then send them out, *simultaneously*, to the ends of the earth."

Edwin asked, "How many is a handful?"

"Considering the defect rate, between seventy-five and one hundred fifty."

"And when you say 'the ends of the earth'—"

"There are 128 cities with populations of five million or greater. I would send my infected carriers to places like Tokyo, Delhi, Shanghai, São Paulo, Mexico City, Dhaka, Cairo, Beijing, Mumbai, Osaka, Istanbul, Moscow. I would know definitively the time frame for contagion, and I would thread that needle so, as my carriers were shedding this highly contagious virus, they'd be passing through airports, going to concerts, festivals, sporting events, protests."

Edwin looked terrified.

"How do you find *willing* carriers? A challenge, no?"

A great question. And I already had a theory.

"For sure," I said. "They have to know exactly what they're doing. They have to know the 13.6 percent chance of death. They have to *want* to help Kara bring about this forced evolutionary event."

"I'm just trying to imagine who would *want*—"

"Geneticists," I said. "Disgraced, disgruntled, frustrated geneticists. People who think the Gene Protection Act was wrong. But also, and especially, those who believe the world is ending anyway, so why not throw a Hail Mary. In other words, geneticists who also identify as hard-line environmentalists. *Believers*."

"You need access to MYSTIC," Edwin said. "You think you can track them down."

"Yes. And I want Nadine in on this. She's one of the few people I trust not to shoot me in the back."

"Done. Do you know where your sister is right now?"

"I have a theory."

"I'll help you find her. Whatever you need."

I examined Edwin's face. Observed his heartbeat. In this moment, he wasn't lying to me, but that didn't mean he wouldn't change his mind later, when he was out of imminent danger. Or allow other forces to turn him against me.

"Why come to me?" Edwin asked. "You took a huge risk."

"Because I don't think my sister will anticipate me returning to the people who betrayed me. And that might just give me an edge in finding her."

"How do I know—"

"You can trust me?"

He nodded.

"You'll look at the data for yourself. You'll confirm the fatality rate. You'll imagine what will happen if that sweeps the globe, and you'll decide that if there's even a chance I'm telling the truth, you have no choice but to help me."

"Fair enough."

"I injected you with a sleeper gene package, which I whipped up in Ty Feld's lab. You aren't in danger right now, but I can trigger it at any time. And if something were to happen to me, it will be activated by an environmental trigger."

"What would it do?"

"Initiate a cascade of awful shit inside of you."

"I have no desire to—"

"I know."

I believed Edwin's intentions. What I didn't trust and couldn't control were the people in power above him, specifically the DoD. The same bosses who wouldn't allow Edwin to arrest and prosecute Ty Feld would be very interested in me if I were to fall back on their radar.

I stood. "Not to put too fine a point on it, but if I'm killed, or captured, or if you betray me again, you'll die."

"That's not going to happen, Logan."

I believed him.

He would try to protect me now. He might even sacrifice his life for it, because a bullet or a prison cell was a knowable horror. What I injected into orbit around his genome was the unknown stuff of nightmares.

We stood on a flat, featureless plain.

The sky was the same stark gray as the land, and there would've been no dimension to the space at all—no horizon, no sense of depth—if the ground wasn't darker by the slightest degree.

Suddenly, it broke open between us.

A black chasm spreading wider.

Ava and Beth were screaming my name as the distance between us grew. Ava looked at her mom. She looked across at me. Then she took several steps back and started running toward the edge.

No! I screamed. *You don't want this!*

But she continued running.

Faster, faster.

I watched as her foot touched the chasm's edge, and she leaped—

Arms pumping, legs still running in midair.

Sailing toward me out over the abyss.

We locked eyes for a moment, and Ava was smiling.

I'm coming, Dad. I'm coming with you.

She crashed into the side of the cliff, clutching the edge with her arms, feet scrambling for purchase. I rushed toward her, but as I reached down to grasp Ava's hand, she lost her grip, her fingers slipping through mine.

On my knees, I stared down into the black abyss as Ava fell away from me.

Plunging down into that endless dark.

I woke suddenly.

My heart was pounding in the darkness of the hotel room.

I was saying my daughter's name, quietly, over and over.

Climbing out of bed, I went to the bathroom and filled my glass.

Drank it down, filled it, then drank it down again.

I was beginning to calm down, my heart rate falling through the 120s. Something had happened during the dream. My emotions had broken free from their Faraday cage, and I felt—for an agonizing moment—the time I had been away from my family.

I crumpled down onto the bathroom floor.

A sob burst out of me. And then another. A dam of grief exploding, and for sixty seconds, I let myself go to pieces, staring unblinking at all I had lost.

Edwin picked me up in front of the hotel at midnight. I climbed into his 911E, and we sped across town.

The Porsche was one of the new "throwback" extended-range electrics with a quad-motor chassis that could do 0 to 60 in .9 seconds and had a range of 1,000 miles on full charge. Edwin kept trying to engage with me, but I was mentally elsewhere, preparing for my time on MYSTIC.

He parked on the curb on D Street SW, and we hurried down the walkway to a door on the quiet side of Constitution Center, which was, incidentally, the same door I'd gone through trying to escape this building more than a year and two upgrades ago.

I didn't think he'd be dumb enough to double-cross me this soon, a mere twenty-two hours after I'd shown up in his bedroom in the middle of the night, but I hoped I hadn't misread him. There was always a chance he could subject me to virtual interrogation and torture, with some choice chemical adjuncts. Take a run at getting me to explain what I'd injected into his system.

As we drew near, the door opened. My old partner, Nadine Nettmann, stood on the threshold, smiling.

"She knows everything," Edwin said.

As I stepped into the stairwell and the door swung shut behind me, Nadine threw her arms around my neck.

"You okay?"

There was a lot to unpack there. I just said, "Better now."

I'd experienced so little by way of physical touch since being kidnapped from this building almost fourteen months ago, and I could feel the interaction trying to lockpick the door to my emotional triggers.

"What?" Nadine asked. "You don't hug anymore?"

I embraced her.

After a moment, we came apart.

She looked up into my eyes. I saw compassion. Pity. Mostly fear. But that was natural in her position—seeing me for the first time in over a year, wondering what I'd become. Wasn't it?

"You look different."

"Made a few changes."

Edwin said, "Shall we?"

"I've got everything ready," she said. "Just what you asked for, Logan."

We climbed the stairs to the second floor, which housed the MYSTIC servers. The corridors were silent. Lights, on motion-activated sensors, flickered on above us as we moved down an empty hallway.

"I've got you set up in here," Nadine said, opening the door to a small, sterile office. The walls were bare. No personal flourishes. It had been empty for some time. The desk was clear except for the two desktops and keyboards I'd requested.

Because of the threat of cyberattacks and the ultra-sensitive data sets at play, MYSTIC could only be accessed via the stand-alone terminals deep within Constitution Center.

"You're logged in on my credentials," Nadine said. "What else do you need?"

"How long do I have?"

"You should probably be out of the building before six A.M.," Edwin said. "We'll keep an eye on the corridor. I don't think anyone will recognize you, but it'd be ideal if as few people as possible know you're back."

"Want me to stay in here with you?" Nadine asked. "Second set of hands."

"Thanks, but probably better if I work alone on this part."

They left, closing the door after them.

Before my second upgrade, I would've been overwhelmed at the prospect of finding Kara with MYSTIC—so many potential avenues of exploration. I wasn't so much looking for her now as confirming that my theory was right. I suspected that Kara was working out of either New York City or Miami. I would know momentarily.

I set to work, dividing my consciousness so I could type on each keyboard simultaneously.

At my fingertips, I now had one of the most powerful search engines ever created, and if I could cross-reference a handful of curated data groups, I would find her.

First things first—she would need a virologist. I had more of a background in genetics and virology than Kara did. Even now, as I was approaching her second-upgrade threshold, I would still need a virologist to engineer the perfect virus to carry the upgrade.

The database returned 378 names. I filtered the group down to 24 ranked candidates based on contributing factors that could lead to criminality. Since they were already in the system, they all had recent photos I could use to scrape the CCTV databases. I labeled the images from the likely-to-be-involved virologist data group "Block A."

At the same time, on the other computer, I was building my second group. In Glasgow, the man I'd performed an emergency tracheotomy on had told me he'd been a friend of Kara's from her military days. And while Kara and I were staying at the motel in West Virginia, I'd asked if she was still in touch with the people who rescued her in Myanmar. She'd answered, "They're some of my best friends."

She had upgraded Andrew, and I suspected she'd done the same for at least some of her other military cohorts. I could see now, looking back, that these were the only people in the world she really trusted.

Andrew had been on the team that freed her from the Myanmar militants. His full name was Andrew Kegan. There had been seven other Green Berets on Kara's rescue mission. Two were KIA during the op, but I ran checks on the remaining five with the clearance Edwin had gotten me for the DoD servers.

Nathaniel Jacks. Alexis Hurley. Rodney Viana. Deshawn Brown. And Madeline Ortega. All still alive.

Nathaniel Jacks was presently stationed in Pyongyang. Alexis Hurley was in jail in Arizona (again) following a drunk and disorderly arrest.

Madeline, Deshawn, and Rodney had all been honorably discharged.

Deshawn Brown's social media posts suggested he was recently divorced and living in Pensacola, Florida.

Rodney Viana was happily married and in his tenth year of law enforcement with the Columbus, Ohio, PD.

Madeline Ortega drove trucks for Freightliner.

I ripped as many photos as I could find of Ortega, Viana, Kegan, and Brown, and labeled this data group "Block B."

Reaching into my backpack, I pulled out the photo-realistic pencil sketch I'd made of Kara yesterday. This was exactly how she'd looked at our mother's house in Colorado, with her updated facial modifications. Kara was "Block C."

To finalize her transmissible upgrade, Kara would have to design a synthetic viral vector and transfect it into helper cells, which would then produce a packaged and potentially infectious virus, purified by column. She would then need to test it to make sure it performed as intended, with a high level of virulence and transmissibility in humans. Arguably, this was the hardest step, and one that would require a *willing* test group.

"Block D" comprised return targets on former scientists in our system who had contributing factors (terminal illness, debt, markers for radicalization, hard-line environmentalist leanings) that might lead them to risk their lives by becoming Kara's guinea pigs. Or her super-spreaders—her frontline fighters she would send to the ends of the earth. I got a ranked list of 291 candidates and uploaded their most recent photos.

I wrote my master query: *Return target = any surveillance camera that has captured images of any element of Block A + any element of Block B + Block C + any element of Block D, within time range T—twelve months.*

I also wanted to know if a ticket had been purchased for anyone in Block D (the potential test group and super-spreaders).

I wrote a subquery: *Return target = airline; hyperloop; bus; train tickets purchased by or on behalf of Block D, within time range T—twelve months.*

The left screen flashed up my master query results. It was a list of CCTV cameras' serial numbers. I called up a satellite map of America and overlaid the serial numbers on their corresponding locations.

While there were a few returns sprinkled around the

country, an inordinate number were clustered around the edges of New York City. There were none in Miami.

I stripped all fields except for my virologists in Block A. Out of twenty-four possible virologist candidates, two had been captured on multiple cameras and occasions in and around New York City.

I did the same for Kara's special forces crew in Block B and got multiple hits for Madeline Ortega, Deshawn Brown, and Rodney Viana, in and around New York City.

Now for my sketch of Kara. Five days ago, her face had been captured in Durango, Colorado. After that, nothing. There was a regional hyperloop station there. She had probably stayed in a motel and augmented her features before hopping a pod out of Colorado. And the face I'd seen in our mother's lodge had probably been modified there, which would explain why there were no hits on that image prior to Colorado.

For Block D, the viral test group and super-spreaders, out of 291 possible candidates, I saw multiple camera hits in and around New York City on 38 people. The number seemed low. Was this because the super-spreaders had yet to arrive in New York to receive their transmissible upgrades? Maybe those 38 were her test group.

I opened the results from my subquery—financial transactions related to travel. There was a list of flight and hyperloop ticket numbers for Block D.

Relief flooded through me.

Out of 291 AI-collated candidates, 94 people from Block D had international airline tickets purchased in their names, with destinations to all of the major cities I'd listed off for Edwin, and many, many more. And they were all flying out of Newark, La Guardia, JFK, Philadelphia, and Boston Logan International, over a period of two days, beginning in seventy-two hours.

I zoomed in on New York City and requested returns on the

surveillance cameras that had the highest frequency of image capture for Blocks A, B, and D.

Three hits came back.

A camera at the intersection of Furman Street and Doughty Street, near a waterfront park in Brooklyn Heights.

A camera at the intersection of Richmond Terrace and Nicholas Street, near North Shore Waterfront Esplanade Park at the northern tip of Staten Island.

And a camera at the intersection of Washington Street and Dudley Street, near Morris Canal Park in Jersey City.

Okay. Before this moment, I'd been operating on a mix of mental models of Kara's thought process and sheer speculation. But that last query felt solid. It built a foundation under my theory of how Kara was building her upgrade in secret.

I suspected those parks—all on waterfronts—were points of departure and arrival, for when Kara and her team traveled back and forth from her lab.

They were boating across New York Harbor, the East River, and the Hudson, into the flooded no-man's-land of Lower Manhattan—the perfect place to finalize her upgrade.

Lower Manhattan checked multiple boxes for Kara. A blackout zone with no CCTVs. Existing infrastructure in the form of abandoned mol-bio labs for Kara to plug into. Proximity to numerous international airports. And the densest population center in America, which would provide ample cover for watchlist scientists traveling to NYC to become beta-testers and super-spreaders, thus avoiding any suspicion from the GPA.

Simply by conjuring a satellite image of New York, I knew there were approximately eleven thousand buildings in the new ghost town of Lower Manhattan. Before it flooded, Lower Manhattan was home to more than four hundred life-science companies—far fewer than before the Gene Protection Act. Only some of those companies would have labs on site. Only some of those labs would be appropriate for Kara's needs. Only some of those appropriate labs would still be intact and accessible.

I could build a query to come up with a target list. It would still be a daunting number of buildings to contend with, and I would never have time to search them all.

But if my theory was right, I wouldn't have to.

Twenty-nine minutes after walking into the office, I walked out again. Nadine and Edwin were sitting across from each other in the long, silent corridor.

"That was fast," Nadine said.

Edwin watched me intently. I walked over and looked down at him. "I need a bio-SWAT team," I said. "Twelve people. Full tactical hazmat gear. Thermal-imaging drone. The works. They'll need rafts. I'll need a two-person kayak. For my load-out, I want NightShades, Chainmail body armor, a dozen C-4 door-breach charges, a flashlight, a Spyderco Harpy, a can of compressed air, and an FN Five-seveN with four magazines of armor-piercing rounds. Oh. And duct tape. Always duct tape." I looked at Nadine. "You'll come with me? One last raid? Like old times?"

"Um . . ." She looked at Edwin, then back at me. "Sure. When are you—"

"Now. We finish this raid before dawn."

"I'm sorry," Edwin said, struggling up onto his feet. "Where are we going?"

I didn't hesitate. "Miami."

14

NADINE AND I WALKED through the vaulted spaces of the great hall, our footfalls echoing in the church-like stillness that was Union Station at two in the morning.

I stopped at a kiosk and purchased two tickets to New York City, paying extra for a private pod.

Nadine said, "I thought—"

"Edwin's compromised."

"How do you know?"

"Saw it in his face."

"You're sure?"

"Positive."

We walked into a passageway, under a sign that read TO ALL NORTHBOUND TRAINS. By the time we got through security, we were second in the queue.

I scanned our tickets at the gate, and the attendant showed us to our pod. We climbed through the open door into a tight space with two facing chairs, sat across from each other, and strapped ourselves into the three-point harness system.

A modulated female voice said, *Departing for New York City in sixty seconds. Time to destination: twenty-nine minutes. Please secure all personal items under your seat. Thank you for riding Virgin Glideways.*

The pod glowed inside with gentle purple lighting and a calming soundtrack of synthesizers played over ocean waves.

We began to move.

There were slit windows built into the hyperloop tube at ten-meter intervals. I got four glimpses of the gates below Union Station and then we were off into the tunnel under the city.

"So what's the plan?" Nadine asked.

"We'll have to do this on our own."

"Do you know where in New York Kara is?"

The lights of the subterranean tunnel whipped past faster and faster until they were nothing but a blurred line of light through the curved smart-glass of our pod. At slower speeds, like now, the effect was distressingly strobe-like, providing jarring glimpses of the world outside. But at cruising speed near the sound barrier, these portholes flowed by so fast that they made a zoetrope, smoothly animating the world outside and creating the illusion that the pod was traveling under a continuous piece of glass.

I woke the touchscreen between the seats and dimmed the glass so we couldn't see the portholes.

"Lower Manhattan."

I could feel the 0.5g acceleration kicking in, watched the speed creeping up on the touchscreen:

300mph.

325mph.

350mph.

375mph.

Nadine took her phone out for the first time since we'd left

Constitution Center. I took out my phone as well, sent the text to Edwin I'd written on the ride over to Union Station.

Nadine looked suddenly frustrated.

"Everything all right?" I asked.

"You have a signal?"

"Yeah. I just sent a text to Edwin."

"Saying what?"

"To shut off your phone."

Her head snapped toward me with a sudden intensity.

I felt our pod lift out of the subterranean tunnel.

"When did she get to you?" I asked.

I could almost feel her body tensing. For a long moment, the only sound was the ocean waves coming through the speakers. Considering our rate of speed, the ride was preternaturally quiet.

Nadine's face remained implacable, or rather trying desperately to be so. But I observed her inner turmoil. The manic-thought train hurtling through her mind, wondering what I knew for sure and where I was still in the dark.

For a fraction of a second, she considered lying, and then I saw her realize that it would be pointless. Leaning back in her seat, she let out a quiet sigh.

"Last summer," she said. "I took some vacation time, went down to Tulum. Saw the ruins. Swam in the cenotes. I was alone. One day, I was sitting by the pool when who walks up but your sister. At first, I thought it was a wild coincidence. And she let me believe that. She told me she was also traveling by herself. Invited me to dinner. We'd had some chemistry that night we spent at her cabin in Montana. It was still there. She was charming and so damn smart.

"We hung out for a few days, and during a hike together in the jungle, she finally told me what had really happened to you. I thought you were dead."

"Weren't you—"

"Confused. Furious. Scared. She told me she had broken you out of a GPA black site. She told me your mother had upgraded both of you. She told me about your fight in New Mexico. And then she made her pitch for what she wanted to accomplish. And why. And how."

"She convinced you?"

"I couldn't deny her logic. When I worked at UNESCO, my job was expanding environmental education. We're in trouble. That night, she gave me the upgrade in my hotel room. How did *you* know?"

"Without MYSTIC, it would be risky, time-consuming, and practically impossible to find an army of willing super-spreaders. And Kara needed them to be willing. In light of the security measures in place, even super-upgraded Kara couldn't have accessed MYSTIC by herself.

"I was sure she had someone on the inside. Someone pulling candidates for her. I didn't know if it was you or Edwin, or someone else. I suspected you. Edwin's a true believer. But you feel the same way about the gene act as I do. And when we were in Montana with her that night, you talked about your job at UNESCO. You spoke *passionately* about it. And . . . you were my friend. You know my wife, my daughter. Kara would've known you'd be furious once she told you what the GPA did to me.

"Then tonight your body language was weird when I first saw you. So I ran one more test. When I came out of that office and Edwin asked where this raid was happening, I said Miami. He flashed surprise. You flashed relief."

Nadine reached for the touchscreen, undimmed the smart glass. We stared out the illusory window as the rolling country-side of Maryland slid past with a swift elegance at 760 mph. Everything brilliant under the moon.

"A billion people, Nadine. Any person who catches the upgrade virus and dies—that'll be on you. People you know and love will die."

"If you stop this," she said, "you may well be responsible for the extinction of *Homo sapiens*. That'll be on you."

"Consider this. For a time, Kara and I were the only upgraded humans on this planet. And what did we do? Immediately tried to kill each other over differences in belief. You got the upgrade and decided to help Kara release a virus that will lead to mass suffering and death. Doesn't feel like intelligence itself is the answer. It terrifies me to think of a world where we have all the same problems, a billion less friends, and everyone thinks they're smart enough to be infallible."

"So you'd rather have no world at all?"

"That's a false binary. We are in trouble, but that doesn't mean this is the only solution. Rejecting something that involves killing a billion people isn't the same thing as sticking my head in the sand while the world burns."

"What happens now?"

"You'll be taken into custody at Grand Central." I tapped the touchscreen, glanced at our trip monitor. "In seventeen minutes. What happens after that, you actually have some control over."

"I won't tell you where she is. You may know the general area. You don't know the building. And there are a lot of buildings in Lower Manhattan."

My phone lit up—Edwin messaging me the results of the Lower Manhattan building query I'd asked him to submit to MYSTIC. It was a list of thirty-seven predictively ranked companies that were candidates for Kara's lab. Too many.

I texted him back:

Cull that list down to buildings that are 500 feet or higher.

Nadine glanced down at her handbag, her pulse rate accelerating. I could smell her beginning to sweat.

We hadn't taken any government-issue firearms through security. But if she knew there was a chance I could return, would she have made advance preparations?

A capsule in her mouth she could crush to release a lethal vapor? Some other method of poisoning contained in that handbag?

She was reaching for the metal clasp that opened it.

I released my three-point harness, lunged across the pod, snatched her handbag.

"What the fuck, Logan?"

"What's in here?"

"Girl shit. Give it back."

For your own safety, please refasten your seatbelt.

I twisted the metal clasp, opening the bag. Nadine watched me closely.

When I saw the black-and-orange bands emerge from inside, my lizard brain took over. I flung the handbag to the other side of the pod.

Shit.

Nadine *had* brought a weapon.

The ultimate weapon.

She reached for the touchscreen, killed the lights.

I registered a hardy 6kHz whine.

"I'm sorry," Nadine said. "I hate this. You're my friend, you were my partner, but I can't allow you to interfere."

I could see a shape hovering between us now. I had experienced fear since receiving my mother's upgrade, but I hadn't come anywhere close to the terror of staring into the two sets of eyes—one compound, one ocelli—of the massive Asian giant hornet that hovered six inches from my face.

Please fasten your seatbelt immediately.

A second buzzed behind my right ear. I could feel the soft eddies from its powerful wings.

Nadine said, "Kara got your DNA from your mother's lodge in Colorado. She hacked these hornets, programmed them to seek out your unique genetic fingerprint by targeting the pheromones in your axillary sweat."

"What did she replace their venom with?"

"The inland taipan's."

I remembered a nature show I'd watched when I was fourteen. The inland taipan snake, endemic to Australia, carries the most potent venom in the world. One bite's worth is sufficient to kill a hundred grown men. It contains neurotoxins, hemotoxins, mycotoxins, nephrotoxins, and hemorrhagins.

The sound of a hornet at my right ear was getting louder.

The other one was drifting closer as well.

They had target-locked me.

Their stingers looked like they could punch through steel.

I saw Nadine's plan—it was a good one. Once the hornets had stung me, she would pull the emergency brake, bringing the pod to a halt under one of the exit platforms. She would escape through the ceiling hatch, leaving me here to die.

I sidelined the fear, dividing my consciousness four ways: hornet one, hornet two, Nadine, and the lights of the Philadelphia suburbs that were racing toward us.

The hornets were moving in to attack, and I was decelerating my perception of time, seeing everything now.

Speed: 589 mph.

Time to destination: 15 minutes.

Racing across pastureland, an old farmhouse glowing in the distance.

Nadine, wide-eyed, in the throes of eight conflicting emotions, but mainly fear and guilt.

Thinking I had nothing to swat the hornets with, and if those stingers nailed me—just one of them, anywhere—I was done. They were a half-inch long, and would easily penetrate my clothing.

I became very still.

If you do not fasten your seatbelt, you will be fined five hundred dollars and barred from future travel on a Virgin hyperloop.

I slowly raised my arms now, the hornets two inches from my skin, their stingers arcing toward my face and neck.

I watched my thumbs and forefingers gently close around their abdomens.

They writhed, buzzing maniacally, straining to stab my hands, the tips of their stingers millimeters from my epidermis.

I watched the shock flood through Nadine's face.

As her left hand reached up to release her shoulder harness, I bit the heads off the hornets, flicked the business ends of their bodies across the pod, and moved out of the way as Nadine launched herself at me.

She crashed into my seat and tried to right herself, but I was already on her, my right hand squeezing her throat, her eyes bulging, her hands clawing at my face.

"Be still," I said.

She kept fighting.

"Be still!"

She calmed herself. I eased my pressure around her neck but didn't let go. I glanced at my phone, praying Edwin had sent the new list. He had. Seventeen contenders.

"AJ Vaccines." I studied her face more closely than I'd ever studied anything in my life. "Alexion. BioCryst. Ennogen."

"What are you doing?" she asked.

"InGenX."

She closed her eyes and looked away from me. I leaned in closer, pinning her to my seat. "Open your eyes, Nadine." She wouldn't. I squeezed. "Look at me!" She looked at me. I continued reciting the list of companies Edwin had sent. "Kora Healthcare." No. "Leyden Delta." No. "Merck. Omega. Phoenix Labs."

Tears were running down her face.

"Ridge Pharma. Stirling-Anders. Teva Pharmaceuticals. Tor. Underell Solutions. Vifor. Zentiva."

"I guess you'll have to kill me."

I sat on her lap, clutched her throat with one hand, her face with the other—a face I had laughed and cried with. A face that had—the last time I'd seen it before my life was upended—comforted me as I grieved in front of a memorial my actions had played a part in building.

"Open your eyes." I said the names faster this time. "AJ Vaccines, Alexion, BioCryst, Ennogen, InGenX, Kora Healthcare, Leyden Delta, Merck, Omega, Phoenix Labs, Ridge Pharma, Stirling-Anders, Teva, Tor, Underell Solutions, Vifor, Zentiva."

And again, faster . . .

"AJVaccinesAlexionBioCrystEnnogenInGenXKoraLeyden DeltaMerckOmega."

I stopped.

Nadine stared up at me.

Trembling.

"It's Omega."

She said nothing.

I let go of her throat and threw myself back into her seat. I had been reasonably confident that Omega Laboratories had elicited a reaction—her racing pulse had increased 5 bpm, her systolic blood pressure spiking. But the look on her tear-stained face as she slumped back into my seat and stared out the window said everything.

I've failed.

I pulled out my phone and texted Edwin:

It's Omega. Get me floor plans for the entire building.

I looked at Nadine, said, "If you'd gone through with helping Kara, it would've destroyed you."

"You're probably right."

Our speed had slowed to 250 mph, and out the window, I could see the skyline of New York City—or what remained of it—glowing in the night.

15

NYPD WAS WAITING FOR us at the gate in Grand Central, and as they cuffed Nadine, Edwin stepped out of his pod, which had been a few minutes behind ours.

He walked over, looking Nadine up and down with a quiet fury that said more than his words ever could. As I watched them lead her away, I feared what would become of her. Would Edwin take her to a black site for study like he'd done with me? Subject her to virtual interrogation? She deserved better than what had happened to me. I couldn't believe it had come to this with her, but I had to push that grief away for now.

"Director Rogers?" We turned to the young female cop who had stayed behind. "I'm supposed to take you to the SWAT team."

We followed her out of the Grand Central underground, up through the main hall and onto Park Avenue, where she'd left her cruiser double-parked.

As we rode south, I studied the floor plans Edwin had sent me for 140 Broadway, the skyscraper that housed Omega Laboratories. Omega had been a beta-phase lab, occupying the entirety of floors 33 and 34. They built flu vaccines for clinical trials, prior to the final-phase product moving into mass production for the market. Of course, that was all before Lower Manhattan flooded.

"Maybe this is a mistake," Edwin said.

"What? This raid?"

"You have no idea what you're walking into. People are going to die. I could probably get authorization for a drone strike. Hit the building before dawn. Just fucking bring it down."

"I've heard estimates that ten thousand people live in Lower Manhattan."

"There'd be some collateral damage."

"And we'd never know for sure that we got her. Or the virus she built. I want eyes on her."

One forty Broadway was an International Style building of glass and black steel, its initial construction completed 101 years ago. I quickly scrolled through each of the fifty-one floors, committing the various layouts to memory.

We rolled past Union Square Park, then down Broadway until it terminated at the intersection of Houston Street, one of the new southern boundaries for inhabitable Manhattan. The flood zone wasn't a straight line across the island. There were variations. All of SoHo was underwater, but there were neighborhoods that high tide didn't submerge, like parts of Chinatown.

Stepping out of the cruiser, I approached the line of Jersey barriers and chain-link fencing that blocked travel farther south. In the distance, beyond the barricade, I could see water lapping at the street where the tide had stopped.

Behind me, the city lights glowed in their iconic shades of white and champagne. Straight ahead, the only thing visible was a ribbon of starlit sky, squeezed between black buildings. I'd seen photos of this ghost city at night, but I'd never been here.

There was something unnerving about the forest of featureless, black monoliths that now comprised Lower Manhattan. Of course, it wasn't completely abandoned. The homeless had taken over three years ago. They called it New Venice. Far in the distance, I could see light sources emanating through broken windows—open fires in high-rise encampments.

Edwin came up behind me. "They know you've got the lead here."

"You trust them?"

"It's just NYPD bio-SWAT. They do what they're told."

I climbed over the concrete barricade and slipped through an opening in the fence.

"Hey," Edwin called after me. I glanced back. "Watch yourself."

Halfway down the next long block, I saw shadows and flashlights.

I announced myself as I drew within range, my inherent night vision overlaying details from the existing star- and city-light.

I saw four rafts and a dozen SWAT officers making final weapons checks. Two people in night-camo hazmat suits finished loading gear into a raft and walked over.

We introduced ourselves. The team leader was Bob Noyes, a burly, bearded man who looked like he could do some real damage. Beside him stood a silver fox named Aaron Brandes, who was presently shoving a lithium battery into a drone.

Noyes called everyone over. "Let's focus up!"

The team hadn't pulled their hoods on yet, so I made a quick scan, trying to establish eye contact with each of them, seeing what I could read in the low light.

Nothing I observed suggested deception. I saw exhaustion. One instance of mild intoxication. Two bored sociopaths, hungry for violence. But more than anything, uncertainty and fear.

And I couldn't blame them. The more I understood 140 Broadway, the more I could see why Kara had chosen it. Up there on floor 33 or 34, she had a perfectly defensible position. It was going to force me to do something crazy.

"The target is Kara Ramsay." No one asked if she was my sister. I suspected they didn't really know who I was. "You should have a recent sketch of her. She's operating out of One forty Broadway, twenty-four blocks due south of our current position. You should also have the floor plans by now."

"How much resistance are we expecting?" Noyes asked.

"Several guards with special forces training. But these aren't ordinary soldiers. They have abilities you've never seen."

"They know we're coming?"

"I don't think so, but they'll be ready. I suspect the lab is on the thirty-third or thirty-fourth floor. Obviously, there's no elevator access. There are four stairwells. Two toward each end of the building. When we get there, I'll want a twenty-minute head start. Take up positions *outside* the stairwell entrances on the ground floor and wait for my signal. Four stairwells. Four teams. There will be motion-activated surveillance cameras, so use your personal signal jammers. I would anticipate barricades. Choke points."

"Shooting galleries," Noyes said.

"Basically. And now you know everything I know. We'll head south, make a pit stop at the intersection of Fulton for drone surveillance and final comms setup. Any questions?"

As the team returned to their rafts, Brandes handed me my loadout. I donned the Chainmail body armor and fastened the magnetic straps. Then I hung my NightShades from the front of my collar and opened the small pack, removing the weapon I'd requested—a Belgian-made FN Five-seveN with low recoil and a twenty-round magazine capacity. I slipped three magazines into my pocket, inserted the fourth into the pistol, and jacked a round into the chamber.

The SWAT team finished stowing their gear, then dragged their rafts to the water's edge. I followed, pulling the kayak behind me until it floated eight inches over the white dotted lines that had once designated a bus-only lane.

I climbed in, got situated in the cockpit, then grabbed the paddle and pushed myself off into deeper water.

Three in the morning now.

A cold street wind biting down the urban canyon.

The four rafts floated a short distance ahead, the sounds of the city behind us echoing through the corridor of dark buildings. The ubiquitous sirens and horns. The drunken cacophony of last-callers tumbling out of bars. And all of it growing fainter and fainter.

After seven blocks, all I could hear were the oars dipping into black water.

We paddled south down Broadway, the water deepening. Past flooded Duane Reades, a Sephora, a Forever 21, a Bloomingdale's, banks, and bodegas.

Occasionally, I would see a flicker of firelight through a broken window, smell the acrid bite of woodsmoke or whatever was being burned for warmth.

We passed City Hall and St. Paul's.

From one of the skyscrapers high above, I heard the fragile notes of a violin—someone playing "Tonight" from *West Side Story*. It echoed down the dark and flooded avenue, between the hulking shadows of what had once been the greatest city in the world. *Tonight, tonight, it all began tonight, I saw you and the world went away.*

Almost two miles from where we started paddling, just beyond the intersection of Fulton and Broadway, the rafts began drifting to the left side of the street, gathering under the old signage of a Shake Shack.

We had made good time—just two blocks now from 140 Broadway.

I eased my kayak alongside one of the rafts. Brandes lifted the drone from the bottom of his, powered it on, then fired up a small laptop. He tossed the drone into the air, its propellers whirling it off down the street.

After a moment, he said, "I've got a visual." I watched him from my kayak. He was hunched over the tiny laptop with a joystick plugged into the side.

"Anything of note?" I asked.

"Not yet. Just a tall, dark . . . Jackpot."

"What?"

"Your intel was solid. Looks like someone put up IR panels around an entire floor."

Infrared panels were built-in defenses against thermal-imaging surveillance, usually in the form of walls that lit up the entire lab, making it impossible to determine where and how many people were working. It also made it impossible to target the people inside with thermal scopes.

He took a few more laps around the building, investigating the lobby, roof, and secondary entrances, before piloting the drone back to us.

Noyes handed me an earpiece and a wireless rig.

"Switching over to comms," he said. "Channel two."

The building loomed black against the starry sky as we approached the intersection of Broadway and Liberty Street. The SWAT teams donned their hoods, and two rafts separated from the flotilla, heading down Liberty.

I followed the remaining two, which peeled off across the

plaza toward the Isamu Noguchi cube—once bright red, now rusting and submerged in six feet of water. It had been the showpiece of the main entrance before the city flooded.

I continued paddling until I reached Cedar Street, between 140 Broadway and the Equitable Building. As I drifted in the darkness between black skyscrapers, Noyes's voice came through my earpiece. *"This is A-team. We're approaching the main lobby entrance. Initiating personal signal jammer. Logan, which stairwell are you taking? Over."*

"No stairwell," I said. "Over."

"There's another way up? Over."

"Nope. I'll be climbing. Over."

There was a brief pause and then: *"Sorry, I thought you said you'd be climbing. Over."*

"You heard right. Over."

"Climbing the building? Over."

"Yes. Over."

"C-team approaching the Nassau Street entrance. Over."

I paddled my kayak to the side of the building and stared up at a sheer black wall.

"B-team in position at the southwest stairwell. Over."

I opened my backpack and dug out a door-breach charge—a candy-bar-size piece of C-4 with a timer and blasting cap. I shoved it into my pocket, then unlaced my shoes, tied them together, and hung them from my pack.

I knew the stairwells—especially the entrances and lower floors—would be under surveillance and likely booby-trapped. The moment someone set foot inside one of them, Kara would know. It would be a race to reach her through a dark, mazelike building with all sorts of nasty shit waiting in the wings. But if I could get inside first, entering a stairwell high above the lower floors, I might have a chance at reaching her undetected.

"D-team in position at the southeast stairwell. Over."

The water came halfway up the ground floor. I stood carefully on the kayak, which shifted precariously under my weight.

Reaching up, I took hold of a vertical beam that separated the window bays. It was a three-inch strip of textured black aluminum, and the only element of the exterior I could actually grasp.

I pulled myself up, clutching the vertical beam with both hands, my bare feet purchased on the cold glass. Reaching my left hand over my right, I squeezed the beam, then lunged for the next handhold.

After three identical moves, I arrived at the first horizontal handhold—a meager lip at the base of the second-floor window bay. It wasn't much, but I could dig my fingers into a half-inch gap and give my triceps a rest.

"A-team in position at northwest stairwell. Over."

"C-team in position at northeast stairwell. Over."

Noyes said, *"All teams standing by. Over."*

I continued to climb, hand over hand, up the vertical piece of metal. I knew I was strong, but I hadn't tested my upgrade to this extent. In my life before, I wouldn't have made it up a single story of this building, but tonight I climbed the first three with effortless grace.

It was only as I reached the fifth floor that I noticed the first tremor of muscle fatigue in my triceps. I knew they'd be fine. The real strain was developing in my adductor pollicis, first dorsal interosseus, and flexor pollicis brevis—the finger and hand muscles involved in pinching and grasping.

Noyes came through in my earpiece: *"Logan, how we doing, buddy? Over."*

I could hear the stress in my voice as I answered, "Five floors up. Need to focus now. Out."

I glanced down, instantly relegating into the background

noise the part of my consciousness that wanted to scream at the vomit-inducing distance between me and the tiny kayak. I reached up once more, pinching a grip on the vertical beam, the balls of my feet scrambling up the glass as I ascended from the seventh to the eighth floor.

Sweat was pouring down my back, my legs, dripping off my heels. I clung once more to the unforgiving, half-inch steel ledge, my gastrocnemius and soleus (calf muscles) quivering. It was my glucose levels, which fueled my muscles, getting dangerously low, veering me into hypoglycemia. While my triceps and pectorals were burning, they weren't the real problem. It was my fingers. They were nearing the end of their ability to keep me on this wall. The pain wasn't the problem. I could wall that off. Eventually—pain or not—my finger muscles and tendons would simply fail.

I looked down.

It would be a 37-meter fall into six feet of water. I weighed eighty-four kilograms. I would fall for 2.75 seconds. Speed at impact 26.93 meters per second. 96.95 kilometers per hour. 30,458 joules of energy at impact. Survival unlikely but possible, although six feet of water was nothing. It wouldn't stop me from slamming at considerable speed into the submerged sidewalk.

Broken legs for sure—I'd probably drown.

I looked up the face of the building, which seemed to meld into the night sky. I'd hoped to reach the tenth floor, but it was now or never.

I reached into my pocket, now clinging to the building with one hand, fighting through another wave of muscle cramps as I dug out the C-4 charge and carefully ripped the adhesive covering away with my teeth.

With one hand, I set a timer on the blasting cap for thirty

seconds. I would've liked more time to climb away from the charge, but I figured I had less than a minute of clinging to 140 Broadway left in me.

I started the timer and stuck the charge on the lower half of the ninth-floor window. Until this moment, I'd been holding my adrenaline back, knowing I'd need it at the end. Now I let the fear creep in, a sliver of blinding panic, and with it the adrenaline I would need to not fall.

I down-climbed fourteen feet to the next floor, got a two-handed grip on the vertical beam.

The blast nearly shook me off the building, but I fought to hold on, glass raining down on me, my grip slipping.

I reached up for the next handhold, squeezing with every-thing in my being, squeezing so hard I was afraid I'd break my fingers, and kept climbing, sweat running down my face, burn-ing my eyes, and I could see the gaping hole the charge had blown in the side of the building. It had twisted some of the metal into horizontal shapes that called out to me for hand-holds. I didn't trust them.

I stayed on the intact vertical beam until the ninth-floor opening was just within reach. With my left hand pinching as hard as I could, I flung myself at the ninth floor, glass slicing through my right forearm as I clung to the edge, my feet dan-gling over open space.

I was *going* to fall.

I shot my left arm into the room, needing something, any-thing, and I clutched what felt like the leg of a desk.

It was the first real handhold since leaving the kayak, and I leveraged myself up over the edge and rolled into a dark room.

For a moment, I lay gasping on the floor—my legs, arms, and hands trembling with exhaustion and strain. After thirty seconds, I sat up and studied the damage to my arm. Eight glass shards protruded from my right brachioradialis—two of them deep in the forearm muscle. I reached into the pack, emerged with the roll of duct tape. I ripped off a long piece, stuck it to the desk, and began removing the glass. Blood sheeted down my arm. Pain threatened; I walled it away. When I'd dug out the final, deepest jag, I carefully squeezed the gashes together and wrapped my entire forearm in duct tape—hoping it would hold until I could properly stitch myself back together.

I put my socks and shoes back on, wondering if anyone on the floors above me had heard the blast.

I was sitting in what appeared to be a library, surrounded by bookshelves filled with legal volumes. Came to my feet, shouldered my pack, and moved around a dusty conference table into a hallway.

I slipped on my NightShades. Straight ahead stood a reception desk. I walked past the bank of dormant elevators to the north side of the building.

I was on the ninth story. The lab was twenty-five floors above me, and I had four stairwells to choose from.

Turning left, I headed for the northwest stairwell.

Seventeen minutes, twenty-nine seconds had elapsed since I'd started my ascent. I pulled my Five-seveN pistol as I approached the stairwell door.

I opened it slowly.

Complete darkness.

With no ambient light to work with, my NightShades were useless. I went to the nearest office, and as I grabbed a stapler off the desk, my phone buzzed in my pocket. I took it out— Edwin calling.

"Hey," I said.

"Where are you?" Something was wrong.

"Why?"

"Are you in the building?"

"Yeah."

"There's a second team en route."

"Why?"

"They're going to land on the roof—"

"No, you can't let that—"

"I was just told . . ." He lowered his voice. *". . . this isn't my op anymore."*

"How is that possible?"

"Your time in Virginia . . ." He meant when he'd held me in a glass cage. *"There was video footage. People found out. People way above my pay grade. I thought if we moved quickly on this thing, we could stay under the radar. Obviously, I miscalculated. They were watching me. I had no idea."*

It had to be the Department of Defense. Had they been searching for me and Kara all this time? The military applications of an enhanced human were the stuff of DARPA dreams, and in some ways even scarier than Kara's plan. At least her motivations came from a place of wanting to help our species. She wanted to upgrade everyone. I had a hunch our government wouldn't take such an egalitarian approach.

"They're about to come in hard."

"Who?" He didn't answer. "Edwin. Tell me what I'm up against."

"JTF-Black." Shit. It was the domestic-based Joint Task Force unit comprised of former Delta, SEAL Team Six, Army Special Operations, Marine Raiders, and federal law enforcement officers from groups like FBI HRT. The elite of the elite.

"High-value target extraction?" I asked.

"I think it's safe to assume they want you alive. Both of you. And whatever Kara has built. I need you to know, Logan, I didn't sell you out. I had no idea—"

"How many?"

"They usually roll in teams of eight."

"What about the SWAT? They seemed fine when—"

"They aren't working for you anymore. I'm sorry. JTF-Black is six minutes out, so whatever you're planning, do it fast and get out of there."

The line went dead.

Five seconds later, another voice came through my earpiece.

"Logan, this is Noyes. You make it inside? What's your position? Over."

I could hear the deception in his voice. It sounded like honey. I ripped out my earpiece and chucked it with the wireless unit over my shoulder.

I opened the door to the stairwell, set the stapler against the jamb. As I shined the flashlight up the next flight of stairs, I heard footfalls and then Noyes's voice drifting up from six floors below.

"I think he made us. Also, we just ran into . . ."—I missed a few words—*". . . third and fourth floors. We're going down to try another way."*

When they began moving again, I turned on the flashlight and started up the stairwell, trying to keep my footfalls from echoing inside the column of concrete.

As I crossed the landing for the fifteenth floor, the building shook. I heard a sound like distant thunder, and dust motes floated in the beam of light. I glanced down, didn't see fire or hear any screams. Whatever had exploded had been in another stairwell, and if Kara hadn't known we were here two seconds ago, she did now.

I flew up the stairs.

17.

18.

19.

20.

Four minutes until JTF-Black set down on the roof. Wouldn't matter how loaded up they were. They didn't stand a chance against Kara's upgraded special forces pals. Worse, all of this incoming mayhem would only serve to slow me down and provide cover for Kara's escape.

24.

25.

26.

I caught an odd scent in the air—was that tar?

27.

Something glinted in the light above me. I slowed to a jog, finally coming to a stop at the landing between 28 and 29.

The smell was stronger here.

Coils of concertina wire had been strung from railing to railing and floor to ceiling, like Christmas decorations in hell. Razors gleamed in the light. From what I could see, they extended up an entire flight of stairs.

I knew what I was smelling—the C-4 that was packed inside the olive-green shell of the claymore, just six feet away from where I stood, on the landing, perched on a stand with wires running under the door to floor 29. The business end of the remote-controlled mine was facing me. It contained roughly 1.5 pounds of C-4 and 700 steel ball bearings. Across the façade, I could read the words FRONT TOWARD ENEMY.

I turned and ran, leaping down to the next landing and continuing my sprinting descent until I reached the door for 26.

Locked.

I dug another door breach out of my bag, slapped the charge on near the handle, set the timer for twenty seconds, and ran down to 24.

After the chest-squeezing explosion, I returned to 26. The door had been blown fifteen feet into the next floor. I stepped through the wreckage, my eyes watering against the heavy C-4 stench of tar and motor oil.

I could see without the flashlight here. The floor was mostly cubicle space, with a few offices and conference rooms along the exterior walls. I hustled to the northeast stairwell, opened the door. The flashlight shone through a thick layer of smoke, and there was another scent in the air: the sickly-sweet odor of charred flesh.

Four floors above me, I saw the glimmer of more concertina wire.

I sprinted down a row of cubicles.

There was no smoke in the southeast stairwell, but I heard voices far below and saw more wire blocking the stairwell several floors above.

As I ran for the last stairwell, I marveled at Kara's planning. She'd built a lethal barricade between any threat and herself. But to get out of the building, she'd have to make her way down these stairwells, fighting through attackers along the way. And no doubt the DoD—or whoever they had hunting us—would have reinforcements guarding the exits too. SWAT snipers on overwatch, at the very least.

Even if all went well for me, I'd be facing the same problem.

I was betting Kara had an escape route up her sleeve. An elevator shaft? Some secret stairwell that wasn't in the blueprints? If she didn't—or if I couldn't figure it out in time—this would be a suicide mission.

Two minutes—if Edwin had told me the truth—before JTF-Black's arrival.

I stepped into the southwest stairwell.

No smoke. No noise. No wire immediately above.

I surged up the stairs, powering my way through 28.

29.

30.

Gunshots erupted somewhere in the building—the racket of automatic fire, and then another blast, not above or below, but lateral to my position.

I kept climbing.

Through 31.

32.

Just two floors away, and I was searching meticulously, but I didn't see a threat—no sign of wire or explosives.

Light bled through around the seams of the door to 34. Was it rigged to blow? I pressed my face to the edges of the door and inhaled—no trace of that motor oil smell.

JTF-Black would be landing in one minute.

I grabbed the door handle, tried to turn it.

Locked. And a breach charge would reveal my presence.

But these were fire stairs. Doors could be locked from the outside, but from the inside, they had to be easily opened in case of an emergency. Usually, this was accomplished by means of an REX (request-to-exit) sensor on the door's interior side, which uses passive infrared to detect temperature changes in proximity to the door. If the sensor detects a change in temperature—caused by a person approaching—it transmits a message to unlock the door.

The keyword there being *change* in temperature. Not necessarily an increase.

I rummaged through my pack, found the can of compressed air. I ripped off the packaging, inserted the straw into the nozzle, and got down on the floor, hoping there would be enough space between the bottom of the door and the threshold plate to slide the straw underneath.

I found a chip in the threshold, worked the straw through, and held the can upside down. If I sprayed it upright, only the fluorocarbon vapor at the top would be released. But when inverted, a liquid is forced out instead. This liquid, under great pressure, quickly evaporates and expands to become a gas at room temperature.

The thermodynamic process of adiabatic cooling would hopefully chill the immediate area on the other side of the door and—if I was right about all this—trick the sensor into thinking someone was approaching from the other side.

I squeezed the trigger, listening as the liquid hissed out on the other side, the can growing cold in my hand.

I took off my NightShades, reached up, grabbed the door handle.

This time it turned.

It occurred to me that there might also be a secondary sensor on the door itself, which, if opened, would break the alignment with its partner sensor on a facing wall and trigger an alarm—something as simple as a phone message to Kara and her security team.

Nothing I could do about that. I was out of time.

As I eased the door open, I heard machine-gun fire high above, followed by the deeper, locomotive chugging of a chain gun.

And then a shuddering *boom*.

I charged into the light, my Five-seveN up, fluorescents burning down on a white corridor, something pulling at my attention from the left—

I turned just in time to see a burning Black Hawk falling past a wall of windows, the rotors still spinning, cutting through the building in a cataclysm of exploding glass and cloven metal, the pilots screaming in the cockpit—and gone.

Then 3.8 seconds later, an explosion rocked the building as the helicopter smashed into Cedar Street.

And I was on the move, jogging down the corridor past

rooms filled with cots and medical equipment, wondering if this was where Kara's viral test group had been given her experimental upgrade for the first time.

On the other side of the elevators, I saw a stainless steel bioreactor.

Glass columns.

Centrifuges.

I crept into a sprawling lab that took up the eastern half of the thirty-fourth floor, unable to escape the thought that Kara was already gone.

All along the far wall, server racks whirred quietly. Behind a metal door, I could hear the louder, muffled humming of the generators that powered the lab.

I moved past a -80° C refrigerator, then two controlled rate freezers.

Through the potent smell of solvents, I caught a familiar scent—it was the same shampoo Kara had been using at our mother's house in Colorado.

I heard something around the next corner: the soft clink of metal. From my pack, I pulled another breach charge and set a timer for three seconds.

I peered around the corner.

Kara stood at a biosafety cabinet, her back to me, frantically loading what appeared to be auto-injectors into a small backpack. Beside her was Madeline Ortega, holding an H&K MP7 that was already swinging toward me, our eyes locking, hers flashing surprise.

But she had the drop.

I wouldn't be able to place her in my sights before—

I swung back behind the corner as 4.6×30mm armor-piercing bullets shredded through the wall at 950 rounds per minute. Ortega's body language had indicated she'd be coming after me, so I engaged the door-breach timer, dropping the charge as I ran.

Three.

Two.

As I approached the elevators, I glanced back.

One.

Saw Ortega rounding the corner, raising her H&K.

She disappeared in a bright, loud bang, and I turned into the bank of elevators as Kara shot past down the north-side corridor.

Where was she going?

The northeast stairwell couldn't get her to the ground floor. Neither could the southwest or northwest. They all had barricades between floors 30 and 32. She'd have to take the southeast stairwell to 26, cut over to the northwest stairwell, descend to 6, *then* over to the southwest stairwell, which was the only one with no reports of wire or claymores in the first six floors.

If she was heading down, I needed to wait in the southeast stairwell, which she'd have to pass through. But that didn't feel right. Even if she got through me, it'd be far too easy for forces to surround the four building exits on the ground floor.

But if she went up, she'd just be trapping herself—right?

No. Fuck. Of course. She *was* heading up. It all made sense now. I knew where she was going, what she was trying to do. And I didn't have long to stop her.

I turned around, rushed back down the corridor toward the southwest corner of the building, leaping over what was left of Madeline Ortega.

Ten seconds from the stairwell, the door exploded.

I recognized Noyes and Brandes through their face shields. They were standing in the doorway, and I was absorbing it all at once:

Noyes's eyes going wide in the clearing smoke.

Brandes raising his assault rifle.

Ortega's blood running down the walls.

Everything decelerating.

I could've put them both down in less than a second, but I didn't want to kill them; these were cops who'd been roused from their beds in the middle of the night, with no concept of what they'd walked into.

I was still running toward them, a half second having passed since they'd blown the door off its hinges, and the thirty-fourth floor layout flaring into focus in my mind's eye—straight ahead, there should be a hallway that bisected the floor.

Brandes pulled his rifle snug against his shoulder, hesitating, aiming for my legs, and Noyes drew an X-30 sidearm—a military-grade nonlethal munitions weapon that fired Taser-like bullets.

I veered left—the smallest feint—and saw Brandes and Noyes overreact, the muzzle flash blooming out of the assault rifle in a flower of fire, rounds raking the wall, and as the recoil pushed both men slightly off balance, I launched right down the other hallway.

Narrow.

Fluorescent lights flickering.

Four doorways on the left, four on the right.

The first two opened into an office and storage closet, respectively, the third a breakroom, which I ducked inside.

Two circular tables. A kitchenette. A water cooler. The smell of old, burned coffee and something rotting in a trash bin.

I stood just inside the threshold, their footfalls coming.

A door opened, closed.

Then another.

Noyes saying, "We found Logan on thirty-four. Get up here if you can. We're engaging."

Their Tyvek suits crinkling.

Close now.

Brandes said, "Cover this door, I'll open it," and the way his voice carried, I could tell they were clearing a room across the hall, which meant their backs would be facing me.

I charged out of the breakroom.

My consciousness dividing—

I'd caught them off guard, Noyes spinning toward me at a creeping pace, and I was accelerating at him, reaching, not for the weapon, but for Noyes's trigger finger, breaking it as he put me in his sights, and Brandes ages behind—I could see the slowly dawning horror in his eyes as he realized he was fucked. Noyes shrieked as I snatched the X-30, ducked a haymaker, and shot him point-blank in the leg to avoid any body armor. As he seized and toppled over, I sidestepped Brandes's frantic firing and shot him in the leg as well. Both men twitched violently on the floor, the electrified bullets short-circuiting their systems. I grabbed zip ties from the bundle on Noyes's waist, then quickly fastened each man's wrists and ankles, hoping I still had time to intercept Kara.

The southwest stairwell was hazy with smoke.

I turned on the flashlight and raced up the stairs.

As I reached the landing between 36 and 37, the door to 38— one and a half floors above me—burst open. I hid my light, glimpsed another flashlight beam streaking the walls, heard the lightning-fast patter of my sister's footfalls rushing skyward.

I followed carefully.

Heard a door creak open.

Her light vanished.

I felt confident she'd left the stairwell at 40, and as I reached it, I eased the door open and slipped through, just as the northwest stairwell door clanged shut.

I ran across 40.

Sweating again, past abandoned offices, a copy room, restrooms, until I reached the northwest stairwell door.

I pulled it open to the sound of footsteps climbing above me.

The walls were strobed with my sister's light, but I didn't give chase this time. Just listened. Counting the floors as she continued to climb.

42.

I modeled an image of her progress up the stairs based on the speed of her footfalls.

43.

44.

I heard a door swing shut and lock. She had gotten off at 44, and I knew she wasn't going any higher. She didn't need to.

I ran the entire length of the building, back to the northeast stairwell, and as I climbed toward 44, I heard boot-falls on the steps above me and two distinct voices drifting down.

Had some of the JTF-Black team made it out of the helicopter? Because that was one thing to deal with. But if these were Kara's people . . .

I strained to hear the voices.

Two men, talking a little too fast.

One saying: ". . . be safe, we'll meet you there. Yeah, we'll be fine."

I knew that voice. It matched the one I'd heard perusing social media tonight—a video of Deshawn Brown from a year ago at his youngest daughter's birthday party. Which would make the other guy Rodney Viana, the happily married cop from Ohio. Both upgraded special forces.

I was trying to think how I would take out the two of them. The chances were better than even, but not by much. In all likelihood, I'd kill one of them and they would kill me, their inherent training gifting them a huge advantage.

So I wouldn't try to take them out.

I cut my light, needing to decelerate everything now more than ever.

Boot-falls, two different cadences, the lighter, shorter man in the lead.

Their scent preceding them—salt and the faintest remnant of a fragrance—Old Spice?—and the pungent reek of nitroglycerin from recent gunfire.

Their flashlight beams streaking across the walls.

I stood on the landing just below 43, and I could see the space perfectly in my mind's eye.

They were fifteen seconds away.

In the pitch blackness, I climbed the steps to 43, hopped over the railing, and lowered myself until I hung from the second step from the top—out of sight from anyone descending.

They were two floors above me.

Now passing 44.

Now the landing between 44 and 43.

Then 43, one of their boots passing within millimeters of my fingers as I clutched the edge of the step. They were heading down to the 43/42 midpoint landing, both flashlights momentarily aimed at the floor, and I pulled myself up as they reached the landing, smoothly swinging my legs over the top of the railing and just out of their sight line as they made the turn, easing down silently, then rolling across the steps as they continued down the next flight.

A beam of light swept toward me, a second away—had one of them heard me?

I slithered soundlessly down the stairs, watching as the light passed over the steps where I'd just been sprawled, and I nestled against the wall as tightly as I could, not breathing, not moving, and their boot-falls still descending.

After a moment, I couldn't see the lights anymore.

I waited, imagining their progress, just wanting them gone before I—

Shouting broke out, muzzle flashes lighting up the corridor eight floors below. They had engaged with someone. I came to my feet and ran up to 44. The door was locked. I pulled out a breach charge, set it for ten seconds, and ran down to 43.

The door exploded.

I rushed back up to 44 and raced through the open doorway.

The floor was wide open—nothing but the elevators and stairwells. It had been abandoned during a remodel, leaving ductwork exposed, electrical wiring hanging from the ceiling.

I saw a figure crouched down at the far end of the building.

I glanced back at the newly doorless entrance to the northeast stairwell—empty.

Eleven seconds from Kara.

She was crouched down, securing something to her back, and when she saw me, she sprang to her feet and began to run—just thirty feet back from a window that was missing an entire panel of glass.

I stopped at the bank of elevators, ninety-eight feet away, letting my consciousness divide and time slowing as I registered the pain in my fingers, gunshots still echoing several floors below, the cold wind blowing through the open window off New York Harbor, the lights of Jersey City in the distance, and a cascade of heartbreak at what I was about to do, which I immediately walled away.

I raised my pistol, focusing on Kara's right leg, which now moved so slowly I had no doubt of my aim.

I fired, she fell—sliding across the floor toward the open window—and then I was sprinting toward her again as she rolled onto her back, facing me now, a weapon in her hand, her finger a split second from squeezing.

I fired again, hit her center mass, watched her punch back,

her arms falling to her sides, the pistol clattering to the floor out of her left hand.

She was reaching for the gun when I arrived, and I kicked it across the polished concrete slab and through the open window frame.

Kara's leg was bleeding, and I could hear in her respirations that her right lung had been punctured. With each breath she wheezed. Blood trickled out of the corners of her mouth, and I forced her right hand open. She clutched a bundle of black fabric, which was attached to an S-folded strap that connected to the pack she wore.

Her eyes were open, watching me, a deep pain exuding from them, and I could not let this emotion touch me.

"Are there still remnants of the viral upgrade in your lab?" I asked. "Something the government could take and—"

"Yes, but the lab won't be here much longer."

"When?"

She glanced at her wristwatch. "Ninety-two seconds."

I loosened the leg and chest straps, Kara whimpering as I rolled her over and freed her shoulders. I awkwardly maneuvered the entire harness rig down her legs. She'd worn the Tumi backward, strapped to her chest. I ripped it off, opened it, stared down at roughly a hundred auto-injectors.

I inspected the harness and container for signs of damage from the bullet. I saw none. It was still inside of Kara. Stepping into the harness, I finally shouldered the pack. Tightened the leg straps. Cinched the chest strap. The cord connecting the pilot chute to the container had become tangled, and I stepped away from Kara, letting the bridle slowly unfurl.

"So this is it?" she asked, struggling mightily to speak. "Just going to let us destroy ourselves?"

I began to refold the bridle. No expertise beyond what I'd

seen in Kara's hand and a video I'd haphazardly watched about BASE jumpers on a bored Tuesday night, many years ago.

I lifted the Tumi bag, strapped it to my chest, said, "You can't kill humanity to save humanity. Human beings are not a means to an end."

Kara took a ragged breath. "Logan."

"What?"

"I can't see a thing."

There were voices in the northeast stairwell. I needed to go. Instead, I sat down behind my sister and pulled her toward me, enveloping her in my arms.

"Don't think of me this way," she said. She was shivering violently, and I could feel the warmth of her blood running onto my leg. I smelled its coppery scent. "We were more than this."

"I don't just see you in this moment. I see you in all of your moments. All of *our* moments. We had some good ones."

"Eighteen," she said.

"What?"

She coughed blood. "We had eighteen perfect moments."

I thought about it.

"Nineteen."

"How do you get nineteen?"

"This one. But I'm sorry to have it."

Kara was crying. She was dying and had let her defenses go. I could feel mine wavering.

I wanted to say something in our last moment together. Something profound. Kara did instead. It was the simplest of things. But it was everything.

She reached back, her hand touching my face.

"You can't do nothing, Logan."

I wanted to tell her how much I would miss her. How sorry I was for every time I almost picked up the phone to call and didn't. For not being more in her life. But the words caught in my throat.

Her hand slipped away.

"Kara?"

I felt something go out of her.

Whatever I was holding wasn't my sister anymore.

I eased her down onto the concrete, closed her empty eyes. I saw her, not as this shell, but in a perfect memory: twelve years old, riding ahead of me on her bicycle down the dirt road outside our grandparents' house. It was late afternoon, and in the golden light, she glanced back at me and Max, taunting us to, *Catch up! Go faster!*

I came to my feet, my pistol in one hand, my other holding the pilot chute. I walked to the edge of the glassless window and looked down.

Kara had come to this side of the building because it was the only aspect that didn't have another skyscraper crowding up against it. I looked out over the plaza and Broadway, and what had once been Zuccotti Park—a 33,000-square-foot oasis in the heart of the Financial District. Now just a patch of dead, flooded trees.

A strong wind was still blowing off the harbor. I would need some velocity to clear the building.

I jogged back forty feet from the window, and as I turned to face my runway, something zipped past my ear.

Hazmat-suited people were flooding out of the northeast stairwell. A projectile struck my pack. I pulled out a tranq dart, tossed it aside, and fired twelve rounds in under two seconds, everyone scattering, and then I was running.

Thirty feet from the window.

Twenty feet.

Two darts struck the pack.

Ten.

I shot past Kara, thinking: *This is the last image I will ever have of my sister.*

Two feet from the edge, I leaped, exiting the building at a dead run, my consciousness dividing—

It was the strangest sensation of my life, falling at one-quarter speed, my stomach lifting, the ground looming toward me, the wind blasting my face, and out of my right eye, I saw a light burst from the roof of One Liberty Plaza. Sniper.

I'd been falling just two of the 6.18 seconds it would take me to hit the ground when I tossed the pilot chute out in front of me. It vanished, the plaza still racing toward me and a main line of animal panic rushing through me as I waited for the main chute to deploy, wondering if it had been damaged by the darts.

I was wrenched up—still descending, but after that splinter of freefall it felt like I was moving horizontally to the ground. Gunshots popped behind me, and that sniper rifle flashed again as I glided over Broadway and the submerged trees of Zuccotti Park.

Reaching up, I grasped two handles. When I tugged on the left, I veered left. Correcting with the right, I straightened myself on a heading that sailed me over the center of the park.

Something exploded behind me in a series of low, concussive booms, and I glanced back as a wall of rolling flame licked through the windows of the thirty-fourth floor.

Even from this distance, I could feel the heat on my face as glass rained down onto the flooded plaza. I hoped no one else had been killed in the blast, but at least the government wouldn't be walking off with any of her work product.

Well played, sis.

There was a building straight ahead. I eased to the left, now four hundred feet above ground and gliding over Cedar Street between skyscrapers, the street wind wreaking havoc on the canopy.

I floated out over another open space, glimpsed the dome of a church in the distance, the light poles and dead trees of Liberty Park, and beyond it all, the hulking black shadow of One World Trade Center.

Ten feet above the water, I took a deep breath and pulled a handle on the main lift web of the harness.

I splashed down into freezing salt water, trying instinctively to swim for the surface, but I sank like a rock—my gear too heavy, all systems redlining.

My boots touched pavement—I was full submerged.

I killed the panic.

It took me a full minute to free my shoulders. In total darkness, I worked the harness down my legs, fighting to pull my boots through the holes as the first sparks of oxygen deprivation kindled in my field of vision. Finally, I tore off my jacket and body armor, bent my knees, and sprang off the street.

Surfacing. Gasping.

I was on West Street, facing the storefront of an abandoned Marriott.

I swam into the lobby, toward a staircase that curved up to the second floor. Dragging myself off the last submerged step, I sprawled across the landing.

Breathless and shivering. Hurting everywhere.

And one thought repeating.

I had killed my sister.

Those words ricocheted through my head, and I tried to stave them off, but a crushing pressure was building in my chest. I didn't know how much longer I could insulate myself from the blast-radius of her death.

The scream was coming.

• • •

Dawn light woke me.

I came to consciousness curled up against the wall, having slept just over an hour, and on the verge of hypothermia.

I sat up, powered on my phone—eighteen missed calls from Edwin.

He answered on the first ring.

"You live."

"Not by much." I couldn't be sure who was listening in. If a trace had already begun on my location.

Edwin said, "Running is pointless." His voice sounded stiff. He was performing and not for me. "We have images of your face. There are BOLOs out to everyone. You'll never make it out of the city."

I understood. He knew this call was being monitored, that he couldn't be seen as helping me. But he was also warning me. *Be careful. They're looking for you.*

Edwin said, "Let's meet somewhere. I'll bring you in."

"I have to tell you two things," I said, "and then I'm going to hang up. First—you better do right by Nadine. Treat her well. Treat her fairly. Second—that stuff I injected into you?"

"Yeah?"

"It was only saline."

I waded down into the water, instantly shivering again. I swam out into the morning light, scrambled up a dead tree, and found a comfortable place to perch in the branches, desperate to warm myself in the sun.

High on the east aspect of the buildings, the glass and steel were shining in the early sun, and a little ways up West Street, I heard voices.

For a moment, I thought it might be a search party, but then

I saw the gathering of boats near One World Trade Center. It was a collection of ramshackle skiffs. Some were laden with fresh fruit. Others with books, magazines, and sundries. One sold beer and cigarettes. From another lifted coils of smoke—an old woman grilling kebabs. Music effervesced from the crowd—someone playing guitar. The sounds of conversation and laughter reverberated off the buildings.

The temptation to swim over was strong. Barter for breakfast. See about getting a boat. But the commotion at 140 Broadway last night must've sounded like Armageddon. Anyone in the vicinity would have heard it, and me stumbling into their midst would only raise an alarm. So I settled for watching them from a distance—this forgotten fragment of humanity making a life together in the most inhospitable of places.

They seemed truly happy, and it made me happy to watch them—a thousand small kindnesses among people who had nothing to give.

I was all day in the water, making my way toward the southern end of Manhattan, steering clear of 140 Broadway.

Progress was slow.

I went from block to block. Patiently. Carefully.

As I swam up the FDR, the first fires of the evening appeared in the surrounding skyscrapers, and Venus wobbled in the sky, the Earth's atmosphere bending its light.

I finally stumbled out of the water, onto the dry ground of the on-ramp for the Brooklyn Bridge.

It was eerily silent.

No one out.

I walked onto the bridge, moving down the empty car lanes, and when I reached the highest point—127 feet above the water—I caught a glimpse of the Statue of Liberty. On this winter evening, she stood in ominous silhouette against a bloodred sky—more time capsule than symbol.

I opened Kara's bag, pulled out an auto-injector. It was light in my hand. Unassuming. Strange to think that just a few of these could alter the trajectory of a species.

I took my time tossing my sister's handiwork, one by one, into the dark waters of the East River, that terrible pressure returning, the scream of grief begging for a voice.

Was this the last vestige of my humanity, shrieking at me to *feel*?

I could've stopped the emotion; I didn't. To feel nothing about my sister's death seemed like crossing a frontier I couldn't return from.

The tears came.

Streaming.

And I let myself break.

Thinking about those eighteen perfect moments, and our last one—her hand touching my face just before she died.

For a moment, I felt like the Logan of old, wondering if I could somehow merge the man I had once been with the man I had become.

I glanced back at the city of darkness, the city of light.

And I was walking again, moving toward the lights of Brooklyn, and my thoughts racing, my mind alight with the flickering of a wild notion, and I could feel the good, warm hope of a new idea taking its first breath.

We were a monstrous, thoughtful, selfish, sensitive, fearful, ambitious, loving, hateful, hopeful species. We contained within us the potential for great evil, but also for great good. And we were capable of so much more than this.

My sister had been right about one thing: I couldn't do nothing.

EPILOGUE

Human nature will be the last part of Nature to surrender to Man. The battle will then be won. We shall have "taken the thread of life out of the hand of Clotho" and be henceforth free to make our species whatever we wish it to be. The battle will indeed be won. But who, precisely, will have won it?

—C. S. Lewis, *The Abolition of Man*

THREE YEARS LATER

THE VALEDICTORIAN HAS JUST finished her speech, and I'm sitting in the highest row of bleachers overlooking the football field and the raised platform on the fifty-yard line.

The principal begins to call out the names.

She's somewhere down there with the other graduates, in a sea of royal blue, though I haven't spotted her yet. I did see Beth as I climbed the concrete steps to the upper reaches of the stadium—sitting with the man I observed her having dinner with several years ago at La Fleur. His name is John. He's an English professor at American University, where Beth still teaches, and his specialty is British literature from 1485 to 1660. I've read all of his publications. They're fine.

"Ava. Gray. Ramsay."

As I watch my daughter walk onto the stage, my eyes well up. When did she start using my name?

After the ceremony, I wait by Beth's car in the high school parking lot.

It's evening now, and I watch the families moving past with their graduates, the air vibrating with ebullience.

John walks between Ava and Beth, each of them holding an arm. He wears a blue suit, and his shoes are newly shined. I'm pleased he dressed up for Ava's day. It speaks well of him.

He stops when he sees me.

Straightening.

Beth senses the change in his body language, glances up at him, then seeing the intensity of his gaze, follows it to me.

There is no facial augmentation I could make that would fool my wife and daughter.

When Beth gasps, Ava looks up from her phone. I was leaning against the hood of their car. Now I stand and walk over carrying a bouquet of pink roses and a small package. Ava drops her phone and diploma and runs at me, throwing her arms around my waist, sobbing uncontrollably. As I hold her, I look at Beth. Huge tears roll down her face against an expression of complete shock.

Cracks running through my heart of stone.

"I'm John," John says.

"I know."

He looks at Beth.

"I'm okay," she says, wiping her eyes. "Maybe the three of us could have a moment?"

"Of course. I'll take a walk."

John looks at me with his kind eyes—extremely unsure of the situation.

"You have nothing to worry about," I say. "I'm glad you're in their lives."

It's the first time we've been together in four years, and I feel our disunity intensely. I am an interloper in their lives now. A discordant note.

We sit in the car—Beth behind the steering wheel, Ava and me in the back seat. The interior smells of the roses and of Beth's perfume, a new brand she never wore when we were together.

I say, "I hope I didn't spoil your day."

Ava shakes her head, eyes red, swollen with tears.

"Is it safe for you to be here?" Beth asks.

"Not particularly." I disabled all CCTV within two blocks of the school, but AI would likely sniff out the virus and have it removed within the next fifteen minutes. I'd be gone by then.

I look at my daughter. "Number three in your class."

"It's perfect," she says, finally finding her voice. "The top two had to make speeches. I hate public speaking."

It's like a dream being in the same space together. Nothing and everything to say. In proximity, I can see the subtle toll the last four years have taken on Beth: deepening laugh lines and a heaviness in her eyes that wasn't there the last time I looked into them—the residency of grief.

And in my absence, Ava has changed. I see far more of the woman she is becoming than the child she used to be.

"I can't believe you're here," Beth says.

After New York, I wrote her a letter—the hardest words I'd ever put to paper. I tried to explain everything. The breadth of my transformation. Kara's plan, and what I'd had to do to stop her. I told her that, as much as I wanted to be her husband, my presence in their life would only be a liability. I encouraged her to move on from me and seek happiness. I told her I would always love her.

I hand Beth the package. "This is for both of you."

"What is it?"

"When I was looking for Kara, I kept a journal. Sometimes I'd write you letters I never thought you'd get to read. Maybe this will help you understand what I've become. There's also a letter in there. To both of you. I can't stay long enough to tell you what I've been doing these past few years. It's not safe. Read it later, after you've celebrated."

Beth stares at the package, uncertain. While it's true I don't have time to linger, I'm also terrified of what they'll say when they learn what I've done.

"We're having a little party back at the house," Ava says.

"I can't, honey. I'd put all your guests in danger. I'm sorry."

She nods, holding back tears.

"You took my name," I say.

"I'm not ashamed of it. Are you still?"

"No."

"Good. You shouldn't be. I mean, you kind of saved the world."

It takes everything in my power not to break down. I had stopped using my emotional Faraday cage months ago. To save humanity, I needed my humanity.

I lean forward, touch Beth's hand. "Does he make you happy?"

She smiles through her tears. "Very much so. But I miss you. I'd rather have you."

I stare through the glass, breathing through the hurt. The loss. All the moments we would never have. All the chess games I'd missed with Ava. The ten thousand dinners with Beth. Late-night soaks in the bathtub, just talking. I would take a bullet over this pain. Would hand back my beautiful mind and return to the 118-IQ Logan of old in a second.

The urge to wall myself off from the ache is acute. But I *want* to feel it. If I lose the ability to hurt, I also lose my grasp on joy—those brief moments of contentment that make consciousness worth the voyage.

Beth says, "You could've left this package at the front door."

"I came for Ava. And to see you."

"You may have transcended to another level of being, but I still know you. So let's try that again. Why did you really come? Why take the risk?"

"I should let you get back to your celebration," I say.

She looks me in the eyes.

I hesitate.

"Logan."

I just stare at Beth.

She says, "I know they might never let you come back to us. And even if they did, you've changed in ways I can't understand."

"I'm so sorry."

"I'm not saying it doesn't hurt—*badly*—but we'll make it. So whatever it is you need to do, go do it. We'll be okay." She looks at our daughter, gesturing to her graduation gown, and behind the tears, I detect a spark of defiant happiness. Resilience. "Because as hard as it's been, life went on."

I look at my daughter.

Her eyes are filling with tears, but she says, "I love you, Daddy."

"I love you too."

Silence. More tears. For all of us.

I finally open the door. We step out of the car, and I go to my daughter and wrap my arms around her. Beth comes over, and we all hold one another in the parking lot, the sodium lamps humming softly above us.

I want to tell them I still love them, and also how that love has been changed and deepened—made infinitely more complex by the intimacy of being able to relive every memory of them in perfect detail.

But I have no words. Or none that would be sufficient.

And so I settle for dividing my consciousness and decelerating my perception of time to the slowest possible crawl, savoring every elongated second of their touch, their warmth, their smell, their presence.

As I walk across the parking lot, away from the two most important people in my life, I feel more alone than I've ever felt before.

But also—more at peace.

My Beth.

My Ava.

Kara and my mother believed they could stop humanity from destroying itself by increasing our collective intelligence and reason. They built an upgrade to ramp up those abilities, and despite Kara's massive intellect, she was still willing to kill a billion people.

But my sister was right about one thing—we will die out in the next century if nothing changes. And I think I discovered why our species seems so willing to let this happen.

One child dies in a well, the world watches and weeps. But as the number of victims increases, our compassion tends to diminish. At the highest number of casualties—wars, tsunamis, acts of terror—the dead become faceless statistics. They call this compassion fade, but in reality, it's our genetic inheritance—old adaptations from our ancestors persisting in our DNA.

In the late-twentieth century, an anthropologist and evolutionary psychologist named Robin Dunbar proposed a theory that Homo sapiens *can only care about, identify with, and maintain stable relationships with 150 people. This number correlates to the size of the social groups in our evolutionary past. When we were* Homo erectus, *we lived in small hunter-gatherer groups bonded by sociality. Back then, only caring about our immediate group was advantageous. It helped us defend our tribe. It helped us advance, and survive.*

But that limitation carried forward. Today, in a given tragedy, we can overlay the faces of our family, friends, and co-workers on only

150 people. Beyond that, compassion fades, but not because we're evil. Our emotional hardwiring can't cope with it. We're living in a global community of ten billion, with brains that can only feel compassion for our immediate clan.

Other factors come into play, such as distance. A tragedy across the world is harder to feel compassion for than one in our own neighborhood. People who don't look like us are more challenging to identify with.

And if our species has a problem with apathy, and feeling compassion for the pain of others in real time, how can we expect ourselves to conjure compassion for a tragedy that hasn't even happened yet? The victims of Homo sapiens' demise haven't even been born. What emotional incentive do we have to make the sacrifices that will save future generations, if our brains aren't capable of caring about them sufficiently?

My mother once posited that we are not rational beings. We read about all the looming threats in the paper, we watch it on the news, and then we get on with our day. And, yes, some of that is thanks to our ability to hide from reality with denial, with cognitive dissonance, with magical thinking.

But she forgot the most important thing: In the absence of compassion, selfishness is the most rational response of all.

Our species' superpower is not caring. We merely exercised that ability.

We don't have an intelligence problem. We have a compassion problem. That, more than any other single factor, is what's driving us toward extinction.

After Kara's death, I spent a year poring over my mother's genetic data from The Story of You, with a focus on gene systems connected to compassion. I found one that programs the volume of key prefrontal cortex subregions, which determine an individual's mentalizing skills, which determines the size of our social group, which directly controls the ability to feel compassion. I also found one that controls dorsal portions of *the medial prefrontal cortex, which light up when people feel empathy for strangers. Our brains evolved to help in-group members for a very good reason, but what we need to survive as a species is the ability to care about strangers. Especially people who haven't been born yet.*

So I built a compassion upgrade.

Our beta group experienced increases in compassion and curiosity. They presented a heightened concern for strangers, and an almost compulsive need to understand one another.

Ten months ago, after extensive testing, I sent a hundred people to the ends of the earth, all infected with a viral vector that carried my upgrade.

My super-spreaders shed virus as they flew across the Atlantic and Pacific. As they walked the concourses of Charles de Gaulle and Heathrow. Listened to the most sublime music in the world at the Teatro Colón in Buenos Aires. Cruised the shopping stalls of Mong Kok District in Hong Kong. Shibuya Crossing. Times Square. Football stadiums from Madrid to Manchester. Red Square and the Forbidden City.

So far, more than fifty percent of the world's population has received my upgrade, and we're already seeing modest changes in public policy and online discourse. I can even feel it moderating the colder effects of my prior upgrades.

We decided against announcing the upgrade, but it's important to me that you both know what I've done.

Will you be horrified by my hubris? Am I no better than my mother, or Kara, thinking my intellect gives me the right to determine the course of humanity?

I don't know the answer to that question. Just as I'm not sure if my upgrade will do what I hope or of what unintended consequences it might reap.

What I do know is that, Ava, you're inheriting a world on the brink of collapse. I came before you, which makes this my fault. I couldn't do nothing.

Maybe none of it matters. Maybe it's just our time.

Humans have had 300,000 years on this planet. We lived from the Stone Age to the space age. We split the atom and sequenced our own DNA and built machines that could think.

But for all our progress, ten million people die of hunger every year. We have hyperloops and rampant nativism. Phones more powerful than the computers that took us to the moon, but no more coral reefs.

And year after year, nothing really changes.

If there's a solution, it has to lie in rescuing us from our ambivalence. Our apathy.

Whatever happens next, I tried my best. I gave up everything that wasn't already taken from me, and I've finally walked out from under my mother's long, long shadow.

As you read this, I'll be driving west. I have unfinished business in Glasgow, Montana.

I want you to know that if I could make things go back to the way they were, I'd do it in a second. But, alas, there are no reverse gears in life.

When I think of the old Logan, it's like considering an entirely separate being, and in moments I choose not to control, I feel a fierce loss for him. I suspect that, if we all had perfect memory, we would all grieve the older versions of who we used to be the way we grieve departed friends.

But even though I'm changed from the Logan you once knew, the part of me that loved you madly remains.

As I finish this letter, I'm sitting in a car across the street from a place I used to call home. It's the night before Ava's graduation, and through the front window, I can see the two of you and John in the living room. I think you're playing a game. There's definitely a lot of laughter, and I cannot escape the thought that you look like a family.

This hurts me deeply; and it makes me happy.

What do you call a heart that is simultaneously full and breaking? Maybe there's no word for it, but for some reason, it makes me think of rain falling through sunlight.

ACKNOWLEDGMENTS

An extraordinary group of people helped me at various stages during the writing of this book, and I'd like to take a moment to thank them.

For every redline, for every note, for every time I interrupted what you were doing to bounce an idea off you, thank you, JACQUE BEN-ZEKRY, my editor and partner in all things. You were down in the trenches with me as I tried to wrestle *Upgrade* to the ground—on the good days, but especially on the brutal ones when I doubted everything. I couldn't have finished this book without you.

For keeping the faith on the most difficult book of my career, a very special thanks to JULIAN PAVIA, who has been my editor now for three books and seven years. Your insights and instincts are sharper than ever. You are the pressure that makes the diamond.

For the counsel, friendship, (and always epic meals!), thank you, DAVID HALE SMITH, my literary agent now for more than a decade. It's been quite a ride, my friend.

And thanks to the gang at INKWELL MANAGEMENT, especially RICHARD PINE, ALEXIS HURLEY, NATHANIEL JACKS, and NAOMI EISENBEISS.

For handling my film and television business with pure aplomb, thanks to ANGELA CHENG CAPLAN and JOEL VANDERKLOOT.

For your indispensable support, which allows me to focus on writing by keeping the details of my life in order, thanks to TYSON BEEM, BRANDON KLEIN, MOLLY FIX, and CARISSA GAYLORD.

For being the rocket engine on my books, thanks to everyone at PENGUIN RANDOM HOUSE and BALLANTINE BOOKS, but especially GINA CENTRELLO, KARA WELSH, KIM HOVEY, JENNIFER HERSHEY, QUINNE ROGERS, KATHLEEN QUINLAN, CINDY BERMAN, and CAROLINE WEISHUHN.

For your tireless work on my behalf, and for being the best publicist I've ever had, thank you, DYANA MESSINA.

For my beautiful covers on *Dark Matter*, *Recursion*, and now *Upgrade*, thank you, CHRIS BRAND.

For publishing me so well in the UK, a big hug to the incomparable WAYNE BROOKES, and everyone at PAN MACMILLAN.

For reading the ungainly early drafts of *Upgrade* and sharing your feedback, which improved these pages immeasurably, thanks to my early readers—CHUCK EDWARDS, BARRY EISLER, JOE HART, CHAD HODGE, MATT IDEN, DAVID KOEPP, STEVE KONKOLY, ANN VOSS PETERSON, and MARCUS SAKEY.

A massive, literally-couldn't-have-written-this-book-without-you bow to the brilliant and witty molecular geneticist MICHAEL V. WILES, PH.D. I learned so much from you. Thank you for your patience, your time, and your deep well of knowledge. You are the gold standard for subject-matter experts. I was so lucky to find you.

For taking a moment to speak with me about quantum computing applications vis-à-vis manipulating genetic data sets, thank you to HOOMAN MOHSENI, PH.D.

For inspiring conversations about the intersection of science and philosophy during the writing of *Upgrade*, thanks to PHIL WEISER, BRYAN JOHNSON, and J. PIERRE DE VRIES, PH.D.

For helping me find the greatest subject-matter experts on my last three novels, heartfelt thanks to THE SCIENCE AND ENTERTAINMENT EXCHANGE, and especially SACHI C. GERBIN and RICK LOVERD.

For being not only my great local bookstore but one of the great independent bookstores in the world, high fives to everyone at MARIA'S BOOKSHOP, but especially EVAN SCHERTZ, ANDREA AVANTAGGIO, and PETER SCHERTZ.

For your love and support as I worked on this seemingly never-ending book, thank you to my wonderful family—JACQUE, MOM, DAD, my brother, JORDAN, and my three talented, kind, and spectacular children—AIDAN, ANNSLEE, and ADELINE. And a special thanks to AIDAN for all the fascinating philosophical conversations, and especially for pointing me toward *The Abolition of Man* by C. S. Lewis, which became essential food for thought during the final stretch of the book.

For giving me an amazing life that allows me to do what I love, thank you, MY INCREDIBLE READERS, especially those who've been with me since the beginning.

Finally, in 2019, my dearest and oldest childhood friend, BRIAN ROGERS, tragically lost his son, EDWIN ALEJANDRO ROGERS. The character of Edwin Rogers is dedicated to his memory.

UPGRADE

BLAKE CROUCH

Random House
Book Club

Because
Stories Are
Better Shared ™

A BOOK CLUB GUIDE

QUESTIONS AND TOPICS
FOR DISCUSSION

1. How does the past influence the present in *Upgrade*? How do the characters try to repress, escape, or even rewrite the pain of their stories?

2. Memory plays a significant role in this book. In what ways does it inform identity? Do you think even the things you don't remember can affect who you become? What are the events in your life that have been important in shaping who you are?

3. In *Upgrade*'s near future, citizens and governments believe that genetic engineering needs to be harshly limited and regulated. Do you think we'll need to adopt similar measures in the future? Why or why not?

4. Logan's mother and sister share a bleak view of humanity and its future. Did you find any parts of their reasoning persuasive? Where do you think their arguments fail?

5. What did you think of the science and technology in this book? Does the idea of editing genetics excite you or scare you?

6. Did you understand Kara's side of the story? Did you root for Logan? Which sibling did you identify with more?

7. Did *Upgrade* change or challenge your own idea of what it means to be human?

8. Was Logan a reliable narrator? Was there anyone else's perspective you wish you saw?

9. If you were offered the chance to "upgrade" yourself, would you? Would you be worried that you'd be different or not even remotely the same person afterward?

10. Did reading *Upgrade* change your understanding of genetic engineering and the role it may one day play in our lives? How so?

11. What did you think about the ending? Were you satisfied with it or were you left wanting more? How do you envision Logan's life after the story ends?

A CONVERSATION WITH BLAKE CROUCH

Q: In *Upgrade*, much of the story revolves around the potential consequences of gene editing and genetic engineering. What inspired you to write a story about this evolving technology?

A: I did an interview on Science Friday for *Dark Matter* back in 2016, and at the end Ira Flatow asked what I was working on next. I didn't know yet. He suggested I look at the technology known as CRISPR-Cas9, a next-generation gene-editing tool. When I started researching what gene editing could accomplish, I was blown away. I knew I had to write about it. As I researched further, I read a book called *A Crack in Creation* by Jennifer Doudna, one of the pioneers of CRISPR. She wrote about having a nightmare that Hitler had gotten his hands on the technology, and I thought, "If the creator of this biotech is having nightmares about its potential applications, this is something I have to write about."

Q: One of the things readers love about your novels—aside from being page-turning thrillers!—is the way you bring such rich, complex characters to life. How did you get into Logan's head as you were writing?

A: It was one of the hardest things about the book—about any book I've written—getting inside his head. I usually write highly intelligent characters, but Logan wasn't just highly intelligent. He becomes superintelligent. Trying to find ways to have him display his burgeoning IQ and stay relatable even as his emotions cooled off was a sort of high-wire act. One of the tricks I came up with was to essentially slow down his perception of time so he could fully evaluate his environment and react. Writing him became about noticing details, which allowed him to anticipate others' actions and behaviors.

Q: Without giving too much away, one of the pivotal moments in this novel comes when Logan and Kara realize they have come to different conclusions in answer to the ethical question posed by their genetic "upgrades." What was it like for you to explore each of their perspectives as you wrote their characters?

A: That moment was the reason I wrote the book. Gene editing represents the greatest invention in the history of our species. It is the ability to remake ourselves. With technology of this power, there are a multitude of paths we as a species can take—utopia, dystopia, and everywhere in between as we rush to save our dying planet. Being at the heart of that discussion gave me a ton of room to play with and fascinating points of view to explore.

Q: Another signature element of your novels is the way that you incorporate elements from different genres to arrive at something new and exciting and different. Do you think consciously about that as you write? Are there any writers or filmmakers who inspired you in thinking this way?

A: Genre-blending isn't something I intentionally set out to do. It sort of just . . . happens. I think it goes back to my love of stories that don't stay in their assigned lane, and to the most impactful story in my development as a writer: *Twin Peaks*. Part soap opera, murder mystery, sci-fi, and horror, that show is the reason I became a writer. I think what appealed to me most about it *was* the genre hybrid of it all.

Q: And, of course, we have to end on a fun question! Some of your past work has been adapted by Hollywood—are there any plans for *Upgrade* that you can share? Any dream casting or directors?

A: I was fortunate enough to sell *Upgrade* to Amblin, Steven Spielberg's company, which is a literal dream come true. I'll be adapting the book into a screenplay for them—another dream come true—and hopefully the good news keeps rolling from there!

PHOTO: © MATTHEW STAVER

BLAKE CROUCH is a bestselling novelist and screenwriter. His novels include *Upgrade, Recursion, Dark Matter,* and the Wayward Pines trilogy, which was adapted into a television series for FOX. Crouch also co-created the TNT show *Good Behavior,* based on his Letty Dobesh novellas. He lives in Colorado.

ABOUT THE TYPE

The text of this book was set in Janson, a typeface designed about 1690 by Nicholas Kis (1650–1702), a Hungarian living in Amsterdam, and for many years mistakenly attributed to the Dutch printer Anton Janson. In 1919, the matrices became the property of the Stempel Foundry in Frankfurt. It is an old-style book face of excellent clarity and sharpness. Janson serifs are concave and splayed; the contrast between thick and thin strokes is marked.

RANDOM HOUSE BOOK CLUB

Because Stories Are Better Shared

Discover
Exciting new books that spark conversation every week.

Connect
With authors on tour—or in your living room. (Request an Author Chat for your book club!)

Discuss
Stories that move you with fellow book lovers on Facebook, on Goodreads, or at in-person meet-ups.

Enhance
Your reading experience with discussion prompts, digital book club kits, and more, available on our website.

Join our online book club community!

[f] [g] randomhousebookclub.com

Random House Book Club ™

Because Stories Are Better Shared

RANDOM HOUSE